FRANCIS KING

THE DIVIDING STREAM

I0639324

With a new introduction by

PAUL BINDING

VALANCOURT BOOKS

The Dividing Stream by Francis King
First published London: Longmans, 1951
First Valancourt Books edition 2014

Copyright © 1951 by Francis King, renewed 1979
Introduction © 2014 by Paul Binding

Published by Valancourt Books, Richmond, Virginia
Publisher & Editor: JAMES D. JENKINS
20th Century Series Editor: SIMON STERN, University of Toronto
http://www.valancourtbooks.com

ISBN 978-1-939140-69-2
Also available as an electronic book

All Valancourt Books publications are printed on acid free paper
that meets all ANSI standards for archival quality paper.

Set in Dante MT 11/13.2

THE DIVIDING STREAM

FRANCIS KING was born in Switzerland in 1923 and spent his early years in India before being sent back to England to a boarding school. A bright student, he earned a Classics scholarship to Balliol College, Oxford, but later changed to English literature, and published his first novel, *To the Dark Tower* (1946) while still an undergraduate. This novel, and his next two, *Never Again* (1947) (an autobiographical novel based on his childhood) and *An Air That Kills* (1948), were published by Home and Van Thal, which then went bankrupt, but not before King had established himself as a promising young novelist.

Beginning in 1949, King worked for the British Council and travelled extensively, including to Italy, Greece, and Japan, all of which would provide settings for his novels. His next book, *The Dividing Stream* (1951), set in Florence, won the Somerset Maugham Award and cemented King's status as one of the bright young literary stars of his generation. During the 1950s and '60s, King published a string of excellent works, including *The Dark Glasses* (1954), *The Man on the Rock* (1957), *The Widow* (1957), *The Custom House* (1961), and *The Waves Behind the Boat* (1965).

In 1966, King resigned from the British Council to devote himself to writing full-time and supplemented his income by writing book and theatre reviews and working as a literary adviser to the publishing house of Weidenfeld & Nicolson. He continued to write prolifically, and notable highlights include the gay-themed novel *A Domestic Animal* (1970), which drew the threat of a libel suit, *The Action* (1978), which narrowly missed the Booker shortlist, and *Act of Darkness* (1983), one of his most commercially successful books.

King went on writing until his death in 2011, making the Booker longlist with *The Nick of Time* (2003) and publishing a revised 60th anniversary edition of *An Air That Kills* with Valancourt Books in 2008; his final novel, *Cold Snap*, appeared in 2010.

Cover: The cover is a reproduction of the jacket art by Leslie Wood (1920-1994) from the 1951 British first edition. Wood studied at the Manchester College of Art and Design and is best known for his illustrations for Diana Ross's series of *Little Red Engine* children's books, published by Faber & Faber between 1945 and 1971. The Publisher gratefully acknowledges the kind permission of Mrs. Elsie Wood to reproduce the cover illustration.

By Francis King

To the Dark Tower (1946)*
Never Again (1947)*
An Air That Kills (1948)*
The Dividing Stream (1951)*
The Dark Glasses (1954)*
The Firewalkers (1956)
The Widow (1957)
The Man on the Rock (1957)*
So Hurt and Humiliated, and Other Stories (1959)
The Custom House (1961)
The Japanese Umbrella, and Other Stories (1964)
The Last of the Pleasure Gardens (1965)
The Waves Behind the Boat (1967)
The Brighton Belle, and Other Stories (1968)
A Domestic Animal (1970)
Flights (1973)
A Game of Patience (1974)
The Needle (1975)
Hard Feelings and Other Stories (1976)
Danny Hill: Memoirs of a Prominent Gentleman (1977)
The Action (1978)
Indirect Method and Other Stories (1980)
Act of Darkness (1983)
Voices in an Empty Room (1984)
One is a Wanderer: Selected Stories (1985)
Frozen Music (1987)
The Woman Who Was God (1988)
Punishments (1989)
Visiting Cards (1990)
Secret Lives (1991)
The Ant Colony (1991)
Yesterday Came Suddenly: An Autobiography (1993)
The One and Only (1994)
Ash on an Old Man's Sleeve (1996)
A Hand at the Shutter (1996)
Dead Letters (1997)
Prodigies (2001)
The Nick of Time (2003)
The Sunlight on the Garden: Stories (2005)
With My Little Eye (2007)
Cold Snap (2010)

* Available from Valancourt Books

INTRODUCTION

In 1949 Francis King (b. 1923) accepted a job at the British Council in Florence, the offer coming, as he tells us in *Yesterday Came Suddenly*, his 1993 autobiography, when "by a curious coincidence . . . I was actually in Florence." He accepted "with alacrity." "I was already in love with Florence—as I have remained, despite the ever-increasing crowds, din and pollution, up to the present." *The Dividing Stream* (1951, the author's fourth published novel) was actually written during the eighteen months Francis spent in the city lecturing and teaching at the British Institute there, and the book is permeated by that never-diminishing love. But this love is not allowed to blur the sharpness of the author's perceptions of society and individuals. Quite the contrary—the novel's rendering of the city's beauties, of the changing light that plays on the surrounding hills and on the abundant architectural testimonies to Florence's unique place in cultural history serves to put in, sometimes ironic, sometimes tragic, focus the sadness inherent in actual Florentine life and, too, the limitations of those foreigners viewing it from their own standpoints. To that acute awareness of human frailties, of the universal drives to self-gratification and self-deception with their inevitable destructive consequences, distinguishing Francis's precociously accomplished first three novels, we find added here another greater quality: empathy, and with it, a recognition that all of us are captives of our own circumstances.

We cannot forget as we read *The Dividing Stream* that World War Two, in which Italy suffered so devastatingly, is but four/five years over. During the war Francis himself, a pacifist, worked on the land as a Conscientious Objector, and though he experienced the air-raids on London, Britain 1939-1945 can have provided no helpful experiential equipment with which to face post-war Italy. Here armies had fought at huge cost of life the whole length of the country, ravaging countryside and city alike. It was also a case, after 1943, of one part of a nation pitted against another, each supported by powerful armies from elsewhere (Americans/ British/Canadians/Poles/South Africans vs. Germans). Though the novel is not overtly political, the word 'dividing' in its title can be taken as referring not just to the differences between the Florentines and their visitors but to the mental divisions between members of a (split) country during the blood-stained chaos of war-time and the Italians of the book's present, facing the uncertainties—above all economic—of a peace arrived at in a state of corrosive exhaustion. (Writing as one who lived and worked for five years in 1980s Italy, I can testify how—especially in the rural regions—memories of the War and its bitter aftermath of hunger, constant worry and doubts as to who were one's true friends still lived on and determined behaviour.) Especially as Francis is himself so visual a writer, conveying general atmosphere and minute particular detail with equal vividness, readers of this novel will be reminded of those influential, unforgettable Italian films of the late '40s/early '50s, in their integration of persons and places, their sense of a community at once unstable and defiantly strong, their paradoxical assertion of passion and stoicism: the creations of Roberto Rossellini, De Sica (*Bicycle Thieves*, 1946, *Umberto D.*, 1952), the young Visconti. Haven't such tense, compellingly slow-motion scenes in *The Dividing Stream* as Enzo and Rodolfo's conduct when bidden inside a smart suite in the (to them) dazzling hotel, Palazzo d'Oro, or Enzo's being dragged off to the police station and detained in a cell, that fusion of external and internal experience we rightly associate with the great years of *verismo*? And tellingly in the very first pages the American Max is trying with his expensive camera to catch two Italian youths in the medium of photography.

Francis King assembles for us—as he will in many of his best later novels, such as that favourite of his, *The Custom House* (1961), set in Japan—a group of wholly representative yet wholly individualised and autonomous-seeming persons. He studies both their interplay and their isolations, to arrive at a composition with—never precisely nameable—metaphoric significance. Max Westfield, he of the camera, stands at the centre of this group, yet—by the author's intention—he is the one we will know the

least, the reason being that he does not really know himself—
or has chosen not to do so. His passion for his wife Karen, who
expressly doesn't love him, who goes out of her way to tease him
and even to make a fool of him, devours his being, to a degree
he cannot bring himself to understand. (Just as he wilfully won't
understand, until very late on, the feelings for him entertained by
his Italian secretary, Lena.) Yet this in no way impairs his acumen
in different fields—in business pre-eminently. Without his money
the novel would be an impossibility, since without its power all
the seemingly diverse characters could not have been brought
together. Without symbolic strain or sacrificing the validity of
him as a flesh-and-blood being Francis makes Max stand for the
American in post-war Europe, a figure of half-reluctant, half-arro-
gant authority, too easily taken advantage of yet unwilling to face
up to the effect of obvious inequality on others.

His foil, his antagonist will be the penniless Englishman, Frank
Ross, his name an echo of the surname T. E. Lawrence used when
he joined the RAF (British Royal Air Force). Where Max is skilful,
even cautious, yet thorough, dedicated, not least in matters of
sexual love, Ross yields to often cruel impulse while being unable
to sustain any consistent interest whether in people or in subjects.
He is a portrait, and a terrifying one, of that extremely British
dilettante-ism which holds itself superior to the rest of the world
and which disagreeably stalks the novels and memoirs of (among
others) Evelyn Waugh.

Nobody detests Ross more than Max's son, Colin, Anglo-Amer-
ican, since Max is having him educated at a prestigious English
public school. Colin's experience of Italy—which includes a painful accident and a crime on his part with something of the *acte
gratuit* about it—is, we are told, of lasting, indeed lifelong con-
sequence. "He did not then guess it, but that evening was to be
the beginning of a devotion to a country and a people and, less
happily perhaps, of a whole way of life." Casually enough put,
but it seems clear to me that Colin, now fourteen years old—with
his ardent feelings of affection for the Italian youth Enzo, his
heightened response to works of art, his detestation of the crude
womaniser, Ross, underneath whose veneer he senses other
threatening psychic elements—is homosexual, and will decide—

as did so many Britons in those years of their country's cruel laws, not changed till 1967—to reside abroad, to be an expatriate with all the alienations and artifice that this role involves.

The portrayal of young people with whom one can identify—Colin's sister, Pamela, named, one assumes, for Francis's own loved elder sister, is most convincingly drawn—is one of Francis's supreme gifts as a writer, and beautifully in evidence here. The two Italian youths—and Enzo's pathetic, coarse-grained, morally ruthless brother, Giorgio, one of the *mutilati di guerra*—have an extraordinary vitality, a vitality so badly needed in a community weighed down not only by poverty but by a code, a system of values with no place in any emergent civilised society. Enzo's father lolls about and swears and swills drink and indulges in petty crime, just as his brother, when not too debilitated, goes whoring and forcing himself on girls, while his mother slaves away at an ill-paid job injurious to her health, while continuing to believe in the rights of the male. Yet in Enzo—and even in boastful Rodolfo, with his Tunisian background and pride in his command of French—one feels a kind of muted hope for the future. With energies like theirs surely their society can manage the resurgence that we know it, for all its deficiencies and difficulties, to have achieved.

I knew the author of *The Dividing Stream* for twenty years and, despite my not living in London, saw him often, talking to him as intimately as I have ever talked to anybody not a contemporary of mine. He was delightful to be with, unceasingly friendly, and his talk made countries, individuals and books come alive. I told him of my particular feeling for this novel, feelings I also entertain for the later novels, *The Woman Who Was God* (1988), *Punishments* (1989) and *Dead Letters* (1997), and they seemed to have been works he was particularly proud of. Yet, just to mention these remarkable creations is to realise what I hope I never forgot at the time—that this outstandingly agreeable man had a darkly penetrative vision of existence and the steely determination to serve it in the art of the novel, to the demands of which he applied himself unstintingly. After his death in 2011 I wrote: "I shall miss his company and his unseen presence immeasurably." I wrote truly, but I trust I will always remember that his spirit was formidable, not just entertaining and kindly mannered. This fourth novel of his exhibits *all* these qualities superbly.

PAUL BINDING

July 21, 2013

PAUL BINDING is a novelist, critic, poet and cultural historian. He studied English Literature at Oxford University and has written more than ten books, including the novels *Harmonica's Bridegroom* (1984; forthcoming in a new edition from Valancourt), *Kingfisher Weather* (1989), *My Cousin the Writer* (2002), and *After Brock* (2012). He lives in Shropshire.

THE DIVIDING STREAM

TO MINA

Love consists in this, that two solitudes
protect and touch and greet each other.
                RAINER MARIA RILKE:
                        Letter to a Young Poet.

Yes! in the sea of life enisled,
With echoing straits between us thrown,
Dotting the shoreless watery wild,
We mortal millions live *alone.*
The islands feel the enclasping flow
And then their endless bounds they know.

. . . Who order'd, that their longing's fire
Should be, as soon as kindl'd, cool'd?
Who renders vain their deep desire?—
A God, a God their severance ruled!
And bade betwixt their shores to be
The unplumb'd, salt, estranging sea.
                MATTHEW ARNOLD: *To Marguerite.*

Chapter One

THERE were three of them there.

Of the two boys outstretched beside the Arno one from time to time shifted or muttered in his sleep, and the American, who had been perched for many minutes on a slab of stone from the ruins of the Trinità bridge, continued to watch him with a vague curiosity. It was that hour when a sudden relenting in the heat of the day lures the bathers out of the shrunken waters and makes those who sleep on the banks awake and reach for clothes with arms that all at once seem cold, hard and stiff. Although at this season no mist arises from the river and the dusk serves only to sharpen the town's outlines as it sharpens the afternoon's once drowsy appetites, yet in a moment the hills appear to be about to dissolve into the receiving sky beyond. The rattle of the trams becomes strangely muted, the balustrades of the Lung' Arno are dark with leaning crowds.

Suddenly, like an animal roused from sleep, one of the boys jerked upright, looked about him, gazed long and carefully at the watching American, and then once more sank his head back on to the rolled shirt on which it had been pillowed. He lay like that for a long time, his eyes half-closed, while the American, a man of forty-six with red hair *en brosse* and a still youthful physique spoiled only by a slight stoop and over-long arms, opened the case of his camera and began to fiddle with its gadgets. He attached a filter and then a lens-hood; but immediately he unclipped the filter and attached another; twice he changed the aperture. At last he rose to his feet, pointed his camera up towards the Ponte Vecchio and seemed about to take a photograph; but with a shake of the head the camera was once again lowered. One by one the stops were changed, the gadgets were unscrewed and placed in their separate boxes.

Through all this routine he had been watched by the Italian boy; but some children had begun to pick their way over the tufts of bruised and burnt grass, their clothes over their arms or trailing from their hands, and seeing them, the boy turned from the American to let out a piercing whistle. They waved to him and shouted greetings, and one of them, a girl of sixteen whose sturdy legs were caked in mud, picked up a flat stone and threw it to where he lay, so skilfully that it skimmed across his naked body without doing him hurt. The boy shouted something obscene at her and they all laughed; then, still laughing among themselves as they attempted to push each other into the water, they moved on until they, too, were lost in the throng about the bridge.

The American, who was called Max, had by then returned to his seat. He yawned twice and looked at his watch, disappointed that it was less late than he had hoped. He was waiting for his wife's return, but it was unlikely that she had even left Viareggio yet; she had said that she would be back at eight, but she was always unpunctual, and on the days when they quarrelled unpunctuality became one of the many instruments used for his punishment. She would know that he was waiting for her, eager for forgiveness, and that knowledge would delay her; usually a reckless driver she would now on purpose drive slowly.

The boy had reached for his shorts over the sleeping body of his friend and having searched in both pockets, he produced an inch-long stub of cigarette, stared down at it for a moment as if about to burst into laughter at the ridiculousness of hoarding such a fragment and then, looking about him in a pretence of not knowing that the American was the only person near, at last sauntered over for a light. He was well-built and he walked gracefully, but it was at once apparent from the leftwards sag of his body and a protruding bone that his collar-bone had once been broken and never properly set. When he was thirteen he had fought with an Arab in a street in Tunisia and had been thrown down a flight of stone stairs; but (he would always hasten to add) he had won the fight. Like this: and he would demonstrate how, bull-like, he had butted his opponent with his forehead, shattering nose, teeth and left cheek-bone. He rarely fought with his fists; this was better. And once again he would demonstrate the butt, the tightly drawn muscles of his neck making it seem coarse and ugly.

"*Grazie.*" He drew three or four times on the fag-end, holding it between finger and thumb. His short toes, widely spaced from walking so often barefoot, closed and unclosed on a dusty clump of goose-grass as he attempted to wrench it from its roots. *"Inglese?"*

"No. *Americano.*"

"Ah, Americano." He stared at Max for a moment and then shook his head. "Don't seem it," he said in Italian.

"Don't I?"

"You speak Italian well." He perched on the stone beside Max but in such a way that, becoming top-heavy, it at once keeled over. He leapt up and then resettled himself; now his body, naked except for the bleached strip, leant against the other's. He drew his knees up and hugged them, and a rank, not unpleasurable odour, such as often comes from the fur of cats in the south, filled the American's nostrils. "You speak Italian well." He repeated the compliment.

"No. Only a little."

"French too?"

"Yes, I speak French."

"Vous parlez Français?"

"Oui, je parle Français."

"Moi, je parle Français." He sucked for the last time at the cigarette and then threw it away with an exclamation as the red-hot tip touched his fingers. "Tunisian, *moi.*"

"Tunisian?"

He nodded. "Three years in Florence. In Tunisia my father had a large house—large, large." He stretched his bare arms to their utmost extent, revealing under each a shadow of the only hair which could be seen on his whole body. "Pastry-cook. Then the French came back and we all had to leave. I was three days in the boat. . . . How many days did it take to come from America?"

"Oh, five or six."

The boy looked crest-fallen at the comparison. Until: "All my family was very sea-sick," he declared. "There was a terrible storm. Everyone was sea-sick, all over the deck."

"Were you sea-sick?" Max asked, already knowing the answer.

"Me?" The boy pointed at himself in incredulity. "Me sea-sick?" He made a contemptuous gesture of dismissal. "I'm never sea-sick." He looked at the case of Max's camera and pronounced with difficulty: "Ko-dak. . . . Is that your name?"

Max laughed. "No. That's the name of the camera. My name is Westfield. Max Westfield."

"Westfield." He repeated the name, but on his lips the *w* became a *v*. "My name is Rodolfo. Rodolfo Binelli. My friend"—he pointed to the sleeping boy who, having now turned over, lay with his face in the dust—"is Enzo. He's a Florentine."

"I was wondering why he was so restless in his sleep."

"He has a bad back, and when he lies down it hurts him. He doesn't know what's the matter."

"Hasn't he seen a doctor?"

"The doctor wanted an X-ray. Three thousand lire."

"But there must be free hospitals."

Rodolfo shrugged his shoulders; he had begun to fiddle with the catch of the camera case, and now he asked, "How much did this cost?"

Max first told him the sum in dollars, but the Tunisian asked for it in lire. Then he whistled. "Can I see it?"

"If you take care."

As soon as he had grasped the camera, the boy leapt up and sprinted away, his bare feet scattering the dust. "Hey!" Max shouted. "Hey!" He rose and gesticulated vaguely and then decided that if he ever wanted to regain the camera he had better start running. But meanwhile Rodolfo had stopped some fifty yards away, his body arched forward and his hands on his knees; he was laughing uncontrollably. "Do you want your camera?"

"Yes, bring it here at once. At once!" Max shouted.

"How much will you give me?"

"Don't be a fool. Bring it here!"

"How much?" the boy shouted.

"Do you want me to call a policeman?"

Still laughing the boy began to saunter forward while Max hurried to meet him. "Thank you." Max snatched the camera.

"Were you frightened?" the boy asked. Again he laughed, but seeing Max's displeasure, he at once attempted to smother the sound by putting a hand over his mouth. A splutter emerged. Max did not answer. "Did you think I would steal your camera?"

"You might have."

"No!" Suddenly serious, the boy raised one fist as if to strike the American in the face; but instead he gripped his arm, his eyes neared his.

"No. I'm not a thief. Not a thief," he repeated. "Never."

"All right," Max said drily. For a moment he still felt angry; then he realized how absurd the scene had been, and a smile broke on his heavy, vaguely Teutonic features, making the green eyes almost disappear under the red brows and showing a large triangular chip in one of the yellow teeth at the side of his mouth.

Rodolfo at once smiled back. "Do you want to take a photo of me?"

"Not very much."

"Like this," Rodolfo suggested, posing with his hands on his hips.

"No, thank you."

"Why don't you want to take a photograph of me?"

"Why should I? . . . . Oh, I'll take one if you like. If it'll please you." Max combined two of the dominant characteristics of the American abroad; suspicion of the foreigner, who apart from being likely to prove more astute, was certain to want something, probably dollars; and at the same time a longing for "matiness", for acceptance in a society in which he never felt wholly at his ease. The boy was a guttersnipe and at best he would cadge a cigarette, at worst steal something; yet his impudence appealed to Max and, in his loneliness, the American responded.

"I'll wake my friend, shall I? Then you can take us both together. You'd prefer that, wouldn't you?"

"I'm sure he'd rather sleep."

But Rodolfo had already leapt down the incline to where the Florentine lay and was prodding him in the stomach with the toes of one foot. Enzo stirred, grunted and rolled over on his back, his hands going down to adjust his slip in a gesture of modesty; but still he did not wake. Scooping some water out of the river Rodolfo scattered the drops over the outstretched body and laughed as his friend shot up.

"What the hell?" the Florentine asked, as with one hand he rubbed his eyes and with the other massaged his back.

"Come, come, come!" Rodolfo beckoned with both hands. "The American wants to take a photograph."

"What American?"

Rodolfo pointed, Enzo looked round; and it was typical of the Florentine's nature that as soon as he saw Max his surliness at being woken should melt into a smile. He jumped to his feet.

They posed against the water, their arms round each other's bare shoulders, and Max photographed them, not once, but three times—he would never risk failures. Rodolfo lacked all self-consciousness, but Enzo, who was shy, spoiled the first snap by shifting suddenly from his left to his right foot, and the second by covering his face with one hand as he was seized with uncontrollable giggles. On both occasions Rodolfo, who held himself erect and motionless, shouted angrily at his friend in a slang which Max, perhaps fortunately, could not understand. The Florentine, his skin gold against the deeper, less glowing brown of his friend, had the better physique, with wide shoulders, a narrow waist, and a straight, sturdy stance, but his self-consciousness denied him the Arab grace of Rodolfo. Max noticed how his body was covered with a number of small, white scars.

When he had finished, the American wondered why he had bothered. The photographs would be developed and printed, and then stuck in an album or left in a drawer or perhaps accidentally thrown away. Back at home when he showed guests his snaps of the trip someone would ask "Who are those?" and he would answer, probably truthfully, "I can't remember." And in a sense all the photographs, so carefully planned and posed, which he had taken in Europe would be equally futile. "What is that?" "That? Oh, that's the Uffizi, and that's San Miniato, and that's Santa Croce—or it may be Santa Maria Novella." He would know the names, or approximately know them, whereas already he had forgotten the names of the two Italian boys; but in both cases the photographs would evoke no real response, no quickening of the pulse, no agreeable rush of memory. For too long he had been emotionally dead to anyone but one person, to anything but one thing.

As he packed away the camera, he asked: "What did you say your names were?"

"I'm Rodolfo. Rodolfo Valentino. You remember him? . . . My friend is Enzo—short for Lorenzo."

"Lorenzo the Magnificent," put in Enzo, in allusion to an exhibition being held that year in Florence; he giggled at his little joke.

"Have you a cigarette?" Rodolfo asked simply.

"Sorry. Not here. I don't smoke myself."

"At the hotel?"

"Yes, at the hotel."

"Which is your hotel?"

"That one. Just opposite."

Rodolfo whistled and nudged Enzo. "He lives at the Palazzo D'Oro. How much would they rook him for there?"

Enzo was embarrassed by a question which it obviously had not embarrassed his friend to ask. "Four thousand lire a day," he muttered in a husky voice which always made it seem as if he ought to clear his throat. "Full *pensione*," he added.

Again Rodolfo whistled, shaking his right hand loosely from the wrist in a gesture which he used to express any superlative. "Enzo's mother works at the Palazzo D'Oro. In the laundry. . . . When are you going back to the hotel?"

"Soon."

"If we come with you, will you give us a fag?"

"What?"

"If we come back with you——"

"Yes . . . all right."

A year ago Max would never have dreamed of taking two half-naked urchins into the best hotel in Florence; but wasn't it one of Karen's chief complaints against him that he was so conventional, so "stodgy", as she put it? These days he was always catching himself trying to "show" her by some action which was wholly untrue to his real self; an admission, if any were needed, that that self had long since ceased to be satisfactory in her eyes.

But, in truth, the reception-clerk at the Palazzo d'Oro saw stranger things in the course of a day and, in spite of Max's fears, their entry passed without comment, probably without notice. They stood in silence as the vast iron and glass cage, flushed to a uniform rosy glow, swung them up and up to the sixth floor, and then, single-file, they clattered their way down a marble-paved corridor. From time to time Rodolfo looked over his shoulder to smile at his friend in triumph at their admission into this exotic world, but the Florentine made no response, thinking at that moment of how through seven layers of masonry, with antique furniture, concealed lighting and all the other expensive, incredible apparatus of civilized living between, somewhere, under his feet, his mother was at this moment touching the iron with a moistened finger to see if it sizzled, was swathed in steam as she lowered one padded half of the trouser-press or (the job of which she complained most) was sorting and counting the soiled heaps of laundry thrown haphazard by the chamber-maids on to the sweating floors. What would she think if she knew that her son was walking above her—was at this moment standing outside one of the terrace suites while the American fumbled with his keys before they could enter? A strange feeling of pity, combined with resentment, shook him momentarily through his whole frame.

While the boys went round the room, whistling their astonishment, Max unlocked his case, fetched out some Camels and threw them to Enzo. The Florentine clumsily drew out two cigarettes, one of which he gave to his friend, and then returned the packet.

"Keep it," Max said.

"What?"

"Keep it, keep it," said Rodolfo irritably. Finding his friend slow, he tended to bully him.

"*Grazie, grazie.*" Enzo pushed the cigarettes into one pocket of his shorts but at once they descended down the trouser-leg. Rodolfo guffawed, Enzo blushed and stooped to recover the gift.

"His only pair of pants," Rodolfo explained. "And he spent all this morning sewing them up. Look." He turned his friend round like a dummy and showed the place where a rent in the seat had been untidily drawn together with a few large stitches. "Too small for him," he said. "He never stops growing." Suddenly his eye was caught by the open suit-case, in which lay Max's passport and a heap of foreign money. He fingered a note:

"French?"

"No, Swiss."

"And this?"

"A florin."

"How much is it worth?"

"About two hundred lire."

Max shut the case and locked it.

"He doesn't trust us," Rodolfo said to Enzo in an aside which none the less reached the American's ears. He laughed: "I don't blame him, with all that money." He turned to Max: "You're rich." It was a statement, not a question, and of course it was true. But Max had never applied that word to himself, being, like most rich people, a little afraid of it. He now shrugged his shoulders, no less embarrassed than if the Italian had suddenly announced, "You're good."

"Nice stuff." Rodolfo had begun to finger the material of the suit which, an hour previously, had been pressed by Enzo's mother in the hotel laundry. He rubbed it against his cheek. "How much?"

"How much?" Max echoed.

"How much did it cost?"

"Twenty-five guineas. It was made for me in England."

"In lire?"

"Oh, I really don't know," Max said impatiently. For some reason he had already lied about the suit; it had, in fact, cost forty, not twenty-five, guineas.

"And these brushes?" Rodolfo picked them up and began applying them to his hair which, according to the fashion of the moment, had been cut à l'Américain and stood up in a dense, coarse mat, black and slightly scurfy at the roots.

"Please don't use those."

Rodolfo went on brushing his hair.

"I said please don't use those."

When Max attempted to grab the brushes, the boy slithered away, with a giggle, and at once began to brush the hair of his friend. But seeing Max's displeasure, Enzo grabbed Rodolfo's right arm and slowly twisted it until the Tunisian squirmed and squealed in pain; the two ivory-backed brushes clattered to the floor. The Florentine picked them up, dusted them between his hands, and returned them to the dressing-table.

"I think you'd better be going now. . . . And please don't put your cigarette-end down the wash-basin," Max added irritably.

"Give it to me." The Florentine took the cigarette from the Tunisian, went out on to the terrace, and there ground it beneath his heel. Evidently it had never occurred to either of the boys that

the two crystal and gold dishes over which they had whistled when
they had first come in, might really be ash-trays.

"What are you doing there?" a voice demanded in English.
"Why are you in my son-in-law's room?"

An old woman who had been sleeping in a wicker chair at the
other end of the terrace, her straw hat tilted so far over her nose
that only her chin was visible, had suddenly awoken, pushed the
hat off her face, and tottered to her feet. She was terrifying, and
Enzo fled back into the bedroom.

"Max, Max! . . . Oh, you *are* here! What was that boy doing out
on the terrace? What's going on?"

Mrs. Bennett was a woman of over six feet, with large hands and
feet, untidy grey hair worn in a bun, and a face whose main features were a long, thin, indeterminately shaped nose, a skin which,
except in moments of stress, lacked any of old age's wrinkles, and
a pair of eyes remarkable both for the paleness of their blue and
the absence of either lashes or eyebrows. She wore a faded blue
cotton dress, shapeless except for the belt which gathered it at the
waist, white plimsolls on her stockingless feet, and dark glasses
which dangled round her neck on a piece of knotted twine. "Who
are these people? I was woken up by one of them, on the terrace.
He frightened me," she added with a sudden smile.

"I met them on the beach and they asked for a cigarette. I hadn't
any on me so I brought them up here."

"Oh, I see. It was silly of me to be frightened," she said, turning
to Enzo. "But I was having such a strange, confused dream, and
then I woke with a start and saw you. . . . Now that I'm old, I've
become silly about sleep—always a little afraid to go to sleep, in
case I don't wake up, and when I *do* wake up, I always think that
perhaps I may be dead. . . . You wouldn't understand that because
you're young."

Enzo had not understood it; not merely because he was young,
as she had suggested, but because the whole speech had been
delivered in English. He was still regarding her with terror.

"They don't understand English," Max put in. "But that one
speaks a little French *patois*—he's from Tunis."

"This one? Yes, I've been looking at him. Partly Arab, I suppose.
. . . He's a fine-looking boy."

Hearing the word Arab, Rodolfo leapt up from the bed where he had been squatting. "Me—Arab!" he exclaimed in French. "Not on your life!"

"He didn't like that." She smiled at him, putting one hand on to his shoulder and gently pushing him back on to the bed. Once she had him there, she stared down at him with her strange, faintly blue eyes, and he, with a sullen hostility, stared back, his palms clasped behind his head. Suddenly she bent down and caught one of his wrists. "He'll do. I want to draw him." She began to pull him to his feet and such was her personality, that Rodolfo, mystified and unfriendly, nevertheless rose. "I'll take him to my room," she announced, beginning to drag him to the door, and commanding at the same time in an appalling French accent: "*Venez—venez! Venez avec moi!*"

"*Mais, je ne comprends pas——*"

"*Venez, venez!*"

Enzo began to shamble after them, but she waved him away, crying in English: "No, I only want the one. Do explain, Max."

"You stay here, Enzo," Max said.

"But——"

"Stay with the Englishman," Rodolfo commanded. He was not sure what was desired either of him or his friend, but of one thing he was sure; it always paid to do what foreigners asked of one. "Stay with the Englishman," he repeated.

"But——" Enzo began again.

"Stay!" Rodolfo shouted. "Keep the Englishman company."

Enzo crossed over to the bed, sat stiffly down on it, and began undoing and doing up the top button of his shirt with one large, clumsy hand. His face was red and he was sweating profusely.

"What are those white scars?" Max asked, saying the first thing that came into his head and then realizing that, even to an Italian and a boy of this class, the question might seem personal.

"Football," Enzo muttered, his voice so husky now that it was almost inaudible. "I play in goal."

"It looks as if football in Italy were a battle, not a game."

"What?"

"Oh, nothing." He couldn't be bothered to repeat it. "Another cigarette?"

"No, thank you." Enzo adjusted one of his ankle socks and then, with a deep sigh, brushed a bare forearm across his forehead so that it returned to his lap gleaming with a number of minute, golden beads of sweat.

"Go on." Max held out the packet.

"Thanks." But the boy fumbled for so long that in the end Max had to shake the cigarette into his own palm and then give it to him. "Thanks," the boy repeated again.

Max rose to his feet. "Come out on to the terrace," he said. "Come."

They leant over the balustrade and were silent for a while, watching the crowds sauntering beside the Arno in the last fume of dusk. Max pondered and at last said in an Italian that was vitiated only by his use of the English open *o*: "I suppose you're unemployed."

"Yes, unemployed."

"For how long?"

"Two years."

"And your family?"

"My mother works. Here." He pointed down between his feet. "In the hotel laundry."

"She probably pressed my shirt," Max said. "But the rest?"

"All unemployed."

"And you can't find work—work of any kind?"

The boy shrugged his shoulders.

"Surely, as a labourer—a farm-worker or a builder or a road-maker——" Max pursued, submitting the Florentine to the kind of slow, logical cross-examination which always irritated his wife. "Surely——"

"I can't do very heavy work, unfortunately. It makes my back worse. But even if I could, I'd probably not find anything. My father and my elder brother can't find anything, and they're much stronger than I am."

"What unemployment benefit do you get?"

"What do you mean? I don't understand." Max explained and the boy laughed: "Why, nothing, of course. My brother gets paid by the State, but he's a *mutilato di guerra*. Oh, I have this." His hand dived into his shorts and, after a certain amount of scrabbling, he produced a green card marked out in squares with numbers printed on them. He handed it to Max as if, in itself, it were an explanation.

"What's this?"

"My food card. I can get three free meals a week with it, not very good meals, just bread and a *minestra*, but it's lucky because I'm not allowed to eat at home. Well, I do eat there," he added with a smile, "when my father is out. But my father says that if I don't work, I can't expect to be fed. Not that *he* works."

"And where do you sleep?" Max asked.

"Oh, at home. He doesn't mind that, because I share my brother's room."

"If you can't do heavy work, how is it that you can play football?"

A deep flush covered the boy's face at a question on which he had so often argued with his family, and Max thought: "Yes, I knew the story was all too glib"; his attitude suddenly changing from complete credulity to a no less complete scepticism.

Enzo put out his cigarette on the stone balustrade, and then carefully hoarded the stub in the breast-pocket of his shirt, before he answered. "Football is my only hope," he said at last, with a slow, painful intensity, *la mia unica speranza*—my unique hope. The grandiose adjective "unique" made the announcement appear even more pathetic in Max's eyes. "Perhaps in the end I shall be able to make money with my football—a lot of money. Next Sunday I've been picked to play in the Coppa di Toscana—it's a chance, my big chance. My back hurts when I play, but somehow when I play—that doesn't matter. I feel it, but I don't really notice it, if you see what I mean." He added, after a moment: "My whole future's in my football."

Now, no less abruptly, Max felt his sympathies shift back; he put one hand on the boy's shoulder, and let it rest there. Then he drew out his wallet: "Your friend told me that you needed three thousand lire for an X-ray. I'd like to give it to you."

Enzo stared at the three notes and once again the deep flush mounted to his face as he attempted, but failed, to say something. He was mystified; that was his predominating emotion at that second. Surely there must be something he should do in return?

Something must be required of him? There must be some catch? And it was this feeling, not habit or avariciousness, which led him surreptitiously to examine the water-mark on each note when he thought Max had turned away; but the American had seen, and had wondered, with a sense of extreme helplessness, if he might not have been deceived after all in someone who so blatantly looked a gift horse in the mouth.

"Remember," Max said sternly, "that's for the doctor, so don't spend it on anything else. For the doctor," he repeated. "For the X-ray."

"Yes, yes, *signore*. . . . *Grazie*." Enzo added this first word of thanks in an almost inaudibly husky whisper.

"Would you like to join your friend now?"

"If you wish."

Max led the way along the terrace to the french windows which opened out from his mother-in-law's room. "You, Max?" Mrs. Bennett said without turning round. "He poses beautifully. A bit stiff at first but he soon got the idea. Pity about that shoulder; you've probably not noticed it but the collar-bone couldn't have been properly set when it was broken." Enzo, standing on tiptoe so as not to come too close, had begun to peer at the drawing; then he looked at his friend, and as soon as they exchanged glances, they both began to giggle. "Now you've upset him—and you're in my light too," Mrs. Bennett murmured, once again in English; Max drew Enzo to one side. "Oh, it doesn't really matter, because it's stopped going right." She tore off the sheet of cartridge-paper, crunched it in one hand and then, on an impulse, threw it at the Tunisian. At once he picked it up, unfolded it, and began to smooth it under his hands; Enzo hurried across. Again they were both swept with giggles. "I agree. It's extremely funny." Mrs. Bennett began to scratch one of her unstockinged legs, on which the veins were swollen like bunches of small blue grapes. "Oh, these bites! I suppose they must be mosquitoes. Surely they wouldn't have bugs in an hotel like this? Would they, Max?"

"It's the mosquitoes."

"Oh, they look charming like that. . . ." The two boys were lying horizontally across the bed, their legs dangling and their heads propped against a peculiarly ugly dado of woods inlaid in a

Walt Disney pattern of reindeer among pine-trees. The fingers of Enzo's right hand were laced in the fingers of Rodolfo's left, and from time to time their bodies were convulsed with a brief spasm as one attempted to twist the other into submission. "Hungry?" she asked, and then in her dreadful French: "*Vous avez faim? Faim, faim?*" she repeated as if she were talking to someone who was deaf.

"*Toujours faim*," said Rodolfo.

"Give them the chocolate on the dressing-table, Max." But Max had already wandered back on to the terrace where, arms on balustrade and face on arms, he stood looking for his wife's return with a concentration that excluded all thought of his visitors. "Where's he got to? Oh—he's not there." She got up, threw a slab of chocolate over to them, and then watched, once again scratching her swollen legs, as they broke the slab in two, tore off the paper and began each to devour a half. She was smiling, as she often did when there appeared to be little reason for amusement, and the smile was accompanied by a nervous tic which, fluttering her left eyelid, gave to her whole face a look of almost idiot *bonhomie*. "Now be still," she commanded. "*Restez tranquille. Tranquille.* . . . No, I can't draw you if you giggle. Stop giggling," she commanded, and attempted to translate the phrase into French. But there was no need. All at once the smile had vanished from her face, the idiot winking of the left lid had ceased, and the strange, gaunt woman, with the enormous hands and feet and the penetrating, faded blue eyes, was once again as terrifying as when she had first sent Enzo running in panic from the terrace. "Oh, but that's charming." she was murmuring. They could hear, like a fingernail scratching wall-paper, the decisive strokes of the charcoal, until suddenly she jumped up, caught Enzo's bare leg, and pulled it out at an angle of forty-five degrees. "That's better. You've got the better thighs. He's too thin, the other; wouldn't surprise me if he'd had rickets at some time." It was all extraordinary, they had never seen anything like this, never experienced anything such as this, and yet that unconquerable desire to giggle had all at once left them and they felt (yes, each admitted it to his own secret self) curiously alone, unguarded and afraid. The fingers which had been linked so that they could contest against each other's strength now remained linked because, from that contact, each drew a confidence without which he felt he might suffer some obscure, yet terrible, disaster.

. . . No, but it was no good. She sighed, put the block aside and replaced the charcoal on the table at which she had been attempting to write letters to her children ever since she had arrived, more than a week ago. The marriage between execution and conception, it never came off. She was too old, she had left it too late; or perhaps the gift had never been there, and what she had all along regarded as a sacrifice—her sacrifice to her husband, the children, and the school—had been a sacrifice of something which, in fact, had never existed. A discouraging thought; for it was true, certainly true, that all those years she had got a secret, slightly shameful satisfaction out of telling people: "Yes, I used to paint. But I haven't much time for it now, none at all really." And they would think how plucky she was, running a boys' school to support an invalid husband and five children, when she had had such artistic gifts. And she herself had believed in those artistic gifts, had never for a moment doubted them. Never, until now—coming out to Florence, with the last of the girls married, the school sold, and an annuity to keep her for the remaining ten or fifteen years of her life. Perhaps it had been a mistake to come; but it was at Florence that, as a young art-student, she had met the middle-aged schoolmaster for whom, with one of those reckless gestures so dear to her, she had sacrificed the life to which she had already made a somewhat naïve self-dedication. . . . Seven months later they were holiday-making in the Dolomites, in the village to which her husband, on another holiday, was to be brought groaning and screaming on a stretcher (his physical courage had always been scant) with his spine fractured from a fall of something less than five feet. . . .

The boys' inexplicable flurry of panic had long since ebbed, and they now slept, their fingers still interlaced, their legs still dangling above the high and gleaming bed. Enzo's cheek had slipped on to Rodolfo's shoulder, and the mouths of both of them were smeared with chocolate. The Florentine's flesh seemed to have hoarded, like phosphorus, the sun which it had drunk during the long afternoon's sleep in the dust by the Arno, and now it gave its treasures back to the apartment, glowing warmly against the cool glow of the coverlet. In comparison, Rodolfo's body lay dim: but the stir of his breath gently trembled the hair at Enzo's temple, from time to time a shudder ran through him, as through a sleeping animal. They were like animals, Mrs. Bennett thought, falling asleep in a strange room, on a strange bed, with a strange old woman scratching away at a block of cartridge-paper in front of them. She admired their beauty and their careless, unselfconscious grace; but above all she admired that ability to shut their eyes, to let go, to drop off over the precipice without a struggle. . . . She thought of the last night she had spent and its confused terrors and anxieties, appeased only by the transparent orange phial which she had at last fetched from her daughter's room. On an impulse she got up and crossed over to the two boys, and lowering one hand, ran it slowly up the cheek of the Florentine. How smooth, how warm it was; and here she could feel some invisible vein throbbing rhythmically against the dry surface of her finger-tips. She gazed at the leaning head for many seconds, her hands still at his temple, and did not notice that all the time the Tunisian was watching through half-closed lashes.

With a sigh she turned from Enzo, once again looked at the block on which she had sketched two sleeping bodies, and then, with a sudden, almost tearful irritability, threw it on the floor. Oh, it was hopeless. In England, when the whole family went on their holidays (to that farm-house in Montgomeryshire or camping at Studland Bay) between nursing Eric, minding the children, and doing the household chores, she had somehow found time to sketch; and she had always sketched with an intense pleasure, and the results, apart from regrets that she could do it so seldom, had always seemed satisfactory. But now. . . . Perhaps it was just Italy, or just Florence, the different light, the heat, or the fatigue of the journey. No one would think from that piece of paper that she had once won the Prix de Rome. But that was forty years ago; and so many people had won the Prix de Rome and never been heard of again. . . .

She wandered out on to the terrace, in the hope of finding Max; but he was gone, and all she found was an incredible, brilliant sunset which filled her with despair. The Piazzale Michelan-

gelo lay like a gutted fortress, with the David an avenging angel.
The Arno, shrunk to a narrow gold thread, half lost itself in dense
and dusty vegetation until suddenly at its furthest visible point to
the west it seemed to swell upward like a vast gold bubble. How
warm the balustrade was from the afternoon sun; like that child's
skin, and how cool the evening air. The long day had burnt itself
out into a healing dew and a faint odour, as of bruised violets. For
a long time she stayed there, the risen breeze shaking the folds of
the old, shapeless, blue-cotton dress and stirring her grey hair so
that occasionally a hairpin slipped, with a faint click, to the floor
of the terrace. She no longer cared that she would now never paint
anything worth while, and she had forgotten that in her room she
had left two boys neither of whom might be trustworthy. Further
down the Arno, beyond the Grazie bridge, was the *pensione* at
which, forty years ago, she and her companion had been greeted
by Mrs. Jennings crying: "I know just what you want, dears—a nice
cup of tea"; and that same evening, in the stuffy dining-room they
had disagreed with the officious Englishman who had told them
how unwise it was to drink the Florentine water. And he had pro-
posed to her four evenings later; no, not on an evening as romantic
as this, but in the Boboli Gardens, during a thunder-storm. And
afterwards he had confessed that nothing terrified him so much as
thunder; but that was not true, for she had learnt that he was terrified of most things in life.

Meanwhile, in the darkened room, Rodolfo had gently shifted
Enzo's weight off his shoulder and had lowered him on to a pillow
which that night Mrs. Bennett would find smelling of cheap hair-
oil; he had then tiptoed up to the table, to examine the drawing,
but he hadn't thought much of it (his face wasn't the least like that,
he decided) and so he had begun to turn over the other articles and
papers that lay on the table: the letters which Mrs. Bennett had
begun but never completed to each of her children, the 1899 *Baedeker* with the crushed flowers between so many of its pages, some
knitting, some needle-work, and lastly, a gold fountain pen. He
examined the fountain pen more carefully than anything except
the *Baedeker* with the crushed flowers: he was fond of flowers. It
was an old pen, cumbersomely heavy, and the nib was so broad
that Rodolfo assumed wrongly that it had been broken. When he

pulled a lever a bubble of green ink slowly appeared at a hole in the nib, and grew larger and larger until it all at once exploded, scattering small green beads over the glass-topped table. He wiped them away with his bare arm; then he put the pen in his trouser-pocket, returned to the bed, pulled Enzo's head once more back on to his shoulder, closed his eyes, and soon genuinely slipped back into sleep.

The tranquillity of the dusk was beautiful; and their tranquillity was no less beautiful, brought a no less acute pang to the heart (their breath so even, their bodies so utterly relaxed). Once again she felt the desire to touch that youthful cheek, and going over to the bed on tiptoe, she repeated the caress. There was a faint dust on the luxuriant eyelashes, pollen-like dust on the eyebrow: and here, where her finger touched the drumming temple, she seemed to feel the boy's whole life under her hand. She drew from her belt a handkerchief smelling of lavender, the scent of old age, and used it to wipe away the chocolate stain from around the wide, slightly over-full lips. Then she looked down, and saw protruding from the trouser-pocket of the other sleeping boy a gold gleam which she knew at once to be her own fountain pen. She stared at it for many seconds but felt no astonishment; it was as if she had all along known this would happen and now accepted it, as earlier she had accepted the knowledge that she would never paint any-thing worth while. I should feel surprised, she thought; I should do something—call Max, or ring for the valet, or take it back while he sleeps. . . . But it didn't seem to matter. Strangely, it didn't seem to matter at all.

She went back to the chair, sat down in it, folding her hands in her lap, and from there watched the two sleeping figures as the sky behind her slowly withered from azure to violet, and then went black. She did not sleep, nor did she move. She thought of nothing, unless the intense yet passive contemplation of their beauty was in itself a kind of thought; and when Max came in to fetch her to dinner and to wake and turn out the boys, she felt irritated with him as she would feel irritated with someone who spoke to her while she was listening to music.

"One can't help feeling sorry for them," Max said when they were both gone.

"I look a sight." She stared at herself in the mirror and then said with a touch of petulance: "Why on earth should you feel sorry for them? I don't feel sorry for them. I shall die soon and they'll go on living for years and years and years; living here in Florence, too. I envy them."

"It's not much of a life."

"And is yours much of a life?" She peered at the travelling clock on her bedside table: "Heavens, what's happened to Karen? It's gone nine o'clock. It's so thoughtless of her to be late for meals. She knows that you won't eat without her and how I hate eating alone. I'm hungry. And I went and gave those children my last slab of chocolate. . . . You know, Max, I was mean with them. I only gave them thirty lire each for all that time here. That was mean, wasn't it?"

"You could have given them more."

"Yes, I'm getting all the vices of old age—curiosity, and irritability, and greed, and meanness. They don't hurt others much, there's that to be said for them. But they're so terribly unattractive—so much more unattractive than the really bad vices. . . . Oh, I've hardly a hairpin left. Thank you, my dear." Max had picked two hairpins off the parquet floor. "He took my fountain pen—the Tunisian."

"What!"

"Just put it in his pocket, when my back was turned. Just like that. It was the only useful wedding-present I was given. Oh, that's not quite true. We were given a dumbwaiter—a hideous thing—which was useful when the children were young. I could never teach them to pass anything at breakfast."

"Do you mean—he's got your——?"

"Yes. The funny thing was that I didn't do anything about it. I don't know why. I could have taken it back from his pocket while he slept. That would have been the thing to do, wouldn't it?"

Meanwhile Enzo and Rodolfo were swinging each other round and round in the massive mahogany-and-glass revolving doors; and would no doubt have continued to do so for the whole evening if the reception-clerk had not shouted at them. They retorted with some rapid and pungent abuse, and then, laughing derisively, turned towards the Piazza Repubblica where, in the evening, an orchestra collected a dense, unpaying crowd before one of the city's most expensive restaurants.

Enzo pulled out the three thousand-lire notes. "Look."

"*Mamma mia!*" Rodolfo whistled. "How did you get a chance to lift them?"

"I didn't. He gave them to me."

"Then he *did*——?" Rodolfo smiled knowingly. "Something told me he was that sort."

"No. He just gave them to me. Just like that. When I told him about my back he gave them to me. For the X-ray."

"Come off it! He must have——"

"I tell you, he didn't. It was a present—nothing more."

"Yes, but why should a bloke like that——?"

"I don't know. It seemed a bit crazy to me. Still, I wasn't going to say, 'No, thank you'."

Rodolfo could never resist an opportunity to out-do his friend. "Well, look what I was given. I bet it's worth more than three thousand lire. Look!" The pen flashed incandescent in the light of a street-lamp. "The old girl gave that to me."

"Liar!"

"What the hell do you mean?" Rodolfo raised a fist. "I tell you she——"

"You pinched it. You did, didn't you?"

"And suppose I did? Thirty lire each after we'd been making fools of ourselves for two hours for her benefit! *And* she came and messed you about while you were asleep. I saw her, though she thought my eyes were shut. It's not a bad pen, either. Heavy." As he weighed the gold barrel in his palm, it once again shot splinters of light into the surrounding darkness. "Solid gold, I shouldn't be surprised."

Enzo snatched at it but Rodolfo leapt aside. Under the lamp-post at the end of the street, the two boys grappled, the night's silence broken only by their heavy breathing, an occasional exclamation, and at the last, a clatter as the pen fell on to the cobbles. Enzo groped for it, and the Tunisian at once stamped on his out-stretched hand. But the Florentine had the pen. Dishevelled and bleeding, they stood for a moment staring at each other as if they were strangers brought together by some arbitrary street accident: Enzo's shirt was ripped from neck to waist, so that a bare, muscular shoulder gleamed from the shadows, while from the place where one sole of Rodolfo's shoe had grazed his hand a number of minute, black beads of blood crawled, like ants, downward to the fingers. Suddenly they both began laughing.

"You win," Rodolfo said.

"I'm going back."

"For Christ's sake!"

But Enzo had already trotted off into the darkness; and Rodolfo, hauling himself up on to the parapet beside the Arno, began to examine his injuries while he waited for his friend.

Enzo had no handkerchief, and as he mounted the service stairs, the blood from his hand, flowing freely now, left a trail of bright red drops on the veined marble. The climb to the sixth floor made him more breathless, and when he stopped for a moment's respite he saw, with dismay, that during his fight with the Tunisian the clip of the pen had been wrenched off and lost. They would never find it now.

As he reached the last step, he was taken aback to see Mrs. Bennett and Max walking down the corridor towards him, on their way down to dinner. He slipped into the shadows behind the lift-shaft; then, as they rang for the lift, he came forward.

"Scusi." He held out the pen to Mrs. Bennett; his hand was trembling, either from nervousness or the exertion of the fight, and when he attempted to control it, he could not do so. "Scusi," he repeated in his faint, husky voice.

"Grazie." Mrs. Bennett took the pen as if he were one of the hotel servants handing her an unimportant letter. Glancing up, Enzo was surprised to find her face lacked all expression; but, suddenly, before he looked down once more, the nervous tic, fluttering her left eyelid, made it appear as if she were gravely and deliberately winking at him. It was terrifying.

"Buona sera," he muttered. "Buona sera."

In the silence of the long hotel corridor they could hear the magnified, echoing thud of his feet as he raced down the stairs.

"He must have had to fight for it," Mrs. Bennett said. "His shirt was torn, and his blood is on the pen. Look." The pen seemed to have oozed red ink, but this ink was sticky. She pulled out the lavender-scented handkerchief and began to wipe the barrel.

"That must have needed courage," said Max.

"And honesty—which is so much rarer. . . . Oh, let's go and eat. We seem to be fated not to."

Chapter Two

IN the hotel-garage Karen switched off the engine of the vast, dusty Packard as Max greeted her. "Back at last, darling! I saw the car pass from the dining-room window. You must be tired. What happened to you?"

"Oh, I don't know." She sat for a moment with her hands on the wheel, staring ahead. If her face had been less pinched, her body less meagre, and her clothes and hair less untidy, her claims to beauty would have been indisputable; as it was, it was precisely these defects that gave to her the waif-like pathos which, for Max, had always been a lure more potent than any kind of beauty. Her wrists and arms were so thin, her collar-bone so fragile; when she spoke it was with the faint lisp of an adolescent. Recently she had allowed her fashionably bobbed hair to grow and it hung, straight and dishevelled from the drive in the open car, about her bare, slightly freckled shoulders. There were shadows beneath her eyes, and on one lid an inflammation which Max had already noticed and knew, with concern, to be the beginning of one of her styes.

"You look tired," he said tenderly.

"Thank you. You know I hate to be told that. Now tell me that I look ill. And you look even more gloomy than when I left this morning. What's the matter? Has the market dropped unexpectedly? . . . Yes?" She turned impatiently to the garage attendant, and learning that he wanted the car moved, exclaimed, "Hell! Oh, all right, all right. But why didn't you say so when I first came in?" Recklessly she swung the Packard backwards so that the rear buffer, lunging into another car, rocked it from side to side.

"Hey, hey hey!" an English voice shouted, and a middle-aged Englishman of over six foot appeared, carrying a motoring-rug, a picnic basket and a bag full of golf-clubs. "Take care of my little bus. She's got to get me back to England."

"Oh, damn!" Karen muttered, grinding the gears: she made no apology.

"Shall I do it?" Max suggested.

"No, I'll——" Once again she struggled. "Oh, all right. You might have offered in the first place." She jumped out of the car, snatched her bag, and hurried away.

The Englishman directed Max with bass shouts of "Whoa" and "Rightey-ho" until the Packard was eased beside his own Hillman. Then he said: "You could take the Minx for a drive in the back of that lorry of yours. Must eat up petrol." He examined the car enviously. "You don't often see the old G.B. plate on anything of that size—not these days. Here long?"

"Another week or two."

"You're not English, are you? Canadian, I suppose."

"No, American. But I've been working in England since the war."

"Then I *was* right! The wife and I had an argument. She swore that you were Canadian." Max himself could not recollect ever having seen the man before. "But your wife's English, isn't she?"

"Yes, she's English."

"And that's her mother, I suppose—the other lady?"

His curiosity was so naïve and good-natured that Max could feel no resentment.

"Yes, that's my mother-in-law," he said.

"Bit of an artist, eh? We saw her sketching on the Ponte Vecchio just after lunch yesterday. Right in the sun, too. She should be careful of sunstroke, you know. . . . Play golf?" he asked as they began to stroll towards the hotel.

"No, I'm afraid not."

"Pity. The wife and I've just spent a day on the links. The Ugolino. They're not too bad, you know, better than I'd expected. We took a picnic lunch with us, seemed cheaper than eating out there. Shame we English should be made to feel such paupers while we're abroad. Of course we could have gone to a cheaper hotel, but the wife and I prefer to do things in style for a fortnight rather than spin out our fifty pounds. We didn't have too bad a picnic either. Flies, of course. Some cold chicken, and those 'paninos' with some 'formaggio'—and of course a bottle of 'vino'. I never miss my 'vino'; I think one's system needs it. I'm a medical man myself, and I'm sure one's system needs it. Well, it stands to reason with all that oil in the food. . . . Going into the dining-room?"

"Yes, I haven't finished my dinner yet."

"Oh, well, bye-bye. I must wash first. I expect we'll bump into each other—literally, I shouldn't be surprised, with your wife at the wheel!" His bass laughter swung back and forth like a bell as: "Maskell's the name," he said, "'Tiny' Maskell"; and once again the bell was shaken out loudly. "'Tiny' Maskell," he repeated. "That's me."

In the dining-room Karen was sitting sideways to the table, one bare leg crossed over the other and her head supported by her left elbow, while, fork in right hand, she jabbed at her food. Max touched her head momentarily as he went to his place, but she did not look up. Mrs. Bennett was peeling a peach, the drops trickling down her forearms and even spattering her dress. "This is the last," she said. "I haven't left you one."

"We can ask for some more."

"I told you I was becoming greedy. I never used to care for food. . . . What have you been doing all day, Karen? Did you like Viareggio?"

"Yes. . . . I don't know why we stay on here," Karen added peevishly after a moment; her hair, falling forward over the hand on which her head rested, made it impossible for either of them to see her face. "It's much pleasanter there, much cooler."

"We decided we should be three weeks in Florence," said Mrs. Bennett, "because I wanted to come here. When the children arrive, of course we shall go to the seaside. But to somewhere pleasanter than Viareggio, I hope. I'd always heard it was the Italian Blackpool. . . . You still haven't told us what you did there."

"There's nothing to tell." Karen pushed her plate aside, only half emptied, and then impatiently looked round for the waiter to bring the new course. "I get so tired of this Italian food. . . . Oh, I bathed, and I ate, and I bathed again, and I sunbathed. And then I ate again."

"Karen's so informative," Mrs. Bennett said to Max. "She was like that, even as a child. I can't understand it, I love to share experiences—and so do you. Perhaps that's why she never reads, and writes such bad letters."

"I wish you wouldn't talk about me as if I weren't here," Karen said.

"Well, I don't feel you are here," her mother replied. "You haven't been here for a long, long time."

"Oh, do leave me alone! I can't bear this incessant prying, questioning, fidgeting. It makes me so self-conscious. Can't one be oneself without having to be subjected to incessant analysis from you and Max? That's all I ask—to be left alone." Max had covered one of her small, childish hands, the nails bitten short, with his own large one. "No, please don't. If it's not this mental mauling and messing about, it has to be the other kind. No, don't!"

"Why use ugly words like mauling and messing to describe things that are perfectly natural?" Max asked softly.

"Because they've become ugly."

"Oh, I don't understand you," Mrs. Bennett sighed.

"Well, don't try to understand me! Leave me alone, I tell you! Leave me alone! ... Now you've spoiled my dinner," she announced like a tearful child, her napkin thrown to the floor.

"Karen!" Max attempted to grab her hand, but she pulled away from him. "Do sit down."

"Scenes in restaurants," Mrs. Bennett murmured. Then she saw the waiter hovering with Karen's chicken: "Oh, put it down here, man—anywhere."

But Karen had gone and Max appeared to be about to go after her.

"Sit down, Max. It's always best to leave her alone. She's overtired, anyone can see that. She's not sleeping well and she won't take those pills."

"She's not happy," Max said gloomily.

"No, I suppose not."

"You know she's not. She hasn't been for ages. Is it my fault?"

"You can't help being what you are."

"That's not very kind."

"Isn't it? I thought it was the kindest thing I could say. .... I should like to eat that chicken of Karen's, but I'm afraid I should shock the waiter."

"Aren't you at all fond of her?" Max asked angrily. "You discuss her in this cold voice, and you make all those upsetting remarks to her, and then it appears that all the time you're only thinking about eating her chicken."

"Yes, you're right to be cross with me. But I find I can care about very little now. And even when I do care, there's nothing I can do. Ten years ago I had the power to alter people and circumstances, and I don't know I often used it well. Now, it's gone—and I doubt if I should want to use it even if I had it. I like to think that in its place I've gained in understanding; but sometimes I even doubt that. . . . You were once very cruel to her, Max," she added suddenly.

"Yes, I know." His misery was plain. "And I've never forgiven myself for it. But it was six years ago. Can't one ever forget and forgive."

"It's usually easier to forgive oneself than to forgive other people."

Seven years before Max had been a widower with two young children and, having been sent by his firm to England, had there met Karen. Only eighteen, she was teaching in her mother's school while her father succumbed to a slow and humiliating illness with none of the fortitude that even the cowardly can usually muster for death. She had been his favourite daughter and she had loved him; but now she had come to resent his incessant demands and complaints, to shrink from going near him, and to dream incessantly of a future in which he would no longer exist and she would be free. Circumstances had driven her to believe in the not uncommon heresy that only the healthy are deserving of love; and because, with a family of three sisters and a younger brother, money was always scarce, she had decided that next to health, she most desired money. Perhaps when she accepted Max, she had really loved him; but the wealthy American whom she had taken round the school, because her mother was busy, had at first appeared as no more than a miraculously offered escape—from the boys, whom she could never control, from a large, bickering family, from her mother who always confessed that she "could not understand her", and, above all, from the quavering and tearful cripple for whom she had to perform so many horrors in the name of love and duty.

Soon Max went to the war; and while he was on active service she met the twenty-year-old boy whose child, whose V.C. and whose handful of books were all she now had of him. He had been killed in an act of reckless courage (because of her father's cowardice she had always admired courage more than any other virtue) three days after Max had returned on his first spell of leave. It was absurd to have looked for sympathy from the husband she had deceived, but in the past Max had always fulfilled her smallest expectations. Now, once she had given up to him the whole secret, she met nothing but a stony muteness; and their separate, solitary agonies had continued up to, and beyond, the birth of the child. They were never to have any children themselves.

"I was suffering as much as she was," Max now said, as if in self-justification. "If she'd lost him, I'd lost her. And she became so utterly remote. It's silly to say that grief brings people together. . . . Besides, there was the deception of it. Until his death I never even knew she knew him. Probably if it hadn't been for his death and the child, I never *would* have known."

"But she never lets one know anything."

"Surely keeping the child was a big enough gesture. There can't be many husbands——"

"Many more than one thinks, probably. Oh, we've been over it all so often before, Max. You did all that could possibly be expected. It was just sad that you couldn't do more—as people sometimes can. That's all." Mrs. Bennett plunged a bunch of grapes into the bowl of water provided for that purpose: "Have a grape."

"No thanks." She was staring at them with a dreamy absorption and he added: "But don't let me stop you."

"Oh, I don't want to eat them. But they look so beautiful with the water on them." Some drops hung opaque like small seed pearls, others glittered like minute splinters of glass on the chill, blue flesh. Mrs. Bennett sighed.

They found Karen out on the terrace, crouched like an animal, her knees drawn up and her back against the railing.

"Come over here, dear," Mrs. Bennett said, patting the wicker sofa on to which she had lowered herself. "That cold stone isn't good for you. Or fetch the rug from my room. . . . Oh, as you wish." Karen hadn't moved. After a moment Mrs. Bennett got up and went across, the evening breeze making her clutch her skirt to prevent it from ballooning upwards. "Cheer up, dear." She put out a hand to brush the hair away from the girl's averted cheek, and was surprised to touch something moist. Karen had been crying. In silence Mrs. Bennett watched her daughter while Max leant over the balustrade, his face in his hands. "That blouse looks charming," Mrs. Bennett suddenly leant over to whisper. "But you know, dear, it's beginning to need a wash." Karen said nothing. "It's funny—you're fastidious about everything except your own appearance."

"Oh, do stop nagging, Mother," Karen burst out.

"Well, what have I said now?"

"Oh, nothing, nothing."

Mrs. Bennett turned away. "It's getting chilly here. And I can hear a mosquito. I think I shall go into my room and play patience. Come and see me, Karen, before you go to bed, don't forget. Good night, Max."

She went through the french windows into her room, and Karen watched her as she cleared a space at the writing-table, took some cards from a drawer, and then, moving the lamp close to her right elbow, dealt out "Miss Milligan". Caught in the long, horizontal shadows thrown by the lamp, her face looked older than her daughter had ever before seen it.

"Forgive me, Karen," Max said. He was going to kneel beside her on the terrace but she stopped him:

"No, please—don't come near."

"I don't understand."

"It's a thing I've got and it's becoming worse and worse—I can't explain. I had it when I was nursing father. He liked me to sit by him and let him hold my hand or stroke my hair." She shuddered involuntarily: "Such hot hands, and yet so weak that I felt I only had to squeeze them in order to break them. I used to think of any excuse in order to get away. I couldn't bear it. Doing the most appalling things for him was far, far better. Once he caught hold of me and began to cry against me—like a baby, it was—and I remember that I pushed him away. That was wrong of me, I know, because he was in such pain." She stopped and then said in a tranquil voice, "Yes, this blouse is dirty, Mother is right." She added after a moment: "I wonder if she'll ever stop having a down on me, Max?"

"A down on you?"

"She doesn't realize it, but she's never been able to forgive me. I can see that it must have been hard for her." Momentarily a smile passed across her face.

"How—hard for her?"

"Father caring so much more for me at the end. It was funny, that—and also so unfair. She did everything for him, and I did nothing. She wanted him to live, and I had begun to wish him dead. Yet he loved me." She gave a small, childish laugh. "Like the parable of the labourers in the vineyard, so terribly unjust. . . . Oh, Max, don't look so gloomy."

"You're not exactly bright yourself."

So they remained for several minutes, she crouched on the floor of the terrace and he standing a few feet away from her, his back against the sky; between them lay his shadow and, gleaming in the middle of it, her white bag stuffed with the jackdaw odds and ends which her untidy, hoarding nature accumulated from hour to hour. Suddenly a voice boomed out from the end of the terrace:

"Ah, there you both are. We thought you might be here. May we butt in on a domestic scene? I want you to meet the wife, Mrs. Maskell."

Mrs. Bennett heard the laughter, swinging out and in like a bell, and then, a second later, the telescoped vowels of Mrs. Maskell's voice exclaiming her enthusiasms: the Uffizi was unbelievable, she raved about Donatello, the Signoria had just knocked her sideways. . . . The old woman got up, shut her french windows and went back to the table where her patience lay. But suddenly she felt dizzy, there seemed to be an oppressive weight at the back of her neck. She clutched the tablecloth and, swaying, pulled it towards her so that a few of the cards slipped to the floor. A high-pitched buzzing had started in her ears, and she looked vaguely round her for a mosquito, but found none. All at once she felt frightened, and her fear becoming panic, she hurried out on to the terrace where "Tiny" Maskell greeted her by exclaiming: "Ah, now the cup is filled to overflowing." To show off his height, he had reached up and swung one of the suspended lamps back and forth, back and forth, with a flick of the hand, so that a white radiance splashed over the frightened, and almost cowering, old woman.

The same light, thus swaying outwards, illuminated the two figures who were perched far beneath on a balustrade by the Arno. Each of them had devoured a loaf of bread sliced in two and crammed with thick, greasy rounds of *Mortadella* and now they shared a cigarette, passing it from one to the other in the pauses in their conversation.

"Let's go to the 'casino'," Rodolfo had just said. He added an obscene allusion to the state of his health. "Come on!"

"And what do we use for money?"

"Money! You've got three thousand lire, haven't you?"

"That's for the doctor."

"Christ! You mean, you really——"

"I promised."

"Bravo! Bravo!" The Tunisian taunted in a soft, singsong voice. Then he noticed the light from the terrace, spurting out over the Arno in a pure milky jet. He looked up: "They're sitting there, I bet. Drinking and smoking cheroots, after their dinner. And what a dinner. They're lucky," he said. "Christ, they're lucky."

Chapter Three

It was eleven o'clock, and Enzo's mother sat out on a straight-backed, wooden chair mending the shirt which Rodolfo had torn. She was alone under the solitary street-lamp which lit the winding, cobbled Borgo, and as she carefully drew the frayed ends of stuff together she was already half asleep. From above she could hear Giorgio, her eldest son, plucking one lazy note after another from his mandoline; he was too careless to do more than vamp out a tune, but when he began to sing in his soft, slightly nasal tenor, she lowered her sewing and listened with pleasure. He was her favourite child.

"Going to bed?" Giorgio asked his brother. He was sitting at the window, the mandoline in his lap, and as he spoke he began to cough, jerking the phlegm up and up from his aching chest until he could lean over and spit it loudly into the empty street below.

"Are you unwell?" his mother asked from the darkness.

"No, no." One hand, the nails long and carefully polished, idly teased the strings; twice he sang over the same phrase, a commonplace one, as if it gave him an extreme, voluptuous pleasure; now he tried it again with a series of trills and elaborations. He laughed: "She's promised to meet me," he said. Then he exclaimed: "Washing again!" as he turned and saw that Enzo was standing naked before a tin basin which rested on a trestle in a corner of the room. "What do you do it for? You haven't got a girl. And look how you're splashing the floor." The cold water, thrown energetically over Enzo's gleaming shoulders, trickled down his body to his feet where the boards gulped it greedily.

"Yes, she's going to meet me to-night," Giorgio repeated.

Looking at him, as he sat, fair-headed and sturdy on a wicker couch beside the window, one would not at first imagine that, having been accidentally gassed through his own carelessness during a field-exercise, he was now a chronic invalid. But then, inevitably, his incessant cough and the intense languor of his voice and all his movements would betray his real state of health. He was good-looking and he was aware of his looks; nor was he slow to profit from them, since his pension as a *mutilato di guerra*, small though it was, excused him from all activity except that of local Don Juan. His vanity caused him to walk through the streets with his shirt unbuttoned to his wide, leather belt; to tend his nails with the care of a woman; even, as he was preparing to do now, to wave his naturally straight blond hair.

As he lit the spirit stove, he said: "I managed to slip into the room while Ma Kohler was out shopping. For once she had forgotten to lock the door. The girl was hot stuff, I can tell you. She liked it all right when she got it—and came back for more!" He continued with his story while the stove whined and spat, and Enzo, in a disgust which he could never dare to voice, continued to splash the cold water over his face, arms and torso.

The Rocchigianis had let out two rooms near the top of their house to a German woman, one of the many destitutes of that nation, who attempt to scrabble an existence in a city where they are now no longer wanted. Fräulein Kohler, who had been manageress of the defunct *Pensione Germania*, took in needlework, gave occasional lessons in German, and offered herself as a guide to bewildered Swiss tourists. With her was a girl, of obvious Italian features, whom she always called her "niece". The niece was nineteen, but being both epileptic and slightly simple, did no work except sewing, and never left the house except in her "aunt's" company. She could have been a beautiful girl, with her large, vaguely melancholy eyes, her soft hair and skin, and her clear features, but for the fit which as a child had caused her to fall on to a stove and shrivel one half of her face. She had always frightened Enzo, particularly when in the darkness of night he would be woken, on a sudden, by her shrill, unearthly screams; so that meeting her on the stairs, he would always hurry past with no more than a glance and a quick *"Buon giorno"*. But Giorgio had long since decided that she was, in his own crude phrase, "a lovely bitch".

Fräulein Kohler, whether through an intense possessiveness, or through fear of what other accidents might befall, always locked the door on her niece when she went out; and the niece herself, Bella she was called, never seemed to rebel or even fret against this strictness, appearing content to sit for hour after hour at an open window, sometimes sewing but more often merely gazing out into the Borgo. If Giorgio or some other of the local boys whistled up to her, she would look down but make no other response. When her "aunt", a big, red-haired woman about whom everything seemed aggressively competent except a pair of small, strangely frightened green eyes, talked to Bella, the girl would answer her in a soft voice without any trace of German accent, usually in monosyllables; she would rarely talk to anyone else. But sometimes, when the two women sat out together with the Rocchigianis on a hot evening, Bella, who appeared to be paying no attention to the conversation, would all at once let out a strange, high-pitched, whinnying laugh at a remark which no one else had thought funny. Only on such occasions, and during her fits, would there be a stir in the dreamy immobility in which her whole life was passed.

Giorgio was explaining how he had found a key that would open the door of the bedroom in which the two women slept, sharing a double-bed, which was covered after the German fashion

in a balloon-top scarlet eiderdown. That evening, he continued,
Bella had told him that her mother would be acting as cloakroom
attendant at a dance at Fiesole and it was unlikely that she would
return until the early hours of the morning. "So it's money for
jam," he said. "As soon as Mum and Dad have turned in, I can open
the cage." He chuckled, and then noticed that Enzo was staring at
him, his face dripping with water and a rag-like towel in his hands.
"What's the matter?"

"Nothing."

"You prig!"

Enzo shrugged his shoulders.

"You don't think I should do it?"

"I didn't say that."

"But you think it. You do, don't you?"

"Well—yes."

"My God!" Enzo admired his brother for many things which he
assumed that he himself did not do because he lacked the courage, and this contemptuous exclamation at once made him wince.
Like most younger brothers, he very much wanted Giorgio's good
opinion.

"If it were an ordinary girl," he tried to explain, "it would be different. But you know she isn't all there. Half the time she doesn't
know what she's doing."

Twisting the tongs in the flame of the stove, Giorgio laughed:
"She knows what she's doing all right. You can take that from me.
And she likes it!"

"Then perhaps that makes it worse. Perhaps she loves you."

"I wouldn't be surprised," said Giorgio coolly. He looked round
for a piece of paper on which to test the tongs and stooped to the
floor. He whistled. "What's this?" The wad he had picked up was
Enzo's three thousand lire.

"They're mine. They must have fallen out of my shirt when I
was undressing."

"Where did you get them?"

"I was given them."

"Oh, yes?" Giorgio still held the three notes in one hand, while
with the other he grasped the curling-tongs. "You were given
them," he mocked. "And by whom?"

The inquisition continued, as the older boy avenged himself on the younger for the disapproval which had somehow blunted the edge of his night's adventure. When he had learnt all the facts, he looked out of the window and, seeing his father, slouched in a chair with his pipe, while his mother still sewed, called down: "Hi, there! Enzo's come home with three thousand lire. He was trying to keep it dark, the little miser."

"What! Where'd he get it?" came back the thick, slurred voice of their father. "What? . . . That's all very fine, but he lives here for nothing, does no work, hasn't done any for two years. The rent's overdue, he knows that."

Enzo had all along guessed this would happen if he showed them the money and now, cursing himself for his carelessness, he determined not to give in. His father shouted up, he shouted down; Giorgio intruded his cool, sharp comments. His mother pleaded—the money was Enzo's, had been given him for the doctor, and should be used for that purpose. Rubbish, exclaimed Signor Rocchigiani. There was nothing wrong with the boy—except idleness. He could play football, couldn't he? Well, couldn't he? The once quiet Borgo echoed with their recriminations, heads appeared at windows, a woman's voice shouted to them to shut up and Signor Rocchigiani shouted to her to do something obscene in return; until, after many minutes, Enzo saw the three notes fluttering slowly down from his brother's smooth, beautifully manicured fingers into his father's grasp. "No, Luigi," his mother once again protested: but the notes were thrust into the purse sewn inside Signor Rocchigiani's greasy belt.

"Thank you," Enzo said bitterly to his brother.

"It wasn't my fault. He told me to chuck the money to him."

"You didn't have to do what he told you."

"That's fine, coming from you. You're always telling me I should have more respect for Mum and Dad." But being naturally good-hearted, in so far as selfishness, vanity and weakness allowed him to be, Giorgio now felt guilty. "I'm sorry, Enzo," he said. His brother had stretched himself out on the bed where they both slept together, and Giorgio went and sat beside him, putting out a hand to ruffle the younger boy's hair.

"Oh, have it your own way, then," Giorgio said. He picked up the tongs which had cooled during the argument and once again twisted them in the flame.

A girl's voice was fluting plaintively: "Mummy! Mummy! What was all the noise about? We can't sleep"; and their mother could be heard answering: "It's nothing, dear. Go back to bed. Back to bed." Giorgio was singing to himself as, standing astride before a blotched mahogany-framed mirror, he crisped his hair; but from time to time his whole body was shaken with a cough and he would yet again lean out and spit into the darkness.

When, an hour later, the house was still and Giorgio had slipped out on his outrageous errand, Enzo still lay naked on the crumpled coverlet, his arms crossed behind his head and his eyes staring at the ceiling. He hated them, he hated them all. The money was his, Giorgio and his father had stolen it from him. They didn't care if his back got worse and worse until he became a cripple. He couldn't help it if he couldn't get work. There were thirty-eight thousand unemployed in Florence alone, it was so unjust. So unjust, unjust. And his father had never done a stroke of work for as long as he could remember. Selling guidebooks in the Signoria, that wasn't work, and he didn't even do that now. Drinking and smoking and playing cards, and talking politics, politics, politics, while his mother worked herself to the bone. Oh, but she was so weak with him, always had been, had only herself to blame. If only he could get away! Why not to England, or to America? There a chap had a chance. That's all he wanted, just a chance. Or Tunis. Rodolfo had spoken to him so often about Tunis. One walked through the orange groves and picked oranges, just put up one's hand. . . . But the French had turned them all out, they weren't wanted there, they were wanted nowhere. He was wanted nowhere. Nowhere. Wanted nowhere. . . . He turned over and lay with his hot cheek against the cold pillow; sweat trickled down between his shoulder-blades, while one hand, hanging over the edge of the bed, rapped on the floorboards. At this moment Giorgio was lying in her arms, here, just here, beneath his fingers. Again he rapped. Oh, it was horrible. He thought back to his first and only visit to the "casino", and how afterwards he had pretended to Rodolfo that he had enjoyed it. But of course Giorgio was right. Bella was beautiful. Sitting at the open window, her sewing in her lap, while she gazed

down. Such fine wrists and the soft shadows under her cheek-
bones, soft shadows between her breasts when she wore that silk
dress and leant forward to pick up a reel of cotton. . . . Feeling an
increasing pressure in his loins, he turned over once more on to his
back, and stared at the ceiling. . . .

"Mother! What are you doing?"

"Sh!"

Her hair now in pig-tails, she slipped through the door, a small
saucepan clutched in one hand; she did not turn on the light.

"Is the back bad? I couldn't sleep for thinking about it. Dad
should have let you have the money. But you do understand, don't
you? He's so terribly worried just at present. And it came so conve-
niently—the rent being due and all," she explained.

"Oh, I'd forgotten about it," he lied. "But it's hot. I can't sleep."

"Where's Giorgio?" she asked, suddenly realizing that what she
had taken to be the shadow of his sleeping form was only the bol-
ster which Enzo had pushed from beneath his head.

"He couldn't sleep either, so he went out for a stroll."

"I warmed this oil to rub your back. Turn over."

"Oh, there's really no need. It's not hurting. You're tired, Mummy.
Go back to bed." Enzo could remember how ten, even five years
ago, his mother had still been beautiful; but the worries and pri-
vations of the war, combined with child-birth and long hours
spent underground in the steam and darkness of the laundry, had
already spoiled her. At thirty-six, her hair was turning grey; her
skin was blotched and sallow, the pores distended; round her neck
there were four or five deep wrinkles as if a length of twine had
been tightly twisted about it.

"I'm not tired. Turn over, dear." Coming from Siena, she spoke
without any of the disagreeably hard and guttural ch's of her husband and her children.

Enzo at last turned over, and she sat down beside him. Dipping
her hands into the saucepan of warm oil, she began to work at
the boy's glistening body with a persistent rhythm that made him
think of lying out on the beach at Viareggio, while the waves broke
and receded over him, one after another, causing him to glow and
tingle from his head to his feet. . . . Now, glancing at her as he lay
with his head turned sideways, he saw that she was working with

her eyes closed, as if in sleep, and that her arms, so strangely white against his brown body, were much thinner and frailer than he had ever imagined them to be. And yet she was so strong. As she bent close above him the crucifix which she wore slipped out of her nightdress and rested for a moment icily against his spine. Now her fingers seemed to be gently erasing his anger and bitterness as if they were things written in pencil, there, on his back; and it was her own spirit, not oil, that she seemed to be rubbing into him, rubbing with a rhythmic, unwearying persistence as her love persisted unwearyingly, in spite of the disappointments and fatigues of the day. Enzo was at last utterly relaxed.

"I wonder when Giorgio will return," she murmured.

As she said the words an epileptic scream flashed like a dividing sword through the night's reposing darkness.

Doors opened, feet thudded down stairs; voices were raised, one of the girls began crying, "Mummy, Mummy, Mummy," over and over again, and then Giorgio could be heard explaining coolly: "I heard the sound just as I was passing the door on my way in. I tried all my keys and this one fitted. . . . A bit of luck, a real bit of luck."

Chapter Four

"YOU'RE later than usual," Karen said to her mother who had only just arrived at the breakfast-table.

"No, not later. Earlier. I couldn't sleep, so I got up at half-past six and went for a walk. Now I'm hungry." She turned round to click her fingers for the waiter. "He's half asleep—always is in the morning."

"What was it like out?" Max asked, without any interest, since the mail had brought him a heap of business letters to keep him absorbed.

"Oh, cool."

"He's not really listening," Karen put in.

"I know. That's why I answered in only two syllables."

Beside the Arno Mrs. Bennett had found the once-dusty vegetation glistening with a heavy dew that wet her bare ankles and made

her plimsolls squelch. She had walked into the sun which had at
first appeared as no more than the tip of an opaque pink finger-nail
through the mist on the hills; but as it rose higher and drank up the
mist, her eyes began to ache from having to look at it and her skin
to prick and itch with its slowly increasing warmth. All at once she
felt tired and decided to sit down. The ground was still damp, but
recently she had ceased to worry about such things, and finding
a small, humped mound, she lowered herself on to it and stared
at the water. How dirty it was, she thought: where it slapped the
wrinkled mud there was a fringe of scum in which bobbed ciga-
rette-ends, paper, and the other human filth of the city. Yet those
two boys who had helped to make this filth—who daily bathed in
it and sunbathed beside it—had been clean, so miraculously clean.
And at the thought, she once more gave herself up—as she was
always now giving herself up—to the recollection of their sleeping
beauty on the dim, high bed.

She stirred from this reverie to notice some sunflowers growing behind her; and since they were larger than any she had seen
in England, the vast orange petals curling outward to the warmth
of the morning, she tottered up to pick one, not realizing, because
there was no fence, that they were grown there for their seed.
While her hand struggled with the stiff, prickly stem, twisting
it from side to side without its once yielding, someone sneezed
from the undergrowth at her feet and, to her astonishment, a voice
asked: "Che fa?"

"Am I not supposed to pick it?" she answered in English.

Like some aged Caliban a man lumbered up out of the grasses
and approached her, dragging a tattered army blanket in his left
hand and carrying some boots in his right. His clothes, with their
innumerable joins and patches, had the appearance of having
once been sewn on to him and then never removed, in spite of
an increase in his girth which threatened to explode them as the
swelling seed explodes its pod. A grey lather of hair frothed from
his head over his chin, the nape of his neck and the space where his
shirt lay open. He wore gold-rimmed glasses, mended at one side
with a piece of rag and cracked horizontally across both lenses.
His mouth had fallen in about two long, decaying eye-teeth, the
bridge of his nose had collapsed. Again he sneezed, and a thin

thread of spittle glittered in the sunlight on his beard. "Ing-leesh," he suddenly said, in a voice which wheezed and scraped as if some old engine had been started up after many years of idleness.

"Yes."

"You-want-the-flower?"

"Yes."

"*Un momentino.* A moment, please." He sat down on the mound where she herself had been seated and began to tug his boots (they made her think of the early Charlie Chaplin) on to his blackened, sore-covered feet. Then, without doing up the laces, he went over to the sunflower and began to wrestle with it, his breath coming painfully in long, shuddering sobs, as if it were some creature he were trying to behead. "*Difficile, difficile,*" he muttered.

"Oh, don't bother, please don't bother."

"*No, no. . . .*" He swayed grotesquely from side to side, and the whole plant now swayed with him; then he tugged, tugged, tugged. "*Ecco!* . . . Please, lady." With a strange little bow, almost as if he were parodying the manners of a dead generation, he held the bruised, battered head out towards her, the nails on his upturned hand curling round over each finger as if they were claws. Now a strong smell of turpentine from the bruised petals was mingling with the sweet-sour, almost intolerable odour from his mouldering body.

"Thank you."

Suddenly, looking into his face and finding nothing uncovered by hair except the collapsed nose and mouth and a pair of blue, blood-shot eyes, whose red, sagging rims were smeared with what looked like golden eye-ointment, she felt an overmastering horror. "Thank you," she repeated. She twisted the stem of the flower into the belt of her dress, and turned to hurry away.

But he was hobbling after her, gesticulating, talking Italian, tripping from time to time over the laces he had never done up, then all at once shouting, running as she ran, clawing at her arm. . . . She knew that at any moment she would fall, collapse, be left wholly to his mercy, and wondered whether to shout for help; until through the stream of Italian she heard, as if she were at last striking some solid object through water, the words "Tip . . . tip . . . tip"; and then, in an enraged, tearful reiteration, "Hungry . . . hungry

. . . hungry." Turning her back to him in case he should try to snatch her bag, she pulled out the first note that came to her hand, unfortunately a thousand lire, and threw it to the morning breeze so that he had to grovel after it as it fluttered over the mud. . . . She did not wait to hear his thanks.

"Well, what *was* it like?" Karen was asking.

"Oh, as I say, cool. Pleasant. There were no bathers, not a soul. . . . I've just thought why I woke up so early this morning," the old woman added.

"Why?"

"Excitement."

"Excitement?"

"Aren't you excited? The children coming," Mrs. Bennett explained.

"Oh, the children," Karen said.

"Evidently not."

"Now please don't try to make out that I don't care for them, Mother. I do. And I've been very much wanting them to come. I just don't get excited over things before they happen, that's all. Unlike Max. I think his most intense pleasures and pains are in anticipation—or in retrospect."

"What's that?" Max asked, looking up.

"Nothing, dear. Mother and I are talking because, unlike you, we haven't any letters to read. I do envy Max his letters. They give him a status—the assurance that he is necessary in the world."

"The children should give you that," Mrs. Bennett said, staring out past her daughter and then suddenly giving a small bobbing nod.

"'Tiny' Maskell?" said Karen.

"Yes, dear. . . . The servants here all speak such good English that I wonder why he imagines he has to shout in order to be understood. Edith Maskell is showing her mid-riff. It looks odd at breakfast."

"May I look round?"

"Yes, but wait a moment. They've guessed that we're talking about them. People always do."

Karen at once swung round in her chair, so that if the Maskells had previously been in any doubt they then must have been sure;

covering her face with a hand, she began to giggle. "She'd never dare in Wimbledon—or did she say Putney? I wonder what Dr. Maskell's patients would say. And all those shoulder-straps—I can count at least three. What do you suppose they all support?"

"Oh, nonsense, Karen." Mrs. Bennett laughed and then added. "If you're going with them to Siena to-day, aren't you being a little rude?"

"You stared first."

"Yes, but I didn't have to turn round to do so."

"You're not going to Siena, are you?" Max suddenly asked, lowering his prospectus.

"Yes. . . . Why not? I told you about it and you said you didn't want to go. You didn't seem to have any objections to my going."

"But the children," Max said.

"Well?"

"You're going to meet them?"

"The train doesn't get in until after seven. Of course I'm going to meet them."

"It's a long journey. Suppose the car breaks down. You know how disappointed they'd be if you weren't on the platform."

"Oh, really, Max!" Karen laughed, but without any kindness. "It's bad enough that we should have to be at the station two hours early when we're catching trains ourselves. You fritter away so much time just waiting for things."

"My own time," Max said. "You prefer to fritter away other people's time, by making them wait." He had taken out a gold pencil and was jotting some figures on the back of an envelope; Karen leant over.

"Counting it again?" she asked.

"Counting what?"

"The money. All the money. . . . I must go and ask the Maskells when they expect to start."

"She's no better," Mrs. Bennett commented, as Karen went away, and added, "I feel so dirty. I can't think why."

Then she knew the reason. The old man's feverish scrabbling at her bare arms had given her the sense of being soiled, almost infected.

Chapter Five

MAX's Italian secretary, Lena, had large, masculine hands, a great deal of coarse black hair on her bare arms and legs, a figure which Mrs. Bennett had unkindly described as being "all anyhow" and a breathlessly efficient manner. Yet in spite of all these disadvantages Max had always thought her an attractive girl. She smiled readily and when she did so her oval, somewhat podgy face at once acquired charm; the teeth she showed were beautiful, her fine dark eyes glowed with good humour, a dimple appeared in her left cheek.

"That's enough for you to get on with, isn't it?" Max had been lying full length on his bed, his hands over his eyes, as he dictated letter after letter to the girl.

"If you'd like to go on, don't worry about me," Lena assured him. "To-day I feel indefatigable."

"Yes, but to-day I feel far from indefatigable," Max replied with a smile. "It's sweet of you to offer, though. I really ought to go on, because I know that to-morrow there won't be a moment, with the children just arrived."

"The children! Of course, I'd forgotten! They come this evening," she exclaimed excitedly. "How pleased you must be. And Mrs. Westfield too! I am so glad for you."

"Yes, we are pleased," Max said, feeling his words to be somehow limp and tepid after the girl's.

She was pushing her dictation pad into the battered portfolio which she always took about with her as she said: "I think you work too hard, Mr. Westfield, considering this is your holiday."

"The work has to be done. Besides I came here partly on business."

"It must be a great strain, feeling that you are responsible for so much money, for so many people. And yet it must be exciting, very exciting."

"Oh, I've long ago ceased to think myself important. Six months ago one of my fellow directors was killed in an accident. He had a

great opinion of himself, obviously considered himself indispens-
able. But apart from a certain amount of administrative fuss and
bother, the difference his death made to the firm was nil. That
made me think."

"I believe you're too modest." She sat looking at him, her portfolio clutched in her hands and her face glowing with the adoration she would never dare to voice. Nor was it necessary that it
should be voiced, since Max had long since guessed.

"Well, I think that's all then, Lena."

"Oh—I—I—wonder, Mr. Westfield," she began as she went to
the door, "I—I was wondering if—if I might be allowed to come
to the station to encounter your children's train. I'd keep in the
background of course, but I should just like to see them. I've heard
so much about them," she ran on hurriedly, her face becoming
more and more red and a chain of small bubbles appearing on her
long upper lip. "I feel I know them really well, and of course you
needn't introduce me or anything, it's just if I can remain there
and observe them, that's all, just observe them. I should consider it
indeed an honour," she concluded breathlessly, and pulled a handkerchief from her sleeve to run across the tip of her nose.

Max felt touched. "Of course you can come, the more the mer-
rier. The children will be delighted to have a reception committee
for them. I can pick you up in the car, if you like."

"You mean I come here?"

"No, I can pick you up at your house. I have the address somewhere, haven't I?"

"At my house?" As she echoed the words, a number of questions collided in her mind. What on earth would he think of the
shell-chipped block of apartments? Should she ask him in? Introduce her mother? Offer him something to drink? "Oh, that's really
not necessary," she said.

"But why should you have the long, hot walk here?"

"I can bicycle."

"Even bicycling exhausts one in this sort of weather. No, I can
easily pick you up. At about seven o'clock."

"I'll be waiting on the steps so as not to delay you."

"Is your mother better?" Max asked kindly as Lena prepared to
go out.

"She still has pain in her abdomen, Mr. Westfield. . . . If I close the shutters, perhaps you would like to sleep? You look tired," she added tenderly. "You are Atlas supporting the world."

She reminded him of someone and when she was gone he lay for many seconds thinking who it could be. Each time that he was almost on to the connection, his mind seemed to shy away, as if it were afraid, until suddenly with an odd, jolting shock, he at long last knew: Ethel, his first wife. . . . Oh, they were not really alike, because Ethel had been frail, with mouse-blonde hair, a soft, almost inaudible voice and small hands which perpetually fluttered as she talked. But the smile, yes the smile; and the same douce, almost cloying, tenderness which at one and the same moment made him want to relax with a sigh and to run far away. . . . For both women his work was a mystic dedication to be spoken about as the wives of politicians speak about their husbands' careers; whereas for Karen it was merely the source of holidays in expensive hotels, a town and country house, and the children's education. Never for a moment did Karen flatter him with the thought that what he did could be done by no one else; but for poor Ethel, as now for Lena, that belief had been implicit.

Not that he had ever really enjoyed being Ethel's hero. Even as a young man, when the taste of adoration is kinder to the palate, he had often wanted to vomit up her sweet, uncritical devotion. And indeed, what had first attracted him to Karen, apart from her pathos, was precisely her refusal to find him impressive, as Ethel had done. Moreover her very scepticism had driven him up and up to heights which he doubted if he would ever have scaled with only Ethel to satisfy. All at once, on marrying Karen, his ambitions had swollen; for, whereas, with Ethel, it had been enough to have made a success out of his uncle's business in Detroit, to own a six-bedroomed house and a comfortable Ford tourer, and to have a single coloured maid, under Karen's grudging eye these achievements soon began to seem small. And so the business ceased to be a Detroit business, or even an exclusively American business; and with a strange mingling of joy and fear he had discovered in himself abilities which, because of the atrophying effect of Ethel's praise, he had never known he possessed. Karen demanded so much, the most ingenious and reckless of deals winning from her no more than a "Not bad, darling", that each success only served to make him struggle higher in the determination that one day he would really show her, one day she would really be impressed. ... And he had come so much to enjoy the tireless pushing upward, that sometimes the thought of attaining this object would make him feel afraid. After that, what would be left? he would ask himself. Would life seem all at once empty?

Ah, but the climbing so often made him feel giddy; and then, like the traveller in the desert who suddenly thinks nostalgically of tea in his suburban home (soggy toast, fruit cake and damson jam in a crystal dish), Max would think of the six-bedroomed Detroit house, of Ethel padding up and down stairs in slippers to "peep" at the sleeping children, of picnics, visits to the cinema, and holidays in a bungalow on the Cape. Perhaps he didn't really wish to go back to these things any more than the traveller really wants to return to his suburb; but there were times when an intense, parched longing for them would fill his whole being. To return, only to return!

As if to break from this craving, he got off the bed and thumbed through some of the letters and papers which Lena had arranged on his desk. The man in Vienna was obviously inefficient, perhaps should be sacked. What news from London? Rome—he'd have to go there. ... Suddenly, a physical giddiness, the counterpart of the mental unease he felt as he turned the typed papers, made him clutch the side of the desk. Up and up, up and up. ... He remembered how at one of his college initiations he had had to climb a pole blindfolded, while below the members of the fraternity had belaboured him with plimsolls, belts and rulers. He had seemed to climb for hours to escape from their encouraging shouts, their laughter, and their sharp, stinging blows; nor had he ever wholly escaped from them, since in the end they had pulled him down and told him that would do. ... "That will do"; he had never heard Karen use the phrase.

He wandered into her room and, as if deliberately to humiliate himself, began to pick up and sort the possessions she had strewn everywhere on chairs, floor, and bed. Dirty underclothes lay on clean dresses which the maid had brought the day previously from the laundry; her last night's evening-dress had been chucked in one corner; on the dressing-table there was a handkerchief stained with lipstick, a confusion of bottles, pieces of soggy cotton-wool and odds and ends of paper, and littered among them, the whole contents of one of her jewel-cases. Suppose the maid had come in and taken something? And if she had, would Karen have ever missed it? Max began to take up the rings, brooches and necklaces and place them one by one in their crocodile-and-gold box. He liked Karen to dress well; and since, in spite of her untidiness, she succeeded in doing so, he never for a moment grudged her the money thus spent. But without being mean, he was naturally careful of money, and it grieved him that she should waste and spoil what he gave her by her indifference to its value. Whereas his own straitened upbringing had made him always "careful", on Karen the same sort of upbringing had had the precisely opposite effect; marrying Max, she had decided that she would never again worry about money.

Sorting out the jewellery, Max came on a circular diamond-and-ivory brooch, in an old-fashioned setting, which he stared at for many seconds, holding it in both hands. It was one of the few, perhaps the only really valuable piece of jewellery he had given to Ethel; and when he had become engaged to Karen, it was the first of his many presents to her. The brooch had been his mother's. Karen had never really cared for it and had talked of having it reset, without ever doing so; but when, the year previously, he had suggested that, since she never wore it, they might give it to Pamela, his daughter, on her sixteenth birthday, Karen at once refused. From then on she had worn the brooch at increasingly long intervals.

Unlike Karen, Ethel had never cared for jewellery, putting on the same few pieces day after day. There was her engagement ring, which he had bought for forty dollars because she wouldn't let him spend more, her wedding-ring, a cultured pearl necklace, a hideous spray of flowers in jet and pearl—the bequest of an aunt—some diamond ear-studs, and of course this brooch. When she died, bleeding stanchlessly after child-birth, she whispered "I've nothing to leave you, dear. Just my few bits and pieces. And of course the kids." He had told Karen this story and she had at once turned away, making him think she was smiling, because the remark had struck her as sentimental. But then she turned back; her eyes were full of tears, and he felt strangely and pleasantly relieved.

Having put the brooch away among the rest of the jewellery, Max set about collecting the soiled handkerchiefs, scraps of paper and cotton-wool. Ethel had been so tidy, so irritatingly tidy. ("What's the matter, darling?" "I can't find my socks. I do wish you'd leave things where I put them." "But they're not lost, darling." And the socks would invariably be produced.) She wore heavily starched white blouses, her skin always smelled vaguely of coal-tar soap, and after each meal she would go into the bathroom to brush her teeth. She kept a Christmas-card list, sent and received. . . .

But now his whole being went out to the dead woman, as sometimes in the lonely years before he had met her, his whole being would go out to his dead mother. Yet, while he thought of her, it was only half her features that he saw. Strangely, the rest were the girl Lena's.

Chapter Six

"I HOPE you don't feel too uncomfortable after the luxury of your Packard," Mrs. Maskell said.

"No, of course not," Karen assured her.

"They're plucky little cars, these Hillman Minxes." On the back of "Tiny" Maskell's head there was a grey-flannel cricket hat such as Karen could not remember having seen since the days at her mother's school. His heavy jowl shone after its morning shave like a slab of purple meat and she noticed, glancing at his massive hands on the wheel, that he wore a broad gold wedding-ring on his fourth finger.

"You must be excited about the children," Mrs. Maskell said, and then, clutching at her hair, "Could you shut the sunshine roof a little, Tiny?"

"What's the matter? Losing the old toupée?" His bell-like guffaw jangled back and forth, deadened only by the stifling upholstery. "Yes, you must be pleased about the brats," he said.

"Have you any children?" Karen asked.

"No," Mrs. Maskell answered in a small voice from the back of the car.

Tiny sighed. "It's not for want of trying," he said. "There's nothing we want more. Still, we have some nephews and nieces, we get a lot of fun out of them. And I always say a doctor has to be a father to his patients."

"I love your dress," Mrs. Maskell said. Unlike her husband she did not care to talk about their childlessness and believed him to be insensitive for doing so.

"Do you? I'm so glad. I got it in Paris when we stopped there on our way through."

"We hurried through Paris as quick as we could, to avoid the temptations."

"What temptations?" Tiny asked jocularly, but Mrs. Maskell's voice surmounted this obstacle, merely by rising a little, as the car was at that moment surmounting the bumps in the road:

"Fifty pounds is so little," she said. "One feels so ashamed, having to niggle and scrape all the time. It can't be good for British prestige." Plumply middle-aged, she had a fresh complexion, a round, indeterminate face and a tendency to wear the sort of clothes and hair-styles which she saw in fashion magazines on girls of half her age. At present, as she leant forward, the white flesh of her bare mid-riff was creased into three rolls. "Someone thumbing for a lift," she said, as out of the dust before them a khaki-clad figure with a rucksack on his back could be seen with raised arm. "No, don't stop," she told Tiny who had begun to slow down. "We're cramped enough here already, what with the picnic basket and those two empty Chianti bottles I keep telling you to throw away."

"Looked English," Tiny said.

"Probably one of those Scandinavian students who would sleep on the beach of our hotel at Nice. They do Europe on a shoe-string. I rather admire that, because I could never do it myself. They've got guts, those Nordic people. Don't you think, Mrs. Westfield?" She fingered her hair which was brushed back in a straggling Dauphin bob. "Don't you?"

"More than the Southerners, you mean?"

"Yes, more than the Southerners."

"Chris always gets romantic about the North," Tiny Maskell explained. "That's why I've never dared to take her for a holiday up there. I think it began with a Swedish medical student she was walking out with before she met me."

"Oh, don't be silly, Tiny."

"What was he called? Tore—Tore——"

"I can't remember."

"Of course you can," he said jovially. "You're only bluffing. I often wondered what happened to the chap? Nice-looking boy, he was."

"I made a list of what we ought to see in Siena," Chris Maskell interrupted. "At least, I made it with the help of an Italian friend of ours." She added impressively: "The Marchesa di Canelelas."

"Oh, yes," Karen said.

Mrs. Maskell felt that some amplification was necessary. "Last year she fell suddenly ill during the night in our hotel at Salzburg and Tiny had to go along to see her. It was sheer over-eating, he says. But she thought he'd done wonders for her, and she told us to be certain to visit her if we came here. Well, when we arrived, of course like most of the best people she'd gone up into the mountains. But she invited us up to Vallombrosa where she was staying and gave us a gorgeous lunch and tea. She's an awful darling, really terribly cultured as they all seem to be, and speaks the most lovely English—much better than the average Englishwoman. Anyway, I asked her about Siena and she gave me a list of 'musts'—and——"
Chris paused for emphasis—"and an introduction to Count Chigi so that we can see the Chigi collection. You've heard of the Chigi collection?"

"Yes, of course."

"Two Botticellis, I think she said, and something we must look at by someone called Sanso-something-or-the-other, and quantities of marvellous furniture, glass and so on. It was particularly kind of her to give us the introduction because, as you probably know, without one, one can't get in."

"Unless one tips the attendant two hundred lire," Karen could not resist saying. "That's what Max did."

"Really?" Chris looked at her in dismay, and then added: "Oh, these Italians are so corrupt!"

"Well, anyway, what's the plan of campaign?" Tiny asked.

"I thought we'd keep the Chigi collection to the last—until the afternoon—and that before lunch we'd peep at the Duomo, the Palazzo Pubblico, San Giovanni"—she continued to read from her list—"and the Accademia, and something here which I can't quite make out." She handed the list to Karen.

"Oh, the Palazzo Buonsignori."

"Yes, that's right," Chris said, without attempting to pronounce the name. "You're not stopping again, Tiny, are you?" It was one of their jokes that he so often had to leave the car.

"I'm not stopping," he said. "But the old bus is. I wonder what's the matter with her. Plenty of petrol."

One by one they all tumbled out into the heat and dust of the road. Tiny pulled up the bonnet of the car and put his head into it, clicking his tongue against his teeth. "Well, what's wrong?" Chris asked, yet again hitching at her shoulder-straps. She perched on a stone by the roadside but at once leapt up. "Christ, it's burning!" she exclaimed. "What's wrong, Tiny?"

"How the hell should I know? Give a chap a chance."

Chris turned to Karen. "He's a kid-glove driver. At home he can't even mend a fuse. I think men should be practical, don't you?"

"Oh, stop nattering, Chris!" Tiny growled, as he surveyed the car, leaning back with his paunch stuck out and his hands at the belt of the crumpled grey flannels which sagged low on his hips.

Two cars had already shot past, covering them with dust and choking them with fumes, but the third, a battered and rickety Fiat, at least twenty years old, drew up and, while two children peered from the back, an old man asked them in Italian if he could be of any help.

"What's he want?" Tiny demanded.

"He wants to know if he can help," Karen said.

"No, I can manage on my own. Please thank him and tell him I can manage. It'll only mean a large tip."

"Oh, don't be so obstinate, Tiny!" Chris exclaimed. "We don't want to be stuck here all morning."

"I can put it right in a jiffy. Anyway he doesn't look as if he knew a thing about engines. He's almost in his grave. I don't want him meddling about, you don't know what harm he mayn't do."

"Oh, all right, all right. Have it your own way." Chris sank down on to a patch of grass under an olive-tree; but once again she had to leap to her feet. "Ants!" she exclaimed. "Oh, you are maddening," she accused Tiny in a sudden fury. "It's always like this. If we get lost, he's always too proud to ask the way. It's so bloody silly. We'll all get sunstroke," she added peevishly. "And I'm dying of thirst."

Karen was not herself sorry for the interruption. The olive-tree against which the two women leant, with its dry leaves that changed colour at each breath of wind and its small, pebble-like fruit, was no less beautiful than the falling landscape whose crowded lines at last blurred into a heat-haze in the distance. Karen appreciated natural scenery, though she could never appreciate "sights". "Is that Siena?" she asked, pointing to the hill that rose up before them.

"One of the hill towns," Chris said despondently. "God knows which." With each minute she saw another item on her time-table disintegrate in the dust until, in the end, the Chigi collection would no less certainly vanish away. "Oh, do something, do something, Tiny!" she shouted in despair. "Don't just stare at the car as if you thought you could hypnotize it into going. Do something!"

Many minutes later Tiny was still gazing at the bonnet, his expression more puzzled and his hands more greasy, but with no other change; Chris had returned to the back seat where she read Angela Thirkell, crossly flicking over the cross pages, one after the other. Karen, her back against the olive-tree, was watching a khaki-clad figure trudge up the road. She recognized their hitch-hiker.

He was older than he had appeared in the dust of their passing, a man of about forty with close-cropped hair, thin, muscular legs and arms burnt black by the sun, and a slender, slightly cruel face, the lips thin and wide, the cheeks marked with two deep, vertical creases. As he walked past, he turned his head to glance at Karen and then stopping, said in an oddly youthful, staccato voice: "Achilles and the Tortoise." He lowered himself on to the grass a few feet away and began to take off one of his army boots.

"Take care," she warned. "The ground is covered with ants."

He laughed. "I'm used to them. My skin's like leather now. They don't seem to bite me. Fleas, too—and bugs. It's rather useful." He tugged off the boot and said: "I hope you appreciate that I got to leeward of you. These socks need a wash. Yes, I thought so. A nail has come through." She noticed that the dust of the road lay thick in his ears, his eyebrows and his hair. "What's the matter?" he asked, pointing to Tiny's protruding rump.

"We don't know." He went on hammering at his boot with a flint, until Karen said: "Don't you think you might offer to help?"

"No. But I will if you wish it."

"Do you know anything about cars?"

"More than your friend, I expect. . . . Is that his wife peering out at me from the back of the car?"

"Yes."

"Why on earth does she expose herself like that? The Italians hate it, even on the beach. They think it indecent."

"You'd better tell her."

He shrugged his shoulders as he pulled at his laces. "None of my business," he said. Then he got up, and brushing the dust off the seat of his shorts, sauntered over to Tiny. Five minutes later he returned. "Well, I think that's done the trick."

"You are clever." Karen was sarcastic.

"Thank you. Could you help me with my rucksack? The strap has got twisted."

"Goodness, it is heavy," she involuntarily exclaimed.

Tiny now joined them, followed by Chris. "Well, she's going all right! Silly of me not to think of the plugs. Anyway you've saved our lives for us, we can't thank you enough."

"Yes, thank you so much," Chris said. "My husband's no mechanic, as you've probably guessed. . . . Can we give you a lift?"

"No, thank you."

"Oh, please!" Chris exclaimed. "We've bags and bags of room. And it's such a climb to the town. I suppose you're going to Siena."

"Yes, I'm going to Siena."

"Then we insist, we absolutely insist! We couldn't possibly let you walk after what you've done for us. No, we insist."

"Thank you, but I should prefer to walk. . . . Good-bye—good-bye—good-bye."

Having given to each of them in turn a small, mock bow, he

adjusted his pack, squared his shoulders, and at once set off.

"Well!" exclaimed Chris. "What silly pride! Anyway, it's his loss not ours."

"Cutting off his nose to spite his face," said Tiny. He clapped his hands together: "All aboard, everyone! *Andiamo!*"

Chapter Seven

WHEN Tiny had finished arguing over the bill for their lunch, he slipped twenty lire under his coffee-cup and then put out a clumsy hand to his wife's bodice: "That shoulder-strap is showing again."

"Do leave it alone. I need a pin."

"I've got one," Karen said, turning over the rubbish in her bag, and added: "If you don't mind, I think I'll call a halt to my sight-seeing this afternoon. I've got a bit of a headache." The truth was that she not only disliked "sights", but she particularly disliked looking at them while Chris read from her *Baedeker* in a loud and tireless singsong.

"Oh, you poor dear," Chris said. "I've got some Alasil in the car. It was all that standing in the sun. But you can't miss the Chigi collection. It's the high-spot of the whole place."

They argued for many minutes and then separated, with Chris saying in a sharp, injured voice: "Well, headache or no headache, it's not the sort of thing *I'd* miss for anything."

Karen wandered out to the Forte Santa Barbara because Max had said that it was the only place in Siena where one could escape one's claustrophobia; but when she approached the entrance, she found a turnstile and a vast poster announcing that a *Mostra di vino* was in progress.

"Can I get in without visiting the exhibition?" she asked the attendant who dozed, fork stuck out and head on chest, in the shade of a tree.

"Hundred and fifty lire," he said in English. He spat into the sunlight.

"Yes, I know. But I don't want to visit the exhibition. I only want to sit down in the Forte."

"Tickets," he said, resolutely refusing to understand her Italian.

"Hundred-fifty lire. *Vino*," he added, and raising an imaginary glass in one hand, he tilted back his head. "*Buono*," he said, and smiled.

"All right, a hundred and fifty lire."

It was the hour of siesta, and the garishly painted booths shimmered in desolation against the bare red brick. There were signposts everywhere of colossal size, directing visitors to Gabinetti, Direzione, Ristorante, Informazione: but there were no visitors to follow these trails, and if there had been, they would have found the places closed. From the centre of the arena three megaphones attached to a tapering white pole tirelessly broadcast American records to the attendants who slept, usually in deck-chairs with handkerchiefs over their faces, under the awnings of their booths. Suddenly a gun-like report shattered their repose; but having looked up and ascertained that nothing more had happened than the explosion of a bottle of Asti Spumante in the Calabrian pavilion, they all once again relapsed into unconsciousness.

Watching the wine fizz and froth from the jagged edge of the exploded bottle, Karen felt thirsty.

"I'll try some of that. . . . No, not that bottle—there may be glass in it." The drowsy boy in the sweat-stained singlet reluctantly opened another bottle and filled a tall glass. It was disgustingly sweet and warm. Karen paid and walked on, leaving the glass half-full for the attendant to drain.

She had heard that Orvieto was good; but the woman, whose snoring she had interrupted, produced at least half a dozen different kinds and Karen was at a loss to choose between them. As she dithered, the woman brought six small tumblers from under the counter, which she then filled, one from each vintage. "*Prego*," she said. But they all seemed to taste alike. Delicious. Karen touched one of the tumblers at random and said: "*Molto buono, questo.*" Whereupon the woman said, "*Si, si, vino finissimo*," and filled a large glass. As an afterthought she picked up a lump of ice in some tongs and dropped that in.

"Isn't that being a little unkind to it?" Karen asked, in English, since she had already begun to feel confused.

"*Si, si*," the woman agreed enthusiastically, while Karen drained the glass.

Vino Santo. . . . That was a dessert wine, and it was lighter—

or was it heavier?—than Sauterne. The attendant was annoyed at being disturbed and he purposely gave her small measure in a glass that had not been washed. But wine is disinfectant, she told herself. Tiny Maskell had said something about that and how it prevented tummy upsets. It was strange that she could drink so much and yet still feel thirsty. But she wished someone would turn off the panatrope. "They should turn it off," she said.

"*Che cosa?*"

"Turn it off," she repeated. "The panatrope. I can't hear myself drink."

"*Signora?*"

"Oh, hell," she exclaimed. "Never mind. The same again."

Her visit to the exhibition had suddenly begun to have all the excitement of a tour through Italy: Sicily, Sardinia, Apulia, Campania, Abruzzi. . . . Had she been into the Calabrian pavilion? She couldn't remember. But, oh yes, that was where the bottle had gone off like a gun in the heat. The sun was certainly strong, her head was feeling much worse, in fact she felt far from well. And that hideous panatrope, grinding out "Did you ever see a dream walking?" . . . It was so old, had been old already when Bill and she had danced to it in a bedroom in the Regent Palace, the portable grinding the tune out until someone banged on the wall. It had been two o'clock. And then the chill, echoing dampness of Liverpool Street Station on a winter dawn. His fountain pen and pencil hurting her as he kissed her, a long dying whistle, running for the train. . . . Her handkerchief fluttering grey in the smoke.

Oh, she felt so giddy; she thought she wanted to cry. A tattooed arm raised the bottle before her and she read "Broglio", peering close to the label and spelling the word out with her forefinger. "Yes, some of that," she said. But she never drank it.

On a bench in the corner of the Forte she was found by their English hiker. "Hello," he said and then, peering down at her face, clammy and green in the shade of an ilex: "Aren't you feeling well?" She was lying full length, her bag on its side in the dust.

"No. I'm drunk."

"Drunk?"

"Yes, it's this beastly exhibition—and the sun. I've been so ill." Suddenly she wrinkled up her face and began to weep.

"Well, you seem to have learned your lesson," he said, squatting on the ground at her feet. "When you feel better, we can go and get some coffee."

"I suppose you disapprove of me? You disapproved of Chris's dress."

"I don't like to see a young girl drunk," he said.

"You are a prig."

He took no notice of this remark, but fetching from his rucksack a grubby, paper-bound copy of *La Chartreuse de Parme*, he settled down to read.

"You have a hole in your neck," Karen suddenly said. "I've only just noticed it."

"Yes," he said, without looking up.

"Is it a wound?"

"Yes, a bullet wound."

"It must have hurt." She turned over on her stomach and groaned: "Oh, I feel so ill! I feel so ill!"

"If you're going to be sick again, I suggest you go into the lavatory. It's just around the corner."

"You're callous," she sobbed. "You're beastly and callous. Oh, I hate you!"

Chapter Eight

"No, not there." The Englishman, who was called Frank Ross, at once objected to the café she had chosen.

"Why not? We had delicious ice-creams there this morning. And we can look at the Palazzo Pubblico."

"Too expensive," he said.

"Oh. . . . I'll pay."

"No," he said in an even voice. "We'll go to this *latteria* and we'll each pay for ourselves."

"But I don't want to go in there," she retorted as she would have done to Max. "It looks sinister."

He laughed. "Don't be silly, there's nothing sinister about it. Come on." Before she could object, he had gone in before her.

"I don't like your manners," she said.

"Don't you?"

"I think you're extremely rude."

"That's the only way to deal with you. . . . What'll you have to drink?"

"I don't want anything to drink."

"Yes, you do." He turned to the man behind the counter. "Two large coffees. . . . How do you feel? Better?"

"I hate to be despised."

"Despised?"

"I know how you despise me. For being drunk in the middle of the afternoon. And then for not going back for my lipstick when I knew I had dropped it under the bench. And now because I don't like being in this kind of place."

"You're rich," he said.

"And you despise me for that."

"No, I have far too great a respect for money to despise those that have it. But you shouldn't let it spoil you."

"What are you doing in Italy?"

"I live here."

"Work here, you mean?"

"Sometimes."

"Where do you live?"

"Oh, all over the place." He laughed: "You say that I'm rude, but your own curiosity isn't exactly polite, is it?"

"I'm sorry. I'm interested, that's all. You interest me," she repeated. But he had turned away to speak to the waiter.

"Sixty lire, with a twenty lire tip. That's forty lire each." He waited for her to pay him her share and when she handed him a fifty lire note, returned her ten lire.

"Now what?" he asked when they emerged into the street. "What about your friends?"

Karen pulled a face. "I'm supposed to meet them at the car at five."

"It's now four o'clock," he said, looking at the watch on his thin, brown wrist. "Are you driving back to Florence?"

"Yes. Do you want a lift?"

He smiled. "No, I don't want a lift. I'm going there, but I don't want a lift."

"Why?"

"Oh, I prefer to go in the S.I.T.A. bus. The company's more amusing."

"Thank you."

"You know I didn't mean you. But they're both pretty good hell, aren't they? One can see that at once. Well, aren't they?"

"They're very kind people," Karen said. She had never thought it before, but now as he criticized them, she knew it to be true.

"Oh, kind! Don't pretend that they don't make your flesh creep."

"You've hardly spoken to them."

"Come to Florence with me, in the bus," he suddenly suggested.

"No, I can't do that."

"What's the matter? Afraid of the discomfort? Yes, it *is* uncomfortable. You may have to stand. And there's the noise and the dust. And, of course, the people."

"I wish you wouldn't sneer at me. I've told you, I don't like it. . . . I can't come with you because I've promised to go back with the Maskells. They'd think me awfully rude if I didn't turn up."

"You could leave a note. I have some economy labels in my rucksack. Write on one that you've met an old friend and we can stick it on the car window."

"I think that would be rather ruthless." As if she had suddenly made a discovery, she added: "You are ruthless, I think."

"Here's the label. Sit down and write on it. Use my fountain pen. . . . What's the matter?" he asked.

"I've something in my eye."

"Don't rub it, that'll only make it worse. Let me see."

"No, it's all right, thank you." She shrank away, as she had always shrunk from the hands of others. "It's all right, really it's all right."

"How can it be all right, when your eye is streaming tears? Do you think I'm going to hurt you? Or are you just being old-fashioned?" He put one hand on her chin and with the fingers of the other opened the eye. She at once squirmed away, making him exclaim angrily: "Oh, don't be such a coward. . . . Here, wait a moment, I can see it. It's a bit of grit." He pulled the handkerchief from her belt, once again making her struggle from him like a wild animal, and with a gentle flick removed the irritation. "All right?"

She had covered her face with both hands and he repeated: "All right?"

"Yes, thank you. I just felt faint for a moment, it must be the drink. Yes, I'm all right now," she said in a flat, subdued voice.

"Well, write your message then."

"There's—there's just one thing——"

"Now what's the matter?"

"I've got to meet a train at seven-thirty. What time does the bus get back? I mustn't be late."

"Oh, I think it should be back by then. I don't know for certain," he answered casually.

"But I must be certain. You see, I'm meeting my children. They're coming out from England."

"You've got children?" he said in surprise. "You look so young."

"Only one of my own. The other two are my stepchildren."

"That means that your husband is older than you?"

"Yes. . . . Why are you smiling?"

"I guessed that he would be."

She moved as if to leave him, but then again sat down. "I must know about the bus," she said.

"Oh, we'll ask when we get on."

But he forgot; and, of course, she forgot to remind him.

Chapter Nine

"MAX must have walked miles up and down this platform," Mrs. Bennett said to Lena.

"He's worried," Lena said.

"Oh, I long ago ceased to worry about Karen and if he was sensible he would follow suit. . . . Oh, do sit down, Max, do stop this incessant prowling. You make me feel so hot."

"Sorry," Max said. "But what can have happened to her? I rang up the hotel and they said the Maskells had returned without her. Unfortunately they went out again almost immediately, so I can't get in touch."

Mrs. Bennett shrugged her shoulders, as if the topic bored her, and said: "How nice you look, Lena. I've seldom seen you look nicer." The girl had no figure and it was sensible of her to wear a plain suit of dark blue shantung, with a white blouse, white shoes and a white hand-bag. There had been days when she had been less sensible. "Doesn't she look nice, Max?" But Max was once again striding up the platform.

Pamela, a tall, thick-set girl with a high colour, large hands and feet, and a mass of straight blonde hair which she wore to her shoulders, was the first to jump from the *wagons-lits*. As the train panted into the vast, cool station, like a dying animal returning to its lair, she waved a handkerchief at her window and screamed in turn: "Daddy, Mummy, Granny." Then she leapt out and threw herself on her father as if she were a dog. "Oh, Daddy, Daddy, Daddy," she squealed. "And Granny—darling! . . . But where's Mummy? Isn't she here?"

Her brother Colin was fourteen, two years her junior, with a small, compact body which made him look even younger, sleek black hair, his dead mother's fluttering hands, and a voice which seemed over-precise because he had once had a lisp. Having spent three years at school in England, both he and his sister had lost all trace of their American accents.

He was helping Mrs. Brandon, who had brought them, and his younger brother, Nicko, down from the carriage.

"Bigger jump than England," Nicko remarked. He was a sturdy, fair-haired child, but at this moment he was tired and travel-sick, and he spoke in a whisper.

"Nicko was sick," Pamela said. "It was awful. All through the journey."

"Wasn't, wasn't, wasn't!" Nicko shouted, stamping his foot in rage.

"Oh, Pamela," Colin rebuked her. "You know he didn't want it said. . . . Come, Nicko. Here's Daddy—and Granny."

"Hello, old chap." Max lifted him up, kissed his cheek and then hugged him, but the child seemed to sense his foster-father's awkwardness and at once screamed: "Put me down, put me down, put me down!"

"He's tired," Colin said, feeling sorry for his father. "Isn't he, Mrs. Brandon?"

"Yes, I'm afraid he hardly slept a wink." Nicko was now clutching Mrs. Bennett's hand, his thumb in his mouth. "How he loves you, Mrs. Bennett," she said with a touch of envy, since she had never herself succeeded in winning a child's affection. She was a woman thin to the point of emaciation, with eyebrows pencilled on gaunt, bony brows, black hair cut fashionably close to a head that was always slightly tilted back on its spindly neck, and hands whose fingers, habitually curling inwards as if about to grasp something, were covered in rings. Her voice was clear yet toneless, with a remarkable carrying power. She edited a woman's fashion-magazine.

"I hope the children were good," Max said, making Pamela and Colin exchange fearful glances.

"Oh, of course they were," Mrs. Brandon said. "They were angels, and I don't know how I should have managed without them. Colin has got the most lovely manners, I envy the girl who marries him."

"Colin says he never wants to marry," Pamela declared.

Mrs. Brandon gave a laugh that sounded like pebbles being rattled in a tin can. "Oh, boys always say that," she exclaimed. "But when they grow older they change their minds."

"I shan't change my mind," Colin said.

Max shifted uneasily, as if he imagined that the example of his own marriage had deterred the boy, while Nicko murmured to his grandmother: "I'm hungry. I'm sleepy."

"Well—let's go!" Max said. "No, you don't have to carry your suit-case," he told Pamela. "The porter can take it for you."

"Yes, put it down, child," Mrs. Bennett said. "It's far too heavy. You'll only rupture yourself."

"He's a very old man," Pamela said, and for the first time the others noticed that what she said was true.

"He'll have to get a buddy to help him," Max said; but when he passed on this suggestion it was at once laughed away. No, no; he could manage easily on his own, the porter declared, he wanted no assistance. Max shrugged his shoulders: "Incredible," he said. "What about you, Maisie? Are you coming with us?"

"Lady N. said she'd send a car for me. I've been warned about it. It's a 1923 Daimler, driven by an aged, aged retainer and it always breaks down or runs out of petrol on the way up to Fiesole. But she'd be awfully hurt if I didn't arrive in it. I wish I were staying at Palazzo d'Oro with you," she added.

"Mrs. Brandon says that life at the villa will be absolute hell," Pamela said. "There's no bath and one has to use things called *bidets* and when somebody-or-other stayed there last year the lavatory wouldn't pull for the whole of July."

Mrs. Brandon laughed. "Don't let Lady N. hear you say that."

"Are we going to meet Lady Newton?" Colin asked dubiously.

"I expect so. . . . You don't look pleased."

"From what you've said about her, she sounds awful," Colin said.

"I don't know why you want to stay with her, Mrs. Brandon," Pamela added.

When Mrs. Brandon had chugged off in the back of the Daimler and the rest of them were in the Packard, Max suddenly exclaimed: "Good God!" He had just started the engine, but now switched it off.

"What's the matter?" Mrs. Bennett asked, easing Nicko's thumb out of his mouth as he slept in her lap.

"Lena," Max said. "What became of Lena?"

"I forgot all about her," Mrs. Bennett said. "The child must have wandered off."

"Who's Lena?" Colin asked.

"She must have thought us terribly rude. We took absolutely no notice of her—didn't even introduce the kids to her. After all, it was very decent of her to come anyway."

"I hope her feelings weren't hurt," Mrs. Bennett said. "I think she's a girl who feels more deeply than one thinks . . . Give me your handkerchief, Pamela. Nicko's dribbling all down my blouse. Oh! What a filthy rag!"

"I'll just slip into the station to see if she's still there," Max said.

"Who's Lena?" Colin repeated.

"Your father's Italian secretary," Mrs. Bennett said.

"Is she nice?" Pamela asked.

"Yes, she's a nice, sensible girl. A very nice girl," Mrs. Bennett answered: "But she doesn't always dress sensibly," she added.

"No one's ever quite right for Granny," Colin said.

Max was dressing for dinner while Colin sat on the edge of the bed and watched him. Recently, father and son had begun to feel more and more awkward in each other's presence. The love between them was still deep, but as Colin grew older, its physical expression suffered increasing restraint without either of them finding the intellectual substitute for which both hoped in secret. Max, frightened by the child's alarming precocity, always had the suspicion that he was being laughed at; whereas Colin, wanting confidence in his ability to command affection, mistook his father's shyness for lack of warmth and sympathy.

Admiringly the boy watched the muscular reflection of his father's naked back and shoulders in the long mirror, at the same time feeling that he should say something to bridge the long silence that had begun to gape between them.

"I'm sorry about the school," he said at last. Although, when writing to his father, he had bravely concealed his disappointment, his failure to win a scholarship to Winchester had by now become an obsession.

"What on earth does it matter?" Max said, drawing his cut-throat down the fold of his cheek. "You're going there anyway."

"I'd like to have got it. . . . Everyone expected me to get it," Colin added. "That's the awful part of it—when people expect you to do things, and you fail." He looked at the back of his father's head, but Max said nothing, continuing to shave. It was silly of him to have tried to explain, the boy decided; obviously his father had other things to think about.

Meanwhile Max was deciding that all the possible answers at which he in turn clutched would sound either patronizing or trite or sentimental or callous to his son's ears, so in the end he said nothing at all. But having finished his shave, he forced himself to cross over and ruffle the boy's hair. "It's good seeing you again," he said.

He was both surprised and touched when, with a strange violence, the boy gripped his bare forearm, muttering no more than: "Yes, father. I'm glad."

But such moments were rare in their relationship; and they were to become even rarer.

"Well, have you forgiven your mother?" Karen asked gaily, as she joined the dining-table. "Well?" she asked, when no answer came.

"Of course," said Colin. He had risen to draw back his stepmother's chair, and now stooped to pick up Mrs. Bennett's napkin. His sleek black hair gleamed under the light; he was wearing a grey flannel suit, the trousers fastened with a snake-belt, and a tie which he had chosen with much deliberation from his father's collection.

"You seem less sure, Pamela."

Pamela's cheeks reddened as she bent over her soup. "Nicko was disappointed," she said. "He was so excited about seeing you."

"Well, he's seen me now," Karen answered in perfect good humour. "And he didn't seem annoyed." She had just left him upstairs in a bedroom which opened out from Mrs. Bennett's.

"You could have been there," Pamela pursued. "You knew what time we were coming, ages and ages ago."

"There's no need to whine," Karen said, in reference to her stepdaughter's tendency to become tearful when she was angry. "I've already explained, it wasn't my fault. I never knew that the bus would take two hours to do a journey which only takes an hour by car."

"Buses usually take longer than cars."

"I don't like your tone. I admit that I made a mistake and I've said that I'm sorry. I can't see what more you expect me to do."

"But why did you come by bus, dear?" Mrs. Bennett asked.

"Oh, Mother!" Karen exclaimed. "I explained that when we first met. I came by bus because I got so bored with the Maskells. They got so on my nerves. I just felt that I couldn't spend another moment with them. I asked when the bus would arrive," she continued, on an impulse, with a fresh lie, "and the man said nineteen forty. Well, I know it was stupid of me, but I always get confused by that way of telling the time and I thought it meant twenty minutes to seven."

"You subtract twelve from the number," Colin said.

"Thank you," Karen laughed, and added: "It's nice to have children who can give one lessons in arithmetic."

"Let's drop the subject," Max suggested.

"Willingly. But before we can drop it, I must go and have a word about it with Mrs. Maskell," Karen said, catching sight of Chris alone in the hall. "Now that I've made my peace with you all, I must make my peace with her."

Pamela examined Chris and then said: "I'm not surprised that Mummy preferred to go by bus. Mrs. Maskell looks quite awful." She and Colin both giggled as their grandmother reprimanded: "You've taken to saying very unkind things about other people. It's something new, and I don't like it. You were unnecessarily sharp to your mother."

Meanwhile, Karen had approached Chris Maskell: "I'm afraid you both must have been awfully cross with me for my rudeness."

To her surprise Chris Maskell at once caught her hand, smiling conspiratorially. "Of course not, my dear! Tiny was a little put out, at first, but I soon squared him. I hope you had a lovely time," she added, squeezing the fingers she still held in her own.

"Yes—yes, thank you," Karen said, taken aback by this un-expected cordiality. "It was such a coincidence. I ran into this old friend——"

"Old friend!" Chris exclaimed. "My dear, I saw you as we passed that café place. His rucksack caught my eye, you know—through the window. Tiny wanted to join you, he's so tactless, but I soon knocked that little idea on the head. He never understands, I've lost all hope of teaching him." Giggling, she added: "And I had my own little adventure, you'll hardly believe it." Suddenly a blush of agonizing intensity swept up her face, as she said: "We climbed all those steps—four hundred and something of them—up the Torre di Mangia, and Tiny wanted a photograph of the two of us against the view, so, as luck would have it, there was this perfectly charm-ing Swede standing there and Tiny asked him and of course he was only too delighted, and then we got into conversation, and it turned out he was coming to Florence." Again she gave a short, breathless giggle as if it hurt her to do so. "It was so funny after what Tiny had said about my having a thing about Scandinavians, because of course it's quite true. Anyway he's staying here, he's the son of a baron, he told us, and I very much—— Oh, here he is, with Tiny!"

A tall young man, so blond that he almost seemed albino, in a suit cut ostentatiously wide at the shoulders and narrow at the hips, was walking down the stairs with Tiny beside him. "May I present—Count Béngt von Arbach," Chris said. This time the giggle came like a convulsive swallow: "Have I got it right?" she asked. "It's such a mouthful. . . . Mrs. Westfield."

As von Arbach bent low over Karen's hand, repeating his name, she at once noticed the oddly Mongolian cast of his features—the cheek-bones high, the eyes at a slant, the nose flat and broad, the eyelids almost invisible when the eyes were open. Yet, for all that, he was an attractive young man.

"Who is that tall person with the Maskells?" Mrs. Bennett asked as Karen returned to the table.

"He's wonderfully glam," Pamela remarked.

"Wonderfully what?" Mrs. Bennett queried.

"Oh, he's someone Chris met in Siena," Karen said absently, busy going over the lies she had told in the new knowledge of the Maskells' having seen her and Frank together. "He's Swedish," she added, "or perhaps she said Danish. He's the second of their discoveries to-day; when the car broke down, an odd Englishman helped to mend it and then we kept running into each other, as one does on such occasions, until we exchanged addresses. He's in Florence," she continued, deciding that, since there was a danger that one of the family might meet him, truthfulness was now the best policy. "He's doing it rough. Funnily enough he was in the bus in which I came back. An odd character, odd," she said, repeating the adjective since it expressed her own baffled estimate of him. "Called Frank Ross."

"Frank Ross?" Max queried. "You don't mean the Burma man? Colonel Ross," he added when Karen looked blank.

"Mummy, you must have heard of Colonel Ross," Pamela said.

"Well, I haven't."

"But *everyone* has heard of him."

"I never met him," Max said. "I'd like to have done, because opinions were so divided. I know that some people thought him a military genius—but others, whom I respected, said that he was a selfish and ambitious charlatan. Of course they said that of T. E. Lawrence, too—and there's no doubt that Ross did almost impossible things in the jungle. . . . The professional soldier always finds it hard to forgive the successful amateur."

"Do you mean you've met him, Mummy?" Colin asked with mounting excitement.

Karen laughed. "I really don't know. He's called Frank Ross, and as he has a wound which he got in the war, I suppose that it's possible. But he seems to have no money, he carries nothing but a rucksack. I thought he was some sort of tramp."

Max smiled. "That sounds like Frank Ross."

"Will he be coming to see you?" Colin asked, and almost simultaneously Pamela exclaimed: "I hope that we can meet him?"

"I hardly know him," Karen said. "We only talked for a moment—as I say, he mended the car in five minutes after Tiny had been trying to mend it for more than half an hour." There was a subdued note of admiration in her voice as she said this, then she yawned: "He was quite amusing but *odd*—definitely odd. I should quite like to see him again," she added. "The people one can't understand are the people one wants to see again—aren't they?" she appealed to the whole company.

There was no one to disagree with her.

Chapter Ten

ENZO and Rodolfo were seated on their perch before the hotel, but when the Tunisian attempted to tease or have horse-play with Enzo, the usual ways in which they passed the time when they had nothing else to do, he noticed a lethargy in all his friend's responses. "What's the matter?" he asked, at the same time turning his head to gaze after two American girls who had passed, skirts swinging from their freely striding thighs. He gave a provocative whistle, and then shouted some abuse when they did not look round. "What's the matter?" he repeated, putting a hand on Enzo's shoulder.

The other, who was rocking back and forth on the balustrade, his arms clasped across his stomach, said no more than one laconic word: "Hungry."

Rodolfo turned out the pockets of his shorts but nothing was to be found except two fag-ends, a lottery ticket and a quantity of dust. When he held out one of the fag-ends in an outstretched palm his friend shook his head: "I feel sick."

"Can't you get something at home?"

"I've had another row with the old man—says I can't even sleep there to-night. It was my fault. I told him what I thought of him. But he's a bastard . . ." He continued with a string of obscenities, his eyes fixed moodily on the swing-doors of the hotel as they sucked in and ejected a ceaseless stream of well-fed, well-dressed foreigners. Already the boys' visit to the Palazzo d'Oro had achieved all the qualities of a dream; and indeed its details had long since merged into the details of the real dreams that had followed it, with a confusion of opulent detail. But, strangely, like most Italians, Enzo felt no resentment when he compared that life of extravagant richness with his own life, but only wonder and a kind of sad, futile desire somehow to better himself.

"Wait a moment," Rodolfo said, and flashing a smile, he sprinted off into the darkness on noiselessly swift feet.

Karen came out of the swing doors, and shuddering slightly in the night breeze, turned to Max who had followed her. "Be a darling, and fetch my fur. I'm feeling rather cold." She crossed the road, dubiously, as if she expected a robber to spring out at her, and standing no more than five feet from Enzo, looked at the water. He looked at her; and then, involuntarily, as it were as a tribute to her beauty, he began to sing one of the popular songs of the day in a soft, barely audible voice. It was "Auld Lang Syne" and all over Italy that year it was being danced as a slow waltz. Karen recognized it, but the Italian words and the boy's light, nasal tenor seemed to blur the melody, to make of it something fluid, insinuating, cloyingly tender. As she listened to it, a strange, romantic longing and despair filled the Englishwoman, though she could not have said for what she longed, for what despaired. She walked slowly back to the hotel and a moment later Max joined her, slipping the fur over shoulders which gleamed white for Enzo through the surrounding darkness.

"Look!" Rodolfo dived into his shirt and produced three cakes, pastry horns, a little battered after their journey and oozing a green, pus-like custard.

"Where did you get them?"

"Eat first."

"You have one."

"No, I don't want one, I'm not hungry." But when Enzo insisted, the Tunisian placed a whole horn in his mouth at one go. Chewing it noisily and laughing at the same time, so that flakes of pastry kept showering from between his small, white teeth, he told the story of how he had gone to the small store at the corner of the street and had found, as he had hoped, that there was no one serving but the old woman, one of whose eyes, sealed by a cataract, bulged from its socket with the greenish-blue sheen of a hard-boiled egg. He had asked for some ink and while she had turned to rummage with arthritic fingers in a shelf below the counter, he had deftly slipped aside the glass panel which covered the cakes, at the same moment releasing a satiated blue-bottle, and had grabbed the three horns. She had suspected nothing, and had even apologized when he had told her that the ink was the wrong colour.

Enzo laughed: "When I have some money, I'll go in and pay her."

"Fool!" Rodolfo spat into the darkness. "You and your conscience! If you hadn't been so honest about the three thousand lire, we could both have gone to the 'casino'—*and* had something to spare."

"Oh, shut up, shut up! I've heard enough of that three thousand lire. . . . I saw the American, just now, while you were away. With a woman—his daughter, perhaps."

"Go on! What did she look like?"

"A lovely bitch." Enzo described Karen in the crude terms in which the boys usually discussed such topics; until, suddenly, the conviction slipped in on him that whatever he said fell somehow short of life, indeed only travestied it. He had never experienced this before, and he at once became silent.

"Well?" Rodolfo prompted. "Go on."

"That's all," the Florentine mumbled. "I couldn't see her even. It was only for a few seconds. But she was beautiful." He sighed, putting one of his hands to his face and rubbing an eye, as if he were tired.

"I could do with a woman," Rodolfo said. "Like that," and he indicated with an obscene gesture yet another American passer-by. . . . "How's your brother?" he next asked, chuckling in reminiscence of Giorgio and the epileptic Bella. "Any more fits?" And he punched the Florentine in the ribs and repeated: "Any more fits?"

But Enzo could not regard that incident as a joke; and whenever Rodolfo mentioned it to him he again felt a shadow of the terror he had experienced when his mother's gentle rubbing of the oil had been interrupted by the girl's shrill scream. That scream had always frightened him, as if it came from another world, but it had never frightened him more than on that night. Now he said nothing, locking and unlocking his fingers and kicking with his heels against the stone parapet.

"You're not much of a companion this evening," Rodolfo grumbled. "That long face of yours! What's eating you?"

"I've told you, I've quarrelled with the old man. . . . Oh, and it all seems so hopeless," he mumbled on. "It'll never be any better."

But these were things which Rodolfo never said, even if he sometimes thought them, and he at once leapt lightly down from his perch and announced that he was going to Piazza Repubblica to listen to the music. "Coming?" he asked.

Enzo shook his head.

"Have this fag now," Rodolfo said kindly, once again offering the grubby, inch-long stub on the palm of a hand whose lines were furrowed with dirt.

"No, you have it," Enzo said. "It's your last, isn't it?"

"I'll find plenty in the Piazza. Have it—go on." Rodolfo peered at it, holding it between finger and thumb, and then read out, pronouncing the words so that they were almost unrecognizable: "Player's Navy Cut. . . . Good cigarette, American," he said, with the certainty of a connoisseur.

"English," Enzo corrected.

"What d'you mean English?"

"English," Enzo repeated.

"Player's English?" Rodolfo asked in scorn.

An argument followed. It was as if they were playing a game which, though it bored them both, had to be dragged out to its conclusion, since neither would give in; and the game was a long one.

But at last Rodolfo trailed off into the darkness, and Enzo, having stayed to smoke the fag-end to the last bitter, scorching puff, also left the Lung' Arno, wandering as the spirit took him back and forth in a zigzag pattern through the darkest alleys of the town. It was thus that he met his mother, carrying under one arm a wicker-basket whose weight made her limp and stumble over the cobbles as if she were drunk. Her head was bent forward from her exertion, a small bald patch, the size of a florin, gleaming strangely white in the reflection of a street-lamp; she did not see him until she was upon him.

"What are you doing, Mother?"

"I've just knocked off. They asked me to take this mending." She drew aside a protective layer of brown paper to display the clothes below. "I thought I'd better not say no."

"But it's far too late. It's gone ten o'clock."

"They mightn't give it to me again, if I refused this time." She put the basket down on the cobbles between them, and began to tidy her hair which was always limp and lustreless from the excessive damp of the laundry. Under her eyes there were a number of small vertical puckers as if the brown skin had been drawn together by an invisible needle. She wore the black dress which she always wore to work, and a pair of black shoes whose surface leather had been rubbed grey at the heels. These shoes, which had been presented to her by one of the hotel guests for having worked all night at repairing an evening-dress, were too large and gave her feet a pathetic appearance of shabby and ill-fitting elegance.

"Well, let them go to hell!" Enzo exclaimed.

She smiled, since even twelve hours of work could not extinguish her spirit. "I wish I could. But they can so easily do without me, and we can't do without them. If I lost the job I don't know how we should manage."

Enzo had picked up the basket with a sigh and she at once attempted to take it from him. "Let me have it. It's not heavy. You were walking the other way."

"Don't be silly, Mother. It's far too heavy for you. No wonder you have back-ache." Each word he spoke seemed to be dragged lifeless out of some secret pit of despair. For, once he had seen his mother stumbling over the cobbles, the light gleaming on that pathetic bare patch of scalp, he had plunged from his former mood of mild pessimism into depths into which his naturally hopeful spirit as a rule seldom penetrated. He had always hated the ugly fact that she should support them, dulling her youth that his father might drink, his brother whore, and he wander the streets and play an occasional game of football; but this hatred had never been so intense as now.

For, to-night, he seemed to have acquired a new vision which made him see things with desolating clarity instead of through the old, good-natured haze; and just as he had suddenly rebelled against the worn, obscene phrases in which he and his friends discussed women, so now he rebelled against the idea, once accepted but now atrocious, that his mother should slave twelve hours a day to support three men.

"But you don't want to come home yet," Signora Rocchigiani protested, still struggling with the handle of the basket as she panted beside her son. "It's far too early for you."

"I'm not coming home at all to-night, Mother."

"Oh, Enzo!" The exclamation of disappointment was pitiful. "Not again! Why do you do it?"

"I did nothing," he said with sudden hardness, removing the arm he had put round her shoulder. "But I won't have him insulting me. Next time I'll hit him," he said, scowling and drawing down the corners of his mouth.

She laughed, but she was almost on the verge of tears. "You look so frightening like that! Please don't pull such faces." He smiled, against his will, and she said: "That's better. . . . But why do you two always quarrel? And always when I'm not at home."

"It's got to stop, Mother, it can't go on like this. I shall have to go away, that's all."

"Oh, don't be so silly, don't say such things!"

"But it's true," he said gloomily. "I must go somewhere else. He hates me," he added.

They said nothing more until they reached the corner of the Borgo, and then Signora Rocchigiani pleaded: "Come back with me and say you're sorry. Just say you're sorry. Enzo—please!"

But he remained stubbornly mute, and taking the basket from him with a light yet inexpressibly mournful sigh and a shrug of the shoulders, she went on her way. He watched her as she moved between the tall, dilapidated houses until she put down the basket, fumbled in a pocket and came hurrying back. "You'd better have this," she said. "It was a tip, so he needn't know about it. I expect you're hungry."

"No, really, Mother——"

"Take it."

In despair he took from her outstretched hand the grubby, tattered bundle of five and ten lire notes; and in despair he found himself wandering on and on through the town, like an automaton, heedless and tireless, while the crowds slowly thinned, the noise from the open-air cafés sank into silence, and the houses, their lights one by one extinguished, stretched upward, narrowed and became less and less friendly to the homeless wanderer. But the Uffizi had always been friendly to such as him. From the deserted Signoria a river of moonlight flowed between the two colonnades until, making a delta of the terrace beyond, where a few lonely figures could still be seen crouching or leaning, it tumbled, like some sudden new tributary, into the Arno below. On the first bench a woman slept clutching a child whose back-tilted head gave the impression of being half-severed from a neck that curved swan-like in the moonlight. On the second bench an old man crouched, appearing to have suddenly woken to face death as one hand pulled what was either a tattered rug or an overcoat up to his chin. On the third bench Enzo lay, and putting his arms under his head as a pillow, gazed up at the dusty, cob-webbed panes of the electric lantern which dangled from the vaulted ceiling on the end of a rusty iron chain. There was interest in the extreme despair of his expression and beauty in the extreme languor of his pose, and so it was not surprising that passers-by, usually foreigners, should from time to time slow their homeward pace to stare. To-morrow they would be staring with the same mixture of bewilderment and admiration at the pictures in the gallery beneath which Enzo, and the rest of the city's outcasts, now sheltered like insects under some vast, elaborate stone. But that was an irony which he, who had never visited the Uffizi, probably failed to appreciate.

Chapter Eleven

"HEAVENS!" Pamela exclaimed when she came into her brother's room and found him unpacking. "All that tissue-paper! You didn't do it yourself, did you?" She was carrying a hair-brush and at once began to brush her hair with long, competent strokes, as "Did you?" she repeated, "did you?"

"Yes," Colin admitted, continuing to place his clothes in cupboards and chests-of-drawers.

"I thought only school-matrons packed like that. You are funny, Colin. Sometimes I find it difficult to believe that you're just a boy. Do you like clothes?"

"If one spends money on them, one might as well look after them."

"I think you do like them," Pamela declared. "I suppose it must give one a feeling of superiority to be well dressed," she added, without intentional malice.

"One feels there's less to be criticized," Colin admitted frankly. He had always been afraid of criticism; and because he knew that, in his inmost being, he deviated so far from what he had been taught to regard as the normal schoolboy, in all external details he was careful to conform with resolute fidelity.

"I'm afraid there must be a lot to criticize in my appearance," Pamela confessed, without apparently wishing it were otherwise. "At school Miss Preston asked me who chose my clothes and when I said I chose them myself, of course she was surprised. She thought Mummy should choose them for me." She sighed: "I wish she did! She does dress well, doesn't she?"

"Carelessly, but well," Colin agreed.

"As she does most things. . . . Oh, I'm tired of brushing my hair! Everyone at school tells me I've got beautiful hair; but that's just a nice way of saying it's the only presentable thing about me." She flung down the brush and, jumping off the bed, picked up a neatly wrapped bundle and began to unwind it, exclaiming as she did so: "What is it? What is it? . . . Oh, it's a bottle of eau-de-Cologne!

You don't use it, do you?" She had unscrewed the cap and now she took a sip. "One of the girls in the dormitory got drunk on eau-de-Cologne. . . . Oh, it burns!" she cried out; and she hurried over to the wash-basin and began to gulp water.

"Serve you right," Colin said.

"What's it for?" his sister asked again.

"For after shaving."

"Shaving! But you don't shave."

"Of course I do. Don't be silly."

"Well, it must be a new idea. I'm sure you don't have to. You've got less hair than I have—at least I've a small moustache! Let me feel." She attempted to touch his cheek, but he at once pulled away from her, and a struggle began.

As usual, Pamela was victorious. "You only shave because it seems grown-up," she taunted. "Your face is quite smooth. I knew it was. . . . Now don't be cross," she added, seeing how he was scowling as he emptied an armful of rolled socks into a drawer.

"We should be in bed," Colin said.

"I know we should. And asleep, after that long journey. But I feel too excited." She stretched out her plumply pink arms to the open window: "Lovely, lovely Florence!"

"You've hardly seen it," Colin remarked drily.

"I know, but what I have seen . . . And Miss Preston says it's the most beautiful place in Europe." She let herself topple head first into an arm-chair, while Colin exclaimed: "Oh, do mind those shirts! You'll crush them, you fool."

"Sorry. Yes, I have crushed this collar." With clumsy fingers she attempted to press the rucked edge smooth once again. "Colin, do you think I was awfully rude to Mummy?"

"She deserved it. It was wrong of her not to be at the station. Not because of us, but because of Nicko."

"She cares for him," Pamela said. "She cares for him a lot. That's what I can't understand. It wouldn't have mattered if it had been just us, because we know we're not really important to her, but Nicko being there made it different. I was furious and I just had to show it, I couldn't help myself. I haven't your control."

"It's not control, only cowardice," he said with the honesty they always showed each other. "I wanted to say the same things."

"Oh, I'm glad of that, Colin. Because I thought that perhaps I'd been unfair to her. And I don't *want* to be unfair. After all she's really been quite decent to us, hasn't she? I mean, she's never been unkind in any way, as stepmothers so often are."

"Sometimes I wish she had," Colin said, drawing a silk tie through his fingers so that it made a gentle swish. "It's not very pleasant not to be cared about, one way or the other."

"Oh, I think this is better than being disliked," Pamela said. "I'm sure it's better." She went out on to the balcony and leant over, the night breeze filling the legs of her pyjamas as if they were sails. "Come out here," she called. "Oh come on! Be a sport!"

Side by side they stood, the thin, compact boy holding himself stiffly beside the relaxed and sprawling body of his sister, until Pamela gathered the saliva in her mouth, and with a muttered "Look!" spat down on to the gleaming semi-circle of light before the swing-doors. "Good shot!" she applauded herself, and as a white-haired man, accompanied by a young woman, emerged from the doors, she spat once again. "You try," she said. "I've no more spit left. . . . Oh, feeble!" She could not help laughing at Colin as he leant gingerly over the balustrade, pursed his lips and, with the utmost deliberation, let fall a thin thread of spittle which the breeze tugged, broke and at last wholly disintegrated. "You spit as you throw a cricket-ball," she said, insensitive, as she so often was, to the shame her brother felt at his own incapacity. "It's funny you can't throw over-arm. You ought to learn. But you're not really interested, are you?"

"No," he agreed shortly. But that was not true. Secretly it worried him that he was so obviously the physical inferior of the other boys at school, being gauche when they were graceful and weak when they were strong. He envied them their ability, and was ashamed for his own lack. But he would never admit this, except to himself, and his pose was not to care for games and to despise those that did.

"Children! What are you doing?. . . . After your bath, too, Pamela." Mrs. Bennett had come into the room, and was calling to them in a high-pitched, scolding voice; but she did not really wish to scold them, as the children well knew.

"Come here, Granny," Pamela said. "Do come here."

"No, you come here." But Mrs. Bennett had already gone across to them. "You'll catch a fearful cold, there's the mist off the river. . . . What are you doing, child?"

"Spitting."

"Spitting! . . . What a disgusting idea!"

"Look, I've just hit that man."

"Come here, at once!" Mrs. Bennett went over to the balustrade and grabbed Pamela's arm. "Which man?" she asked, suddenly peering down.

"That one."

"That's Mr. Maskell." Mrs. Bennett exclaimed with a mingling of horror and delight, and the two children at once burst into giggles. "No, it's not funny, not in the least funny. It's a disgusting, insanitary game. Come in at once. You don't want to get the reputation of being street children, do you? Come in, Pamela! Pamela! . . . No, it's not nice, that sort of thing," Mrs. Bennett repeated more quickly as the children at last obeyed her. Then, as if she had completely forgotten about their misbehaviour, she went on: "I'd have been in earlier to tuck you both up, but Nicko was crying. He wouldn't stop."

"Whom did he want?" Pamela asked.

"I think he was overtired," Mrs. Bennett answered evasively.

"Didn't he want Mummy?"

"Little children always call for their mothers when they feel miserable," Mrs. Bennett said, as if she had to defend Karen's absence.

"Mummy might have stayed in to-night, she might have guessed that he would want her."

"He was asleep when she went in to see him."

"I think she's selfish," Pamela said. "Don't you, Colin?"

"I suppose you're talking about me," a voice said behind them. "It must have been an absorbing topic to have kept you up so late. . . . You look tired, Mother, you really should go to bed."

"Granny has had to sit up with Nicko," Colin said coldly.

"Has she? What's the matter?" Either Karen wished to ignore the oblique accusation or else she had not felt it. "I expect he's overtired," she answered her own question, in the way that was most satisfactory to her conscience. "It was a long journey. And you, too, have had a long journey," she continued to the children. "I think you should turn in."

"Yes, bed," said Max, who had been leaning silently in the doorway, his whole weight on one flexed arm.

"I hadn't noticed you, Daddy," Pamela said in surprise.

"Am I as small as that?" Max asked with an awkward attempt at humour. "Am I?"

Karen had wandered out on to the balcony and was standing there, gazing at the river. She beat a small tattoo with the palms of her hands on the stone parapet, and gave a deep sigh; then she walked up and down the balcony two or three times, her arms crossed over her breast. The wind blew her fair hair across her face, and her flesh gleamed, blue-white, like snow in the moonlight.

When she returned to the room, Pamela asked: "Why are you so restless, Mummy?"

Karen gave a laugh: "I'm not restless."

"You looked as if you were waiting for someone."

"I wish I was!"

"You're restless," Pamela repeated.

"Now back to your room, Pamela," Max put in. "It's past eleven o'clock. . . . Pamela—do what I say!"

"This bed is hard," Colin said, bouncing up and down.

"Be thankful you have a bed," his father retorted. "When we came through the Uffizi we saw one of those two boys asleep on a stone bench. How would you like that?"

"Which two boys?"

"Oh, you haven't met them. I forgot."

"Which two boys?"

"It wouldn't interest you. They were two boys we met. I'll tell you about it some other time. . . . Good night, old chap."

Max stooped clumsily and kissed his son on the forehead, and then watched while Mrs. Bennett also said good night. He noticed how, with her, there was none of the same stiffening on the boy's part, as if for an irksome duty, and in the comparison a swift mingling of grief and anger swept through his being.

Chapter Twelve

"WHAT a strange thing to do, Mother," Karen said.

"Is it strange? Yes, I suppose it is, but it never really struck me. I saw them in the Signoria, and I stopped to have a word with them, because they're nice children. And then I remembered that tonight we were going to the Piazzale Michelangelo, and I thought they might like to come too. The music," she explained. "I expect they'll like the music. But whether they'll come or not is another matter. I spoke to the Tunisian in French, but perhaps he didn't understand me."

"Frankly, I rather hope he didn't," Karen said. "I don't much fancy going up there with two boys off the streets."

"They're nice children," Mrs. Bennett repeated.

"One of them stole your pen," Max reminded her.

"And the other returned it."

"Yes," Max said. "That's true enough."

"Be careful of confidence-tricks," Mrs. Maskell put in. They were all seated in a circle in the lounge, but whereas the other chairs were at some distance from each other, hers was so near von Arbach's that whenever she leant forward to pick up her drink, her knee could touch his. "They all play confidence-tricks. The Marchesa was telling us about one of them when we had tea with her. It's all to do with a bale of cloth, and a Greek merchant who has to catch a plane, and you've to lend him some money on the security of the cloth—and an Italian friend will pay you back. Isn't that how it goes, Tiny? But, of course, the cloth is practically valueless and the friend doesn't exist. They're such crooks," she said. "I wouldn't trust them an inch. . . . Have my cherry," she continued to von Arbach, fishing the Maraschino out of her drink on the end of its wooden stick. "You know that you adore them."

Von Arbach looked embarrassed, his long white eyelashes fluttering over his oblique eyes and his cheeks reddening at this attention; but he docilely accepted the proffered gift, opening his mouth for Mrs. Maskell to push the cherry in.

84

Tiny, who had obviously been thinking for some time, now announced, biting on his pipe: "Look at it this way. Taking those two lads up to that swagger place at the Piazzale is the equivalent of taking two barrow-boys into the Ritz. Well, isn't it?"

"As bad as that?" Mrs. Bennett asked in a dismay which was not without its hidden irony.

The comparison seemed to please Karen: "Then it may be more fun than I had expected."

"Perhaps I've made a mistake," Mrs. Bennett sighed. "Perhaps I shouldn't have asked them."

But, at any rate, Colin and Pamela were delighted with the prospect of meeting the two Italians. At this moment they were seated in the entrance hall, one on either side of the vast central pillar, purple and veined like horse-meat, and were scrutinizing everyone who entered. When, at last, two boys in shorts thrust themselves round the doors and then looked about them, as if dazed by an excessive brightness, before lumbering across to the desk, the American children leapt to their feet and rushed into the lounge. "They've come," they announced. "They're asking at the desk."

"I'd better go and see," Max said.

"Are you joining us?" Karen asked Mrs. Maskell.

"To the Piazzale? Oh, I don't think so," the other woman returned, smiling agreeably and yet managing to indicate by no more than an inflexion that really she couldn't be expected to take part in this kind of social prank. "No, as a matter of fact, we're thinking of going dancing again to-night. Béngt took us to a wonderful place, on a roof near the station, with a floor-show and an American band and simply marvellous food, and we thought we'd pay another visit. You ought to come some night."

"My God, they fleece you!" Tiny said unexpectedly.

Chris looked at him for a moment with intense distaste; then she laughed. "That's so like Tiny, always counting his pennies. I don't see what's the point of coming on a holiday if one doesn't want to spend money on the things one enjoys."

"I didn't say I didn't enjoy the place," Tiny retorted. "I merely said it was expensive."

"Oh, it's so vulgar always to discuss things in terms of expense," Chris said.

"Well, one's got to be vulgar with an allowance of only fifty pounds."

"Thank you, Béngt," Chris said, turning to beam at him, as he extricated her greying Dauphin bob from under the collar of the musquash coat she had just dragged on. "Béngt has such lovely manners," she boasted as a mother might of her child. "Have you noticed his family crest?" And she at once caught his little finger and showed it to the company. But before they could all see, Max's arrival with Rodolfo and Enzo made her hurry away her men-folk. "Ta-ta for now," she called. "Ta-ta!"

Colin and Pamela stood with legs apart and fingers clasped behind their backs, like awkward soldiers at ease, waiting to be presented; nerves made them both want to giggle. Hands were shaken all round, even by Karen who, looking down, was amused to see that the muscles in Enzo's bare knees were unmistakably twitching with panic. Although she was naturally unobservant, for such things her eye never failed her. When she glanced at his face, his gaze swerved away, as if they were two cars coming into collision. "I heard that one singing 'Auld Lang Syne' the other night," she said; and Rodolfo, understanding at least the word "singing", took it up with his unfailing desire to please by announcing, in Italian: "Si, si, Enzo sings beautifully."

"No, I don't. Don't be such a fool." The other boy dragged one toe of his plimsoll across the parquet floor so that it made a long grey smear, and then lowering his head, began to blush.

"Yes, he has a beautiful voice."

"Oh, shut up!"

They all laughed, even Mrs. Bennett and the children who could not understand what had been said.

"Well, let's go," Max suggested; and like a crocodile at school, the party at once formed up. Karen walked indifferently with Max, while a loquacious Rodolfo chattered beside them; Mrs. Bennett followed with Enzo, leaning her weight on his shoulder when they came to the steps and occasionally attempting to say something, either in French or English, which he could not understand; last, there were the children who, when they were not helping to push their grandmother from behind, carried on a conversation in excited whispers.

"One of them smells rather," said Pamela.

"Yes, the Arab one. But it's not really an unpleasant smell. Like an animal."

"The other looks stronger. He's the one that brought Granny's pen back."

"One can see he's the nicer of the two. He was awfully embarrassed when they first came in. I smiled at him and kept smiling at him because I thought that might make him feel more comfortable. But then it struck me that he'd think I was making fun."

"He has a hole in his trousers," Pamela remarked. "They're terribly old, they look as if they might fall to pieces at any moment. I suppose it's unkind to notice such things."

"One can't help noticing things."

"No, but to remark on them. He plays football, Daddy says. . . . I like the way he takes Granny's arm—and the way Granny lets him."

"Children, look at this lovely view," Mrs. Bennett said, pressing one large hand over her heaving side, as if something were liable to burst out. Although it was night, her dark-glasses still dangled from her neck on their length of grubby twine and her other hand was fiddling with them. "Isn't it lovely?" she asked.

"*Molto bello*," Enzo announced without looking at it.

"It's better at the top," Colin said.

"Now you're being tactless," Mrs. Bennett said with a laugh. "That's unlike you. I asked you to admire the view because I was out of breath."

"I'm sorry, Granny."

"But it *is* beautiful," Pamela said, making the discovery for the first time. She had plucked an ilex leaf on their way up and it lay between her lips as she looked down on the city. Far away the terrace of the Palazzo d'Oro floated, a cool square of light above a tramcar which at that moment passed, scattering it with grains of fire. The air was resinous and close.

A piercing whistle, which they guessed was Rodolfo's, followed by a "Holloh", summoned them onwards. "I knew he'd be the sort of person who arrives at places first and then shouts to one to hurry," Colin said. He turned to his sister: "That's usually your job."

"Come," said Mrs. Bennett, the dry surface of her hand scraping on the Italian's smooth forearm. "Let's go on." And they began to trudge onward to where they were awaited by the leaning crowds, Michelangelo's colossus, and finally, the overture to *Traviata*, played by a string quartet on a shell-dilapidated terrace.

"*Ah, la bella musica*," said Rodolfo, as they arranged themselves at a table; but secretly he was wishing that they had gone to the other restaurant from which came the sounds of an Italian woman crooning an American song into a microphone which relayed it, even more horribly distorted, to the whole shadowy hillside. He was in no doubt what to order when Max asked him: "A *cassata*, please, and an orangeade, and some cakes." He smiled impishly and put out a begging hand: "And a cigarette."

"Well, that's plain enough," Max said in English, not sure whether to laugh or be displeased. "And you, Enzo?"

"Whatever you wish." The Florentine was overawed by Karen and the splendour of the setting, shy of the children, and aware, for the first time, of the hole in his shorts. He could barely get out the three words.

"Give him the same as the other boy," Mrs. Bennett said, and added: "This air is suffocating. I feel I can't breathe."

"Perhaps the climb was too much," Pamela said. She drew her handkerchief from her pocket and wiped her grandmother's forehead.

"Still that filthy rag," Mrs. Bennett said, smiling wryly. But she caught the girl's forearm before she could stop, and said: "Go on. I don't mind a little dirt. You're a good child."

"Oh, this dreary music," said Karen, evidently sharing Rodolfo's opinion of the string quartet. She kept glancing around her as if she were expecting someone else to join their party, until Pamela, having watched her for several seconds, her chair tilted back, at last remarked maliciously:

"You're still waiting, Mummy."

"Waiting? . . . Oh, don't start that again, please!" Karen exclaimed with a mixture of amusement and exasperation. But she continued to look uneasily from table to table, her chin supported by her right arm.

After the children had gorged in a silence broken only by their occasional exclamations of pleasure and approval, Colin who had a flair for entertaining others, suggested they should play "Up Jenkins". "Count me out," Karen said, but the children insisted: "No, Mummy, you must play, it's no fun with only a few people," and Mrs. Bennett said quickly: "Yes, dear, you must play." After a short period of bewilderment, the two Italians soon mastered the game, their excited shouts of "Bangs!" "Creeps!" and "Window-boxes!" sending the two English children into explosive shrieks of laughter. Enzo sat between Karen and Colin, and often his hand would touch hers, her flesh seeming wonderfully cool in comparison with the hot, sticky penny. At such moments of contact he would feel a strange, jolting collision within himself, as if an invisible blow had been struck upward through his whole body.

Beside Enzo's hands, not merely Karen's, but even Colin's looked absurdly fragile. Usually so quiet, the English boy had lost his reserve; he kept jumping to his feet, issuing orders and then joining with his sister in yelps of derisive laughter. "Sh! Sh!" Max attempted to quiet them. But the pandemonium increased. Rodolfo fell off his chair intentionally, though the others did not guess this; Pamela accused him of cheating and they began a good-humoured scuffle; the weird Italian shouts of "Up Jenkins" were seriously competing with the mournful contralto who had now begun to sing with the quartet. . . . Guests at other tables were glancing round, some in amusement but more in disapproval; the two waiters had the look of being prepared for any emergency.

"Enough!" Karen suddenly said, slipping the penny which Enzo had just passed her into her bag. "You're getting too excited, children."

"Oh, please, Mummy," Colin pleaded.

"No, I think we'd better stop," Max said quickly. "Let's all have something else to drink, eh?"

He clicked his fingers for the waiter, and as he gave the orders, did not notice that Karen was gazing with a sudden, almost frightened tension at the Piazzale, her brows drawn together and her hands, still lying on the table, clenched tightly. "Yours, darling?" he said.

But she had already risen to her feet: "Excuse me for a moment," she murmured. "I won't be long."

Max rose, too, and watched her in bewilderment as she hurried down the steps that led from the café to the Piazzale. He turned to Mrs. Bennett: "Where's she going?"

"I haven't an idea. She's left her bag so she must be coming back."

"Did we annoy her?" Pamela asked.

"Perhaps we made too much noise," Colin said, already subsiding into his usual grave manner. "Do you think that was it?"

"Oh, I don't think it was anything to do with you all," Mrs. Bennett assured them, with more truth than she realized. "Perhaps she wanted to see the view. Or to be alone."

"I hate being alone," Pamela said.

The children soon forgot about Karen as they gulped *cassatas* and competed in blowing bubbles with their straws in tall, misty glasses of iced orangeade. "Children, your manners," Mrs. Bennett reproved. "Such a bad example for the Italians." But they took no notice of her. Colin put out a hand to the amulet which hung, on a fine silver chain, around Enzo's neck: "He wears a necklace," he said.

"*La Madonna*," Enzo said.

"It's the Virgin," Pamela explained. "He must be a Catholic."

Colin twisted the chain until it bit into the flesh of the Florentine's neck, and then released it with a laugh in which Enzo joined, glad to have provided some amusement. "I wonder if he'd take me to church with him."

"You don't want to go to a Catholic service," Pamela said.

Colin blushed. "Yes, I do," he said with a sudden sulkiness.

"Granny, Colin wants to go to a Catholic service. He can't, can he?"

"What, dear? . . . Oh, I don't see why not."

"But it's Popish!"

Mrs. Bennett laughed and looked towards her grandson, only to find that he had already ceased to be interested in the discussion. He was looking at Max, who sat sideways in his chair, one leg crossed over the other, as he stared at the Piazzale. His heavy, Teutonic good looks seemed to have the consistency and greyness of dough; under the thick red eyebrows the small green eyes peered out unhappily; the fingers of one hand beat an incessant tattoo on the underneath of the table.

Colin knew that his father was suffering and he guessed, though he could not be sure, that it was somehow because of Karen. He wanted to comfort Max, to touch his ceaselessly drumming hand or to say some word that would cheer him; but he could not do it, was too awkward, even feared a snub. Then his impotence in the face of the misery of someone whom he loved expressed itself in a sudden hatred of Karen. He thought of the cutting phrases he would like to use to her; she was an outsider whom Max had brought in, she didn't belong, she was not part of them. . . . In this baffled mixture of love for his father and hatred for Karen, he remained staring at Max until Mrs. Bennett said: "A penny for your thoughts." The boy did not answer, and Mrs. Bennett said: "Such a strange expression. You frighten me when you look like that."

"Karen has gone," Max said.

"Gone?" Mrs. Bennett queried.

"I've just seen her. She's walking back to Florence."

"Alone?"

"No. I think there was someone with her. I can't be sure."

"Mr. Westfield," a voice said behind them. "Welcome to the Piazzale!" It was Lena, in a full purple skirt, a blouse of elaborate *"Broderie anglaise"* worn off the shoulders, and a pair of jet ear-rings that swung back and forth, tugging at her almost lobeless ears, whenever she spoke. This was evidently not what Mrs. Bennett would call one of her "sensible" days. "Hello, children," she said, having long since made friends with them. "Mr. Westfield, I wish to present——" She put out an arm as if she were tugging on an invisible rope in order to get her young man to come nearer—"Signor Commino."

They had all heard of Signor Commino, who worked at an English travel agency, collected stamps, butterflies and fossils, and wished to marry Lena. The children now stared at him with interest. . . . But, oh dear, he wouldn't do, they at once decided, they knew they were going to giggle. He was short and he was almost completely spherical, with two rabbit-teeth in front, a bulging dome of a forehead, and a brief nose half-way down on which there rested an enormous pair of horn-rimmed glasses.

He was a person of extreme good-nature, but the children did not realize this, imagining that his ugliness must be stamped through and through him like the lettering on Brighton Rock.

"Won't you join us?" Max suggested apathetically.

"Oh, no, Mr. Westfield, we do not wish to infringe the family gathering." But Lena had already pulled back the chair beside Max, waiting only for him to repeat the invitation. As, of course, he did.

"Well," said Signor Commino in English to the two children, "and how do we like our Florence?"

Colin and Pamela exchanged agonized glances, until choking back her giggles, Pamela said: "Very much, thank you."

Signor Commino took a small, enamelled box out of the pocket of his greasy brown suit and, watched by the Italians and the two English children, proceeded to take a pinch of snuff. He grunted two or three times, cleared his throat, and then, pulling out a handkerchief, began to dust the vast, uniform, outward curve of his chest and stomach as if it were a mantelpiece.

"What's that?" Pamela asked.

"*Starnutiglio.* I don't know how you say it in English. *Starnutiglio,* Lena," he said, interrupting her in a one-sided conversation with Max.

"Sneezing-powder."

Colin and Pamela stuffed handkerchiefs to their mouths, and catching the infection of their mood, the two Italians now also began to shake with suppressed giggles.

"What have we seen of our beautiful city?" Signor Commino asked, unaware of the amusement he was causing. He scratched with his forefinger at the tuft of hair that divided the bald, shiny front of his head (at the back there was a luxuriant bush, which lay over his collar and scattered dandruff almost to the waist of his jacket). "Have we visited the historical Palazzo Vecchio? H'm, h'm? Or the Uffizi Galleria? Or the magnificent and stony Pitti Palace? H'm?" The children only continued to sway and shudder soundlessly before him, their hands to their lips. "Perhaps we are too young for such treasure." He trumpeted into the handkerchief with which he had been dusting himself, and suddenly raising his left arm above his head, began to click the fingers as loudly as if they were castanets. A waiter hurried over. "What for you all?" Signor Commino asked.

"I think they've had all that's good for them," Mrs. Bennett answered for the speechless children, at the same time giving them a scolding glance and kicking Enzo by mistake for Colin under the table.

When the waiter had taken the order, Signor Commino turned to Pamela: "To-day I have been to Viareggio," he announced. "Do you also bath?"

It was too much for them. Like water from a geyser, their merriment hissed and scalded out. They bent double, they clutched themselves and then clutched each other, Enzo and Rodolfo joined in, the glasses rocked and rattled on the table, Mrs. Bennett expostulated, Signor Commino looked surprised and then hurt, Lena appeared to be about to burst into tears. . . .

But it was soon over. Mute and white-faced, as if they had just been sick, the two children sat in shame before their elders. They knew that they had set the Italian boys a bad example, annoyed their father and grandmother, and hurt poor Lena. About Signor Commino they unfortunately did not care.

"After that exhibition, I think we'd better go," Mrs. Bennett said, suddenly looking even more tired than Max.

"Yes," said Max. "They're obviously over-excited."

"I'm sorry," Colin muttered, in genuine remorse.

When they had said good-bye and were making their way to the steps, Lena ran after them, brandishing Karen's bag. Colin and Pamela were walking last of the procession, and she gave it to them; saying at the same time in gentle reproof: "That wasn't amiable of you. You made Signor Commino very unhappy. No, it was not amiable. I was surprised."

"I'm sorry, Lena," Pamela said. "We didn't mean to be rude. We just couldn't help ourselves. We tried to stop, but that only made it worse and worse. . . . But, Lena," she rushed on, "you mustn't marry him—you mustn't, mustn't, mustn't! Promise!"

A strangely different Lena answered in a cold voice, "Please mind your own business," and turned and walked away.

"Pamela—what a thing to say!" her brother exclaimed in horror. "How could you?"

"But he's awful. And I'm fond of Lena, and I can't bear to think of her married to someone like that. He's fat, and he's ugly, and he's *old*."

"Lena told us he was only thirty-three."

"Well, he looks old. And that awful sneezing-powder that he takes. And did you notice how his hair grew behind? Oh, he's an ogre. Lena *can't* marry him. Besides," she added, "she doesn't love him. She loves Daddy."

"Loves Daddy!" Colin laughed. "Oh, bosh!"

"No, I'm sure of it," Pamela said seriously. "You remember how Miss Phillips loved him too—Mummy was always joking about it. I suppose he's attractive to women of that sort. They want to mother him, and they're afraid that they're getting old and unattractive, and it may be their last chance. I feel sorry for Lena. It must be terrible for her. And having that awful mother, too, with the pain in the abdomen."

Mrs. Bennett, walking with Max, while Rodolfo and Enzo followed behind, suddenly gripped her son-in-law's arm on a narrow path which wound down through a tangled mesh of bushes. "What's that?" she exclaimed.

"What's what?"

"There! There's someone walking there, on the other side. I can hear him. . . . Look, his face! There! There!" In a patch of moonlight between the branches of a tree she momentarily thought she saw the face of the old man of her walk; he was smiling, revealing the two long, decaying eye-teeth which gleamed, like the collapsed bridge of his nose, his forehead and the lenses of his glasses, through the surrounding darkness. Then he moved on. "He's following us," she said. "I knew that he was." Max rushed to where she pointed, plunged into the bushes and searched up and down. "No one," he said. "You must have imagined it."

"But I didn't imagine it! I tell you, I saw him. I couldn't mistake him. How could I?"

"Mistake who?" Max asked in bewilderment.

"Oh, nothing." She sank on to a grass mound and put a hand to her forehead. "Perhaps I did imagine it," she said.

"You're tired," Max assured her. "It was the moonlight on a branch, or a cat, or something."

Meanwhile Rodolfo and Enzo had come up to ask what was the matter. When Max told them, they both began to look excitedly among the bushes where Max himself had already searched. Suddenly Enzo gave a triumphant whoop. *"Ecco!"*

"Have you found him?" Max asked, hastening to the spot. And then, in disappointment, "Oh, it's only a pair of spectacles."

The Florentine emerged carrying the familiar gold-rimmed glasses, fastened at one side with a piece of rag and cracked horizontally across both lenses. He showed them to Mrs. Bennett, but she at once turned her head.

"*Rotto*," he said.

"Yes," said Max. "No good to anyone now. I should throw them away."

The Florentine raised his right arm and, silhouetted against the illuminated city, hurled the spectacles downwards and outwards into the dark void. For a moment, they flashed as the moonlight caught them, then they were lost.

"That's how you should learn to throw," Pamela said to her brother. "But where did he find them?"

"In the bushes."

"Is that why you stopped? . . . Do let's go on, Daddy."

"You go on, children. Wait for us at the bottom. I'm feeling a little giddy and want to sit down," Mrs. Bennett said.

"Oh, Granny, let me stay with you," Colin offered.

"No, you heard me telling you to go on," Mrs. Bennett answered with an unwonted asperity. "Your father will stay with me."

"Granny, are you really all right?" Pamela asked, coming over and putting a hand on the old woman's head.

"Yes, yes—don't fuss so!" Mrs. Bennett cried in exasperation. "I only want to rest."

"Let's have a race—to the bottom," Colin said.

"Yes, to the bottom, right to the bottom! Enzo and Rodolfo must play too," Pamela exclaimed. "A race, a race!" she exclaimed excitedly. "But no unfair starts." She caught Enzo's shirt and pulled him back beside her; and the Florentine, momentarily puzzled, at once understood, crouching like a trained athlete for the word to be off. Meanwhile Rodolfo, examining the wall which ran beyond the path, realized that by jumping down its easy seven feet he would save a hundred yards. He was sure he would win.

"You start us," Pamela said to her father.

"All right." Max raised a handkerchief in his right hand and shouted, "On your marks—get set—go!" The handkerchief descended and they all thudded off into the darkness, except for Rodolfo who, with the agility of a cat, jumped on to the wall and then, like Tosca flinging herself off the battlements, leapt out of sight.

"To be young," Mrs. Bennett sighed. Looking down at her Max saw that she was weeping, he supposed from her fright, large tears glittering like beads in the innumerable folds and wrinkles of her face.

"Why, what's the matter?" he asked. "You mustn't worry about that scare of yours. It could have happened to anyone."

"But not the glasses," she said softly.

"The glasses?"

Before he could search this mysterious reply further, a high-pitched yelping, as of a dog in pain, broke the close and resinous silence of the hill. The yelping went on, and through it Pamela could be heard calling: "Daddy, Daddy," in a voice which grew louder and louder until it ended in a despairing wail.

Max hurried down, leaping the steps two and three at a time, and Mrs. Bennett with a remarkable agility hurried behind him.

"Colin's hurt," Pamela said. "He's in awful pain. He won't stop screaming." Her face gleamed white and panicky in the moonlight.

Enzo and Rodolfo were bending over the English boy, one on either side of him, while he writhed and twisted between them so that they could not see the extent of his injuries. Suddenly he stopped his inhuman yelping and began repeating with a strange hiccoughing sound: "Granny, Granny, Granny!"

"Yes, I'm here, dear. What have you done to yourself? What's the matter?"

The old woman knelt on the path, the Italians making room for her, and took the boy in her arms.

"What is it, darling?" she repeated. "What did you do?"

"Fell," he gasped. "My leg. It's awful—awful."

Other children might have been brave, but he had never had any capacity to bear pain, and now he showed none. Afterwards, lying in the ambulance, he hated himself for having given way with the uncontrolled, abject screaming of an animal in a trap. He was sure the Italians had despised him.

. . . But with what consideration and gentleness they had car-

ried him between them to the bottom of the steps, both talking to
him in soft, coaxing voices which somehow soothed his outraged
nerves though he understood not a word. He did not then guess it,
but that evening was to be the beginning of a devotion to a country and a people and, less happily perhaps, of a whole way of life.

Chapter Thirteen

"I've left my bag at the Piazzale. I've just remembered. I hope
somebody has the sense to bring it back."

Karen and Frank Ross were leaning over the parapet of the
Lung' Arno while from time to time he would excavate a grain of
masonry and flick it, in a wide arc, into the black water.

"Last time it was only a lipstick," he said. "Now it's your bag.
You're careless, aren't you?" He turned his face towards her, with
its two strange vertical creases down each cheek, and all at once
smiled.

"When I saw you, I rushed down without thinking," she confessed.

"And you thought you'd be going back?" Once again a piece of
masonry plopped into the water, its rings spreading out and out
until they grounded and snapped on the bank.

"I didn't know," Karen replied.

"Did you tell your husband where you were going?"

"No. Why should I?"

"Why indeed?" He laughed; but as always his laugh seemed to
express, not amusement, but some less creditable emotion. "I like
that," he said.

"Like what?"

"Oh, your spirit. . . . Why do you dress so carelessly?" he continued. "You obviously spend a lot of money on clothes and you
know how to choose them. You're beautiful, too," he added, as if
he were assessing the points of a horse. "But look at your finger-
nails." She looked at them, holding them to the light that fell from
the hotel. "Good hands, but the nails are dirty and that spoils the
effect. Besides, you bite them. Your hair, too. When did you last
brush it?"

"How gallant you are!" Karen said, in a pretence at being offended. But strangely she was not offended, only curious, surprised and perhaps even pleased.

"Oh, you won't get gallantry from me. I don't pay compliments. And you like compliments, don't you? You like to be admired and petted and spoiled by a husband for whom you care that much"— he clicked his fingers together—"and to whom you yield not an inch. I'm right, aren't I?"

"You have a very low opinion of me."

"No lower than of most people. You obviously have all the usual faults of the beautiful woman." He laughed: "And you're enough of a narcissist to enjoy having even your faults discussed."

"My husband says you're someone famous. Is that true?"

For the first time he seemed to topple momentarily from the heights of his self-assurance. "Was he a Burma man?" he asked shortly.

"Yes. . . . But well behind the front line," she added with contemptuous untruth.

"You've no right to despise him," he retorted coldly. ". . . I'd like to meet him."

"If you wait, he should be back soon."

Ross raised his slender shoulders in their khaki-drill blouse, and smiled: "Is this the best moment—when you've run away from him without an explanation to join another man?"

"Oh, he's not like that. Max is never jealous."

"You've trained him too well?"

They both turned round at the screech of the ambulance swerving to a halt before the swing-doors; a taxi stopped behind, from which Max, Pamela and the two Italians jumped down. "What's happened?" Karen asked, at first with no more than an amused curiosity. Then she exclaimed: "Oh, my God! It must be Mother. I thought she didn't seem well." She gripped the bare flesh of Ross's forearm. "Come with me and see."

"No, no," Colin was exclaiming petulantly, as two clumsy stretcher-bearers jolted him down from the ambulance. "They don't know how to do it. Oh!" He let out a sudden angry scream. "Granny, tell them to put me down! Granny! Let the boys do it, they know how to do it. Granny, the boys . . ."

Reluctantly the stretcher-bearers yielded their burden to Enzo and Rodolfo, who came forward like two awkward understudies before the audience that had already thronged round to watch. But there was no awkwardness in their movements as they raised the English boy, and he at once fell silent, closing his eyes. Meanwhile Karen was questioning Max and the doctor, and Mrs. Bennett was attempting, with the help of a flustered and inefficient porter, to make a way for the stretcher through the crowds.

Frank Ross strode forward.

"*Fate largo*," he shouted. He put out both arms and shoved the people back; and at once all resistance left them, so that murmuring, it seemed in approval, they made a wide lane up the hotel steps as if for a bridal procession. And "Further, further," he commanded. Now he spoke in a conversational voice since he knew they were listening to him. "That's a bit better," he said. "Back. Back. Back."

Colin passed and Ross stared down at the boy's face—green, tear-spattered, and puckered with dread and pain. The boy opened his eyes, looked up for a moment, and then, with a grimace and a sudden hiccoughing sob, turned his head away. His whole body was rigid.

Chapter Fourteen

THE Italian doctor who was to set Colin's leg was a young man of charm and skill who had found, to his surprise, that neither of these qualities took him far in an overcrowded profession. For that reason he was delighted, in spite of the lateness of the hour, at being summoned to the wealthy American family at the Palazzo d'Oro. While he examined the fracture, with Mrs. Bennett, Max and Pamela looking on, he explained that he had been a prisoner-of-war for three years at a camp near Newcastle. "Do you know Newcastle?" he asked Colin, who could do no more than gasp "No" between clenched teeth.

"It is ugly."

He had soft, cool hands, the nails manicured with generous half-moons, and his voice was soft and cool also. His perpetually

fixed smile, his black-and-white shoes and his chalk-coloured tropi-
cal suit, with its wide shoulders and pinched waist, all gave him the
appearance of a member of the male chorus in a London "revue".
"This may pain you," he coaxed. He looked round at the three
onlookers. "Would you like Mummy with you?"

And for the first time the others realized that Karen was not
there.

"Yes, where is she?" Mrs. Bennett said. "She was downstairs
when we arrived. What's happened to her?" She felt it to be
extraordinary that Karen had not come up with Colin to learn the
extent of the damage.

"Shall I get her?" Pamela said.

"Yes, slip down, there's a good girl. Tell her the doctor is just
going to set Colin's leg."

"No," Colin said, raising his head from his pillow. "No, don't
call her." The abrupt movement made him again grimace with
pain.

"Well, why ever not?" Mrs. Bennett asked.

"Because—because that man will come with her. I don't want
him to come. He mustn't come in here!"

"What man?" Max queried, mystified as they all were, since in
the tumult of their arrival none of them had noticed Frank Ross.

"The man who cleared a way for the stretcher. The soldier
man—you know, the one you were talking about, the Burma
man." It was strange how he had at once known Ross's identity;
it was the sort of thing that only happens when we fall into love
or hate with another. "I don't want him here," he reiterated, and
added in sudden resolution: "I don't want anyone here while I'm
being hurt. I want to be alone with the doctor. Could you please
all go? Please, Granny!"

"Very well, dear. If you prefer it so." Mrs. Bennett passed a dry
palm across his forehead, and gazed down at him, her pale blue
eyes into his suffering brown, as if she hoped by doing so to pour
some of her own spirit into the frail vessel which she knew him to
be. "Come, Pamela, Max."

They went out on to the balcony and, leaning over the rail into
the coolness and dark, waited without speaking for the screams
which they felt must inevitably follow. "Poor Colin," Mrs. Bennett

sighed, with the natural compassion the strong feel for the weak and the brave for the cowardly. Pamela, who was trembling as if with cold, could no longer bear not to look and she turned her head to peer through the open window. But all she could see was a gigantic shadow thrown by the bedside lamp—the doctor's stooping head and shoulders; it looked like some enormous, grey wolf, crouched above her brother's prostrate body, and she felt suddenly faint and sick.

But the scream they had expected never sounded. Soon the doctor came out through the french windows, the revue actor taking his curtain, and flashed his brilliant smile: "All over. I have given him something to help the sleep. I shall come again to-morrow. . . . He was very brave," he added with an upward inflection of astonishment which exactly matched their own.

Chapter Fifteen

THAT morning, five days after his accident, Colin was to have many visitors.

After breakfast, he sat up in bed, some half a dozen pillows piled up around him, and worked at a jig-saw puzzle while from the corridor he could hear one of the hotel servants sweep the stone floor with a broom dipped in water. First there was the splash, then a sputtering, and last a series of tearing sounds as of someone trying to draw one long, agonized breath after another . . . ah, ah, ah.

The door opened and an old man in hotel uniform, the tunic unbuttoned to reveal what appeared to be a soiled blue-and-white flannel pyjama top, put his head into the room, said *"Scusi"*, as he did every morning at this hour, made a pretence of retreating and then returned with pail and broom when Colin shouted to him to come back.

He smiled at Colin with his whiskery, slightly fox-like face and then asked, *"Come sta, signorino? Sta meglio?"*

"Si, meglio, meglio," Colin said.

"Bene, bene," the old man said, giving a little cough after each word. He at once set to work, energetically rolling up the carpets, taking them out on to the balcony and beating them one by one,

scrubbing the wash-basin, and fussing over the piles of books, jig-saw puzzles and sweets with which visitors had littered the room. Meanwhile Colin watched him. He must be very old, the boy decided, with his twiglike arthritic hands, the thumbs growing into his palms almost at right angles, the deep, dirt-ingrained furrows which ploughed his whole face, and his curved back out of which his shoulder-blades sprouted like two clipped wings. He wheezed, grunted and blew small bubbles from between his chapped lips as he worked.

After some minutes, a piece of the jig-saw puzzle fell out of the boy's hands and leaning over to pick it up he so jarred his leg that he gave an audible whimper. The old man at once dropped the mat he was carrying in from the balcony and hurried across to the bed, stooped to recover the piece, one hand to the small of his back as if it were turning an invisible handle to make his spine bend, and then returned it to the board with a gasped *"Ecco!"*

Without any diffidence, he next smoothed Colin's hair from his forehead and asked: *"Fa male? . . . Poveretto!"*

Colin said: *"Non capisco."*

"'Non capisco'," the old man chuckled, an unusually large bubble swelling between his lips. *"Sempre 'non capisco'."* He picked up two pieces of the jig-saw puzzle and attempted to force them together, twisting and pressing them between his hideously deformed fingers.

"No, no," Colin cried in English. "You'll break them." He took the pieces from the old man, and said: "Look," fitting them as they should go.

"Bene, bene," said the old man with a kind of amused wonder. Like pistol-shots his knee-joints cracked as he went down on to his haunches to see the board better; and thus he continued to watch Colin while the boy slowly built up the puzzle, until Chris Maskell, Karen and von Arbach came in. Then the old man hurriedly got to his feet, bobbed to each of them in turn with a rapid *"Scusi, scusi"*, picked up his broom and rags, and scuttled from the room.

"You mustn't encourage the servants not to work, you naughty boy," Chris said. "They're lazy enough already. My room wasn't *touched* until after lunch yesterday. Would you believe it? . . . Well, and how's the leg to-day? You've got a lovely colour in your cheeks," she hurried on, with the fear of silence that afflicted her whenever she was with children. "Hasn't he, Béngt? A lovely colour."

The Swede remained leaning against the doorway, his only movements being to transfer his weight from one haunch to another or to pick at his front teeth with the nail of his forefinger. He had a rolled towel under one arm and another towel appeared to have been used to make the open-necked shirt which he wore above his blue linen slacks.

"I hope the Italian doctor knows his job," Chris said to Karen. "Tiny says that compound fractures are pretty tricky things. If they're set badly there's no end of trouble."

"Don't frighten Colin," von Arbach said, with a lazy, good-natured laugh.

"I'm not frightening him, don't be silly. But I wish you'd asked Tiny to do it."

"It didn't seem fair on his holiday," Karen said. "He must be glad to forget all about his work."

"Oh, nonsense. Besides," Chris added frankly, "a few extra lire would have been a great help to us." She hurriedly laughed in an attempt to make a joke out of a remark which she now realized might not have been in good taste.

"You think so much about money," von Arbach said.

"If you thought a little more about it, young man, you'd write to your father to ask what had happened to your allowance."

"Oh, it always comes in the end. But there are hitches. It is not strictly legal for the currency to be sent and so——" he made a sinuous, weaving movement from left to right, right to left, with one hand—"things must be arranged. That is all."

"You should be ashamed," Chris said playfully. "You foreigners are all in the black market. I think it's disgraceful—don't you, Karen?" she appealed, boldly using the Christian name for the first time.

Karen shrugged her shoulders, while von Arbach straightened himself in the doorway and, catching sight of the crutches that had just been brought for Colin, picked them up and attempted to use them.

"What *are* you doing?" Chris demanded in delighted amusement. "Whatever next! You naughty boy!" She giggled and remonstrated at one and the same time, while the Swede hopped back and forth across the room. "But they're too small for you! You'll break them."

"Yes, please take care," Colin said. "If you'd like a chocolate," he added in conciliation, "there's a box open on the table."

"Frigor!" exclaimed Chris. "Swiss chocolates! Well, you are lucky." She had always found it difficult to conceal her greed, and she now stooped above the box, barely able to restrain herself from clutching a whole handful.

"Do take one," Colin said.

"H'm—heaven, *heaven*." She closed her eyes and swayed from side to side, as she did when she and von Arbach danced together. "Have one, Béngt. Go on."

"Yes, do have one," Colin said.

The Swede did not refuse.

"Have you seen my birthday present to Béngt?" Chris said. "It was his birthday yesterday. Fancy, he's only twenty-three. Doesn't that make us all feel ancient? Except you, young rascal," she added to Colin. She had taken the towel from under the Swede's arm and now unrolled it to display a pair of gleaming white-satin bathing-trunks, with a monogram embroidered in red silk in one corner. "Aren't they the twee-est you ever saw?" she asked Karen. "But I tell him that when he wears them everyone will think he's a pansy. . . . Not that he cares—he just loves to be looked at and admired. He's so vain. Aren't you?" she said to the Swede, who, once more slouching in the doorway, did no more than shift his stance with a faint, slightly contemptuous smile and a downward flutter of his Mongolian eyelids.

"Well, we mustn't tire the patient," Chris said, feeling that somehow she had been deflected from her purpose in the visit and that, for that reason, it had been a failure. "Is there anything we can get you?"

"No, I don't think so, thank you."

"Sure? . . . Well, bye-bye for now." She raised one hand and waggled the fingers, so that her three "chunky" bracelets clattered against each other.

"Won't you have another chocolate?" Colin said.

Chris glanced at the open box, and then said: "Well, if you press me. . . ." She giggled: "Aren't I a pig? But you must be a pig, too, Béngt."

Béngt had no objection to being a pig.

This visit was followed by one from Maisie Brandon who entered the room, taking excessively small, tottering steps on giddy high-heels. She was laden with presents. The pebbles once again rattled in their tin can as she laughed: "What a relief to dump that lot! The chauffeur offered to help me carry them but I felt sure he'd drop stone-dead of heart-failure if I let him. He's ninety if he's a day. Oh, good lad! You've eaten nearly all those chocolates." She peered into the box of Frigor which had come as a present from her the day before. "I've got some more for you here, and a sort of miniature tank which climbs over anything when you wind it up"—it was characteristic that she should have chosen a gift that was wholly unsuited to Colin's tastes—"and here's another jig-saw, the *Queen Mary*, or is it the *Queen Elizabeth*? . . . Well, how are you?" She cut short Colin's polite speech of thanks. "Oh, my poor feet! I could use those crutches myself. How are you?"

Colin said that he was feeling better, and then asked about life up at the villa; he was always amused by Maisie Brandon's stories of Lady Newton.

"Oh, hell! Absolute H-E-Double-L, my pet. There are all those lavatories, row upon row of them, and one just clanks and clanks and clanks, and not a trickle comes! It was not so bad before all the servants except the cook and chauffeur left, because one could have buckets of water carried up—I insisted on it, in spite of all Lady N.'s objections. But things get worse and worse each day. Heaven knows when any more servants will be found, because, of course, she's notorious all over Florence. She hadn't paid the last lot for over three months; she says she can't think about anything while she's working—and that means me too. Every morning after breakfast she locks herself into her study and I don't see her until eight o'clock dinner—by which time she's usually in a vile temper because the book won't go right."

"The book?"

"Yes, it's her life work, her last tribute to the memory of Amberson Lane. She was a painter, you know. And Lady N. is writing her life—that dreadful life of hers." She had almost said "that dreadful

Lesbian life of hers", but had checked herself, realizing that the adjective might be too sophisticated even for Colin's ears. "Can you believe it? God knows what the Italians will make of all that sex among the V.A.D.s." She made a little grimace and drew her bony shoulders together. "But I don't honestly suppose a single page will ever see the light of print."

In the knowledge that Colin was one of the few children she could entertain merely by being herself she rattled on agreeably enough until Enzo and Rodolfo came in. Then, with an awkwardness strange in a woman of her experience, she nodded to them, mumbled *"Buon' giorno"*, and clumsily excused herself before hurrying out.

Rodolfo gripped Colin's hands and Enzo followed, all three of them giggling in a mixture of excitement and embarrassment. Rodolfo was carrying a jam-jar crammed with large, dusty leaves and he now presented it to Colin, twisting it round to reveal an enormous hairy, purple caterpillar which lay supine against the blurred glass like a large pod of beans. Emerald pellets, the size of hundreds and thousands, were scattered around it. It made Colin feel squeamish but from the excited gestures and exclamations of the two Italians he understood that the caterpillar would one day become a rare butterfly. Enzo had found it by the river.

In return Colin offered the boys both fruit and chocolates, and while Rodolfo sucked an orange with noisy intentness, he and Enzo began to play draughts. The Florentine always lost, acknowledging defeat with an amused shrug of the shoulders and a laugh. He was stupid, he seemed to be declaring; the English were so clever.

"I've a visitor for you," Karen suddenly announced round the door in the middle of one of these games. "You probably won't remember him from the night you broke your leg."

The two Italians leapt to their feet, Rodolfo concealing the half-sucked orange behind his back, while Colin blinked at his stepmother three or four times in rapid succession as if a handful of dust had been thrown into his eyes.

"I don't . . ." he began. "Please, Mummy, don't let him——"

But Frank Ross had already entered the room and now strode across to the bed to squeeze the child's limp, reluctant hand in his

own. He was wearing the khaki shorts and tunic in which Karen
had first seen him on the road to Siena, and a pair of grey plimsolls; Colin noticed that his knees were covered in scars. "Let's
have some fresh air," he said, and going to the french windows,
he pushed both halves wide open. "That's better. There's an awful
fug in here." In Italian he asked the two boys what they had been
doing, and they explained falteringly, with blushes and downcast
eyes, that they had been having a game.

"Colonel Ross has come to play chess with you," Karen said. "I
told him you were the school champion."

"We were in the middle of a game of draughts," Colin protested.

"I don't think that's very polite, is it?" Karen said. "You can play
draughts any time. The boys are always here. Besides, it's a babies'
game, it's not like chess. You know you can always win at draughts
easily and that's not good. Things are not worth doing unless they
cost an effort."

Frank Ross laughed. "How strange to hear that sentiment from
you—the attraction of the difficult." Karen flushed as he continued: "Oh, let the blighter do as he likes. If he'd rather finish his
game of draughts, that's O.K. by me."

But Colin knew that he would have to play. "Perhaps Rodolfo
would like to finish the game with Enzo for me," he said. "It
shouldn't take him more than five moves," he could not resist
adding with a touch of pride.

Karen picked up the draughts board and carried it across to the
corner where Rodolfo was once more squatting, and then watched
as the two Italians self-consciously took up the threads of the interrupted game. Enzo, who had already decided that evening by the
Arno that Karen was the most beautiful woman he had ever seen,
felt too dazed by her nearness to play with any skill; his hand trembled whenever he touched one of his pieces. The Englishwoman
noticed this and was amused; physically Enzo was not unattractive
to her.

Meanwhile Frank Ross was attempting to beat Colin, and finding the task more difficult than he had supposed. He despised himself for the importance he set on a victory, as he always despised
himself when he caught himself out in some simple conceit or

ambition; it was only to his more subtle conceits and ambitions
that he remained strangely blind. Twice he thought he had the boy
checkmated and twice, to his irritation, he realized he had been
mistaken. He had begun to bite the nails of his left hand in the
intervals of waiting for his opponent's moves. "Heavens, you are
a slow-coach," he exclaimed. "It takes you a month of Sundays to
make up your mind."

"Winning is always important to Colin," Karen put in. It was
untrue, except on this occasion, when to defeat the stranger
seemed to the boy a matter of extreme urgency, he could not have
said why; but he made no answer to the taunt, continuing to frown
down at the board until Karen said: "Enzo and Rodolfo have had
seven games of draughts since you began."

"Draughts isn't chess. You said yourself that draughts was a
babies' game."

"Suppose we talk a little less and get on with the move," Frank
Ross said, now leaving his nails and beginning to crack the joints
of his left hand in the powerful grip of his right. He sat on a cane-
bottomed chair, leaning forward with his legs wide apart so that
the short golden hairs on the inside of his naked thighs glistened
in the sunlight.

"That's not very clever," he said, only to realize that the move
was far cleverer than he had imagined.

"What's the matter with you?" Karen said, coming and putting a hand on Ross's shoulder, so that she could feel the bone
through his thin khaki tunic. "I thought you were supposed to be
good."

"Oh, shut up, do. It doesn't help to have your ill-informed comments," he answered in a voice so matter-of-fact that for a moment
it took the sting out of his rudeness.

Karen said "Thank you," using a phrase which is always the
most feeble of retorts, and then slowly went back to the game of
draughts, while Frank Ross muttered: "That's more like it. I never
could stand being shouted at from the touchline. Particularly by a
woman."

The game was still uncompleted when Mrs. Bennett came in
half an hour later. She had already been introduced to Frank Ross
and she gave him a curt nod and an almost irritable "Please don't

get up" before she went across to Karen. "It's about Nicko," she said. "The maid tells me that he again wet his bed last night."

"You say it as if it was my fault," Karen answered.

"He hasn't done it for years," the elder woman pursued.

"It's very naughty of him. It's sheer laziness. . . . Oh, really, Mother, I know in the old days at the school you always used to say it was the parents who should be scolded for that sort of thing, not the children. But I can't see how either Max or I can be blamed. Well, can we?"

"The child's not happy. He hasn't been happy ever since he came here."

"The heat and the food have upset him, that's all." Karen looked round, as she heard the click-clack of the chess-pieces being tumbled into their box. "Well?" she said.

"Stalemate," Frank answered her. "He almost won."

"Good for Colin!" Karen said. She had ceased to want Frank to win after he had been rude to her. "Well done, darling."

Frank was standing over the two Italians, his hands tucked into his wide belt, as Karen said: "What do you think should be done with a child who keeps wetting his bed?"

"Oh, beat him," he threw out, in a way which made it impossible to tell whether he was joking or in earnest.

"Full marks for that suggestion," Mrs. Bennett said, sinking into the chair which Ross had just left. Where his bare thighs had rested the wood was unpleasantly warm and moist with sweat. She took Colin's hand between her own and said: "I'm worried about Nicko. Be nice to him, dear."

"I always am nice to him," the boy returned truthfully.

"I know you are. But be extra nice."

Frank Ross had picked up the sketch-book which Mrs. Bennett had thrown on to the dressing-table when she had first come in, and had been quietly flicking over page after page. Now he sauntered over to the bed, sat down and said: "Some of these are fine." He was holding the book open at the sketch of Enzo and Rodolfo asleep. "This for instance. Karen told me you painted, but I never thought—never for a moment . . ."

Mrs. Bennett stared at him, one hand making the familiar gesture of scratching the grape-like swellings on her long, bare legs;

then she shot forward, the book was twitched from his grasp. "I'll thank you for that," she said. A crimson flush swept over her, concentrated on her forehead and her cheek-bones; she was trembling with rage. "Another time please ask my permission before you look at my private belongings."

"Mother, don't be so silly," Karen protested, while the two Italians lumbered up from the floor, realizing that something had gone wrong without knowing what.

"I'm sorry," Ross said with a rare, and genuine humility. He liked Mrs. Bennett and wished to be liked by her in return, as he always wished to be liked by those he could not impress. Sometimes she reminded him of the aunt, now dead, who had been responsible for bringing him up with a discipline few fathers could achieve; she had the same ability to be both tender and hard, without the one interfering with the other. "I'm sorry," he repeated. "It was rude of me. It was lying there, and it seemed so harmless to look. I didn't think you'd mind."

"Oh, it doesn't matter," Mrs. Bennett said, shutting the book and pulling across the elastic which kept it closed; but she spoke without either friendliness or forgiveness. For the first time for many years she had found herself detesting another human being, and the discovery had frightened her. She tried to be pleasant: "But it was nice of you to say you liked my work. Not that it's up to very much, I realize that now."

The attempted gesture at once renewed his self-confidence, since he was too little perceptive to recognize the dislike that lay behind it. "May I"—he leant forward eagerly, his brown hands clasped as if in entreaty—"may I—could I possibly have that sketch of the two sleeping boys? May I?" he cajoled with all the charm of which he was capable. "Please?"

She looked aside and down, as if she were examining some slightly repulsive insect on the floor; then she looked up at him, but that same expression did not leave her face: "No, I'm sorry. That's something I'd rather not give."

"Oh, not give——" he misunderstood her.

"Or sell. I'm sorry." She gave a strange, breathless chuckle as she added: "Perhaps when I'm dead Karen will give—or sell—it to you. That's if you really want it."

"But of course I really want it."

She shrugged her shoulders and went out on to the balcony, where she soon fell asleep in a deck-chair, her arms hanging limply to the ground.

"You mustn't mind Mother," Karen said. "She's got very old this last year or so." Once again her hand felt the bone of Ross's shoulder through his thin khaki tunic. "I'm sorry she was so rude to you, but she's like that now. You mustn't take any notice of her. You know what old people are." She gave a small shudder. "Oh, I think it's terrible to get like that."

"Terrible?" He looked up at her, a sharpness in his voice making her withdraw her hand hastily. "I don't feel that about your mother. I don't think that at all. She's very much all there."

"You don't know her," Karen sighed. "She's so irritable—and disagreeable. I lose all patience."

"How can you say that?" Colin put in angrily. "It's not fair. It's not fair," he repeated, because he could think of nothing else to say.

"Very chivalrous," Karen laughed, without concern. She looked at her small sapphire-and-diamond watch on her wrist: "If we're going to meet Chris and von Arbach at the bathing-pool for a drink we'd better go now."

"Oh, those two!" Ross said with contempt. "Doesn't Maskell realize what's going on? The man must be an idiot."

"Of course not. Nothing *is* going on. Chris and Béngt are good friends——"

"Let's face it, von Arbach is nothing better than a gigolo. Chris pays for everything."

"Only until his allowance comes through."

"Anyway it's quite obvious that the pair of them——"

"*Prenez garde à l'enfant,*" Karen put in hurriedly. She had continued to use this phrase even when Colin and Pamela had obviously surpassed her in command of the French language.

"He looks as if he knew all the answers," Frank said drily, causing Colin to blush with resentment at what he took to be a taunt. The boy considered for a moment and then, sitting straight up in bed, his fine dark hair on end, stammered out angrily:

"If you mean that they sleep together, that's obvious."

"Colin!" Karen exclaimed; but when Frank Ross laughed, she laughed too.

"What did I say?" Frank said; and then, his amiability suddenly freezing into contempt, he added with barely parted lips: "You have a well-educated step-son. I must congratulate you."

"You're not going to lie in bed all day, are you?" Karen asked Colin, who had tumbled back on to the pillows as soon as he had delivered his outburst, and now lay with his burning face turned away from them towards the wall. "The doctor said you must get about as much as you could. You must practise with the crutches."

"The boys are going to carry me down to the river bank, when they bathe," Colin answered in an almost inaudible voice.

"Carry you! How can they carry you?"

"By making a chair with their hands. They've often done it."

"How useful to have two coolies at your beck and call," Frank put in; he was standing by the two Italians and he now lowered a hand, without saying anything, and made a move for Enzo; one, two, three pieces were taken from the board. Rodolfo was furious.

"But you must learn to use the crutches," Karen pursued. "It's so lazy to be carried everywhere."

"I have tried to use them. But it hurts."

"The doctor said it was bound to hurt to begin with, with a fracture so high up. It's just one of those things. You must grin and bear it. Don't you agree, Frank?"

Ross shrugged his shoulders as if Colin's welfare were something with which he could hardly be expected to concern himself.

"Don't you agree?" Karen pursued, as if it gave her a secret pleasure to humiliate her step-child before the man she now knew that she loved. "It's no use his molly-coddling himself. He must make an effort with the crutches. Of course it will be uncomfortable to begin with, but he must just put up with that."

Frank glanced at her for a moment and then said in his slightly staccato voice: "Why do you keep saying the things you think I should like you to say? That sort of remark isn't in your character—it's in mine."

Karen had never been able to parry Ross's verbal thrusts, and perhaps, secretly, she really enjoyed them. With those she loved

two attitudes alone were possible to her; to humiliate or be humiliated. Only Nicko's father had escaped this general rule. "I don't
understand," she contented herself with saying.

"You're not very bright," he jeered, but he had taken her by the
wrist and that was enough for her. She deliberately stood close to
him so that his bare thigh touched hers through her light summer
clothing. "Shall we go?"

"Yes, we're terribly late," she sighed. "Good-bye, Colin."

"Good-bye," Frank said; he flicked at one of the boy's ears with
a forefinger, a gesture which, intended to be playful, in fact caused
pain.

"Now don't pretend that hurt," Karen said, seeing how Colin
pulled a face. "Good-bye. . . . Good-bye," she repeated, when the
boy did not answer.

"Good-bye."

Enzo had looked up at Karen expectantly when he saw that she
was about to go; but she had forgotten about him and Rodolfo,
and went out without giving either of them a glance.

Chapter Sixteen

"GRANNY," Colin said softly, and then louder: "Granny! I say,
Granny!"

As if she were about to have a convulsion, the old woman
opened her eyes, shook her head three or four times from side to
side, snorted, and took gulp after gulp of air.

"Granny . . . what's the matter? Aren't you well? . . . Granny!"

"Oh, it's you, it's you," she said, her agitation all at once stilled.
"I was asleep. You gave me a surprise, that's all. The sun had
moved, and when I opened my eyes, it was shining right into them.
I'm sorry."

"Enzo and Rodolfo are going to take me down to the river.
They're going to carry me as they did yesterday. I just wanted to
tell you in case you wondered what had become of us."

"That was very thoughtful of you, very thoughtful," she said,
unpinning the ugly garnet brooch, set in Victorian silver, which
fastened her lace collar, and then pinning it on again, in precisely

the same spot, with trembling, disobedient fingers. "Take Pamela, there's a good boy."

"Pamela?"

"Yes, I think she'd like to go. I think she may have been feeling a little out of things these last few days. You and the boys, it's natural you should want to do things together. But it's lonely for her, on her own, and you and she have been friends for such a long time."

Colin felt ashamed, realizing for the first time that he had been neglecting his sister.

"Anyway, ask her," Mrs. Bennett said. "No harm done in asking," she added drowsily, her eyes already closing. Her jaw dropped, revealing two rows of astonishingly unstopped, undecayed teeth; she was once more asleep.

Pamela was cutting out some material from a pattern on the floor, and at first pretended, from pride, to be reluctant to join them.

"I ought to finish this," she said. "Lena's coming this afternoon and she's going to bring her sewing-machine for me to use. I've cut it badly," she added with the frankness which was at once one of her more endearing and her least comfortable qualities. "The scissors slipped here. It was to be a night-dress for Miss Preston—for a Christmas present."

"Miss Preston?"

"She's the music-mistress," she answered, blushing. "Don't you remember—you and she argued about Richard Strauss at the school concert? She was awfully cross with you. You did say some silly things."

"So did she."

"I think I'll leave it to Lena to finish the cutting-out. I'm glad she's forgiven us. She says that the boy-friend, Commino whatever-it-is, has a surprise for you."

"A surprise?"

"Oh, I expect it's a present of some kind," Pamela returned drily. "Everyone seems to be giving you presents just because of your leg. . . . Let's go."

At the Trinità Bridge Enzo and Rodolfo were both so puffed from carrying Colin that, placing him like a ventriloquist's dummy on the stone balustrade, they decided to have a rest. Pamela indicated that she could take a turn as coolie, but they laughed at the suggestion; they were not tired, only hot, Rodolfo explained in French, and to show what he meant, he drew away the shirt which stuck, drenched with perspiration, to Enzo's broad back and shoulders. At the same moment three other youths, dressed in the same shorts, khaki shirts, and plimsolls, brushed deliberately close against the two English children, gave Rodolfo a push from behind, elbowed Enzo, and hurried on, flinging a series of ribald obscenities at the quartet. Rodolfo sprinted after them, Enzo followed slower. The Tunisian tripped up one from behind, and butted a second, so that the skin split apart over his nose as if it were an over-ripe banana, while the Florentine punched the third systematically in the belly. It was a neat exhibition of street-fighting but one which filled the two English children with fear and dismay.

"Get someone to stop them," Colin said. "Do something. Do something, Pamela. They'll be hurt. Don't you see, I can't move. Do something!"

Pamela had covered her face with her hands.

"Pamela!" her brother shrieked at her.

When she next looked up, Enzo was sauntering back to them, with Rodolfo behind, while two of the youths were carrying away the third as if he were a corpse. Enzo massaged his bruised knuckles, smiling broadly at the same time; a bubble of blood swelled at his eyebrow, elongated itself, and splashed downward on to his plimsoll.

"You've hurt yourself," Colin said in English; he pointed.

"*Niente.*"

"*Mais pourquoi? Pourquoi tout ça?*" Pamela asked.

"They were making fun of us," Rodolfo explained. He used an obscenity to describe their opponents.

"What sort of fun?"

"Oh, because we know you, because you are our friends."

"Then you fought—you fought because of us?" Colin said with a mingling of pleasure and alarm.

"What does it matter?" Enzo said in Italian; he now appeared to be embarrassed and to wish to forget the matter. "*Andiamo.*"

But Rodolfo said: "*Nous sommes amis. Toujours amis. À l'éternité.*"

He put out a hand and shook, first Pamela's hand, then Colin's. He loved to make such gestures. "*Amis,*" he said again.

"*Andiamo,*" Enzo repeated.

When Colin had been deposited in a cool place beside the river, the two Italians hurriedly stripped behind a sweet-corn plantation, chattering excitedly to each other, and then emerged, Rodolfo in a grey woollen slip, Enzo in a pair of elastic-topped pants which left little of his physique unrevealed. Rodolfo at once made the inevitable allusion to the indecency of his friend's dress, causing Enzo and Pamela to blush simultaneously. This fact, too, he did not omit to point out; he was on top of his form.

"I wonder if he's right for Enzo," Pamela said, when the two Italians were half-way across the Arno in a race which Rodolfo had suggested in order to impress his two English friends.

"How do you mean—right?"

"Oh, he's persuaded Enzo that he's a complete fool, and that can't be good, can it?"

"I like Enzo best," Colin said. But it was already more than liking; he would never confess it to anyone, least of all to the Florentine, and he attempted to conceal it from himself, but he was already committed to Enzo to the last farthing of his intense, but reticent emotions. At night he lay awake imagining absurd, magazine-story predicaments from which he rescued the Florentine by his courage and love; yet he knew, in his heart of hearts, that if anyone rescued anyone else, it would be the Florentine who would rescue him. He was feeble, he was cowardly, and there was nothing he could ever do to prove his love; that was the bitterest part. "But Rodolfo's nice," he added.

"Yes, one can't help liking him. But I can never really forget that he once stole that fountain pen."

Colin considered. "Stealing is bad, I suppose. But I wonder if it's really as bad as——" He broke off and said no more.

"As what?"

"Oh, I don't know." He was juggling with two stones. "But now that we know somebody, really know somebody who is a—is a thief, it seems much less awful. I don't really mind. I think I could steal myself."

"Colin!"

"If I was in need. Or for someone else, someone for whom it mattered. Perhaps Rodolfo stole for Enzo," he suddenly said, with the enthusiasm of a new discovery. "Enzo's terribly poor, you know. I'm sure that was it. And in that case I think it was a good thing to do, I don't think Rodolfo was at all to blame. I admire him for having the courage. . . . Oh, here they are. And Enzo has won."

Standing waist-deep in the yellow, scurfy water, the two Italians argued, Rodolfo accusing his friend of cheating because he had not touched some particular stone at the other side of the river. "He doesn't like losing," Pamela said. "Oh, I wish I could go in! It seems so silly to get into a bathing-costume and then do nothing but lie around in the sun."

"Enzo's terribly strong," Colin said dreamily. "Look at his muscles."

"You haven't any muscles at all," Pamela answered with her usual brutal frankness. "Brains instead of brawn," she added and then exclaimed: "Oh, look! Aren't they silly?"

The two Italians were taking it in turns to dive under the water, get between each other's legs, and somersault each other over and over. Rodolfo shouted breathlessly: "*Regardez, regardez!*" in case they were not being seen, and then, pushing aside the dripping black hair which stuck to his forehead: "Lookee!" he shouted. "Lookee!"

"We're looking," Pamela shouted back. "Oh, he does show off."

"So the coolies got you here," a voice said behind them. They both swung round. "And now they're performing for you."

"I—I thought you were going to the swimming-pool with Mummy," Colin stammered.

"It was packed with the most awful people, and it seemed stupid to pay three hundred lire when I could bathe for nothing here. Besides I find the Maskells boring. I left your mother there," Frank Ross added.

"The river water is dangerous," Pamela said.

"Oh, nonsense! Is that why you're not bathing?"

"I'm not allowed to. Granny says it's all right for Italians, they're used to it, but English people can catch all sorts of diseases—diphtheria and typhoid and infantile paralysis and all that."

"You children are molly-coddled."

"Do you think so?" Pamela asked equably, as if the idea had never occurred to her before. "Perhaps Colin is, but I don't think I am. At least nobody's ever said so before. At school most of the girls are far more faddy than I am. . . . Are you going to bathe?" she asked, seeing that Frank Ross had pulled off his khaki tunic and was now removing his shorts to reveal the bathing-slip he wore underneath. "Goodness, you are brown! You don't look English at all."

"Why do you lie in the shade?" Frank Ross said to Colin; he had removed his watch, and where the silver strap had lain the skin was strangely white and puckered as if the wrist had been severed and then rejoined.

"I don't like the sun. It's too hot."

"It's good for you. And why do you want to clutter yourself up with all those clothes?" He put out a hand and tugged at Colin's pull-over: "Fancy a pull-over on a day like this." Then he drew back Colin's sleeve and held his own arm against the boy's fragile one. "Look! You look as if your mother had washed you in Persil." Pamela laughed, and Colin eyed her with a hurt resentment for this betrayal. "You ought to sunbathe; do you good."

"I don't like the sun," Colin repeated stubbornly.

"Colin isn't like other boys," Pamela said. It was impossible to tell whether she was joining in Frank Ross's attack or whether the remark was intended to be some sort of clumsy defence of her brother's attitude.

Frank laughed: "I had guessed that for myself." He got to his feet and hitched at his trunks; then he yawned and stretched luxuriously, scratched the hair under one armpit and dashed for the water. He challenged the two Italians to a race which involved swimming many hundreds of yards, most of them against the current.

"I hate him," Colin said simply.

"He was only trying to help you. The sun *is* good for you, every-one says that."

"He's as bad as Rodolfo, showing off his swimming. I hope he doesn't win. . . . He didn't win at chess," he added with subdued triumph.

"He did wonderful things in the war," Pamela said. She ran her stubby fingers through her luxuriant blonde hair and then drew a strand of it through her mouth.

"Oh, don't," Colin remonstrated; it was a habit which revolted his fastidiousness. "I wonder why he came," he mused.

"Who came?"

"Colonel Ross. It was funny his coming just here, it couldn't have been a coincidence, could it?"

"I don't see why not." Again Pamela put some hair in her mouth.

"Please don't!" Colin said irritably. "You know it makes me feel quite sick. . . . I think he wanted to find us," he added slowly.

"Wanted to find us! Don't be silly. Why?"

"I don't know. I wish I did. It's not as if he likes me," he went on. "I know he doesn't. He thinks me a milksop, I can see that. But he wanted to find us, I'm sure he wanted to find us. After all, when he found us, he needn't have joined us, need he? Need he?"

"That was just friendly."

"But he's not a person who does friendly things. . . . Oh, Enzo's winning. Good, good, good!" Suddenly, in a strangely shrill voice, he began to shout in English: "Come on, Enzo! Enzo, Enzo, Enzo! Come on!" He banged the iron on his broken leg against a stone so that it rang like a bell in time to his reiterated: "Enzo, Enzo, Enzo!"

But, had he known it, it was precisely that shouting which gave Ross the energy to drive himself onward like a flogged horse, pass the Florentine, and fling himself, breathless, exhausted, but first, at the feet of the children. "Oh, well done!" Pamela said, in admiration. "But I knew you would win."

"That current," Ross gasped. "Judged it all wrong. Should have known better." He rose to his feet to greet the Florentine as he came from the water. "Well done," he said in Italian, and he gripped both his hands, put an arm round his shoulder, and led him up the sand. "You nearly beat me," he said. There was a real cordiality in his voice, for in Enzo he had found what he always sought in men; a physical prowess which almost, but not quite, matched his own. He hated easy victories; he even more hated defeat.

Rodolfo came from the river a sulky third. He massaged his leg, pulled faces, and gave an excellent performance of someone who has cramp. But no one, except Pamela, took him at all seriously.

"You swim beautifully," Enzo said to Frank Ross in naïve admiration. "Doesn't he?" he turned to Rodolfo.

Rodolfo waggled his right hand loosely from the wrist as he always did when he wished to indicate a superlative; then he again doubled himself in simulated agony.

"Beautiful," Enzo repeated, lying on his naked side in the sunlight and looking at the Englishman. He closed his eyes and at once, like a dog, fell asleep.

Colin experienced an agony of jealousy. The Florentine, stretched still and glistening in the dust, had forsaken him for the enemy; they had all forsaken him, Pamela had forsaken him, he was alone. The iron rang out on the stone as he turned over on his stomach and lay with his face in a clump of grass.

Frank Ross sprinted up and down the bank three or four times to get dry and then began to pull on his clothes. As the watch covered the white patch on his wrist, Pamela suddenly asked: "Did you find us here just like that—by accident?"

He laughed, but he seemed unusually clumsy, for one so deft by nature, as he fastened the strap. "Of course. Did you think I'd followed you? I often bathe here. And I don't get diphtheria or typhoid or any other of those diseases," he added, as if to taunt her.

"That's what I told Colin," Pamela said.

"Oh, shut up, shut up!" her brother shouted, suddenly raising his face.

"Told him—told him what?" Ross asked.

"Nothing," Pamela said.

"Well, I must be going to my lunch." He felt in his pocket, took out a cigarette, broke it in two with scrupulous exactness, and then dropped a half by each of the sleeping Italians. "Tell them," he said, before he sauntered away.

"He might have given them one each," Colin said.

"Perhaps he isn't rich," Pamela said. "In fact I'm sure he isn't. His clothes are terribly shabby, have you noticed?"

"You like him," Colin said.

"Yes, I do like him. . . . Is there any harm in that? Well, is there?" Her brother did not answer.

Chapter Seventeen

"THAT's where Enzo lives," Rodolfo said, pointing down the tight, claustrophobic Borgo.

"There?" Colin looked at the plaque, blue lettering on white, and read out "Borgo Canto Rivolto."

"What does that mean?" Pamela asked. "The Street of the Revolting Song?" She alone laughed at her own joke.

"Can we go down there?" Colin asked. Then, when the Tunisian appeared to hesitate, he addressed himself to Enzo: "*È possibile andarvi?*"

"*Dove?*"

"*Alla sua casa.*"

The two Italians looked at each other and Rodolfo said: "But why?"

"It would be interesting."

"There's nothing to see."

"It's always fun to see where others live."

"But this street is ugly."

"*Brutto, brutto,*" said Enzo.

"That doesn't matter. . . . Oh, come on," Pamela said, already striding down the Borgo. "It's a shorter way to the hotel anyway. Come on, do!"

After the Italians had followed her for some yards, Colin said apologetically: "If you'd rather not, let's turn back." He knew now that he had forced them to do something which, inexplicably, they did not wish to do. "Let's turn back," he repeated.

"Turn back? But why turn back?" Rodolfo asked; and his tone was one of such astonishment that Colin wondered if he had been mistaken after all. "But why?" Rodolfo said.

"Oh, nothing."

The street was deserted and there was no movement either outside or within the narrow, bare house where the Rocchigianis lived. "That's it," Enzo said.

"That? It looks big."

Rodolfo explained that others lived there also and then, to amuse his English friends, he tried to tell them about the epileptic girl; but their French was not equal to it and he had to give up. A pity, he thought. A good story that. . . . But—perhaps Bella was in?

"*Ecco!*" he jerked his head up to one of the windows, unable to point because his hands still supported Colin.

"*Ecco, ecco!*" Bella sat at her usual place, her sewing in her hands, and she was looking down at them, her face held in profile so that the shrivelled half where she had burned herself could not be seen. Rodolfo whistled and she quickly turned away.

"Oh!" Pamela exclaimed. "She looked so beautiful before, and now. . . . Look, Colin."

"I've seen." The crimson, puckered skin had made him feel slightly sick. "Who is she?"

"A lodger, I suppose."

The boys were about to carry Colin on when Signora Rocchigiani appeared at a downstairs window, her head bound in what appeared to be a dish-cloth. She asked Enzo a question in Italian, he answered, there was much use of the word "*Inglese*", Rodolfo joined in, and eventually Signora Rocchigiani came out carrying a rocking-chair in which they deposited Colin. A moment later she brought another chair, one leg mended with two splints of wood, and motioned Pamela to it. "*S'accomodi,*" she said. "*S'accomodi.*"

"What is going on?" Pamela giggled. But she nevertheless sat down.

"*Un momentino,*" Signora Rocchigiani said. They noticed for the first time that she was wearing no shoes.

Rodolfo and Enzo squatted on the steps, and Rodolfo cleared his throat and spat at two flies that were locked together on the cobbles. He laughed and nudged his friend; then he blew his nose between two fingers.

"Daddy said that was how the Indians did it. I tried once, but it didn't work. There was an awful mess," Pamela said.

Signora Rocchigiani emerged carrying two cups which seemed to have come from a doll's tea-service, and handed one to each of the two children. Colin sipped his cautiously and restrained himself from pulling a face. "I think it's coffee," he said. "But it's awfully bitter."

Pamela tried hers and said: "Oh, Colin, I can't!"

"You must."

"It'll make me sick."

"You must," he repeated. "She'll be awfully hurt. Gulp it, in one." He put back his head and poured the thick mixture down. "It's not so bad like that," he said. "Go on. Don't be a coward."

Pamela gulped, looked as if she were about to retch, and then somehow returned Signora Rocchigiani's questioning smile with a smile of her own. "*Buono*," she said.

"*Buono?*"

"*Molto buono.*"

"*Si, molto buono,*" Colin said.

"That teaches you not to be inquisitive about other people's houses," Pamela said, as they moved off again. "But it was kind of her, wasn't it? Enzo takes after her, they have the same voices and the same blue eyes. She looked awfully ill and tired though."

"She works in the hotel laundry. Rodolfo told me."

"*Our* hotel laundry?"

"Yes."

As they came out into the Signoria, they saw ahead of them a grey alpaca coat, with horizontal creases from arm-pit to arm-pit, a protruding rump below it and a bush of grey hair above. "Signor Commino," said Pamela. Both shoes, once black but now grey for want of cleaning, had split their seams at the heels, and one of the shaggy socks had a hole the size of a florin. Under one arm was a parcel, wrapped in newspaper, while the other swung vigorously, fist clenched with the thumb between the fingers. Suddenly, as if he had seen them in a mirror, Signor Commino turned. His two rabbit-teeth were revealed in a grin; the fist was unclenched and extended to greet them. The spherical stomach seemed to swell with good nature, as he shouted: "Coleen, Coleen. . . . I was coming to speak with you." He nodded briskly to the two Italians and then held out his parcel. "It is for you, Coleen—a loan," he added quickly, in case of misunderstanding. "I cannot give it, because it is antique and therefore costly and belongs to my mother." He began to tear off the sheets of newspaper with a reckless disregard for the tidiness of the city, backing at the same time towards the Loggia de' Lanzi. Once there, he placed his treasure on a stone seat, and the last sheet of the *Corriere della Sera* was ripped off and away. There was a box.

"What is it?" Pamela asked. A crowd was collecting.

"Wait." Signor Commino raised the lid, touched something within, and after a grind, a whirr and a series of clicks, a tune, infinitely faint and tinny, penetrated to their ears.

"Bravo!" someone exclaimed.

"Listen." His head tilted to one side, so that his neck made a roll of fat against his stiff collar, Signor Commino raised a hand. They were silent. And the small, golden comb continued to yield up its melody at the touch of the revolving pins.

"What is it?" Pamela whispered.

"'The Bluebells of Scotland,'" Colin whispered back.

But the music had ceased. Hands were clapped; there were shouts, laughter and calls for an encore.

"This must have belonged to an English lady," Signor Commino said, making his familiar gesture of scratching with his forefinger at the single tuft of hair on the front of his scalp. "The machine is Swiss, the music is English. No?"

"Scottish," said Pamela.

But he took no notice of the correction. "And therefore it seemed just to me that I should give—lend it to your brother. There is also"—he stooped to examine the inside of the lid which framed a list of the tunes in the handwriting of the early nineteenth century—"there is also—ah, yes—'Drink to me only', 'Cherry Ripe', and—but you may see for yourself. See, see?" His stubby forefinger, with its thick, spade-shaped nail and tuft of black hair, pointed to the list, while he drew Pamela closer. "See?" he repeated.

She squirmed away from his grasp; she could not bear to be touched by him.

"Take good care of it, young miss, young master. . . ." He began scrabbling for the paper off the floor of the dusty loggia and twisted it untidily round the box. "There! And a speedy recovery, a speedy recovery." He pulled off his trilby hat and his grey bush of hair opened out like an umbrella and flopped about his ears. "*Arivederci,*" he said; and he continued to back away from them, repeating "*Arivederci* . . . young miss, young master . . . speedy recovery . . ." until he had disappeared from sight. The children all burst into extravagant laughter in which the spectators soon joined.

"But it's bad to laugh," Colin said at last. "It was kind of him to bring it after the way we behaved that night."

"Oh, he's only trying to smarm up, because he knows that Lena takes notice of what we say and wouldn't marry him if we said we didn't like him. I bet you it's that."

"No, I don't think so," Colin said.

"You don't want Lena to marry him, do you?" Pamela challenged.

"No—no, I don't," Colin had to admit. "But I like him all the same."

"You didn't that night."

"Well, I do now. I've changed my mind."

"Because he brought you a musical-box?" Pamela said with contempt. "A loan," she added, imitating his accent. "Because it is antique and therefore costly and belongs to my mother."

"You don't understand," Colin said. And that was always to be his complaint against her; there was so much she did not understand.

"I must eat now," Colin announced when the boys had carried him up to his bedroom. "I suppose you both must eat too." Rodolfo and Enzo looked at each other and laughed, and Colin said: "Don't you eat now?"

Enzo pulled out his unemployment card. "Monday, Wednesday, Saturday," he said.

"And Rodolfo?"

"I have a hundred lire." In fact he had three hundred.

"But that's nothing."

Rodolfo shrugged his shoulders.

"I haven't any money," Colin said. He always spent his pocket-money as soon as he was given it. "How will you manage?"

"Oh, we can buy some bread—and perhaps some *mortadella* or some cheese."

"But that's not enough. Here, wait a moment." Colin had seen the box of chocolates which Maisie Brandon had brought him that morning, and he now picked it up and held it out towards them.

"No—no," said Rodolfo, eyeing the box greedily.

"Yes, you must take it. I want you both to have it." (He wanted Enzo to have it; it was terrible that he should starve.) "Go on, take it."

Rodolfo put out a hand, but Enzo said sharply in Italian: "Don't take it. We mustn't take it. Thank him and say we can't."

"Yes, but——" Rodolfo said.

"Don't take it!"

Colin was still holding it out. "Why shouldn't you take it?" he asked, his usually precise French becoming ungrammatical as his excitement mounted. "You've spent the whole morning looking after me, and if it weren't for you, my father would have to pay someone to do it. I want you to take this, as a return for what you've done."

"He says it's to pay us," Rodolfo said. "That's fair enough. We sweated our guts out carrying him to the river."

"Pay us! Who does he think we are. We didn't do it because——"

"Well, I'm going to take it anyway." Rodolfo's hand closed on the large and expensive box, and Colin smiled with relief.

"I'm glad you've decided to be sensible," he said. "It was so silly to refuse. I've got everything here, and you've—you've got so little. . . . Is work very difficult to find?" he asked as they prepared to leave.

Rodolfo laughed. "Impossible."

"But you do really want to work?"

"Who, me?" Rodolfo pointed to himself, as if incredulous at what had been said. "Of course I want to work, I want nothing more."

"And Enzo?"

"He, too. He's strong, he's a good lad. But there's nothing for us. Damn all." Using the English phrase he made a derisive gesture with both hands as if he were smoothing down a tablecloth.

Rodolfo sold the chocolates back to the sweet-shop where Maisie had bought them, for half the price she had paid, and then, after much argument, took Enzo to the Ristorante Popolare where they both gobbled two plates each of *pasta al sugo* between draughts of wine. Meanwhile Colin was letting his lunch-tray get cold, as he wrote a letter:

DEAR MRS. BRANDON,

When you came this morning you said that Lady N. found it difficult to find servants. I have a friend, I think you have seen him here with me, and I was wondering . . .

Chapter Eighteen

THEY had visited a monastery on a hill outside Florence, and having been shown innumerable paintings by Sodoma and Dolci, had now descended to eat an execrable dinner in a restaurant by the roadside.

"Another *strega!*" Chris exclaimed to Béngt. "You must have had a dozen."

"Mind your own business."

Chris gave the laugh she always used when she had not the courage to appear to mean what she said. "But it is my own business—until your allowance arrives. Isn't it?"

"You are vulgar," Béngt said, turning the glass between his fingers.

"And you're drunk," Chris retorted, again with the laugh.

"Look here, old boy, I'm not going to have that sort of thing said to my wife," Tiny Maskell announced. But he continued to draw on his pipe, scattering sparks into the dark corners of the terrace.

"Oh, keep out of this, Tiny," Chris said irritably. "Please don't do the heavy husband. . . . But seriously, Béngt," she went on with a sudden, maternal softening in her voice. "You're too young for so much drinking. It'll grow on you. It's awful to see a young man putting away glass after glass like that—it really is awful." She tipped into her own glass a thimbleful of the green liqueur which a monk had persuaded her to buy at the monastery. She had bought a bottle of red liqueur, too; the monk had assured her they both tasted alike.

"And how you can drink that stuff!" Béngt said contemptuously. "You are vulgar, I told you, and you have no taste."

"That's enough, Arbach," Frank Ross said quietly but decisively, omitting the "von". "Hold your tongue, if you've nothing civil to say."

Karen smiled down at the tablecloth, as if this intervention had given her extreme, but secret, pleasure and then looked across at him: "Don't you ever drink?"

"No."

"Smoke?"

"Sometimes."

"And you eat some *tagliatelle* and say you've had enough," she added in reference to his meal.

"You should be up there," Max said, pointing to the monastery.

"Oh, but he isn't dirty enough," Chris protested, while von Arbach belched loudly. She glanced at him and then continued: "How that monk smelled! Did you get near him? He would keep button-holing me, not that I could understand a word of his lingo until he spoke French, and there he was leaning over me, right over me, and his breath was like a blow-lamp, and one could tell it was weeks, well, months or even years, since he'd thought of changing his clothes. I always thought cleanliness was next to godliness."

"*Next* to godliness," Frank Ross said. "But if you're godly, why worry about the next best thing?"

"Hold tight, my dears," Chris said, glancing over her shoulder. "Prepare for a shock. Here's the bill, here's the bill. Who's feeling strong?"

"My party," Max said, taking the grubby paper from an even grubbier hand.

"Oh, but no," Chris said. "And all Béngt's *stregas*, and Tiny's *cointreau*. And I ate much more than any of you. I don't call that fair."

"My party," Max repeated.

Well, of course, he could afford to pay; he was rolling, absolutely rolling in it. And there they were with their wretched fifty pounds each. It was not as if he had even been particularly generous to them in the past. But they were all like that, all these Americans. Mean, just mean.

Chris smiled. "It's terribly sweet of you. Tiny, Max insists on treating us to dinner. We really oughtn't to let him, because I'm sure it's something fabulous." She watched Max closely as he counted out eight thousand lire, and was disappointed that the sum wasn't more. "You are angels," she said. "You've been so good to us. Béngt, aren't you going to say thank you?"

"Gratitude spoils what one's given," Béngt said, his head lolling on to one shoulder; he smiled vacantly, raised a hand to his mouth as if he were about to sneeze, and gulped some more *strega*.

"What an original idea!" Chris laughed. "Anyway, Max and Karen, thank you very much from all of us."

"I only wish it had been a better dinner," Karen said.

"Oh, but that wasn't your fault, you weren't to know," Chris said clumsily. She looked round her: "I wonder if there's a ladies' room anywhere. I awfully want to spend a lira." Eventually she got up and going across to the proprietor who was sitting in the deserted dining-room within, reiterated: "*Gabinetto, gabinetto,*" insistently until she and Karen were led off through a labyrinth of corridors.

"Cigar?" Max said, producing a case.

Béngt helped himself, Ross declined, and Tiny Maskell announced, oddly subdued: "I think I'll stick to the old pipe." He was slumped in a blue blazer which seemed far too big even for a man of his girth, as if the joviality had all run out of him through some invisible puncture. Suddenly he looked across at Béngt with his slightly bloodshot eyes and said: "I'd like to have a word with you alone, old man."

"With me?"

"If you don't mind." He gritted his irregular, brown teeth on the stem of his pipe. "Come for a little stroll."

"Can't we——?"

"A stroll will do you good."

Béngt tripped on the three steps down from the terrace and was only saved by Tiny, who put out an arm. The Swede giggled stupidly at this accident, and repeated, "Almost, almost, almost", as if he could not believe his luck. He and Tiny began to walk down the whitely glimmering road, Tiny's arm still round the Swede's shoulder as he swayed and stumbled forward.

"Fat lot of use talking to him when he's in that condition," Frank Ross said.

"I suppose it's about Chris."

Ross laughed. "Oh, I imagine something far more important." When Max looked at him in interrogation, he said: "Money."

"Money?"

"Hasn't Karen told you that Chris told her that the allowance
has still not arrived. This is the third week that they've had to pay
his hotel bill."

"At the Palazzo d'Oro? But how on earth do they manage it?"

"Precisely."

"You mean——?"

"There are ways of making 'arrangements'. Two years ago it
was pretty safe—if one used one's common sense. But now . . ."
He shrugged his shoulders.

"Chris is a fool. We would have lent her some money, if it meant
that."

"She's a little afraid of you," Frank Ross said. "She probably
thought that it would be hard to explain. In Wimbledon, married
women don't keep their lovers."

"Poor devil," Max said, with genuine compassion, pulling at his
cigar.

"Oh, I don't think she really deserves any pity, do you? She's
making such an ass of herself. Everyone must notice."

"Certainly the hotel staff do. I've seen them smile behind her
back."

"And your children," Ross put in softly.

But whether from disinclination or because he had not heard it,
Max left this last remark alone. When he next spoke it was of the
war in which they had both shared. It was an inexhaustible subject,
and the only one which made them feel wholly at ease in each
other's company.

Meanwhile in the ladies' room, Chris was saying: "Oh, I can't.
It's one where you have to squat, you know. In the Gare du some-
thing-or-other Tiny used one back to front and he went and fell
in." She began laughing and then all at once burst into tears.

"Chris, what on earth's the matter?" Karen asked.

Strangely, Chris's crying had given to her the youthfulness
which she had never been able to achieve by the Dauphin bob,
her teen-age clothes, and her artificial girlishness. Like a child, she
pressed her cheek against the flaking whitewash of the lavatory
wall and blubbered without restraint.

"Chris!" Karen said sharply.

"It was awful having him speak to me like that, just as if I was dirt, nothing but dirt. Sometimes he can be so kind and then a devil gets into him and he hurts me all he can. It's not fair!"

"Who do you mean?" Karen asked.

"Well, Béngt, of course," Chris snapped irritably. "Who else could I mean?" For a moment she stopped crying, but then once again she began: "He knows I love him and would do anything for him and instead of respecting that, he just trades on it, just trades on it, and uses me as he pleases. I might be a door-mat for him, really I might. Oh, I'm so unhappy!" Splinters of whitewash were lodged in her hair, and an enormous chunk lay on her cheek like a mound of sticking-plaster.

Karen hated this sort of emotional intimacy no less than physical intimacy; Chris's outburst had affected her as she would have been affected if she had been called in to witness a surgical operation. But she steeled herself, and put an arm round the other woman's shuddering body. "Chris, you mustn't be so upset, you mustn't make mountains out of molehills." No, she mustn't; it made one feel sick, absolutely sick. Oh, why wouldn't people show some guts, pride, control? Instead of parading their filthy little emotional wounds and abscesses as she had seen lepers in Egypt parade their sores. Shut up, shut up, she wanted to scream. "There there, Chris, Chris, do try——"

But like most women who have been spoiled by their husbands, Chris was a connoisseur in sympathy and at once recognized the synthetic flavour of what Karen was feeding her. She was now horrified at her previous admission, and hastily whimpered: "Oh, I know that I'm being silly, because it's not as if I were *in love* with Béngt. I mean, I care most awfully for him, and of course people being what they are, they think what one would expect. It's just—just that having no children of my own—oh, it's ridiculous of me—but I like to have someone to mother, and he's always been so sweet and thoughtful to me, always, always. Except, of course"—she gulped, and began to wipe the plaster off her cheek with a handkerchief she first licked—"except when he behaves as he behaved this evening. And that upsets me, I don't know why. I just can't help it. I suppose I'm too sensitive. Tiny always says I'm too sensitive." She blew her nose hard until it was the colour of the crimson varnish on her nails, and all at once giggled: "And now I suppose, I'd better try and use this thing. I'm sure I shall fall in."

Later, she and Karen wandered out into the overgrown garden which straggled behind the house until it eventually petered out in a tangle of briars, nettles and rusty barbed wire. "Moths!" exclaimed Chris, and then more shrilly "Bats!": but she did not wish to be seen by the men until her eyes were less red, and so she endured these tribulations, walking up and down a dusty gravel path, her arm in Karen's. "Let's sit down," she said, pointing to a stone seat which glimmered in the moonlight. "What stars!" she exclaimed. "What a moon! Don't they make you feel romantic, Karen?"

Karen laughed, but her whole being shuddered from this kind of sisterliness; she could tolerate it with no woman, least of all with Chris. "I'm not very romantic," she said at last.

"No, I don't believe you are," Chris said.

They sat mutely on the warm, pocked stone, one at each end, as if in acknowledgement that between them there was really no sort of contact. Yet the contact was there, had they both known it, since each was thinking the same kind of thoughts, each was hugging the same kind of secret. And the thought and the secret brought an extravagant bloom to Karen's usually subdued beauty and gave to Chris a beauty she had never before possessed. For now she was beautiful, as she watched the bats wheeling and felt the gnats sting her ankles and mused, giving her whole being up to this voluptuously intense remembrance, of a few agonizing moments after a picnic in Epping Forest sixteen years previously, and of the weeks of lonely fear that followed. He had Béngt's loose movements and hair of the same colour, the colour of condensed milk, and he, too, smelled of cleanliness, yes, smelled of it as these Italians smelled of dirt. He had worn a ridiculous white student's cap which made him look like a petty-officer, and had boarded with her aunt in the flat off the Finchley Road. He had promised to write to her, and she herself had written, times without number; but all she had received was a postcard from Stockholm. The Town Hall and on the other side "Best wishes, Tore". Oh, it had been cruel. But the smell of the crushed leaves, and that clean smell above her. . . .

Karen mused less sentimentally. But she, too, had stumbled on the lost, impossible ideal: discipline, heroism, austerity. And how she had despised her father through all those years, wishing that he would die. For when she was seven she had heard him scream out with pain and she, who could bear agonies without crying, had decided that he was no father of hers. She repudiated him, she cast him aside. Men were brave, men were strong, and he was not one of them. Year by year, he weakened and softened before her eyes, clutching at her with his insatiable demands, whimpering, moaning, sobbing out his complaints. And at the end screaming: "I won't die, I won't, I won't, I won't!" as he would scream when the doctor had to cause him the slightest discomfort. . . . Oh, if one must die, one should have the courage of the beasts of the field and go and die alone. All this emotionalism, this give and take of sympathy, handing it back and forth like some flabby, liquescent horror: no, no. . . . But Frank, ah, Frank: and she thought of him standing and watching the game of draughts, his shoulders thrust back, his legs wide apart, his hands under the wide leather belt, and those deep, vertical lines which furrowed either cheek. . . .

"Did you notice how Béngt smoked the cigar you gave him?" Frank suddenly asked.

"No," Max said. "Why?"

"Oh, I don't know. He was watching you to see what you did. As if he didn't know which end to put in his mouth. And then he left the band on. Odd."

"Odd?"

"Well, with his background. I mean, you've heard his stories, haven't you? Father Ambassador in Prague, later Paris. The vast estates. All that sort of thing."

"Do you think he's a phoney?"

Frank shrugged his shoulders. "Wouldn't be surprised."

"But in that case we ought to tell Chris."

"She wouldn't believe it." And he added, in his own mind: "Serve her right, anyway, if she wants to make a fool of herself."

"I'm going to make some enquiries," Max said. "I can do it through our Swedish office, and find out if there really *is* a Count von Arbach—and if he's here in Florence."

"As you like," Frank said.

The two women appeared slowly out of the darkness, walking arm in arm; and because each still wore her secret like some transfiguring garment, the men thought, with astonishment, how beautiful they looked. Throats, arms, foreheads gleamed like snow in the moonlight: there was a soft swishing, as they climbed the steps.

"Where's my old man got to?" Chris said; and as she spoke, the garment disintegrated. She looked plain, dowdy and not a little pathetic. "And Béngt?" she added.

"A stroll," Frank said. "They said they'd be back soon."

"Oh, there they are!" Chris exclaimed. She pointed up the road. "What are you two up to?" she shouted out, and there was a note of anxiety in her voice. "We're all ready to go." Béngt and Tiny turned on their heels and continued their even pacing, this time away from the restaurant. "Oi," Chris shouted. She gave a piercing whistle.

Béngt looked round, and touched Tiny's arm.

"That's more like it," Chris said. "He's walking awfully steadily for a man who was drunk. Awfully steadily," she repeated, as if she had made some nasty discovery. "What have you two been doing?" she asked again, as, blinking at the lights, they mounted the terrace.

"Oh, chatting," Béngt said.

"Chatting—about what?"

"This and that," Tiny said. "I can't really remember."

"Anyway it's made Béngt sober." Chris swung her bag over her shoulder like a satchel, picked up her two bottles of red and green liqueur, and then said: "Well, shall we go?"

Chapter Nineteen

In the car, Karen stared at Max's head for many minutes without speaking to Frank who sat in the back beside her. Chris Maskell had claimed Béngt for the Hillman Minx, though he would obviously have preferred the Packard.

"Where would you like to be dropped?" Max asked, as they drove through the Porta Romana.

"Oh, the other side of the bridge."

"But can't we take you to your door? It'll be no trouble."

"The bridge will do."

Karen again stared at Max's head; it irritated her, the way he allowed his hair to grow on his neck before having it cut.

"You must have your hair cut," she said, and then turned to Frank: "Don't be silly. Let us take you all the way. Why not?"

He laughed. "Because you want to do it out of inquisitiveness, not kindness."

"Well, it *is* funny that I've known you all these days and I still don't know your address. Well, isn't it?"

"I don't mind your knowing it." He mentioned a street and a number. "I haven't asked you there merely because there's no reason for doing so. I have one room, at the top of the house, and you have to climb seventy-six stairs. No lift," he added. "You wouldn't like that. To-morrow I'm going to look for somewhere else. Oh, not because it isn't comfortable. But I'm getting involved."

"Involved?"

He smiled. "Not in the usual vulgar sense in which one gets involved with one's landlady's daughter. They're a nice family and they've been very kind to me. But I'm too much one of them now. If they drive out in the car on a Sunday I'm always asked, the children keep coming up to my room, and I can never get out or in, without a conversation. He's a dentist, and a bad one. Can't bear to hurt a soul, and so when he drilled a tooth of mine, left half the decay untouched. Two weeks later I had an abscess. Oh, they're nice enough people, as I say, and the house is clean, and I have my room for a song. But I can't bear that kind of proximity—the identities of others pressing on one so. No privacy. It just doesn't do." He looked out of the window as the car drew to the kerb. "You've brought me all the way. You shouldn't have done that. How did you find the street?"

"When Max comes to a new place, the first thing he does is to buy a map," Karen said contemptuously. "He's terribly thorough. And then he goes over square inch after square inch."

"Good idea. I do the same." When Karen attacked Max, however obliquely, Ross never failed to put in a word of defence. It was something Karen could not understand.

"Good-bye." Frank hurried away, waving one hand, and then ran back and put his head through the front window. "And thank you, thank you for everything—the drive, the dinner, everything." He turned his head to the back seat where Karen was waiting: "If you're really inquisitive about my room, come and see it for yourself."

"Now?"

He laughed. "No, not now. I've told you they're a very respectable, bourgeois family. But to-morrow, to-morrow afternoon—if you really want to."

"To-morrow afternoon," Karen said, with no more than an appearance of equanimity. "All right. The address?"

He once again repeated it.

She and Max did not mention Frank until she lay in bed. Then, as he brushed his teeth while she turned over the pages of a book which she had no intention of reading, she said: "What do you make of him?"

"Of whom?"

"Frank Ross."

Max took the toothbrush from his mouth and spat before he said: "Now that I've met him, I think they were probably right, the journalists. He must have had a sort of genius."

"Oh, I don't mean as a soldier," Karen said irritably.

Max looked surprised. "But that's the most important part of him."

"The war is over."

"Exactly. And that's why he can settle to nothing else. A man like that is never really himself except during a war. One can see he's not happy."

"I don't understand him," Karen said.

"You said that the first day you met him."

"Did I?" she asked in astonishment. "Funny your remembering that. He's—so totally unlike all the other men I've ever known, doesn't care about the same things—money, a career, family life."

"He cares about nothing," Max said. "To me that's rather frightening. It gives a man so much power." Methodically, he rinsed his toothbrush, wiped it on a towel, and placed it in the rack: the whole routine, repeated night after night, made Karen want to shout at him.

But: "Power," she mused. "Yes, one does feel that. And the power is the greater for being so curtailed. One feels that if the switch were turned on, anything might happen. Anything. . . . Oh, this is a stupid, boring book," and she threw the copy of *Vanity Fair*, one of Colin's prizes, on to the floor. It fell, open and face downwards, in a tangle of India paper pages. Max stooped to pick it up and straighten it, as she asked: "What did you two talk about?"

"Nothing. The war."

"Oh, the war," she laughed, "that dreary old war. I believe we only have wars every twenty years in order to give you men a topic of conversation. Heaven knows what you would do without it. . . . Damn!" She threw back the bed-clothes and said: "Bring me my dressing-gown, would you? And my slippers."

"What's the matter?"

"I promised Mother to put Nicko on his pot. She wanted to go to bed early because she was tired, and it's the girl's night out. I'd almost forgotten. Not that it's any use," she went on, as he helped her into the dressing-gown. "He does it all the same. It's such a beastly habit. I wish I knew what to do about it. Mother believes it's our fault."

"Our fault?"

"She never says so in so many words, but I know it's what she thinks. She's had those sort of theories ever since I can remember. There was a boy who used to steal at the school. . . . Strange, her being so much more *modern* than any of her children."

She went into the child's darkened room and said "Blast" loudly when her foot kicked a table.

"Granny," a voice said, on the edge of hysteria.

"It's me—Mummy."

"Oh, Mummy." All at once there was the sound of noisy weeping.

Karen continued to grope for the light as she said, more cross than alarmed: "Nicko, what on earth is it? What's the matter? . . . And where's the light?"

"I'll turn it on." No less abruptly the tears ceased.

A pillow had fallen to the floor, and the sheet and blankets had ridden up so high that the child's feet stuck out from beneath them. His face was scarlet under a criss-cross tangle of fine blond hair, his thumb was in his mouth.

"Well!" said Karen. "You have got yourself into a mess. What was the matter?"

"I couldn't sleep." He put out his tongue and licked the tear which trembled by his mouth. "So hot. I was waiting for you," he accused. "Waiting and waiting. Never come."

"Don't be silly, how could you have been waiting? Look at your pyjama-jacket." Karen straightened it and began to do it up, her fair hair brushing the child's face. "You didn't know I was coming. Granny didn't ask me until you had gone to bed."

"I was waiting," he said stubbornly.

"Now, don't be silly. How *could* you have been waiting? Don't suck your thumb, dear. Boys of six don't suck thumbs." Inexpertly she began to remake the bed.

"But I was waiting, was, was, was!" In a sudden tantrum the child began screaming until his face became purple and someone in the next bedroom banged on the wall.

"Nicko! Stop that! Nicko!"

All at once the child became silent. "Was, was, was!" he hiccoughed; and turning over, he began to sob quietly into the pillow.

At last Karen was touched. She sat beside him, and eased his reluctant body round; kissed his forehead, his cheeks, his hands; rocked him from side to side as she asked: "But what is it? What's the matter, darling?"

But Nicko did not answer. He pressed himself against her, his sturdy body nestling against her breast, and lay still except for an occasional sob which shook him all over. Karen, being unsentimental, had never before looked for resemblances; but at this moment she thought how like his father he was, and she hugged him still closer. Her breasts ached as if someone had struck them.

Soon the child's body went limp, his head slipped sideways, and he gave a small snort. He was asleep and she had not fulfilled the purpose for which she had come. But she had not the heart to wake him. Nor, as the morning proved, was it necessary that she should do so.

When she returned to her own room, she climbed into bed without saying a word.

"All right?" Max said. He was still fiddling with his preparations for the night.

"Oh, yes," she said. She lay on her back, her hands outside the sheet, like a patient in a hospital, as she repeated: "Oh, yes. I'm all right."

"You look done in," Max said, going across to the bed and looking down at her.

"Do I? You know I never want you to tell me how I look." But if she said the words it was only from force of habit; she had said them so often before. "I feel perfectly well. And I'm not in the least tired."

He shrugged his shoulders at this rejection of his sympathy. "Blinds down or up?" he asked. He put the same question every night, because while Karen said that it was impossible to sleep with the blinds down, he himself always woke at dawn if the blinds remained up.

"Up," came the inevitable answer; and yet again the blinds remained up.

"Light off?"

"I'll do it." She fumbled for the switch, her head still on the pillow, and at last managed to find it. The room was in darkness now except for three blades of moonlight, one of which grazed her face.

Max undid his dressing-gown and threw it across his bed, took off his slippers, and pulled back the sheet; then, on an impulse, he crossed the two yards that separated them and sat down beside her. He kissed her hair, her throat and forehead, and she suffered him to do so; but when he attempted to kiss her mouth, she drew away, not as she usually did, with an exclamation of disgust, but with a light sigh. He tried again, and her hands pushed him from her. A tear trickled out of one of her eyes, and others slowly followed; but she made no sound and her face did not move.

He climbed into his own bed, turned his back to her, and drew the sheet to his chin; it was a warm night but his teeth had begun to chatter. He wondered if he were going to have another attack of malaria. Suddenly she said:

"Oh, all right. But get it over quickly."

He did not move, except as the fever made him shudder; and Karen did not repeat the invitation.

Chapter Twenty

FRANK ROSS pulled off his boxing-gloves and threw them at the sixteen-year-old Italian with whom he had been sparring: "That's enough for one day." He patted his shoulder. "Run along now."

"Better?" the boy queried hopefully.

Ross stuck out his lower lip. "You're still leaving yourself wide open whenever you use your left."

"To-morrow?" the boy asked, attempting to conceal his disappointment.

"No, not to-morrow."

"The next day?"

"All right, Wednesday. The same time. Ten o'clock. Now beat it."

As the boy leapt down the stairs Ross crossed the landing from the empty attic where they had been boxing to his own room. He dipped his sponge in the earthenware pitcher of water which stood in an enamel basin, slipped off his shorts, and began briskly to rub the sweat off his body. He had told the boy to come again on Wednesday and now he remembered that he had decided to look for another room. Something like regret came over him. He had so often thought Tonio and his sister nuisances for perpetually interfering in his life, but he wondered if he would really like to live somewhere where he would not have them near him. It's my vanity, he thought. I like their admiration. I like it when Tonio stares at me in that strange way after I've got home a blow. I like it when Margaretta sits on the floor at my feet and I talk about Burma. I like their respect and their obedience and their obvious fear of me. And, yes, I like their love.

He had pulled on an open-necked shirt and, leaving it unbuttoned to his waist, he now sat himself at the folding card-table which stood before the window, a typewriter resting on its faded and moth-eaten green baize. He picked up a sheet to read what he had last written, but soon put it down. In the jungle someone unimportant, a lieutenant of twenty-three, had died of typhus in circumstances of extreme pain and ugliness, and to the last moment, when a noisy evacuation of the bowels had announced the boy's death, Frank Ross had had to nurse him. He had begun by caring little for his patient since he had neither intelligence nor stoicism, and to Ross these qualities were essential in those whom he loved. Yet as, hour by hour, for two long days, he had listened to the boy's grumbles, demands and feverish soliloquies, the thing which he had always feared once again happened. The snare had snapped shut; he had found himself committed. Before, he had wanted to get the whole beastliness over as soon as possible; better for all concerned, he thought, and he had speculated on hastening that end. But now he fought as with an implacable enemy, in a new war and against even longer odds. The old war was forgotten, in those two days he gave it not a thought. Indeed, in his patient's last racking agony Ross's desire for victory had been so strong that he had clutched to him what was now no more than a bundle of sweat, sores, vomit, pain and fear, in complete heedlessness to his own infection. Jacob wrestled with the angel—and Jacob lost. It was the central experience of his whole campaign.

He was trying to say this now, but somehow it would not come. What he had written seemed insincere, sentimental and over-literary; and yet it was an incident whose importance must be realized for the truth of the whole book. For, in a sense, he regarded those days of nursing the sick boy as a period when he had for the first time discovered the weakness at the heart of his own strength. Others suffered from such weakness, of course he well knew, mistaking the smaller contest for the greater, and caring more for the fall of a sparrow than the fall of a nation. And by such people little could be achieved. But he, too, it now appeared, was also "human", and his humanity, like the bias in a bowl, had swung him from his aim. Temporarily, of course. But might it not happen again? That thought now obsessed him.

. . . He read another sheet, thinking: We all come to it in the end. After the cheers and the flags and the conference tables, we slink away, take up our pens and hope, if not to glorify, at least to justify ourselves. Lawrence did it best. And but for him, how different I might be! When I was fifteen, picking up *Seven Pillars* and reading of that horrifying beating, while the rain streaked the drawing-room windows and, in the conservatory, Aunt Lucy potted bulbs. The lawn so green, the branches rubbing incessantly against each other, and the sea, always the sea, thudding beneath the garden. A moment I have never forgotten. "What are you reading, dear?" I held it up. "Oh, General Mennen sent it this morning. It's his subscription copy. It looked awfully boring." "No, it's not boring." And after that his life was as if he were clumsily tracing a map on transparent paper, as he had learned to do at school. . . .

"Come in!"

Tonio's head appeared. "There's a lady to see you," he announced on a note of astonishment. "Shall I send her up?"

"Yes, send her up," Ross said, and began to thump at the typewriter, so that when Karen arrived, she had to apologize breathlessly:

"I'm afraid I've disturbed your work. . . . Oh, what a climb!"

"I warned you. Seventy-six steps. It wasn't really worth it, was it?"

"That's to be seen." She took off her cart-wheel straw hat and threw it on the bed, and then, inexplicably self-conscious, began to shake out her hair, at the same time glancing round the room. There was a single window, two feet by two, and she went to it and looked out. But there was nothing to be seen but innumerable roof-tops jostling to the sky. Next she examined the books which lay neatly piled on top of each other beside the camp-bed.

"You have the books of an English master at a prep. school," she said. "All those Everymans and Oxford Standard authors."

"Ever read a book twice?" he asked.

She did not answer but continued her scrutiny. It was one of those bare, cramped rooms in which she herself had often lived before she had married. All its possessions seemed to have been collected there for some express purpose, and she knew that the calendar which hung from a drawing-pin above the card-table had been placed there, not because of its twelve sepia views of the Thames valley, but because from time to time its owner might wish to know the date. Across one corner of the room a line had been stretched and from it were suspended a singlet, some pants and two pairs of socks. The floor was uncarpeted, and the plaster of the walls was pocked and cracked as if from a bombardment,

but everything was scrupulously neat and clean. In another corner
there was a primus stove, above which three nails supported a
frying-pan, a saucepan and what appeared to be an old army billy-
can.

"You cook for yourself?"

"Yes. But they will insist on my eating with them. It's embar-
rassing because they won't let me pay my way. I go out sometimes,
too—to a *latteria* round the corner."

"Where do you keep your clothes?"

"My clothes?" He laughed. "There's a spare pair of shorts, some
grey flannels which I keep meaning to mend, and a sweater behind
that curtain. The rest are in the rucksack."

"Who's this?" For the first time she had discovered something
which had no practical use. Tucked into the heavy mahogany
frame of the mirror above the wash-stand was a small, faded snap-
shot.

"That? My sister."

"Do you ever see her?"

"Sometimes."

"Is she the only one?"

"Yes. She's my twin. There weren't any others." An impulse to
confide, such as he rarely experienced, made him add: "She's ill. I
have to support her."

"Ill?"

"Oh, they think she's going to get better now, for a long time
they were doubtful. They're giving her some kind of shock-treat-
ment."

"How did it happen?"

He shrugged his shoulders: he could not be expected to talk
of his father, the discovery and the suicide. It was he, then only
fourteen, who had first spoken to his aunt and he remembered her
horrified: "What are you saying, child?" But she had clutched at
the information as at a proffered weapon; even before her sister's
death, she had hated her brother-in-law.

"She's not like you," Karen said. "Yours is a strong face, and hers
is weak. But she's beautiful."

"Not now," Frank said. "Look, suppose you stop being so inquisitive and sit down somewhere. I'll make you a cup of coffee."

"Give me your trousers and I'll mend them for you."

He seemed doubtful about this suggestion, but going to the curtain, he raised it and brought out the trousers. "I can't give them to you," he said, "they're absolutely filthy—covered with grease."

"It doesn't matter." She took them from his reluctant grasp, and, as he fetched her a needle and cotton, ran her hands over them. They might have been worn by a mechanic, they were so stained, but strangely she did not care.

"Oh, my God!" he exclaimed, when he brought her the cup of coffee. "Is that the best you can do?" Sewing on a button, she had drawn the flannel into a tight, ugly knot, and now, darning, she was circling the hole with a number of loose stitches, two or three times, as if uncertain what to do next. "Haven't you ever been taught how to darn?"

"Of course I have."

"You must have forgotten then. I could do better than that myself."

"That's gratitude for you!" She tugged at the thread, and when it wouldn't snap, put it between her teeth. "If you're so clever with a needle, you can finish it yourself." She gnawed at the thread until it was soggy, and at last got it to break. "I shouldn't have thought it mattered anyway with such a pair of trousers."

"Drink your coffee before it gets cold," was all he said. He took the trousers and the needle and thread from her, and then, fetching his own mug of coffee, sat beside her on the bed. "Nice dress," he said, taking the flowered chiffon between his fingers. He gulped at his coffee, and then looking over the raised mug said: "You know, since we met you've begun to look much tidier. Is that because of what I said to you?"

"You're insufferably conceited."

"I just wondered," he answered, again with complete equanimity.

"I don't know why I go on seeing you," she continued in a sulky, aggrieved voice. "You do nothing but insult me. I don't think you like women at all, you just regard them as so many cows. You're the typical Fascist."

"Fascist!" he laughed. "My dear Karen, if you knew."

"Knew what?"

"My politics."

"Well?"

"I'm a Communist."

"Oh, it's the same thing," she retorted irritably.

He smiled and said: "I don't think you're really unintelligent. It's just that you're too lazy ever to use your brains."

"I'm going." She got to her feet, but seemed deliberately to wait for the hand with which he tugged her back on to the bed beside him.

"You don't want to go," he said. "Do you? Not really?"

"Oh, I don't know. I don't know what I want with you. I don't know what I feel about you." She kicked out a leg and upset the mug of coffee which she had placed on the floor beside her. "Damn! Where can I find a cloth?"

"It doesn't matter."

"Of course it matters. You're so tidy, I must mop it up."

But he held her arm so that she could not struggle to her feet. "Let me go," she said. "Oh, don't be a fool."

"Relax."

Suddenly she turned to him and said in a small, petulant voice like an aggrieved child: "You know why I came here."

"Because you're so inquisitive."

"No. Because—oh, because—— Oh, it's no good!" She reached for her hat, and then suddenly, changing her mind, slipped a hand through his open shirt. "Oh, Frank," she said, caressing his bare flesh. "Don't you see? Don't you understand?"

He laughed. "Of course—I see." With unexpected violence he pulled her hand away and then thrust her head down to the pillow; he kissed her on the mouth. "Listen," he said, and she noticed how he trembled. "Let's get this clear first, in case of misunderstandings." He looked down at her, the vertical furrows in his cheeks seeming even more exaggerated than before. "It means nothing. To me it means nothing. Do you understand that? It might be you, it might be some other woman. You're beautiful, you attract me, I admit all that. But it means nothing more. See? See?"

"You don't love me," she said. "Oh, what does it matter?" She put her arms round his neck and attempted to draw his mouth to her own. But he resisted her:

"You have no claims on me. I don't belong to you, you don't belong to me. All right?"

"Yes, yes. I understand," she said impatiently.

"Good," he replied with something of the satisfaction of a man who has struck what he considers to be an advantageous bargain with a prostitute. "Now let me remove your hat—and lock the door."

Compared to Max, he was neither a skilful nor a considerate lover; but whereas her body always rejected Max, as it would reject some intolerable degradation, now it lay calm, open, yielding. His was the passion of a man who cares more for his own satisfaction than the object by which he is satisfied, and she knew that, and in part, welcomed the knowledge. He hurt her, and she loved him the more for it, and it was she, not he, who wished the scene prolonged.

Afterwards, when he was seeing her out, he said casually: "I won't come down with you. You can find your own way, I expect? It's such a climb back."

She laughed, as she began to run down the stairs: "You are a chivalrous lover!"

"Karen!" he called. "Karen!"

"Yes?" He beckoned to her, and she rejoined him on the landing.

"Not lover," he said. "Not lover. Don't forget what I said."

Chapter Twenty-one

WHEN Karen entered the hotel, Chris and Béngt were coming down the wide sweep of the stairs together. Their little fingers were linked but, noticing her, they at once swerved apart in extreme self-consciousness:

"Hello, dear," Chris said. "You haven't seen Tiny, have you?" Karen shook her head. "I don't know what can have happened to him," Chris continued. "He went out before breakfast and hasn't been back since. I'm not really worried, but we did have a little tiff—he's terrible in the mornings. So many men are, aren't they?" She spoke jocularly, but it was obvious that she was anxious; her skin looked even more blotched than usual, and her eyes, usually so keen and inquisitive, had the strained expression of someone whose glasses have been broken. Perhaps she had been crying. "I hope no harm's come to him," she said.

"What harm could come to him?" Karen asked.

"Oh, I don't know." Chris ran her small, dimpled hand up and down the banister, and the corners of her mouth all at once slipped into despair. "It's so unlike him," she said.

"How you worry!" Béngt exclaimed. He touched her arm and gently propelled her forward. Once again grief had given to Chris the youthfulness which she so often sought in vain, and now as the Swede stood behind her, so much taller than she and so full of authority, she appeared like a small child in charge of a school-master. But she resisted his forward impulse long enough to say to Karen: "We're going to the Post Office. Béngt thinks the allowance may have been sent Poste Restante."

"The whole hotel must know about my allowance by now," Béngt said acidly.

"Oh, my dear, you don't mind my mentioning it to Karen——? Do you? Béngt, do you?"

He shrugged his shoulders: "Oh, it doesn't matter." But his expression was a mingling of irritation and contempt.

"I suppose Max is at work," Chris said, hurrying on to this new topic as if she now dreaded being left alone with the Swede. "He never seems to rest. I hold him up to Tiny as an example, you know. Tiny's so lazy. . . . Won't you come out with us? We can just slip into the Post Office and then go to the Piazza Repubblica for a long, cool drink."

Karen excused herself: she was tired, the sun was so strong, and she must find the children.

"Oh, don't worry about the children," Chris reassured her. "They're playing cards in the upstairs lounge. I heard them from my room. Bless their hearts!" she added, in case Karen should think her last remark had been a criticism. "What fun they get from life!"

Karen passed the lounge, and then turned back and opened the door. Mrs. Bennett, her grandchildren and the two Italian boys were all playing a version of Snap in which each of them chose an animal and made an appropriate noise when two cards of the same kind appeared on the table. As Karen looked in, Mrs. Bennett rose to her feet and let out a triumphant "Cock-a-doodle-doo!" followed by a belated and feeble bleating from Enzo.

"What are you doing, Mother?"

"I've won again!" Mrs. Bennett exclaimed, excitedly scrabbling the cards into her pack; then she glanced up and repeated: "Look how much I've won, Karen." She brandished the pack aloft. "Look! These children are so slow. You all were much smarter when you were young. . . . Play a round without me," she ordered, as Karen remained in the doorway. "I wanted to catch you before you went out to visit that—what's his name?"

"Frank Ross," Karen said.

"Ross, Frank Ross. I wanted you to give him something from me."

"Give him something?"

"It was this—only this." She began to turn out the canvas bag which she carried about with her, and at last produced the sketch of the two boys asleep. "He asked for it once and I'm afraid I was rude to him. I don't like him. I don't know why. But there was no reason to speak as I did. If he still wants it"—she held out the sketch—"there the thing is. Give it to him, when you next see him."

"Oh, I don't know when that will be," Karen said. "He talks of moving."

"Out of Florence?"

"No, I don't think so. I don't really know." Karen was aware that her mother's eyes were gazing into her own, and at once she became flustered. "You'd better keep the sketch for the moment," she said. "I'd only lose it."

"You look happier," Mrs. Bennett said, still fixing her with the same penetrating gaze.

"Do I? I can't say I feel it."

Mrs. Bennett put out a hand, and her dry finger-tips scraped on smooth flesh. "Your neck is red."

"It must be some irritation. . . . Perhaps I've been bitten," she added recklessly.

"I must get back to the game." Once again the old woman brandished her pack: "Look at all that! I'm going to beat them," she said. "My eyes are sharper than theirs. I tell you, I'm going to win."

Karen at once went up to her bedroom to powder the marks

which had caused her mother's comment; it was strange that at the time she had not felt any pain. She smiled to herself, remembering how, playing hockey in a match at school, she had smashed one of her finger-nails and had only noticed it under the showers afterwards. She continued to tidy herself, changed some of her clothes and then wandered through the suite into the other room where Max did his work.

"Hello," she said. "No Lena?"

Max was sitting at the table on a straight-backed chair, with his back to her as she entered; his chin was in his hands, and he was slumped in such a way that his right shoulder almost touched his ear. It was an unattractive ear, Karen had long since decided, like a prize-fighter's, with a large, flabby lobe that curled slightly forward, and freckles sprinkled like grains of sand over the skin. He looked slowly round at her when she spoke, cleared his throat and said: "I sent her away."

"Why?"

"Didn't feel like work."

"You seem to have enough of it there." She went across to the table, perched on an edge, and picking up a letter, read out: "'Dear friend, I am an ex-service man of both wars with a wife, two children, one of whom has tuberculosis, an invalid mother, and no work. We live in two rooms——'" She chucked the letter back on the heap and asked: "Do you ever do anything about that sort of thing?"

"What? . . . Oh, sometimes, if it seems genuine."

"But how do you know?"

"Know? Know what?" He had picked up a pencil and was drawing on the letter a pattern with which he amused himself. There was a circle and inside the circle a triangle, and inside the triangle a circle, and inside the circle . . . It went on and on.

"Whether it's genuine, stupid. You are being dense today. What's the matter with you?"

"Oh, one knows, one learns how to tell. This letter's obviously a fraud."

"Why?" she pursued.

"Because it stinks to high heaven of deceit. I can't tell you why. One knows, that's all."

She flushed, looked at him narrowly and at last said: "Your eyes are bloodshot."

"Are they?" He covered them with his fingers in a gesture of weariness; even in this hot weather the skin of his hands looked cracked, as if from an east wind. They were always like that. Ugly, she thought.

"You've still not had your hair cut," she said.

He gave a vague smile, followed by a sigh: "That's what Lena said."

Karen laughed. "So she's taking an interest in your appearance! She shouldn't make it so obvious. Poor girl, she'd do far better to marry her boy-friend. What's his name? Pamela always calls him Signor Enos."

"I can't remember."

"He obviously adores her, as much as she adores you. All this unreturned devotion—it's rather frightening when you come to think about it. All over the world it's being poured out, streams and streams of it. And all useless, all for what?" She put out a hand and with her forefinger twanged one of the elastic arm-bands with which he kept up his cuffs while he worked. "More grey hairs," she said, and suddenly she wrenched one out.

"Don't," he said, looking straight ahead of him, while his hands gripped the edge of the table.

"What *is* the matter? . . . Max, what is it?" she repeated.

He got to his feet and began clumsily to stack the letters and papers that lay strewn before him; he picked up an armful, began to carry them to the card-index that followed him about Europe, and then, returning to the table, dropped them in a loose heap. Some slithered to the floor, as Karen asked: "What on earth are you doing?"

Instead of answering he walked across to the bed, with the movements of someone who had just started a long convalescence, and fell on it, face downwards. What was as much a grunt as a groan emerged from the pillow.

"Max!" Karen said, her uneasiness all at once changing to alarm. "Aren't you well? Max!" She attempted to pull him round so that she could see his face, but obstinately he resisted her.

"I'm all right," he said. "Go away. Leave me." He twitched irritably at the seat of his trousers because in his fall they had become rucked up and were now making him uncomfortable. "Go away," he repeated.

"Oh, very well," she said, laughing. "If you want to be moody, be moody. I don't mind." She went across to where his coat lay on the back of a chair, and fished out his wallet: "I've run out of money," she said. "I've taken five thousand lire. All right?" He did not answer, and she repeated: "All right?"

Still he did not answer, and when she went out, slamming the door behind her, she felt she genuinely had a grievance.

Chapter Twenty-two

IN appearance there was little impressive about Lady Newton. She was slight, with small, sharp features, and she wore her grey hair still shingled in a manner reminiscent of the years during which she had been Mayoress of a town in the Potteries. Her hands with their innumerable calluses and far from clean nails were those of a gardener's boy. Whatever the season she always wore the same tweed skirts, usually with at least one press-stud unfastened at the side, flat-heeled strap shoes and grey blouses knitted so unevenly that at a first glance one assumed the moth had helped with the pattern. It was usual for those who did not know her to mistake her for a governess or lady-companion.

Yet this was a woman whom English and American visitors to the city invariably wished to meet. It would be hard to say why. Except to a few chosen friends like Maisie Brandon she behaved with a gross, and sometimes even a foul-mouthed, incivility; in summer her dilapidated villa smelled and in winter the damp streamed down its walls; once a brilliant conversationalist, she now preferred to talk only about dogs, gardens and the postage-stamps whose collection had become a mania of her life. Yet still she was visited. True, she was said to be a wealthy woman, and the reputation of her dead husband's fortune, long since squandered on gaming, litigation, and that most lost of all Italian lost causes, the prevention of cruelty to animals, still somehow persisted. Such reputations always die hard.

For example, the young man from Cambridge who was to visit her that morning had gleefully informed the friend with whom he was travelling: "She's said to be fabulously rich. Her husband left six hundred thousand." He tossed out the remark as he sipped at his coffee, but at heart he was deeply impressed. In his wallet was the letter of introduction which would take him to all this imagined wealth.

He was typical of the many visitors who climbed the steep, dusty path in the heat of the day, and Lady Newton knew how to deal with him. She was shrewd and she guessed at once that here was yet another undergraduate who was using a slim artistic gift to help himself up the Italian social ladder. He explained how his interest in painting had taken him to some of the leading Florentine houses; and he hinted, tactfully, that her introduction would take him to the rest. He wore a bright shirt and linen trousers, and fanned himself with a panama hat with a wide green-and-red band. He talked of the author who had sent him to visit her, without realizing that she had long since taken one of her unaccountable dislikes to the man, and he exclaimed extravagantly on the beauties of a garden which she knew to be out of hand and pictures which she knew to be negligible.

He was only nineteen and it was therefore perhaps unkind of her suddenly to cut him short:

"But I mustn't keep you any longer, Mr.—— Mr.—— I'm afraid I've forgotten your name. It was so kind of you to trek all the way up this hill to see a lonely old woman. I won't come with you to the gate because there's a bus which goes"—she looked at her watch—"in exactly ten minutes and I'd only delay you. I'm not very quick these days. . . . Good-bye, good-bye."

She turned abruptly; and then, with none of the feebleness she had just ascribed to herself, proceeded to march back to the villa where she poured herself the drink her guest had not been offered. "Jackanapes!" she said, and bawled with fearful stridency: "*Senta*, Maria!" She paused, a glass of gin gripped in one fist, but no answer came. "M-a-r-i-a!" she shouted again.

After many seconds there was a rustling, scraping, shuffling noise from the corridor as if some vast wounded animal were dragging itself along; but the old woman who eventually appeared was of paradoxical minuteness. She was filthy, with greasy white hair slipping out of a rag-like turban, feet in what had once been a pair of Lady Newton's discarded bedroom slippers, and a few teeth so rotted that they looked like burned-out matches stuck haphazard in her gums. One claw-like hand was already cocked over her ear in expectancy of what her mistress would say.

"I—am—working," Lady Newton said loudly and slowly in Italian. She gulped some gin. "I—am—working," she repeated, and with each word the old servant's nose twitched as if she were smelling rather than hearing what was being said. "Lunch—will—be—at—two. I—must—not—be—disturbed." She then gestured the woman out of the door, turned the key and, curling herself up on a sofa where an ancient spaniel already wheezed and snuffled, at once went to sleep.

She was woken by the sound of Maisie Brandon knocking, rattling the door-handle and calling: "Are you there, N.?" The spaniel was languorously scratching a tattered ear. "I say, N.?" Lady Newton jumped up, pulled open one of the card-indexes on her desk and arranged some sheets of foolscap-paper; then she growled: "What the hell is it?" Her voice had an amazing range, from the soft, apparently timid soprano of the governess or lady-companion she so often appeared to be, to a *basso profondo*.

"It's me—Maisie. I'm sorry to disturb you, but I've brought that boy."

"Boy? What boy?"

"The boy I told you about. At breakfast this morning."

"You never told me about any boy." But the door was at last unlocked. "Really, Maisie, once and for all, you must understand that when I'm working, I'm working. And must not be disturbed. *Must—not*," she repeated slowly and emphatically, as if she were talking to the deaf Maria.

"Yes, I'm sorry, but it's past one o'clock, so I knew you'd be breaking off for lunch."

"To-day lunch will be at two," Lady Newton said, without any further explanation. She looked Enzo up and down as he stood, in the middle of the hall, his head bowed and his hands clasped before him. "And who is that?"

"Oh, don't be tiresome, N.," Maisie Brandon said. Weary, hot and hungry, she had just asked at the Palazzo d'Oro for a room at the week-end. "You can't have forgotten in these four hours. I told you that I had a servant for you."

"Well, why didn't you say so in the first place?" Suddenly Lady Newton sniffed: "What's that scent you're wearing," she demanded.

Maisie told her.

"Well, I don't like it," Lady Newton replied as the dog thudded down from the sofa and tottered towards them, stopping at every yard to scratch at its ear with short, staccato yelps. "What is it, darling? What is it then?" Lady Newton picked up the animal and holding it like a baby kissed each of its paws in turn and then kissed its nose. Suddenly she looked up at the impatient Maisie: "I told you not to use the car in the mornings. You know I explained that I must have Giorgio for the kitchen while Maria is single-handed. It's so thoughtless of you, Maisie, really it is. You can easily take the bus."

"But I asked about the car, and you said——" Maisie began in a voice of controlled rage. But she was at once interrupted:

"What were you doing in town anyway? The hairdresser? That's the second time this week."

"You know I've got to dine with the Consul——"

Lady Newton threw back her head and guffawed so loudly that the dog squirmed and wriggled in her arms, rolling its puffy, red-rimmed eyes. "Who ever heard of spending money on a hairdresser before taking pot-luck at that household? Don't be ridiculous, my dear." The story was that when the Consul's wife had asked her to dinner Lady Newton had written back that she would be delighted to come provided that she was not expected to return the invitation. "Well, let's see the boy." She dropped the dog and strode across to Enzo, looking him up and down. He blushed, shifted like a startled animal, and eventually raised his eyes to give her an embarrassed smile. That morning he had put on clean clothes and his mother had given him the money to have a shave and hair-cut. "Looks as strong as a horse," Lady Newton said with approval. "He'll have to be, with all there is to do." In Italian she said to him: "From eight to eight. All meals. Six thousand lire a month. All right?"

The boy nodded but Maisie cut in:

"My dear N., six thousand lire—that's a beggar's wage! It's less than three pounds a month."

"Mind your own business," Lady Newton said casually and then, after a moment's deliberation, twisting her lower lip between her gardener's-boy fingers, she added: "Let me tell you that there are thirty thousand unemployed in Florence alone. I'm going to feed the boy. I shan't feed him well, but at least he won't be hungry."

"I don't know how you have the face to offer anyone such a— such a——" But indignation came naturally to Maisie only when her own interests were involved. "Well, I'll leave him to you," she said. "I must go and get ready for lunch."

"It's not till two, don't forget."

"But I'm famished!" Maisie wailed, with far more distress than at the mention of Enzo's wages. "No, really—it's going a bit far!"

Lady Newton merely ignored this protest. "Come," she said to Enzo, and going to the end of a corridor, lined with large brass pots, some empty, some containing umbrellas or the yellowed, trailing remains of plants, she again bawled: "Ma-ri-a!" But though she continued to shout the name down the echoing passage, on this occasion no shufflings, scrapings and rustlings announced the woman's approach. "Damn! . . . Oh, well, you can start scrubbing this floor. It hasn't been done for months. Come on." And because Enzo, in his confusion, was slow to follow, she caught him by the arm and began to push him before her towards a door. "Open the door," she commanded. "Bucket—cloth—soap. Don't be so clumsy, put the soap in your other hand! Like this." Suddenly she grabbed all the articles from him, only to give him back the bucket. "Tap over there. No—use your eyes. Over there! Fill the bucket—good lad. Never mind if the water splashes on the floor, you have to scrub it later. All right? Now, down on your knees. . . . No, no, no!" she expostulated in irritation. "Give it to me, give the cloth to me." She pulled up her shapeless tweed skirt and then knelt beside him. "Like this." Energetically she began to scrub the cracked and dusty tiles. "Put all you've got into it." She panted, obviously doing this herself. "There's nothing like hard work."

In the end she left him and there was silence in the corridor except for the splash of water, the swish of the cloth, and the boy's heavy breathing. Now that he was alone he worked with a violent efficiency, as if he were scrubbing out the traces of a crime, never once pausing, never once slackening, though the sweat poured down his face. He was working, and he had not worked for two and a half years; in that knowledge he experienced an exaltation of the spirit, he recovered his essential manhood. The blackened tiles were slowly polished to whiteness; the water in the bucket foamed with dross and scum. His knees were already sore, his arms and back ached. But he was hardly aware of these things; and it was with the sense of being roused from a long dream that he at last heard Lady Newton bark:

"Boy! I say, boy!"

"Yes, *signora*."

"Go and find that woman. Ask her what's become of lunch, tell her it's half-past one."

"Which woman, *signora*?"

"There's only one woman," she retorted irritably. "Oh, not the Englishwoman. Maria, you fool."

"But where can I find her?"

"Where? In the kitchen of course."

"The kitchen?"

"Yes, the kitchen."

As Enzo walked stiffly down the corridor, peering into empty room after empty room, Lady Newton shouted after him: "Don't dawdle. Get a move on. Tell her she's over half an hour late."

Maisie, hearing the strident voice as she lay on her unmade bed and read a book in an effort to forget her hunger, muttered to herself, "The bitch is quite mad," and then got to her feet with a sigh. Perhaps, after all, lunch would be before two.

Chapter Twenty-three

ENZO was fortunate and was paid his week's wages; and when Colin asked him how he liked the work, he would nod his head vigorously and repeat, "*Va bene, va bene.*" But it was a strange household; and particularly strange now that Maisie Brandon had left to join her friends at the Palazzo d'Oro. Until her departure she had been, in an ineffective, sporadic way, the boy's protector and guide, shielding him from the worst of Lady Newton's eccentricities and giving him advice when he was baffled by her contradictory orders. "He's a nice kid," she used to drawl when she was asked about him, "and he has the patience of an angel." While she was still at the villa, she used to like to sit in some room he was cleaning. Pretending to read, she would watch the muscles in his broad back and arms as he scrubbed and swept before her, and from time to time she would let fall some remark in her slovenly Italian or toss him a cigarette. Once she said casually, "I want a puff of that," and took the cigarette she had just given him from between his lips to put it to her own.

"I'd like to visit the villa," Colin repeatedly told her. "It sounds so extraordinary. Please mayn't I?"

"Not an earthly, my dear. I've blotted my copy-book well and truly. She never wants me in the villa until I decide to go; then she does. I'd rather break out of Holloway any day than make that escape again. It was hell, sheer hell. Every door was slammed, but every door."

Nevertheless Colin decided that he would go to the villa. "No, no," Enzo said, echoing Maisie's words. "È impossibile." He was genuinely alarmed. "I shall lose my job. You must not come. She would not forgive me."

"But when she's out," Colin pursued.

"She never goes out."

"She must go out sometime."

"Never."

But this was not true. Lady Newton had for many years been a member of the Committee of a British relief organization, attending its meetings with unfailing zeal and regularity. It was not that she was interested in the work of the organization or even, as once, in the exercise of power for its own sake; but there were feuds of long standing between herself and most of the older members and whatever the cost in boredom she could not now bear to leave them the field. So whenever the Committee met, she was there, like a prizefighter who should long ago have quit the ring, to join issue with foes of twenty, twenty-five and even thirty years' standing.

Colin had heard other members of the English colony talk of these meetings to Karen and Max, and having discovered when the next took place, decided that on that afternoon he would pay Enzo a visit.

At twelve, on the day he had chosen, the sky had begun to descend, and the hills had been united with it. On the terrace of the hotel, a sudden, convulsive shudder would pass through the flowering shrubs in their square green boxes, a few dead leaves would scrape on the stone-paved floor. Apparently without reason, a branch all at once snapped from its stem and hung, like a badly severed limb, from a ribbon of green skin. The brown surface of the Arno was pocked with an occasional cascade of raindrops and then congealed into its usual muddy tranquillity. A blind man was seated on the pavement opposite the hotel, his long, emaciated legs stuck so far out that the passers-by either had to climb over them or walk on the road. He was playing a harmonica, but in the heavy air the quavering notes seemed barely to have strength to rise from his lungs. He had turned up his coat collar in expectation of the storm, while those who might have given to him hurried regardless past.

"At last it will rain," Mrs. Bennett said with satisfaction, drawing a handkerchief across her face.

"It was like this last Tuesday, and it didn't," Pamela warned. "But I hope it does. Then we can have electricity for the lift all through the day, and the taps may run faster."

"You and Colin are real Americans," her grandmother laughed. "You never think of anything but comfort. But I should like it to get cooler. Yes, that I should like. . . . Don't lean too far over the balcony, Nicko," she added sharply. "Nicko!"

"Mummy's friend has arrived," the child announced, kicking his shoe against one of the stone columns.

"Don't do that. Nicko, don't! You'll ruin your shoe."

"Don't care."

Mrs. Bennett sighed and turned away; at this moment she felt neither the desire nor the ability to deal with him, although she knew she should scold. She looked hopelessly at Pamela, who at once cried: "Stop it, Nicko," and dragged her brother, now screaming loudly, away from the balcony. To console him she began to kiss his hair and cheeks until his tears stopped. "Draw for me," he said.

"Oh, Nicko, you know I can't draw."

"Draw for me, Granny," he turned to Mrs. Bennett.

"I'm too tired, dear—and too hot. Not now, another time."

"Nobody will draw for me," he said, again on the verge of tears. "I'll have to draw for myself."

"But I'll watch," Pamela encouraged. "Colin, come and watch Nicko draw."

"I'm busy." Colin was pasting stamps into his album, kneeling on a rug; by his side was a heap of "swops" which he had decided to give to Enzo.

"Oh, Nicko, what a horrible drawing!" Pamela exclaimed. "What's it meant to be?"

"Bomb," Nicko said with satisfaction. "All killed. Arms—legs—blood." He drew in a large smear with a red crayon. "More blood."

"Why do you draw such things?" Pamela asked; but Nicko was too absorbed to answer. He continued to scribble with the red crayon, and then made some circles of blue. "Eyes," he announced.

Mrs. Bennett frowned, smoothing her hair away from her forehead where perspiration had made it stick in a number of loose strands. She knew that the child was unhappy and she feared for his future; but she had no idea what to do for him, and the consequent frustration was poisoning her days. For she loved him more than anyone else in the world. Wearily she got up from the wicker-chair where she had been seated and went and knelt beside him, putting an arm round his shoulder.

But he at once jostled her arm away. "I can't draw like that," he said.

"Your collar's all crumpled." When she began to straighten it, he at once gave her a violent push from him. She toppled, tried to regain her balance, and fell on the rug. He gave an excited squeal of laughter.

"Nicko! Naughty boy!" Pamela slapped him across the face.

"You shouldn't have done that, Pamela," Mrs. Bennett said, clumsily hoisting herself from the rug. She was surprised to notice that Nicko had received the slap without a sound. He was staring down at his drawing, with its splashes of violent bloodshed, while his blue eyes filled with slow tears. "That was wrong of you, Pamela," Mrs. Bennett added.

"He must be taught a lesson," Pamela said stubbornly. "He treats you as he pleases."

"I don't mind," Mrs. Bennett said.

"That's not the point," Colin put in, slamming his album shut. "You mustn't spoil him, Granny."

"I don't think children are often spoiled by affection and generosity and forgiveness," the old woman said, fingering the branch that the wind had snapped as if she were thinking of how she could mend it. "Those aren't the things that spoil children." The green ribbon of skin lay between the old, dry fingers. "I'm sure they're not."

Nicko had come across to her and suddenly he put out a hand and clutched the belt of her dress; he buried his face in her side. "Poor Nicko," she said; and at the same moment she wrenched at the green skin so that it ripped from the tree. The branch fell to the floor. "Poor Nicko," she repeated.

"Rain," said Maisie Brandon, clicking on her high-heels towards them. She was fanning one large-boned, emaciated cheek with a copy of *Vogue*. "I tried to have a snooze, but I couldn't. I just sweated and sweated and sweated." She held out the box which she had been carrying under her arm: "A present for you, Nicko."

"For me?"

"Yes, for you."

"What is it?" he asked, taking it with some reluctance. He did not like Maisie and she knew that he did not like her.

"Well, open it and see," she replied, sinking into a wicker-chair and shuddering as she said: "Br-r-r! A moment ago I felt hot and now I feel cold. Fetch my fur, there's a dear, Colin."

"Colin!" his grandmother reprimanded, when he continued to read.

"Yes, I'm going. Just let me finish this book. . . . Which fur do you want?" he asked Maisie.

"Oh, the old fox," she said.

"No, you can't!" he declared. "It would be all wrong with that dress. Mayn't I bring the mink?"

Maisie laughed and shrugged her shoulders, obviously delighted. "As you please, dear," she said. "Well, do you like your present, Nicko?"

"I have a monkey already," he replied.

"Then this will be a companion for it," Mrs. Bennett said.

"Say thank you," Pamela added.

"I like it," Nicko said, as if contradicting them. He clutched the animal to him, and then mumbled mechanically, "Thank you, Auntie Maisie."

"Not *Auntie* Maisie—please!" Maisie protested. "For the hundredth time! I've told you. I don't want to be an aunt"—she laughed—"not even your aunt, Nicko."

"It's bigger than my other monkey. Look, Pamela!"

Maisie yawned, stretching her bony arms and extending her fingers high above her head. "Oh—oh—oh! I'm so tired, but so tired! I didn't sleep a wink. And neither did Chris's Swede from the noise he made next door. Poor boy, I suppose it was the thought of her that was keeping him awake. Sometimes the thought of Chris keeps me awake, too." She gave her pebbles-in-a-tin laugh. "It's priceless, I do think! But I can see what she sees in him. Can't you, Pamela?"

She appealed to the sixteen-year-old girl who at once felt enormously flattered.

"Well, I don't know, Maisie," Pamela deliberated. "I don't know. . . . Yes, there must be something about him. I suppose he *has* got sex-appeal."

"You bet," Maisie said, yawning and stretching once again, while Mrs. Bennett scowled at her for attempting such a conversation with the children.

"Oh," an anxiously high-pitched voice said from one of the bedroom doors. "Oh, there you all are. I suppose Max isn't here, is he? Is he?" It was Chris, in the state of anxiety which appeared to have become habitual with her during the last few days. Her hair was unkempt, and the skin of her face, covered inexpertly with powder, was curiously blotched and greasy. She had a boil on her chin which she had covered with a piece of sticking-plaster. There was a terrible pathos about her which even the children felt, though they could not have said what caused it.

"Max has had to drive to Pisa on business," Mrs. Bennett said.

"When will he be back?"

"I don't know. Probably not until this evening."

"Oh, Lord." Chris swayed, as if about to faint, and put both hands to her temples.

"Is it something urgent?"

"Yes—no," Chris hastily corrected herself. "Oh, it's not urgent but I ought to see him. Immediately. I don't know what to do," she added.

"Can I help?" Maisie offered.

"No, I must see Max." Then, feeling that perhaps she had been rude, Chris added, in the same mumbled, noncommittal voice that Nicko had used when given the monkey: "Thank you, all the same."

"Sit down," Maisie said. "You look all in."

"Gosh, I feel it too." Chris slumped into a chair and again put her unattractively large hands to her greying temples.

"Headache?" Maisie said. She clicked open her bag: "Let me give you one of these pills. They're the latest thing."

"I don't want a pill," Chris exclaimed petulantly. Her voice broke: "I haven't slept for nights—not a wink."

"Neither have I," Maisie said in a voice which was intended to soothe. "It's this weather. Wait until we have this rain."

"Oh, it's not the weather!" Chris flung out, creaking from one side to another in the wicker-chair.

Mrs. Bennett came across and said softly: "It's money, isn't it?"; and her sympathy was so evident that Chris's whole manner at once changed. Hopelessly, she confessed:

"Yes, it's about money. I've been such a fool. Oh, I can't tell you about it all. But I want Max's advice." She picked up the branch which had snapped off the tree and gave herself two or three stinging cuts across the hand. "He understands that sort of thing. I don't, and Tiny doesn't. But I've been such a fool—such a fool."

"What have you done, Aunt Chris?" Colin asked with interest. But a sudden gust of wind scattered the cards with which he had begun to play patience and he had to hobble after them. "Oh, help me, Pamela!" he shouted. "They'll be blown into the street. You know I can't walk properly yet." So Chris never explained; and Maisie, though she had wanted to ask the same question herself, did not dare to repeat it.

Suddenly they were all startled by Pamela shouting: "Nicko, you wicked, wicked boy! What have you done? *Nicko!*"

The child burst into paroxysms of tears.

"What on earth's the matter?" Mrs. Bennett asked. Only Chris was not interested in the scene, sitting with one hand over her eyes while the corners of her mouth sagged slowly downward.

"It's the monkey," Pamela explained. "He's thrown it down. Mummy and Colonel Ross were coming out of the swing-doors and he threw it down. He threw it down."

They were never to discover whether by the gesture, Nicko had intended to reject Maisie's gift, to make his mother and Frank bring the monkey up to him, or to strike them with the first missile that came to his hands. He screamed, he wept, but he would not explain.

It was Rodolfo who at last appeared with the monkey.

"Your mother gave this to me to bring up to you," he explained. "We met outside the hotel." He bowed and smiled to each of the ladies in turn, saying: "Good evening" in his fearful English pronunciation. "Well," he said to Colin. "Shall we go?"

"You can't go out in this weather," Mrs. Bennett said.

"It's not raining. And we have our mackintoshes," Colin replied. "And umbrellas, and goloshes. Where's the harm?"

"It's dangerous for you on the slippery pavements with that iron."

"But Rodolfo will support me—and Pamela."

Mrs. Bennett shrugged her shoulders: "Oh, do as you please."

"When you say it in that voice, it means 'Don't do it'," Pamela said. "Now we can't go."

"Yes, go, go, go," Mrs. Bennett urged. "Go by all means." For suddenly she had changed her mind, as she so often did. "Yes, go," she repeated. "A little rain will do no harm."

"That was easy," Pamela whispered excitedly, as they made their way downstairs. "When I saw the rain coming, I was afraid she'd say no. I was crossing my fingers all the time. I knew it was our only chance before we went away. . . . You're cold," she said to Colin.

"No, I'm not."

"You're shivering."

"Am I?"

"It must be nerves," she said laughing. "You do get het-up over the smallest things. Look at Rodolfo and myself. We're quite calm. . . . How are we going to go?"

"In the filo-bus."

"What's that?"

"Oh, it's like a trolley-bus. It goes from San Marco."

"Can you walk that far?"

"Of course I can." Normally Colin complained if he had to walk a hundred yards with the iron on his leg; but his desire to see where Enzo worked had miraculously stiffened his courage.

Suddenly the rain descended; and seemed, not merely to descend, but to rise from the pavement, spattering their legs as they jostled through the crowds. A mushroom-growth of umbrellas covered the Signoria, and the city's archways were dense with figures who peered out hopelessly at a black sky fissured from time to time by jagged strokes of lightning. When the thunder followed it seemed as if the whole city were subsiding under the rain. The three children hurried with bowed heads, jumping puddles, shouting to each other, and making extravagant detours to avoid the cascades of water which poured, at every few yards, from broken or blocked water-courses. They were in the highest spirits.

"Are we going too fast for you?" Pamela shouted to her brother, thrusting her umbrella between two people who were approaching along the pavement.

"No, no," Colin panted and laughed at the same time. "I can manage." But as he said the words, one of the two advancing umbrellas pressed against him, his iron slipped, and he fell sideways in the gutter. "Oh, I'm soaked," he moaned. "Look! Right to the knees. And all this sleeve, too."

"We'd better go back," Rodolfo said.

"Yes, you must change," Pamela agreed. "We can't go on."

"We must go on," Colin said with a determination that neither Pamela nor Rodolfo could ever remember him to have displayed before. "I'm all right. It doesn't matter. It doesn't matter at all. Come on!" He hobbled ahead of them, beckoning at the same time.

"But, Colin——"

"Oh, come on! We'll only get more wet if we argue."

"You know you're frightened of lightning, too," Pamela said; and at the same moment a fiery arrow seemed to dart downward to the topmost point of Giotto's Campanile. "Oh, Colin!" she wailed. But her voice was lost in the staccato rap-rap-rap that followed.

All at once Rodolfo began to shout, "Run, run, run!" and without waiting for them, he careered down the street. A trolley-bus clattered and hissed out of the darkness, sparks spinning downward from its black arm and Rodolfo, having gripped a handle, swung himself up on to a precarious foothold outside the platform, shouting, "Quick, quick, quick." He extended an arm, but it was an obviously hopeless attempt, since the doors remained closed.

"I can't!" Colin shouted, and muttered: "The fool! The bloody fool."

Rodolfo flung himself downward, landing in a puddle so that water splashed outward, and then sprinted back to join his friends, with a panted: "I forgot. I'm sorry. I forgot about your leg, Colin."

"Anyway we couldn't all three have hung on to that one bar," Pamela said.

"The next bus doesn't come for twenty minutes. That's why I ran."

"Twenty minutes!" Colin exclaimed. "But I'm soaked already."

"We can shelter," Pamela said.

"And get pneumonia. I'm going to walk."

Rodolfo laughed: "Walk! It'll take you half an hour." His usually smooth black hair had tumbled over his forehead and he now put out a tongue to catch the raindrops which trickled from it down his nose. He was wearing shorts and a waterproof U.S. army jacket which reached no further than his thighs. His thin, muscular legs were splashed with mud.

"Oh, what are we to do," Pamela exclaimed, for once at a loss how to deal with a situation. "We'll have to wait, that's all. Or go home. Wouldn't it be better if we went home?" The hair which straggled from her green oilskin cap now looked black. "Colin, I think we'd better go home."

"You can, if you like. I'm going on." But his spirit, so inflexible till this moment, now began to droop. He could feel a cold, clammy chill move from his shoulders slowly down his spine. He looked desperately about him and then: "I know," he said. "We'll take a cab."

"A cab?"

"Yes, one of those *fiacres*."

"And how are we going to pay for it?" Pamela asked sarcastically. "Oh, don't let's stand here and argue!" she exclaimed before any answer came, and retreated into a doorway.

"I'll pay him," Colin said, joining her. "Don't worry."

"*Mille lire*," Rodolfo said, having guessed what they were discussing. "Let's go another day."

"But don't you see, there won't be another day," Colin exclaimed in renewed exasperation. "Hi!" He beckoned with one arm from the gleaming oilskin sleeve off which drops of rain cascaded downwards. "Hi, there!"

Rodolfo put both fingers to his mouth and let out a piercing whistle.

The hood of the cab which trundled towards them looked like an inverted antique coal-scuttle, and in spite of its protection, the rain had made the seats so damp that their worn green leather might have been moss. An old man, huddled under an umbrella which he had fixed in a bracket beside the front seat, leant forward to hear the address, his trilby hat emptying a noisy stream of water on to the floor of the carriage.

"*Quanto costa?*" Rodolfo asked.

The man rattled some phlegm in the inmost recesses of his being, hawked for it without success, and then at a second attempt, succeeded in voiding it on to the pavement where it lay like a blue piece of gristle.

"*Mille cinquecento.*"

"*Troppo*," Rodolfo said, and the two began to haggle. Meanwhile Colin and Pamela had already climbed in.

"Oh, do leave it," Pamela said. "Let's get moving."

"As you wish," Rodolfo said huffily, with a shrug of the shoulders. "It's all the same to me. *I'm* not paying."

Pamela laughed. "I still don't know who is going to pay. Colin, how *are* you going to do it?"

Colin unpinned the tie-pin which held together the two flaps of his collar, running under the tie: "I'll give him this."

"But you can't!" Pamela exclaimed. "Mother gave it to you for your birthday."

"I don't care."

"She's sure to notice that you've lost it. She always notices that sort of thing."

"Let her. It's not my fault if the tie-pin she gives me falls off."

"Perhaps he won't take it," Pamela said.

"He won't get anything else."

"I still think it's wrong."

For the rest of the drive they sat in a silence broken only by Rodolfo whistling "Auld Lang Syne" in desolatingly slow tempo. Colin still clutched the pin. From time to time one or other of them would peer either out of the small back-window or round the vast extinguishing hood to see if the rain slackened: but the sky remained livid, the water fell vertically out of it with a destroy-ing malevolence. Stones rattled down the hill-road up which they were now driving; water-courses appeared, fissuring the surface, as if there had been an earthquake; combined with the swish of rain and the click of stones there was the roar of water pressing through the gutters. A flash of lightning lit up Rodolfo's face, his eyes gleaming like a cat's, and then the whole carriage seemed to rock from side to side in the reverberation that followed.

Suddenly Pamela began to cry.

"What's the matter?" Colin asked irritably.

"I don't know. I can't help it."

She pressed her damp cheek against the dry, creaking interior of the hood so hard that when she at last removed it one of the struts had made a red, diagonal furrow. She continued to cry softly until they reached the wrought-iron gates of the villa.

"Tell him not to go up the drive," Colin said to Rodolfo. "We'd better walk from here, just in case. And quickly! Quickly!" he repeated as Rodolfo began to argue with the old man about the tie-pin.

At first they argued whether it was gold, and then they argued about the propriety of a tie-pin being accepted instead of lire; finally they argued because Rodolfo maintained that the tie-pin was worth more than the agreed thousand lire and that the old man should therefore give them some change. Perhaps he would have gained even this last point, if Colin and Pamela had not been impatient.

As the cab creaked, rattled and swayed from their sight, all three of them felt suddenly and overwhelmingly forlorn. Even Rodolfo was subdued as he said: "That pin was worth five thousand. You were a couple of fools."

"Let's get moving." Colin began to limp up the steep path, picking his way over the zigzag streams of water, and slowly the two others followed. A single light burned in the house, and glancing up when they paused for breath, Rodolfo and Pamela exclaimed together: "Enzo!" They pointed to the window. Oblivious of his visitors, since from where he stood they were all three in darkness, he peered at the storm; one hand held the curtain while the other grasped a duster.

Pamela laughed and the boys joined in. The spectacle of Enzo at the window, staring out and not realizing that they were staring at him, filled each of them with a hidden rush of power. Rodolfo tapped on the window; and Enzo who by then had seen them, motioned them, finger on lips, not to made a noise. He had been warned that they would come that day but had decided, with a mingling of relief and disappointment, that the storm would keep them away. Now he did not know whether to be pleased or angry.

"Wipe your shoes," he said as he opened the garden-room door. "On this mat. Oh, take care!" Rodolfo had stumbled into a heap of garden-pots, most of them cracked or broken, and they were now rolling noisily about the marble floor. All of them, even Enzo, sniggered: but it was more from nerves than amusement.

"Is she out?" Pamela whispered.

Rodolfo repeated the girl's halting Italian phrase in a louder voice and Enzo said, "Sh!" Then he said: "Yes, she's gone out. She only left about ten minutes ago. The car wouldn't start, because the garage leaks and there was water in the engine." Again they all sniggered. "But Maria is here. So you must be careful."

"You said she was deaf and blind," Rodolfo reminded him.

"She notices things, in spite of that."

"Oh, it is cold," Pamela said, shuddering. She stared down at the alternate black-and-white lozenges of the hall which seemed to carry their burden of potted umbrellas and orange, trailing plants into a damp infinity. "How big," she sighed. She touched one of the plants and pulled a face: "It's dead. It's all mildewed. They ought to be cleared out."

In a small room, piled with back numbers of the *Manchester Guardian*, *Time and Tide* and Staffordshire local papers, all yellowing under dust, Rodolfo had found a bag of golf-clubs, and was now swinging a mashie back and forth.

"Mind!" Colin warned. But it was too late and a bulb tinkled downwards.

"You fool, you bloody fool!" Enzo exclaimed.

It took them many minutes to clear up the glass and to decide from where they could take a bulb without it being noticed. At last they picked on one of the many lavatories which could not be used because they were out of order, and Rodolfo did not fail to make his inevitable joke about the stench, holding his nose between his fingers.

"Show us the house," Colin said.

It was vast and depressing, full of dust, old photographs, horses' hooves mounted in silver, Tauchnitz novels, typewriters, gramophones and clocks which no longer worked, and stacks of old papers. In short it was just as Maisie had described it. Yet Colin felt disappointed. He had expected something more, though he could not have said what, and as he went round the house with the others, it was as if, with a growing despair, he were seeking for something which he now guessed he would never find.

"I'm not allowed in there," Enzo said, pointing to a door. "That's her bedroom. Maria always cleans it."

"Can't we go in?" Pamela asked.

"It's locked."

"Another key would fit it," Rodolfo said.

"But no one's allowed in," Enzo objected.

"Oh, come on! Try this key."

"No." The Florentine stood with legs astride as if to bar the way.

"Try this key," Colin said, pulling one from a hideous mahogany armoire.

Pamela gave a high-pitched laugh which reverberated strangely down the corridor. "It's like the story of Bluebeard. . . . Try the key, Enzo." She covered her ears: "Oh, this thunder! I do wish it would stop."

"Yes, try the key," Colin said.

Reluctantly the Florentine pushed the key into the lock and turned it from side to side. "No good," he said.

"Let me try." Rodolfo began to rattle the key so violently that Pamela had to grasp him by the arm in order to make him stop: "There's no point. You'll only break the lock. It obviously doesn't fit."

Meanwhile Colin had fetched another key from the door of the bathroom, and inserting it, discovered that it turned without difficulty. "It works, it works!" he exclaimed excitedly. He opened the door only a few inches, as if afraid to take advantage of this success, and it was Rodolfo who in the end pushed it wide and swaggered his way in.

"What's that?" Pamela said, clutching Colin's hand.

"What's what?"

"That sound."

"What sound?"

"A sort of whining."

They both listened in the doorway, the colour seeping away from their faces, until Pamela called:

"Enzo!"

The Florentine now joined them: "Yes?"

"Listen."

For a moment he, too, seemed to share their alarm as he stood listening with his head slightly on one side. Then he laughed: "Mister," he said.

"Mister?" Colin repeated.

Enzo went to a door at the far end of the room, and opening it, whistled to Lady Newton's spaniel; the dog at once creaked slowly out of its basket and, cringing so much that its tail scraped the floor, came up to each of them in turn, its ears laid back, and rubbed a sand-paper tongue over their hands and bare legs. The two American children began to laugh hilariously in their relief, until Enzo silenced them with a repeated "Sh, sh, sh!"

Meanwhile Rodolfo was going round the room, opening cupboards, pulling out drawers, and peering at the innumerable
photographs, mostly of the same eton-cropped woman with the
face of an intelligent dray-horse. One by one the others joined him
in this exploration.

"That must be Amberson Lane," Colin said, pointing to the
dray-horse.

Pamela examined the photograph in the Edwardian silver
frame: "She's everywhere," she said.

In one drawer Rodolfo had found a box of musty cigars and in
another a depilatory; but there was little else to excite their interest. He made them laugh by lying on the mahogany four-poster
bed, a cigar in his mouth, though Enzo was too much afraid that
the coverlet would be muddied fully to appreciate the joke. Jumping off the bed, Rodolfo went to the dressing-table and began to
dab his cheeks with rouge and smear his lips with lipstick: then,
putting one hand on his hip, he minced and grimaced about the
room and spoke in a falsetto voice. Again the two English children
laughed, while the Florentine tried to restrain them. The dog had
meanwhile taken Rodolfo's place on the bed, and was scratching
its tattered ear; but whenever the lightning flashed it lowered its
greying muzzle on to its paws and began a whining like the noise
of telegraph-wires in a high wind.

"This drawer is locked," Colin suddenly announced. He still felt
that he had been somehow cheated by what he had found in the
house, though everything was exactly as Maisie had described it to
him. "I can't open it. Let me have that key."

It was a marble-topped console table, as elaborately ugly as the
rest of the furniture, with a single deep drawer. Key after key was
tried; and with each failure their desire to see inside became the
more importunate. Even Enzo, who had at first tried to get them
away, now ran down the corridor fetching keys from rooms that
lay under dust-sheets, from cupboards that filled the landings on
the disused upper storeys, and even from Lady Newton's desk in
her study below. But not one would fit. Rodolfo fetched a hairpin
from the silver tray, covered with mythical Indian monsters, that
lay on the dressing-table, but even that failed.

Such was their excitement that they did not notice that the electric light was shuddering like a candle in a high wind. "I know," Pamela said. "Couldn't we take off the top. This marble unscrews." "No, no," Enzo protested in alarm.

"But why not?" Colin urged. "We can screw it on again. We won't do any harm."

Now, with its alternations of bright and dark, the lamp made it appear as if the room were a railway-carriage rushing at speed through one brief tunnel after another: an illusion which the incessant roar of the storm served only to fortify. Enzo was still protesting:

"It's better to leave it. There won't be anything there. What's the point?"

But without heeding him Rodolfo produced a penknife and began to loosen one after another of the large, brass screws. He was working on the last when, with a tremendous crack of thunder, overhead as it seemed, the light for the last time shuddered, and then went out. Pamela gave a small wail: "What are we to do? There must have been a fuse."

Peering from the window, Rodolfo said: "No, all Florence is dark. It's the whole electric system." He laughed: "If it doesn't rain, they cut the electricity. And if it does rain, the electricity ceases altogether." He clicked his fingers at Enzo: "Fetch a candle. . . . And shut up you!" he shouted at the dog which had set up a piteous, high-pitched whining. "Shut up!"

"Where can I find a candle?" Enzo said.

"There was a torch in that drawer over there," Colin remembered. "Perhaps it still works."

Pamela fetched it and a feeble glimmer was reflected from the marble of the table, a small S of fire which burned fitfully as if buried deep. "That'll do," Rodolfo said, commencing at the last screw. "Now give me a hand with the top," he panted. "Enzo!" He looked round and when the Florentine did not come to his assistance, let out an expletive. "Colin!"

Between them they removed the marble slab and carried it over to the bed where they put it beside the dog which was still whimpering softly. Pamela shone the worm-like wriggle of light into the interior and said, as the others crowded round her: "Cardboard boxes, that's all."

"But what's inside?" Colin said.

"Open one," his sister suggested and almost dropped the torch as a flash of lightning for a second restored the day-light.

"You open one. I don't think it's right."

"Oh, don't be silly." But still she did not move, and it was Rodolfo who at last took the largest of the boxes and eased off the lid. "What is it?" she said; and they all peered together, as the torch lit a row of neatly packed glass phials.

"It must be a medicine," Colin said.

"This one's the same." Pamela had jerked open another of the boxes. "What have you got there, Enzo?"

"I don't know."

"Let's see," Pamela said, while Colin urged at the same moment: "Perhaps we should put them back. We ought to go, Pamela. They're just a lot of medicines." At first he had felt cheated; but now, having discovered something of which Maisie had said nothing, his one desire was to turn back to the familiar and ordinary. "Put them back," he repeated. "Screw the top back."

"Not on your life. This has just begun to be interesting. What is it, Rodolfo?"

Rodolfo held up a hypodermic syringe, while Pamela shone the torch on to his hand and the gleaming metal. "Take care you don't prick yourself," she said.

"What is it?" Enzo said. He had never seen one before. "Oh, they give you injections with it—doctors do. Isn't that what it is, Colin?"

But: "Leave it, leave it!" was all her brother's answer.

"Dentists use them, too. You must have had an injection at the dentist."

Suddenly the dog heaved itself off the bed, like a seal entering water, and waddled to the door where it began to scratch with both paws, whining and at last yelping as it did so. They all stared in amazement, a chill sweat breaking out over them, until they heard the click-click, at first faint, then louder, of feet climbing stairs.

"It's her! It's her!" Pamela exclaimed in panic. "Quick—put the thing away." And because Rodolfo still stood dumbfounded, the syringe in his hand, she grabbed it from him and herself put it in

its box. But before she could restore many of the other boxes, the
door had been opened.

"Enzo!" a voice said indignantly. Then, peering at the torch's
worm of fire: "Who's there? Who are you?" Lady Newton cried in
a mingling of fear and indignation. "Who let you in? What are you
doing here?"

But they were all afraid to move.

At that moment a flash of lightning revealed the four cowering children, the boys behind Pamela who seemed least afraid; the
rifled drawer; the scattered cardboard boxes, out of one of which
Colin had taken a glass phial. "How dare you!" Lady Newton said,
still in Italian. "What is the meaning of this?"

"It was our fault," Pamela replied in English. Her voice broke
the sentence in two, but with a gulp she continued: "It was nothing
to do with Enzo. We insisted on coming. We wanted to see your
villa."

"English!" Lady Newton exclaimed; and as she said the word
the light slowly flickered upwards, making them all blink, until it
had returned to its usual brightness. "And so you've been breaking
into my possessions." She turned to Enzo and suddenly the
small, timid-seeming woman in the dripping burberry and tam-
o'-shanter began to tremble and go white with rage: a stream of
Italian poured from her mouth, as if she were vomiting.

"*Via!*" she concluded. "*Via!*" And then in English: "Out! Get out
of here! And you're bloody lucky I don't call the police! Go on!
Out!" As she shouted at them, one of her gardener's-boy hands,
with the bitten nails, never ceased to pluck at the clammy folds of
the vast black umbrella she was carrying with her. "Don't let me
see you again," she shouted after Enzo in Italian. "And you won't
get last week's salary, nor this week's. Not a penny! Do you understand?"

They all felt too sick with fear to say anything until, white-faced
and soaked, they found themselves on the bus. Then Colin said:
"You were wonderful, Pamela," with a mingling of admiration for
her and disgust for himself.

"Wonderful?"

"The way you told her that it was our fault, not Enzo's. And
then going back to speak to her and leaving us in the porch."

"She wouldn't listen, it wasn't any use."

"But that's not the point—whether it was any use. The point is that you did it. And I didn't," he added in a low voice. He knew he had betrayed Enzo.

"I expect you would have done it if I hadn't been there," Pamela said, in a clumsy attempt at comfort. "The awful thing is that we've lost Enzo his job."

"That was my fault. It was I who made you go. You and Rodolfo would never have gone if I hadn't been on at you both. Pamela, what am I to do?"

"What do you mean?"

"To make it all right. I've got to do something for Enzo. Well, I have, haven't I?"

"We'll think about it later. When we're less wet." She drew her habitually filthy handkerchief out of a pocket and began to pull through it strand after strand of her hair. "What interests me is that medicine. What do you think it was?"

But this was the problem whose solution at that moment seemed to Colin the least important of all.

Chapter Twenty-four

WHEN the two English children had said good-bye to Rodolfo and Enzo, who returned to their houses, Pamela remarked: "Heaven knows what we're going to tell them when we get back. There'll be hot baths and hot drinks and all the usual fuss."

But Colin was not listening. Allied to the misery of damp clothes, and dwarfing it to nothing, was the knowledge that he, and no one else, had been responsible for losing Enzo his job. Nor did the irony escape him that in his long waking fantasies it was the Florentine for whom he always performed some service against impossible odds. A fine service this! The rain had now ceased and the late evening was revealed in misty pinks, blues and yellows; there was only one cloud in the sky and it seemed not to move above a new moon which lay faint and far in the west. There was a sense of relaxation, as after some tremendous contest; it seemed as if the whole earth had spent itself and had now sunk exhausted.

Only the river still thrashed turbulent and muddy under the quiet sky.

"To-morrow it will be cool," Pamela said, "and then it will be hot again. It will be as if we had never had the rain. What are you thinking about?"

"Nothing."

"You're worrying."

"No, I'm not."

"Well, I am."

But she had no cause to worry about anything the grown-ups might say to them, for their truancy during the storm had been swallowed up in the far more momentous events of that evening. When the children reached the hotel, they at once went up to their grandmother's room and were astonished to find it full of people. Chris lay on the bed with her face to the wall, while Mrs. Bennett sat beside her and Max stood near. Tiny was staring moodily out on to the terrace.

"Oh, there you are, children," Mrs. Bennett said absently. She was treating them as if they had been in the hotel all through the storm, and having been prepared for her anxious scoldings, they both felt a vague disappointment, even a resentment. "You'd better run along for the moment. I'll come and see you later. We're busy just now."

"Ought we to have hot baths?" Pamela asked. "We were both drenched through." She was determined that the scene should approximate more closely to what she had imagined.

"Oh, did you get wet? Yes, have hot baths, that's a good idea. But run along now. You'll find Maisie in her room, if you want anything."

"What *has* happened?" Pamela burst into Maisie Brandon's solitude. "I'm sorry, were you busy?"

"That's all right, my pet," Maisie assured her: she typed two more words of the article at which she had been working and then said: "Such a hoo-ha. All about poor Chris."

"Yes, but what *is* it?" Colin demanded. "Tell us, do tell us."

"Well, I don't know that I ought to. I don't know what your grandmother would say." But Maisie was bursting to confide in them. "It's not really for ears as young as yours."

"Oh, go on, Maisie." Pamela put an arm round the older woman's thin, bony shoulders. "Tell us, please tell us."

"Well, my dears——" Maisie began; and with her forefinger she picked out another two words on the typewriter before she continued. "It's all rather a sad story," she said. "And it must go no further. Promise?"

"Yes, promise, promise," they both said excitedly.

"Well, poor Chris has made an awful fool of herself. It seems she's been lending the glamour boy money to pay his hotel bill— oh, and for a lot of other purposes, too. She soon ran through her poor little fifty pounds so she started cashing cheques. That's dangerous, of course, she could get into a hell of a row. But that's not the worst. It seems that last night she lent him more money to pay his week's bill, and this morning he upped and went early. He just can't be found. And now your father has returned from Pisa and there's a letter for him, from Stockholm, saying that there's no such Count—he just doesn't exist. So poor Chris will never see her money again, if you ask me. . . . Of course she was terribly, terribly taken with him," she added. "Which doesn't help any."

Meanwhile Chris was still sobbing on Mrs. Bennett's bed.

Tiny turned from his gloomy contemplation of the terrace to exclaim in exasperation: "What the hell are we waiting for? Why don't we tell the police? Time's the important factor. The sooner they get on to the bastard——"

"Oh, don't, don't, don't!" Chris wailed.

"Well, be reasonable," Tiny said. "He's taken a cool two hundred off you. What I can't understand is that you never even told me that you were cashing those cheques—and cashing them with shady characters to whom he introduced you. You must have been barmy! Hang it all, if they'd cash your cheques, why in the world's name couldn't they cash his?"

"Don't!" Chris screamed, and then covering her ears with her hands, she sobbed hysterically: "I won't listen to you! I knew you wouldn't understand. You never do. Oh, why did I ever marry you? I might have known."

"Good God!" Tiny strode over to the bed, and stood over her, his six-foot-two of loose flesh quivering with indignation. "You have a nerve. When you've been carrying on with that bounder under

my very nose—your—your—gigolo—cheques—my money, too—
money I've earned with the—with the sweat of my brow——"
Not naturally eloquent, he swung his arms in wild gestures as he
attempted to find words.

Max went up to him: "Look, old man, how about you leaving
her until she has recovered? Let her get over the shock of it all.
Come and have a drink with me. Come." He put an arm round the
massive shoulders, heaving under the blazer with the crest of the
minor public-school, and coaxed him from the room. "You look
after Chris," he said to Mrs. Bennett.

"Oh, he's awful," Chris said, her sobs ceasing as soon as Tiny
had left the room. "If he'd been different, it all would never have
happened. Never!" She turned on her back so that the tears trickled down her temples and lodged in her hair. With one hand she
kept clutching and unclutching the crumpled bedspread, while
with the other she pressed her handkerchief to her nose. "He was
so boring," she said. "I felt I had to do something or I should have
gone off my head. And coming to Italy, to Florence, where one
feels so free and everything is so—so——" Mrs. Bennett hoped
she would not say "romantic" but unfailingly the word came. "So
romantic," she gulped. "At first I thought Béngt loved me. He was
so sweet, you know, so attentive, in a way Tiny had never been.
And—and I thought it was my only chance. Probably no one
would ever love me just like that again. I'm not young, you see,
and I know I'm not pretty, and I don't dress well. . . ." Her candour
was appalling, and it appalled Mrs. Bennett; and yet there was a
pathos in it which made the older woman feel she would do anything to help the younger. "Bit by bit, of course, I began to realize.
I couldn't help it. I knew that it wasn't the real thing, but by then
I'd ceased to care. I was content to have him with me, to have him
make love, even though I knew . . ." She covered her face with her
hands. "Oh, you must look down on me!"

"Of course I don't." Mrs. Bennett thought of the years of ugly,
laborious devotion she had given to a man whom she despised and
in the end hated. She had never been unfaithful to him; but unlike
many other women, she did not believe that that fact gave her the
right to be Chris's judge.

"It was awful to give him all that money, and there were times I was suspicious. But I so wanted to believe in him, I so wanted him to be all the things he said he was. Perhaps, all along . . . Oh, I was blind. I blinded myself, because I didn't want to see."

Max came in: "How is she? I've left Tiny downstairs with Karen and Frank Ross. They've just got in. . . . Cheer up, Chris," he said clumsily; he put out one of his large, freckled hands and attempted to touch her forearm. "But look—what about the police? Don't you think we ought to tell them?"

"Oh, no!" she at once wailed, huddling herself round so that she again faced the wall. "Let him go. What does it matter?"

"But the money——" Max began, genuinely baffled.

"I don't care about the money. And I don't care if I find myself in the—in the Old Bailey, for passing those cheques. I don't care!"

"Then why all these tears?" Max asked brightly.

"Oh, Max, do try to understand——" Mrs. Bennett began quietly, but Chris had sat up in bed and had begun to spit out in Max's astonished face:

"Because I loved him. And love him still. And because I shall never see him again. Never, never, never. And because I shall have to go on living with Tiny to the end of my days, knowing he always has this against me. Now do you see?"

"Yes, I'm sorry," Max said humbly.

He, alone, of all those concerned had never realized the true nature of the affair. "But I'd never thought it was serious," he said to Mrs. Bennett afterward. "I'd never guessed. I thought it was just one of those things."

Mrs. Bennett looked at him closely; then putting both her hands on his shoulders, she said: "Just one of those things so often becomes serious before you realize it."

He knew, then, that she referred to Karen and Frank Ross.

Chapter Twenty-five

LENA was on her bed, staring up at a ceiling painted garishly with acanthus leaves, red and white roses and, in the centre, the head and shoulders of a woman. She had hated this ceiling ever since they had come to the flat, but they had never been able to afford to have it painted over. One day, Lena had decided, she would paint it herself; but that decision had been made more than three years previously. She now lay, thinking of nothing but experiencing a vague, persistent desolation of the spirit. It was hot, and she sat up on the bed and pulled off her blouse, and then she kicked off her shoes; finally she removed her skirt. Each of these actions she performed as if the objects removed were things extremely distasteful to her. . . . Oh, Max, she thought. For now he was always "Max" to her in her thoughts about him. She turned over on her side and stared at the wall, instead of the ceiling. She crooked one arm over her head, revealing a moist patch of hair, and drew a deep sigh. . . . She and he were driving in a fiacre along the Viale Michelangelo and the night was late. A light breeze had risen to quicken the dying air; the scent of box eddied all about them. From far off there penetrated to their ears the music of a cheap, sentimental waltz coming from the Piazzale; but heard at this distance, with the whole city suddenly revealed to them, far below, through the breaks in the foliage, it had a solemn kind of nostalgia. The horse's hooves struck a constant echo from the hill on their right: plock, plock, plock. It was as if someone invisible were striking a pick-axe into stone. The hand with the small, reddish-brown freckles and the lighter red hair was resting on hers; she could feel the weight of his shoulder, the pressure of his knee; his lips at her throat. . . .

Now they were walking, down the ghostly hillside, their feet sometimes scattering small granules of earth after them, the place was so steep. Each of the olive-trees was like a puff of mist, and either they or the earth itself gave out an odour of mustiness and age. She shivered a little, in her light silk dress, and he drew her closer to him. They came to a water-course, where like a scar in the hillside, the ground felt all at once tender under their feet. There was a subterranean murmur, seeming strangely loud in the loneliness and the darkness, as if some imprisoned spirit were crying to be released. "The grass is soft here; it must be green. . . . Oh, and the water's so cold." Under the wide sky she lay open to his love. She kissed the place where that morning he had cut himself shaving; a blade of grass tickled her ears; the intense throbbing of the water seemed to have become a no less intense throbbing within her own being. . . .

Oh, but it was disgusting! She jumped off the bed and pulled on her clothes; but a recollection of these waking fantasies still persisted, giving a dazed languor to each movement that she made. From her mother she had inherited a disgust with the physical demands of love, from her father a spirit which perpetually craved to yield to them. For many weeks now, through this long, breathless summer, her mind had been filled with nothing but such thoughts of Max; and only in intense activity could she escape them. As a result she wore herself out with work that was often unnecessary, turning out cupboards, making preserves or mending clothes she had long since discarded, with an angry impatience which left her weak and limp when each task was finished.

Often she would stride out for a walk; and it was now a walk she took, thrusting her way through an afternoon that was listlessly declining into evening. Few people were about in the Cascine where she went, and most of these lolled on the stone benches or lay full length in the grass. A *vespa* churned past, the stench of stale fumes making her feel vaguely sick. She walked on and on, with the sun in her eyes, until at the far end of the park she came to the hideously pathetic monument to the Indian prince who, dying of tuberculosis in Florence at the age of twenty-one on his way out from Oxford to India, had been buried where the two rivers, the Arno and the Mugnone, joined their parched streams. The turbaned head, modelled in terra-cotta with a daubing of gold paint, stared at the dustily drooping foliage with eyes as blank and characterless as all its other features. There was a dreary, forlorn sadness about it all, and Lena quickly turned away, taking a path that would bring her down to the Arno.

Suddenly, against the peeling brown of the river's edge, she saw a figure, legs apart and the whole body slouched in a posture characteristic of a young boy. She hesitated, and then called: "Hello."

"Oh, Lena," Karen said without either pleasure or surprise. "What are you doing here?"

For no reason, Lena suffered an acute embarrassment; and her face became red. "I was taking a walk," she answered; and it was almost as if she imagined that Karen knew of the afternoon's long fantasies about Max.

Karen had begun to bite the nail of her middle finger and her small, white teeth could be heard clicking like a pair of scissors. "What an odd time to walk," she said.

"It is hot," Lena agreed feebly. Then, gathering courage, she retaliated: "But you must have walked here, too."

"Me? Oh, we bicycled here."

"We?" Lena thought; and her whole spirit seemed suddenly to cleave to the back of her mouth as she guessed that Max must be near.

"You know Frank Ross?" Karen went on; and swinging round, Lena saw Ross walking towards them from a clump of trees, a hand still fumbling at one of the buttons of his khaki shorts.

"Yes," Lena said, and as Ross drew near, she nodded to him, attempted to smile and said "Good afternoon."

"Hello," he said, like Karen without either pleasure or surprise. He lowered himself on to the grass and, clasping the lean brown wrist of his left hand in his right, he too gazed at the opposite bank until Lena said with a certain forlornness:

"Well, I suppose I must be going."

They did not contradict her.

"Bye-bye," she said.

"Good-bye, Lena," Karen responded, without even turning her head. Then she shouted after the retreating girl: "Oh, Lena."

"Yes?"

"I quite forgot the most important thing. Max tried to ring you at your home, but the number was engaged and he had an appointment. I think he wanted you for something, though I can't remember what. Perhaps he wanted you to type something for him? Yes, that was it. He sent you away early this afternoon, didn't he, because he was feeling tired? Well, now he's stopped feeling tired and he awfully wants to get whatever it is finished. And so he wondered if you could look in this evening, after dinner, say—about nine or half-past?"

Having delivered this message, Karen at once turned away, as if there were nothing more to be said.

"Yes, I'll do that," Lena said. "Would you please tell him I'll come as soon as I can after dinner?" But she might have saved her breath; for neither Karen nor Frank took any further notice.

Angrily she began to trudge up the bank, but her anger soon

melted into a deliciously voluptuous pleasure. That evening she would see him; and the fact that she had accepted an invitation from Signor Commino to go to a concert worried her not at all. She was not naturally inconsiderate or selfish, and in the past she had always shrunk from the pain she must cause this man whom she could not love; but since she had begun to work for Max, she had found a secret, shameful release for her pent-up frustrations by humiliating her Italian suitor. It was not pleasant and she knew it was not pleasant; indeed she despised herself for the manner in which she treated him. But she could not help it, she told herself; she just could not help it.

Having reached the top of the bank, she halted, not to regain her breath, but because a thought had suddenly come to her. She was smiling to herself, like a mischievous child, as she walked into the clump of bushes from which Frank had emerged. No, they had not seen her; and from here, holding down this branch, she could see them. She waited, straining on tiptoe, while the perspiration on the arm she had raised to hold the branch glistened in the sunlight. Near her, among the bushes, some creature—lizard, bird, or snake—pattered and rustled. It was even more suffocating here than out in the sun, and a faint whiff of corruption was rising from the soiled scraps of newspaper that stuck to the ground. Lena's arm began to ache, her eyes to prick; her whole being felt an intense, physical oppression. Unconscious of her Ross and Karen talked, several inches between them; and still Lena waited.

Oh, she knew it! Suddenly Karen put a hand out to ruffle Frank's hair, he caught her by the wrist, and they both began to wrestle. Lena could hear Karen laughing, and as she laughed, exclaiming: "No . . . no . . . that hurts, that hurts." The scrimmage was brief, for Karen had already thrown herself on Frank and having pretended to be about to bite him in self-defence, had pressed her lips to his. Thus they remained locked for what seemed to Lena interminable seconds.

The bitch, the little bitch! But there was a wild, animal exultation in the way in which Lena said the words. Hers was a plain face except at such moments when her response to some other person was intense enough to change it. It was changed now. Her fine, dark eyes glittered; the slack outlines of the figure which Mrs. Bennett had described as "all anyhow" were now drawn taut. But the exultation was momentary. She let go of the branch her arm held down, and her view at once obscured, leaned with her back against the hard, crinkled trunk of one of the trees. She thought she might faint in the heat, the closeness of the foliage, and that pervasive, sickening odour of decay; she thought she might cry.

Grief flooded her; and as she gulped for air, it was as if she were gulping that grief in, with the element which she breathed. Grief seemed to saturate the whole atmosphere, as it was saturated with heat and with dust. Mouthful after mouthful she swallowed, until her whole being drowned beneath its oppression, and still out of the invisible air it poured into her body.

Suddenly she screamed; she could not control herself. A snake, no bigger than her own index-finger, had wriggled across her shoe in a flash of brown and purple spots. Or so Lena thought. Afterwards she told herself that it must have been a leaf. She put her hand to her mouth, appalled at the thought that Karen or Frank might have heard her. She waited. Until, at last, she again pulled down the branch and peered cautiously out.

The two bicycles had gone.

Chapter Twenty-six

"I HOPE you don't mind," Mino said when he called round for Lena. "I've asked an Englishman and two Americans to have dinner with us."

"That's a good beginning to an evening."

"You *do* mind?" he exclaimed in immediate distress, holding his mouth open long after he had finished what he was saying, as if he expected Lena to pop a letter in. It was a mannerism which always annoyed her.

"Oh, I don't really care," she replied languidly.

"This is terrible, this is terrible. What was I to do?" He paced up and down the room in his light green suit whose trousers were hitched too high and whose coat rode perpetually above his buttocks, while the lines came out one by one on his bulging dome of a forehead as if drawn in by an invisible hand. "They came into the American Express, they came to me for advice. They were lost, Lena, completely lost; they were terrified—terrified of this city of ours." He made a dramatic upward gesture with his right hand, as if he were pulling at something in the air. "They had come to Italy to learn to be painters and they knew nothing, did not know where to turn, what to do, how to live. I felt sorry for them. You would have felt sorry for them—you *will* feel sorry for them. So—what could I do?" He turned to her, his shoulders raised expressively, and the green coat, covered with darker stains, bulged about his collar-bone. "I had to do something. Do you know, they are thinking of returning to America and England. After coming so far, with eleven trunks in bond in the Florence Customs, they are thinking of going home! I felt that I must dissuade them. Don't you agree? And how could I do that better than by some act of friendship. 'Here, friends'——" He put out one of his small, plump hands as if to greet an invisible person—"'Florence, our city, greets you. We greet you.' What else could I do for them? If you could have seen them!" He came across and attempted to take the girl's arm, but impatiently she pulled away. "Say you're not angry, Lena."

"I've told you, I don't care."

"It's not as if we have to spend the whole evening with them," Mino went on. He opened his snuff-box and scrabbled at the powder. "They understand that. They just want some advice, the sort of advice that you can give so well. About flats, and cheap pensiones, and the price of food and fuel. The Englishman has no money and the two Americans must keep him and themselves on the grant the American Government pays them. You must help them—you will, Lena, won't you? They are very young, very inexperienced, very unsophisticated. This old world of ours terrifies them. Everything terrifies them."

Lena knew that he was genuinely stirred by the plight of these exiles, and on any other day she would have liked him the more for it. He was generous and kind, and she herself shared in those qualities and admired those that had them. Indeed, she would probably never have been able to have borne with his physical peculiarities and ugliness if it had not been for her knowledge that if anyone was good Mino was good. . . . But he was such a fool! And at this moment, her irritation made her want to hurt him. "And how do

you propose to get rid of them after we've stood them dinner?"
She purposely emphasized the word "we", making him hurriedly
assure her:

"My dear, I'm the host. . . . Oh, I've cared for all that. I told them
that we're going to the concert afterwards."

"Oh, the concert."

He beamed in anticipation of the pleasure he would give her, as,
scratching with his forefinger at the single tuft of hair that divided
the front of his massive head, he announced: "For once we shall sit
in style. I bought two *poltrone*."

"I'm afraid I can't manage it."

"Can't?" Once again the mouth hung open long after the word
was said. "But you said—Lena, you promised——"

"I know I did. I'm sorry. It just can't be helped. I have to go and
work at nine this evening. Emergency," she added.

"But surely it's not necessary—dammit, you can wait
until——" He choked and grimaced as if he had swallowed something unpleasant. "Claudio Arrau," he said at last. "Claudio Arrau."

"Yes, I know, don't rub it in."

"Me rub it in! Me!" He pointed to himself. "Oh, Lena! Really,
Lena!"

"There's Mother calling. Come up and see her."

"But, Lena——"

Lena had left the room; and dragging one foot after the other,
like a reluctant child, Mino began to follow her.

"Good afternoon, Signora." He went across to the bed where
Signora Bacchi lay, and prepared to kiss her hand. But ignoring
him, she burst out:

"And what am I going to do all evening, Lena? Oh, really, it is
too bad. I ask a little thing of you—a thing that would take you no
more than five or ten minutes—and you just forget to do it."

"The library," Lena began.

"Yes, the library," Signora Bacchi cut in. "And it closes at six. I
know it's troublesome to go out of your way, but Anna says you
were out for over two hours, and surely surely . . . Oh, I mustn't get
angry like this. I'm sorry, please forgive me." All at once her voice,
previously so strident, sank to a whisper as if it were muffled by the
pillow into which she had pressed her head. A look of patient, even

benignant, martyrdom came on her face. "Poor girlie—I do make life a misery for you. I know you have so much to think about. Of course it doesn't matter. It's lovely just sitting here and doing noth-ing—watching the sunlight and the people in the street and—and those beautiful flowers you brought me, Mino." She gave him a gentle smile. "They are beautiful, aren't they?"

"Oh, I feel a beast," Lena said, when she and Mino had at last left the sick room.

"Which was what your mother intended," he said in a soft voice.

As they looked at each other they both appeared to experience equal surprise at this last comment.

"Just *pasta* for me," Mousey, the American girl, said, pronounc-ing the first *a* short. "I can't take anything else, really I can't. I guess it's all that oil. I just throw up."

"You should have seen her yesterday," Bill, her husband, said gloomily. He was tall, with a drooping head whose hair was sheared close, a putty-coloured complexion, and a charmingly embarrassed smile. "Boy, was she sick!"

"I just threw up for two hours solid," Mousey said.

"It was terrible," the English boy put in. He looked at the menu greedily, and then asked his friends: "What's my budget this eve-ning?"

"Go ahead, go ahead, Tony," Bill said magnanimously. "Eat all you want."

"But please," Mino put in. "I am the host. Please."

"That's jolly decent of you. But really—I feel bad about——"

"Please," Mino said.

The young man scanned the menu with an even more avid interest, fingering, at the same time, at a red silk bow-tie which the Americans had just bought for him at Ugolini.

"Maybe, Signor—Signor——" Mousey began.

"Commino."

"Commino! I guess I just will never remember that name. Well, I guess our kind friend here has told you all about our problem."

"A little," Lena said.

"It's terrible," Mousey sighed. She had been ill, and having lost herself in the streets of Florence that same evening, had had no time to make herself up. The result was that with her bluish complexion, her little nose and the downward curves of her mouth, she had the appearance of a sick pigeon propped up on its back. "We just can't figure it out. You see, we've got a hundred and forty dollars between us—between the three of us, that is, because of course Tony, being a Britisher, can't take his money out. Not that he's got it," she laughed.

"That makes me sound like a real cadger," the boy said, looking up from the menu and giving a disarming smile. He had fluffily soft blond hair, a complexion so smooth that it appeared that he never needed to shave, and fragile, slightly girlish features. He was only nineteen. "But I'm going to pay it back."

"Well, of course the kid's going to pay it all back," Bill said, clapping a hand on Tony's shoulder. "We know that. That's nothing to do with it."

"We have to budget pretty close," Mousey said. "A hundred and eighty dollars a month—that's only about a hundred and twenty thousand lire."

"How much?" Bill demanded.

"I said a hundred and twenty thousand lire."

"You're crazy!" he exclaimed.

"I beg your pardon, Bill McKittrick."

"Here, look here——" He snatched the menu from their English friend and began to scribble on the back; their calculations continued until the first course was over, with a great deal of heated argument, loud laughter and complaint from Mousey that Bill was getting her all balled up.

"Well," Mousey said at the end, "I guess that's how we stand." She turned to Lena. "Now what would you suggest?"

"Yeah, what would you suggest?" Bill seconded.

"Friends—I have a plan," Mino suddenly announced, withdrawing the toothpick on which he had been ruminating. "My mother and I live in a small—*come si dice?—appartamento*, Lena?"

"Apartment."

"Yes, apartment. Apartment." He savoured the word as if he suspected it were not really correct. "We have three rooms, kitchen, bath, lavatory. One room for me, one for my mother, and one as a *salotto*."

"A *what* did you say?" Mousey asked.

"A lounge," Tony replied in his clipped, falsetto voice, his fork raised to his mouth.

"Oh, a lounge," Mousey said.

"Now you could have that lounge, you and your husband. We could place two beds in; it is a large, large room. We could place in two chairs, a table, a——"

"Yeah, yeah," Bill cut him short. "But how much? *Quanta costa?*" He rubbed two fingers together to make sure that Mino realized they were talking about money.

"We pay a rent of thirty-five thousand lire—for one month. We halve the thirty-five thousand. Fifteen thousand lire. You use the kitchen, bath, lavatory——"

"But look, my friend." Bill leant forward, an elbow on the cloth, fingers outstretched. "You have two rooms—*due camere*—your *madre* and yourself. We have one, *uno.*" He spoke in a loud, slow voice as if to an idiot. "That's not fair, now is it? Halves is not fair."

Mino looked startled. "It is our flat," he said simply. "We are two, you are two. But if you like"—he gave a winning smile, though his eyes retained their hurt expression—"you will pay ten thousand lire. I do not wish to cheat you."

"Now you're talking," Bill said.

"But what about me?" Tony asked petulantly. "Now you're both fixed up, I suppose I can jolly well do as I please?"

"Tony, Tony," Mousey reprimanded. "Don't be such a silly boy. You know we wouldn't desert you."

"It looks as if that's what you have in mind."

"I have a friend," Mino said and added to Lena, who was staring at the door of the restaurant, wholly uninterested in the conversation: "Giuseppe."

"Giuseppe?" Lena said. "What about Giuseppe?"

"He would take Tony," he said. "He is a painter," he exclaimed. "He makes very little moneys, he is also perhaps a bit—a bit——" He shrugged his shoulders until Lena rescued him:

"Eccentric."

"*Si*, eccentric. He is a little eccentric. But kind, very kind. You could live with him for two or three thousand a week."

"What sort of room?" Tony asked morosely.

"A little room. But clean, very clean. Isn't it, Lena? Very clean indeed, very nice, cosy."

"What sort of heating?" Tony pursued.

Mino shrugged his shoulders. "A stove," he said. "That is always best. Electric is very, very dear."

"Oh, a stove." Tony pulled a face.

"And in your place?" Bill asked. "Stoves too? Stoves *anche?*"

"*Sì, sì,*" Mino agreed eagerly.

"Oh, that's too bad," Bill said. "Isn't that, Mousey? It's just too bad."

"Yes, that's just too bad. We take cold so easily," she said. "We must have electric fires, or central heating, maybe. Besides, I don't think I'd like to share a kitchen as I guess I would have to at your place. I'm funny like that. It was sweet of you to offer, though," she added, looking more than ever like a moribund bird.

"Besides, this painter," Tony said. "I'm a painter, too, and two of a kind seldom agree. And I'd like to stay with Bill and Mousey."

"Well, of course!" Bill said.

"We feel kind of responsible for him," Mousey explained confidentially to Lena. "We met him at school in London, and we really persuaded him to come along. We've got to look on him as a kind of kid-brother. Haven't we, Bill?"

"That's right. He's one of the family. A sort of kid-brother."

Tony smiled gratefully at them, blinking his long-lashed eyes, and then turned to Mino: "What's that cake on the counter over there?"

"*Fedora.*"

"I think I'd like to sample some of that. It looks jolly good."

Lena glanced at her watch and, though it was only half-past eight, got to her feet. She said good-bye to each of the guests in turn, and then, followed by Mino who was baffled by her early departure, she made for the door.

"They're insufferable," she said.

"But they're nice people, Lena."

"No, they're not. They'll never be happy here. The sooner they're back in wherever-it-is the better it'll be."

"Why do you say such hard things?" Mino asked in distress. "It's so unlike you, Lena."

"Because I get tired of seeing you make a fool of yourself. That's the reason why. Oh, you're good, you're kind, and you're worth ten times what those three are worth. But you're an awful, awful fool."

Having said this, she strode off to see Max.

But when she reached the Palazzo d'Oro, she was handed a note:

DEAR LENA,

I hope you will understand, but my wife insists that I take her out dancing. However, I've left some rough drafts on the table upstairs and perhaps you'd get on with those. So sorry to have caused all this trouble. . . .

Chapter Twenty-seven

THAT day Enzo's brother Giorgio had bicycled out into the country with a gun and had come back, a bunch of sparrow-like brown birds swinging from his handle-bars. He was too lazy often to make such expeditions, but when he did, he felt so acute a sense of physical well-being that he would resolve—of course fruitlessly—to return the next day.

He now lay on the bed, still wearing the canvas gaiters, corduroy jacket and heavy army boots in which he had come home, and puffed at the stub of a cigar while he talked to Enzo. His long nails, which he usually kept so beautifully manicured, were soiled with earth and dry blood, and the two, compounded, had stained the leather of his boots and his worn breeches. A fragment of a dead leaf was lodged in his thick, blond hair.

"Yes, it was wonderful," he said. "Absolutely wonderful."

In the town he did not hanker for the country; but strangely, once he was in the country, he could not believe how he had ever existed in the cramped, sunless Borgo. Alone with his gun, he would experience a sudden flood of generosity and benevolence; much that he had done would, all at once, seem mean and he would make new resolves for the future. Such resolves he never kept. For he was weak and could not for long resist the exploitation of his undoubted, if facile, personal charm. But he had been happy on that day, as he was seldom happy when playing billiards or cards with his friends, going to the cinema or the "casino", eating, teasing his mother, bullying his brothers and sisters, or seducing some local girl. He had devoured a hunk of unsalted bread and sour, vomit-tasting cheese in a tavern on the hillside, gulping it down with some dark, chalky wine whose astringency made his mouth dry. He had joked with the peasants, but had felt no desire to linger with them, for once being content with his own company. All the time, as he brought down one after another of the crumpled bundles of feathers, he had whistled to himself. Nor had he once coughed.

Now, as he lay on the crumpled bed, his shirt unbuttoned to his waist with the self-exhibition which was so essential a part of his character, his eyes had a dreamy, half-bemused look, like that of someone who has woken from a narcotic. Usually so fidgety, he was utterly relaxed; and this relaxation substituted for his charm something more rare and monumental—a kind of grave beauty such as is rarely found except in wild animals at rest. Momentarily he seemed all the things he was not; noble, strong, exceptional.

"Any luck?" he asked Enzo. The phrase always meant the same thing: had Enzo found a job?

Enzo shook his head.

"Anyway you'll have a square meal this evening." At this moment Signora Rocchigiani was frying the sparrow-like birds. "You were a fool to get chucked out of that place, though."

Ever since Enzo had left Lady Newton's his family had been telling him what a fool he had been. As if he didn't know; as if he hadn't learned that lesson, bitterly, through hunger! "Yes, I was a fool," he said.

"Can't your American pals do anything for you?" Giorgio asked, inserting a hand into his open shirt and scratching luxuriously.

"They got me the job."

The Rocchigianis always spoke of the American family with a mingling of envy, admiration and contempt. "Well, let them get you another," Giorgio said.

"They can't."

"Of course they can! Have you asked them?" Enzo did not answer. "Well, have you?"

"Oh, leave it! It doesn't help to talk about it."

"As you like."

Giorgio shrugged his shoulders and continued to scratch, his eyes fixed, with that same dreamy, half-bemused expression, on the cracks on the ceiling.

The meal was good, and to Enzo, who had not eaten since breakfast, it seemed a real banquet. But his father, who tore at the birds with his fingers and crunched their bones between his teeth, spattering the cloth, the stained handkerchief he had pushed into the collar of his shirt, and his unshaven chin, never ceased to grumble: "You should have rolled them in bread-crumbs. And a sprig of salsafi. There's no flavour otherwise. The little bastards might be fried mice for all the taste they have. Salsafi, bread-crumbs. You knew that, didn't you? You've always done it before. Good God, it's not as if it were the first time . . ."

Through this growl, punctuated by hiccoughs, the crackle of bones, and prolonged sounds of suction, Signora Rocchigiani said nothing but "I'm sorry. . . . I'm sorry. . . ." Some indeterminate complaint, for which she would not see the doctor, was turning her sallow skin even more yellow and making her eyes protrude so far that it seemed as if she were in a state of perpetual astonishment.

Fräulein Kohler and her "niece" had been invited to join the party, and the German woman had dressed herself for the occasion in a black silk frock, so unfashionably short that it showed both her podgy knees, a white lace fichu, and a pair of black shoes with diamanté buckles on them. The extra chair which had been brought into the kitchen for her was so low that, although she was a large woman, she looked somewhat deformed as she stooped greedily over her food, her chin, with its wisps of reddish hair, only a few inches from the table. She had contrived to get the largest of the helpings, and was now racing for another; until she looked up to notice that her "niece's" plate remained untouched. Bella sat, the smooth hands whose fragility contrasted so pitifully with her "aunt's" resting in her lap; she was staring down at them.

"What's the matter, Bella?" Fräulein Kohler asked, picking a bone from between her teeth. "Eat up, there's a good girl."

Bella said nothing.

"Bella!" Fräulein Kohler said loudly. "Eat up your food. It's good."

Bella sat immobile, her head still lowered.

"Bella!"

There was a splintering of bones in Signor Rocchigiani's mouth and the sound of his rejecting fragments back on to his plate as his wife said: "I should leave her, if she doesn't want to eat."

"But I can't think what's come over the child."

Giorgio nudged Enzo and winked; but the younger boy had reached a state where he could not even bear to look at the epileptic, much less to laugh at her. When he was in a room with her he always now experienced the same mingling of pity and an inexplicable kind of dread.

"Bella," Fräulein Kohler was saying in the voice used by nannies who have decided to be "sensible" with their charges, "you don't want to waste all that good food, do you? You don't want to be hungry to-night? And think of Giorgio who spent hours shooting the birds for us—and of Signora Rocchigiani who cooked them. . . . *Lieber Gott!* What is the matter with the girl?"

Two tears had welled out of Bella's fine dark eyes and were followed by others which came more and more rapidly. Her face remained impassive as if this grief, like her epilepsy, were some divine visitation beyond her control. Without shame or attempt at concealment, she accepted these tears; and that very acceptance had the effect of intensifying the mood of nervous dread which Enzo was suffering.

"Bella, do stop snivelling."

With a sudden shudder and a grimace, Bella turned her head aside as if purposely to reveal the red, corrugated scar, its texture that of a coarse piece of horse-meat, which disfigured her so terribly. She said something inarticulate (Enzo heard: "I can't . . . let me go . . . don't . . .") and then in a noisy paroxysm of tears she rushed from the room.

Fräulein Kohler sighed: "I don't know what's the matter with the girl. These last few days she's been even worse than ever. It's so worrying. And to-night I have to go out and leave her alone again. Ah, well, we all have our crosses to bear." Signora Rocchigiani had been waiting to serve Fräulein Kohler with a second helping and as soon as the German woman realized this, she held out her plate: "Only a few, dear," she said. "I might as well finish up what that stupid child has left."

After dinner Fräulein Kohler locked Bella in their room and set off for Fiesole; and soon after the Rocchigiani family, with the exception of Enzo, went to an open-air cinema.

"Come, Enzo," his mother said to him as they waited for Signor Rocchigiani who had retired to the lavatory after his meal.

"You know I can't come, Mother. I haven't any money."

She looked in her purse. "I've nothing either. . . . Giorgio?"

"No use asking me, Mother. My pension isn't due until next Friday." Giorgio drew deeply on his stump of cigar and then began coughing.

"Why do you smoke that shit?" Signor Rocchigiani demanded, doing up his braces as he appeared. "No wonder you can't stop coughing."

Giorgio did not answer.

"I wish you could come, Enzo," Signora Rocchigiani said, looking with her painfully protruding eyes in the direction of her husband.

"Oh, I've told you, Mother," Enzo began impatiently.

"It would have been so nice, all the family together. We don't often all go out like this." She looked back at her two sallow, lanky girls who stood silent behind her, and then said mechanically: "Wipe your mouth, dear." They were children who had, prematurely, something of their mother's air of suffering, and this set them, as it set her, apart from the menfolk. They spoke little and were always playing quiet, adult games or reading comic papers.

"Let the boy earn some money and then we can think of nice family parties." Signor Rocchigiani raised his hand as if he were going to yawn, but it was a belch he delivered. "Let's go," he said thickly.

"Couldn't we—couldn't we perhaps lend——?" Signora Rocchigiani began, but she was cowed into silence by a massive:

"No, damn you, no!"

Giorgio stamped out his cigar under his shoe, and smiled at his brother, while the others went on: "Tough luck," he said; and he put his hands in his pockets and followed them whistling.

Enzo lay on his bed for a while attempting to read a copy of *Picture Post* which Colin had given him. He was trying to learn English but, unlike Rodolfo, who picked up phrases with the same facility that he picked up belongings, the Florentine made little progress. He ran a slow finger under a line and then scrabbled the pages of a dictionary, which had also once been Colin's. Physically, he felt sated after a meal of such unaccustomed grandeur, but spiritually he was experiencing a complete sense of emptiness. When he had worked for Lady Newton, though he had often to do unpleasant and even degrading things, he had felt that he "belonged"; he had his place in the world and in his own family. Each week he had surrendered the major part of his wages for his father to drink; and though he had resented this, it had bought him his rights. Those rights no longer existed. Once again he was loose, like a vessel so worthless that no one goes out to retrieve it; and until he again bound himself, he knew that he would suffer from this perpetual sense of unreality and waste.

But with Colin he sometimes escaped this feeling and that was odd, for the English boy puzzled the Florentine as much as if he belonged to a totally different species. Enzo did not even know if he liked Colin, and the kindnesses he performed for the English boy seemed sometimes to be performed out of a compulsive sense of duty rather than as acts of friendship. Perhaps, after all, he felt happy when he was with Colin because he guessed that the English boy needed him; though how great was that need Enzo must never have realized. If he had analysed their relationship (which, of course, he never did) Enzo would have discovered that it was at once more, and less, than a mere matter of liking or disliking. They "belonged"; the English boy needed him, if only to help him to hobble on his crutches, and he, more subtly, needed the English boy to give him the assurance he existed in a world where his apparent uselessness had made him doubt that fact. Colin was the first person to whose happiness he had been a vital necessity; and being that, Enzo had recovered a long-lost belief in his own powers.

Now he decided to go and see his English friends, and having plastered his hair with water and splashed more water over his face and his arms, he took up the *Picture Post* and the dictionary and went out to the landing.

From above a voice shouted: "*Chi è? Enzo?*"; and the face of the upstairs tenant, a small, vitally garrulous woman with neat features and grey hair, was looking down at him.

"Yes, it's me," he said. "What are you doing?" He ran up the stairs two and three at a time, and found that at this already late hour she was scrubbing the encrusted tiles before her front door. Those she had not already washed were grey with dirt, but the others glowed red, as if inflamed into that colour by her ceaseless friction.

"I want it all to look nice for the wedding." The next morning her only daughter was going to be married at Santa Croce church and for weeks past she had been working at her preparations. "See, I've polished the knocker. It looks a treat, as if it were gold. I can't tell you how long it took me. And inside I've got a whole heap of flowers my brother-in-law brought me from Antella."

They talked for a few minutes more, though no doubt she would have liked to go on talking for the rest of the evening, and then Enzo left her, once again hearing, as he jumped down the stairs, the hiss and scrape of her brush on the tiles and the ring of her bucket. But when he passed Bella's door he heard another sound too. The girl was making an inhuman kind of moaning, one low, prolonged cry following rhythmically on another, like the keening of women at a funeral. A chill came over him, as he stood by the door, irresolutely wondering whether he should call out and ask her what was the matter. Probably nothing, he decided, for he had long since decided that there was no logic in anything she did. But it was eerie, and he felt that he wanted to run far, far away. "Bella!" he called. "I say, Bella!" No answer came.

He shrugged his shoulders, turned back once as if to make another attempt, and then ran on.

He picked up Rodolfo by the Uffizi, where he was slouching in the hope of cadging a cigarette or a meal from some foreigner, and together they made their way to the Palazzo d'Oro. They found the children in, playing cards in one of the lounges, while Maisie played patience separately on a small table. She threw each of the Italians a cigarette out of her tortoise-shell case and then, peeling off a piece of cigarette-paper which had stuck to her lower lip, asked Enzo: "Any luck with a job?"

"None."

"I wish I could think of something." She rested her spidery, heavily ringed fingers on the edge of the table, the skin round the thumb-nails gnawed and chewed from nervousness, and at last said: "Haven't you any ideas?"

"Plenty," Rodolfo grinned, with the kind of pertness he knew that she liked.

"Such as?"

"If we could go to Tunisia," he said, thinking of the idea for the first time. "We could run away together and begin a new life. But it needs money—plenty of money," and he rubbed the finger and thumb of his right hand together.

"I thought your family was turned out of Tunisia," Pamela interrupted. "I thought Italians weren't allowed to work there any more. I thought that was what you said."

Rodolfo grinned, making a weaving movement with his left hand: "Everything is possible," he declared enigmatically.

"You mean you could go back?" Colin asked.

"If we had the money." Rodolfo used his little finger to flick the ash off his cigarette into the glass bowl which stood at Maisie's elbow, and then peering over her shoulder at the patience said: "Everything can be arranged."

"His breath is something terrible," Maisie said in English; but she was enjoying the proximity.

"How much money?" Colin pursued.

"A hundred—a hundred and fifty—thousand." Rodolfo was about to pick up one of the cards and place it somewhere else, but was stopped by Maisie who gave his hand a slap as she exclaimed: "Leave it alone, boy. I want to do it myself."

"For the two of you?" Colin said, with a tense kind of persistence.

"For the two."

Later Mrs. Bennett joined them, leading Nicko by one hand and carrying one of his fairy-stories in the other. "Read, Granny," he

said; but she sighed, "No, dear, I'm really far too tired," and sinking on to a sofa in the shade of a distant corner, she at once closed
her eyes and appeared to fall asleep. But there was no relaxation
in either her face or her body. She slept like a soldier waiting for
an attack. A nerve throbbed incessantly in one of her eyelids and
every line seemed to be drawn taut, almost to breaking-point. Her
chin was tilted upwards, her hands were clasped tight; and her
whole body, erect on the sofa, gave the impression of a monumental straining forward, as if life were struggling in a vast piece of
statuary.

Most of her days had seemed to be passed in this kind of strained
sleep; she read little, ate little, and spoke only under a weary com-
pulsion.

Pamela had begun to read to Nicko, and Enzo, like a child,
had seated himself by the boy to listen to the story. He must have
understood little, but he followed every expression on the face of
the English girl, and when Nicko laughed he, too, joined in.

Colin got up and went across to his grandmother. "Granny!"
he said. But the only answer was a long, hissing whistle from Mrs.
Bennett's half-open mouth. "Granny!" he repeated louder.

Without any apparent transition from one state to another,
Mrs. Bennett was all at once awake. "What is it?" she asked.

"Granny, you know I have some money on trust?" He had heard
about this money, though he did not know what "on trust" meant
or how much it was. "You know that, don't you?"

"Yes."

"Well—well, would I be allowed to use it?"

"Use it? What for?" she asked without any apparent surprise.

"For something, something private. Something important," he
added.

"But if it's on trust until you're twenty-one, you're not allowed
to touch it."

"Not allowed? But I thought—it is my money, isn't it?"

"Yes, it's your money, but you can't use it until you're twenty-
one."

"Oh."

"Not unless your father lets you."

"He has to say yes?"

"I suppose so, as he made over the money. But I don't really know."

"I'd better ask him."

"Yes, that would be best."

Still without curiosity as to why the boy should want the money, Mrs. Bennett again closed her eyes and slipped back into unconsciousness; and the long, hissing whistle, like a kettle on the boil, started once more.

When Max came into the room many minutes later, he exclaimed, "Nicko, you should be in bed! What are you doing here? It's very nearly ten."

Nicko did not answer; he tugged at the thick pile of the carpet on which he was seated and kept his eyes still fixed on Pamela's face.

Mrs. Bennett said in a drowsy voice, without opening her eyes: "He obviously wasn't going to sleep, so I thought I'd let him up. After all the Italian children go to bed at all hours, and look none the worse for it."

"But he needs sleep," Max said. "Otherwise he gets whiney and overtired."

Mrs. Bennett rose: "Come along, Nicko."

Nicko did nothing.

"Nicko!"

"Did you hear what Granny said, Nicko?" Max asked in a slow, loud voice. "Nicko!"

Nicko did not answer, but continued to tug at the carpet.

"Nicko, I don't want to speak again. Do as Granny says." Max's face was slowly darkening.

When Nicko still made no response, Max suddenly strode across the room, put his arms round him and dragged him to his feet. "No, no, no!" the child screamed, and Mrs. Bennett said: "Put him down, Max!"

"He must learn his lesson."

As he was half-carried, half-dragged to the door, the child put out arms and legs to anchor himself to each person or object that they passed. He clutched Maisie, kicked at a table, and at the last, lunging for a vase containing some vast white and red peonies, brought the whole thing in a crash and tinkle to the floor. Water

streamed outwards; and half-insane with fear at what had happened, the child gulped, was momentarily silent, and then emitted
a long, piercing wail.

"That's enough," Max said. When roused, his temper was terrible. "I've just about had enough." He threw the child over the
arm of the sofa, and holding him down with one hand, began savagely to beat him with the other. Nicko was silent; and it was only
this silence that, in the end, made Max stop, fearing he had struck
the child senseless. Pamela was pulling at her father: "No, Daddy!
Daddy! Don't, don't, don't!", the tears streaming down her cheeks.
Rodolfo and Maisie both watched from the patience-table with an
air of alert interest. Colin was pale.

"Come, Nicko." Mrs. Bennett picked up the child, who began
to sob as soon as he felt her, and carried him from the room. Max
went across to the french windows, opened them and stood looking out. His loins and back ached, as if in a fever; he was covered in
a chill sweat.

"Why did you?" Pamela asked, going across to him. "What was
the point? It won't make him any better. You know that it won't."

"Oh, shut up!" Max said thickly; and turning from the window,
he strode from the room.

"I wanted to ask him something," Colin said. "It won't do now."

At the same moment Maisie exclaimed: "Oh, clever boy!"
Rodolfo had discovered a way to make the patience come out.

As Enzo walked home after saying good-bye to Rodolfo he
began to think of Bella. It was a beautiful night, with a wind that
touched and then left the water as if afraid of any long fusion with
the element that it wooed. Sauntering, Enzo experienced a vague
romantic longing, compounded of desire for the epileptic girl,
nostalgia and the determination to escape—to Tunisia, perhaps,
as Rodolfo had suggested, or to America; to anywhere where he
would be free, and have work, and be able to live the life of a man.
Even the clothes he was wearing, the brief pair of shorts, the open
shirt and gym-shoes, suggested the uncomfortable physical state
in which he now found himself, neither man nor boy, but something of both; and as his body seemed to be about to burst through
the outgrown structure of the shorts and his muscular, hairy legs

looked absurd thus revealed, so he felt the closeness and the absur-
dity of the life he now lived, and longed to put it aside like an outgrown suit of clothes.

It was strange that Bella should be a part of these musings; and
yet, often, when he had nothing else to do, he would begin to think
about her. She was beautiful; and yet it was a beauty which left
him full of dread and hopelessness. For he knew that, in spite of
his brother's momentary possession of her body, she would always
be, in her inmost depths, unattainable, unpossessed. She was like a
cup so cracked that it will not hold water; a ground so barren that
no seed will grow there. Nothing human touched her in the inac-
cessible silences of her being, he was sure of that. Her griefs were
not human, any more than her sudden fits of laughter or those
more terrible fits when she writhed and frothed before him, filling
him with a ghastly physical malaise as if the whole human creation
had suddenly been turned into wild beasts. Yet he loved her. He
did not know it, but as he walked home, sauntering through the
evening, the desire at the heart of all his other desires—to go away,
to be rich, to begin a new life—was his desire for her.

He called in at the Bar, kept by the old woman with the eye
like a hard-boiled egg, and pleaded with her for credit, remembering how Rodolfo had stolen for him the damp, flaky horns of
pastry with their oozing of pus-like custard. The woman said no,
but then, as he was about to go out, she summoned him back, and
sighing, prepared a cup of coffee. "I go into hospital to-morrow,"
she said.

"Yes?"

"It's my eye," she said. "They say they roll it off as you roll off
the top of a sardine-tin. Well, I shan't be sorry to lose it."

"I expect not."

"I'm eighty-six, but I'm not afraid. They won't give me a general, just a local to make it not hurt. Well, I don't mind that, provided there's no blood. Blood makes me turn right over. Even my
own blood. Would you believe it?"

Did he imagine it, or as she nodded her head, did the whole
cataract wobble like a piece of semi-transparent jelly? It seemed as
if, at any moment, it would slither to the floor.

"You can pay my grandson," she said. "Don't think because I'm going into hospital that you needn't pay." To indicate that she was joking, her mouth, with its vertical, dirt-encrusted furrows, fell open to reveal the stumps of a few blackened teeth.

"I hope all goes well," Enzo said, running his tongue round his mouth as he put down the cup.

She looked offended as she said: "They say he's the best one in Florence—and only thirty-two. Studied in America," she said. "Oh, I was determined to have the best."

When Enzo let himself into the house, the family had evidently not returned; but still, from high upstairs, he could hear the sound of sweeping and scrubbing. She would work all night, he supposed, and in the morning the dusty feet of her guests would obliterate all she had done. Then the tiles would be left and they would again slowly blacken. It all seemed so pointless.

He climbed, and the coffee he had drunk still tasted sweetly bitter in his mouth as if a tooth were bleeding. Outside Bella's room he halted, standing with his face only two or three inches from the door as if his mere presence would undo the lock. It was probably because his whole body was wrought to such a pitch of concentration that at last there penetrated to his ears a sound from within. At first it seemed no more than the sound of deep breathing, and he imagined it was his own, after the steep climb; but punctuating it at irregular intervals was a sound too indeterminate to be called a hiccough—the sound of a bubble breaking or the snapping of a string. He did not know why these two sounds in conjunction should all at once drench him with cold sweat and make his scalp prick. He knocked on the door, saying, "Bella, Bella," softly; and then, raising his fist, he hammered for entry. "Bella!" he shouted.

"What is it?" the woman called from the upstairs landing, and her startled face could be seen peering, while a few drops of water from the cloth she held in one hand suddenly spattered downwards.

Enzo took no notice of her. "Bella!" he shouted; and it was as if his whole life were locked in behind that door. "Bella!" He listened: and at last heard a faint rustle, a click and then a brief gasp. All at once was silent.

He hurled himself against the door, retreating to the banisters and running up to assault it, not once but repeatedly. The door creaked and shuddered and finally, with a splintering of wood, tore from its hinges. Enzo fell almost headlong in.

Horror. Bella lay on the floor, half-undressed, flung down like a doll, her legs wide apart and her head resting against the side of the bed. Her hands were smeared with blood, there was blood on her cheek, and blood was congealing on the black-and-white tiles as it slowly pushed towards Enzo. Her eyes were shut, but all the time he was aware of that sound, now terribly magnified, of deep, gulping breathing punctuated by what appeared to be the bursting of one bubble after another in the white, tilted throat.

He gave a sort of cry, more animal than human, not unlike the cry which had always so frightened him when she had her fits. He dragged her on to the bed, and once again cried out, now with the vexation of a child who has a task too difficult for it, as he saw the blood, blood everywhere, bright arterial blood which her body had covered. Her eye-lids fluttered and her mouth all at once clicked: "Gior—ior——" He knew the name she was trying to say, and a sudden wild, destroying hatred of his brother filled his whole being, casting out all the other devils of horror, fear and anguish. "I—*mamma*——"

The woman from upstairs had screamed; she put both hands to her temples and gave one short, yelping scream after another like a wounded dog. Then she hid her face against the splintered lintel of the door, and burst into a loud paroxysm of hysterical weeping. "To-morrow," Enzo could hear her saying over and over again, "to-morrow . . . to-morrow . . ." And then, as if she were accusing either him or the dying girl: "Oh, what a terrible thing . . . terrible . . . terrible. . . . And the wedding—the wedding!"

Chapter Twenty-eight

THE American family had stayed on in Florence through August and into the middle of September without there seeming to the children any reason for doing so. When they had first come out they had been told that after a few days in Florence they would be going to the seaside. Colin's accident had apparently postponed that plan, though what he did not realize was that, when his stepmother expressed so much confidence in the doctor who was attending him and urged the inadvisability of making a change to another, she was in fact seizing on the best excuse for remaining with Frank Ross.

Nicko and Mrs. Bennett both fretted against the enforced stay and Max himself would talk of "pushing on", though with little conviction; but Colin and Pamela felt no such desire for change. They were happy in Florence; and whenever Colin thought of being separated from Enzo a chill came to his heart.

One day Max drove the children, Lena and Mrs. Bennett out to the sea. Karen pleaded an appointment with the dentist, but Max knew that she would, in fact, spend the day with Frank Ross, and she knew that he knew. Yet the strange thing was that neither of them had ever openly discussed the affair. "You must have it out with her," Mrs. Bennett frequently urged him. "You must do something before it is too late"; and he would always respond with the same shrug of fatalistic melancholy.

"But you must, you must. The whole thing is becoming so ridiculous."

"I don't honestly believe in the value of 'having things out'. I've never found it worked. You have them out, and then all at once, you have them over. There's nothing to do but to wait; to wait quietly and hopefully. He'd never do for her, of that I'm quite certain. And she'd never do for him—no woman would."

But in his heart was a stone-like weight of doubt which he now dragged with him wherever he went. Except on those rare occasions when he lost his temper, he always avoided scenes. His father and mother had bickered all through his childhood and, though he now knew that they had loved each other as he and Karen had never known love, yet the memory of those quarrels had rooted itself so deep in his nature that nothing could drag it out. Anything was better than that people should savage each other in that bloodless, useless way.

Karen, too, stayed dumb; at first because she thought that Max had not guessed and later because, until he mentioned the subject, her morbid reticence made it impossible for her to do so. Besides, she was not sure of Ross, and was never to be sure. He had possessed her many times, but their affair seemed to her like a telephone conversation in which the other person is for ever hanging up. No sooner were they wholly in communication than he all at once eluded her. And so she was afraid. Never in her whole life, not even when she was waiting for news of Nicko's father after the announcement that his plane had not returned, never, never had she experienced such a persistent anxiety. For she knew now she loved him, as she had loved no one else, and she knew that without his love, her whole being would shrivel up and die.

"Mummy should have put off the dentist," Pamela said as they unpacked their picnic lunch in a bay beyond Livorno. "It was silly of her." She handed round napkins, plates, forks and spoons, and ugly plastic beakers. "You've taken more than your share," she told Lena, who was helping herself to cold chicken. "And now that's too little. Let me do it." She began to separate the meat on to the six plates and then gave them round.

"You have such a sense of justice," Mrs. Bennett said. "That is something one learns at school, where everything is 'fair'. And then one goes out into the world where nothing is 'fair' and of course one is outraged."

Nicko, who was still peevish from being car-sick, all at once cried: "Oh, there's a worm in my chicken!"

"Don't be silly, that isn't a worm," Pamela said. "It's a bit of sinew."

"Don't want it, anyway"; and before they could stop him, he had flung the leg of chicken into the sea.

No one said anything; and soon he began to whimper, clutching the plate with both hands to his chest, his face turned sideways. Max gave a brief exclamation, but he was too inhibited by the memory of the scene with Nicko to do anything more. He was now ashamed of that act of savagery, particularly before Pamela and Colin, and wondered if they remembered and held it against him.

Lena said: "Here, Nicko. Have half of mine."

"Don't want it."

But she knew that he did, and having separated a piece of the wing, she shifted it to his plate. In her white silk dress, against which the brown of her bare arms and legs glowed in the sun, she looked more attractive than any of them had ever seen her.

She never ceased to watch Max, and whenever he made one of his jokes, so dry that the children never laughed at them, it was as if her whole body were being consumed by mirth as, at the other times, it was as if it were being consumed by devotion.

Such a response would inevitably either flatter or madden a man; and Max was in a mood for flattery. Dear Lena, he thought. She was so capable and sensible and kind, and yet, unlike most people who possessed those qualities, she had such a sense of humour. Physically she had always a little repelled him in the past, with the thick black hair that covered her arms and legs and made a small moustache on her upper lip, and those ugly feet, calloused and misshapen, which she insisted on exposing by wearing no socks and sandals; but these details no longer worried him. They were "all of a piece". He decided she was charming.

"Oh, it's so hot," Mrs. Bennett exclaimed. "I feel I shall suffocate." She got up from the party and wandered away, some twenty or thirty yards, where she placed herself on a small rock in the shadow of a larger one. The two rocks were covered with a greenish-purple moss from which seeped a vaguely disinfectant smell, reminiscent of the wards of public hospitals. Seen by the others Mrs. Bennett's faded blue dress merged into the shadow cast by the rock overhanging her; but the straw hat, bought at a street-market when they had motored through Arles and worn by her ever since whenever she went out, made a bright, shimmering hole in this peace of coolness, depriving the eye of rest. She sat huddled, her knees wide apart and her arthritic hands clasped between her knees, as she watched the sea pounce inwards on the smooth, hard sand. In spite of the heat, her headache and a feeling of suffocation, she was now completely happy. A month ago she would have fretted with a pencil and a sketch-book, attempting some communion with the landscape before her; and the communion would have been impossible, and the realization of this would have filled her with a vindictive kind of frustration. But now she was resigned; such communion had at last ceased to matter. Here she was, and here under her fingers was this greenish-purple moss, as if the rock had grown a diseased skin, and there before her was the sea, hurling its glittering knives against the quiescent sand. And there were Max, Lena, and the children, with their white napkins,

their red, plastic beakers, and their green picnic basket. No, she no
longer wanted communion with them either. They looked beautiful like that, the sunlight glinting on Nicko's fair hair and Lena's
ready smile, and it was enough to see them, without that desire to
be identified with what one saw. Like the sketching, intimacy was
too costly, too frustrating, too great an expenditure of oneself—
and all for what, for what?

"I think I shall go in now," Pamela said.

"Is that wise," Lena asked, "so soon after a meal? What do
you think, Mr. Westfield?" She leaned over to Max, who lay outstretched, his arms behind his head, so that her face was only some
six inches distant. He opened his eyes, and the red eyelashes flickered in the dazzle as he said: "Wait for half an hour."

How strong he seemed; and how clean, in his white silk shirt,
at the opening of which she could see the coarse hair growing.
His hands were so clean, with the wide, beautifully kept nails and
the palms whose skin, even in this weather, had a slightly chapped
look as if from too much scrubbing. He was wearing some beige
linen trousers, with a silk scarf twisted round his waist, and as he
lay there in the sunlight, the trousers were rucked over his thighs,
as if they were too small. She wanted to twine the hair at his throat
round her large, competent fingers; to pick at the knot of the silk
scarf.

But how sad he looked, even in repose. And all because of that
minx, who was willing to spend his money, though it was obvious
she refused to sleep with him. Lena hated Karen; and now, as she
thought about the other woman, a sullenly voracious expression
came over her face, making Colin say: "A penny for your thoughts."

She ran some sand through her fingers and said: "Oh, nothing."

"I bet you were thinking about Signor Commino," Pamela
laughed.

All at once Lena was inexplicably angry. "Oh, you children, you
really are absurd! It's so ill-mannered, Pamela, to talk in that way.
Don't you see that it's ill-mannered? I don't understand you." Then
she fell silent, and again brooded on Max's shut face.

Nicko had wandered off into the heat of the afternoon, and
Mrs. Bennett called: "Put on your sun-hat."

"I don't want to, Granny."

She said nothing more; and soon he walked back to the others, picked up the hat, and pulled it over his ears. He began to grub for shells. "Look," he called. "Look what I've found!" He ran up to his grandmother and held to her ear a shell so gnarled and brown that it looked like a fragment of old bone; and to fortify this impression, brown strands of dry seaweed hung from its orifice like attenuated sinews. It smelled of salt and decay.

From its depths came a strange, high-pitched singing; at first Mrs. Bennett supposed it was some noise in her own head. "Strange," she said; and the child, hearing the word, chanted out, "Strange, strange, strange!" as he wandered off from her, bearing his trophy. But soon he tired of it and let it drop from his fingers; in the bright glare it lay like the rotten, half-buried remains of some man or animal, deep orange against the lighter orange of the sand. Mrs. Bennett imagined that she could still hear its high-pitched trilling in her ears.

After a while Lena disappeared behind a rock and reappeared, shivering a little with excitement, in a white silk bathing-costume for which she had had to pay nearly a quarter of her monthly salary. "Oh, it's wizard," Pamela exclaimed, as Lena had hoped she would, to attract Max's attention.

His eyes flickered up: "Very nice, Lena," he said, as she placed herself, somewhat self-consciously, on the sand beside him. "It's like that one of Karen's," he added and of course did not notice the immediate darkening of the girl's face.

"Are you coming in with us, Mr. Westfield?"

He yawned: "Oh, I expect so—later. I feel so sleepy. Don't wait for me now. I'll join you when I'm ready."

"Colin?" Lena asked.

Colin pulled a face, as he flicked one stick after another, with a plop, into the sea.

"Ready, Lena!" Pamela called, and she emerged from behind a rock while she was still pulling up one shoulder-strap to cover her right breast. Her back was red and peeling and the sun had brought out freckles on her arms and legs. But as she and Lena ran down to the sea together, she had acquired an effortless speed and grace and beauty which made Lena seem all at once dull by comparison. These were the qualities of youth, and in a year, or two years, or three years, she would inevitably lose them; but because of them, Max was now watching his daughter and not the woman who imagined she was being watched by him.

He peeled off his shirt, rolled it into a ball to put under his head, and was about to close his eyes again when Colin said:

"You're going to peel terribly. You know you always do." He was sitting with a bored, slightly disconsolate expression as he still threw stones at the waves.

Without opening his eyes, Max said: "I brought some oil, but really I can't be bothered."

Colin scrabbled in the picnic basket, and having found the bottle containing the oil, went across to his father: "I'll do it for you," he said.

"Oh, don't trouble."

"No, I'll do it." He spoke almost sullenly, tipping some of the amber liquid into the palm of his hand.

"I think I'll have a dip first," Max said, raising himself on an elbow. Colin felt cheated, as he let the oil trickle into the sand; he watched it as it glinted downward, large, rich drop by drop, and was then sucked into the universal, glaring dryness. "Oh, all right," he mumbled. He wiped his palm on his own bare leg; he had a slight headache.

"What about you?" Max said.

"I don't think I want to."

Max was pulling his trunks over his naked thighs as he said gently: "You must learn sometime."

Colin had the impression that this had all happened before; and then he remembered the scene by the Arno, with Frank Ross's malicious taunts. The connection once established, a connection of mood also took place; he wanted to defy his father, as he had attempted, so feebly, to defy Frank Ross; and because he was not afraid of his father, whereas he had dreaded Ross, he hoped to atone for having been so weak then by being firm now.

"I'm not interested in learning," he said abruptly, still massaging his greasy palm against his leg.

"That seems to be rather silly."

"I dare say it does."

Max looked up from fastening the belt of his trunks. "Come

along, come along!" Lena was shouting, but Max took no notice of her as he wondered, sadly, what he had done to deserve his son's hostility. He hesitated and said: "I'm sorry if sometimes I don't seem to try to understand you." Colin remained silent, his eyes focused on the anchor which his father had had tattooed on his arm during his service in the Navy during the Great War. "Because I *do* try," Max continued, now gazing out to where Lena and Pamela were splashing and screaming. All at once he hated their high-pitched, hysterical fun. "I *do* try," he repeated, like a stubborn child in a school classroom. He put out an arm, the muscle swelling beneath the anchor, and attempted to draw his son to him; but the boy had moved away.

At that moment, Colin longed to be folded in that embrace; and yet, at the same time, he was filled with a savage pride which would not let him yield. He could not understand it, and he was frustrated almost to the point of tears.

"When I've had my bathe, let's go for a walk, shall we?" The iron had been removed from the boy's leg three or four days previously. "Just us two. Shall we?"

"I thought I'd go to the cinema."

"The cinema!"

"They're showing *Johnny Belinda*—I saw as we drove through. It begins at three. It's a good way of learning Italian."

"But not on a day like this," Max protested.

"All days are like this in Italy."

Max gave a not altogether happy laugh. "That's true. But you could have gone to the cinema in Florence, couldn't you? There's not much point in driving all the way out here——"

"Oh, well, if you want me to sit on the beach all day!"

"Don't be silly. Do just as you like."

"I shall need some money."

"Yes. How much?" Max reached for his trousers and put a hand in one pocket.

"Two hundred and fifty lire, I expect. That's what it usually is."

"Well, here's three-fifty."

Colin took the notes and pushed them into his shirt-pocket, mumbling, "Thank you" almost inaudibly.

"Enjoy yourself!" Max called after him.

When the boy did not answer, or even turn, his father dropped the trousers which he had been holding, as if his whole firm, sinewy body were oppressed with a sudden fatigue. Then he straightened himself, and began to sprint over the glaring sand, scattering a fine drifting wash behind him.

Lena and Pamela both raised their arms at his coming, and shrieking and laughing, began to scoop at the water and splash it towards him. But he took no notice. He plunged into a breaker, and then with long, powerful strokes swam far, far out where he knew that neither of them could reach him. Then he lay on his back, floating, his eyes closed and his face strangely white against the redness of the hair on the rest of his body.

Meanwhile Colin was tramping up the innumerable steps which wormed between heavily scented bushes of oleander and syringa, to the glitter of the town above him. His breath came short and he was on the verge of tears. He stopped and looked back behind him, and saw Lena and Pamela still playing their games and Max, barely discernible, like a log of wood in the deep, distant blueness. Nicko was building a sand-castle; but he had started it too near the incoming tide, and each time that a breaker pounded downwards, he would scurry away in terror. It made Colin smile. Mrs. Bennett he could not now see, for with the moving of the sun the shadows of the two rocks had slowly opened like some vast, purple jaws and she, yellow sun-hat and all, had been swallowed downward. If he strained his eyes, he thought he could just see her; but it was something infinitely blurred and transparent, like a bad image on a television-screen. Suddenly he wanted to shout to her, for he felt, he did not know why, that she would never come out. She would dissolve there, in the shadow, as jelly-fish dissolve in the sun, and when they went to look for her they would find nothing but a pool of sticky liquid and the yellow straw hat. He felt sick with dismay at the thought; and it was only by an effort of will that he at last conquered the irrationality of such a mood. For, of course, she was still there, he told himself; and of course they would find her.

In the main street a woman was standing with a boy of four or five asleep in her arms. She seemed only a girl herself, though her swollen figure made it obvious she was expecting again to be mother. She had a small, puckered face, greasy black hair, and clothes which were almost repellent in their filthiness and disrepair. She carried the child towards a smartly dressed woman, and then when she hurried past, towards a man, an obvious tourist from his camera and binoculars, who hesitated, looked her up and down, both nostrils twitching in his long, bony face, and eventually exclaimed: *"Via! Via!"* in a high-pitched, American accent. At this she began to carry her burden over the road, heedless of a car which all but ran her over. The brakes screeched and there was a burning smell of rubber on the hot, heavy air; the driver shouted at her, in Italian, and when she said nothing, he drove on, apparently disappointed. The child had woken and now began crying, fumbling with one hand to grasp her breast while she tried to pull him away from it.

Colin was watching the whole scene, with a fascinated horror. At last, despairing of her attempts to control the child, she unfastened the torn, black dress and, retreating into a doorway, allowed him to suck from the breast. He was so avid that he paid no heed to the flies which she lethargically attempted to brush from his eyelids at intervals of one or two minutes. Her feet were bare.

Colin went across to her and held out the three hundred and fifty lire his father had given him. She stared back, but either because she was astonished at this generosity or because she needed both hands to support the child, she made no attempt to take the notes from him. The child was making greedy, gulping noises, its palms opening and shutting convulsively as it sucked. Colin let the notes flutter downward to the woman's bare feet and then hurried away, before she put out a hand to tuck them into some recess of her filthy clothing. All at once he had lost the desire to see the film; and indeed, he now wondered if he had ever wished to see it. He had wished, from some irrational cause, to alienate himself from his father, and the cinema, on such a day and after they had been driven so many miles to the sea, had seemed the best way to do so.

There was a square of grass, divided by two intersecting gravel paths into four triangles, and Colin went and sat on one of its wooden benches. Its paint gave forth a vaguely unpleasant smell as it burned in the afternoon sun. There were few people about. There was a lethargy over the whole town, and the girl who sold tickets in a cage in the cinema was asleep on her elbow. Two dogs circled each other, sniffing, and then from sheer weariness, each went to sleep under a separate bench. Colin scratched his ankles where some gnats had evidently bitten him and stared at the dust-grey tops of the trees round the square.

He thought of his father, floating far out in cool depths of blue, of the woman who suffered the voraciously sucking child, and then of his own stupid rebelliousness when his father had wished only to be kind. Finally, and as it were as a last clue, he thought of how Enzo had described to him the scene of his mother rubbing his back with oil. . . . Perhaps he would have wept, if he had not felt so tired. He lay full-length on the bench, and stared at the glaring sky; and at last fell asleep, and dreamed of Frank Ross.

Throughout the drive back, Max ignored Colin; and though he wished to apologize, the boy could not bring himself to do so.

"You were silly, going to a cinema, after we'd come all this way," Pamela said.

"Oh, shut up."

"Well, it was silly, wasn't it? And the sea was so wonderful."

"Mind your own business."

"You *are* in a good temper."

Colin turned from her and looked out of the window, his eyes filling with tears. Mrs. Bennett continued to snore in the other corner, with Nicko on her knees. Lena, in front, turned to Max:

"It *was* a lovely day, Mr. Westfield. I can't remember ever having enjoyed myself so much before. You are so kind to me," she added, her voice strangely vibrating as she clutched at her hair; the water had taken all the grease out of it and it was blowing across her face. "So very, very kind."

Max only replied shortly: "I'm glad that you liked it."

When they reached Florence, everyone but Colin again thanked Max. Colin saw his father glance at him, while the others exclaimed "Lovely . . . delightful . . . so kind . . ." and he knew, with a mingling of shame and devotion, that Max was not listening to them, but waiting for him. And he could say nothing, nothing at all. The words would not come. At last Max turned away, and the opportunity was over.

Later that evening, after he had changed for dinner, Colin decided to go and apologize to his father. But still his courage failed him. In the end he wrote a brief note, in the over-correct, stilted English he always tended to use in correspondence, and having waited until an hour when he knew that Max habitually went down to the bar for a cocktail, he made his way to his father's room. The door was ajar; and the boy experienced a brief thrill of pleasure as he looked at his father's ivory-backed brushes; his typewriter on the table, with the neat stacks of letters all about it; his shoes, with their wooden trees, in a gleaming row on the bottom of the half-open cupboard, the packet of cigarettes he had thrown on the dressing-table, and the discarded clothes left, here and there, for the valet to pick up. And everywhere there was the peculiar male smell which he always associated with Max; the smell of a certain kind of soap, and of tobacco, and of something less definable.

Colin tiptoed about the room, examining one object after another; then having taken a cigarette from the packet to give to Enzo later, he glanced at the first letter on one of the stacks.

> . . . You were *so* kind, and I shall never, *never* forget what you did for me, all that money and not only that, your consideration and understanding just how I felt—and trying to make Tiny see what hell I was going through. Not that you had much success there! But I mustn't complain, must I?—After all, I brought it all on my own self. And it was *worth it*, of that I am *sure*. Whatever I have suffered—and God alone knows what mental *and* physical torture these last days have been—whatever I have gone through, I have *no regrets*. And no hatred for Béngt, *none whatever*. Only love—now isn't that crazy? But it has all been so sad, coming back to the house . . .

Suddenly he put down the thick sheet of dark blue note-paper, with its large, rambling characters underlined with splashes of ink. Through the closed communicating door which led to Karen's room there penetrated a male voice. His father's, he thought; and he went nearer to hear what was being said.

"That's the third brooch you've put on and then taken off."

"But they're all so ugly. Don't you think they're all terribly ugly?

Poor Max, he had such little taste for such things. Look at this. It belonged to his first wife. Don't you think it's just too pathetic? I couldn't wear it, really I couldn't. How on earth do you think they ever came to choose such a thing?" There was a burst of laughter and an exclamation of "No, no, don't!" followed by silence for many seconds. "Really, you are naughty, Frank. No, I'm not at all pleased. No, I'm not. I'm not!"

Colin was trembling and his whole back ached. He stooped again to the keyhole.

"Now hurry, hurry up," Ross was saying in that staccato voice of his which made whatever he said sound like an order. After a moment, he asked: "What did *he* say to another evening out?"

"I didn't ask him."

"Liar!"

"I didn't. Why on earth should I?"

"Because you'd hate it if for once you didn't get your allowance. What an allowance!" he added contemptuously. "Do you know that it would pay the rent for my *villino* for over six months?"

"Are you serious about the *villino*?"

"Yes, I think so. Why?"

"It's so far out."

"But you're going to leave Florence soon."

"Must I, Frank?"

"Must you—what?"

"Leave Florence soon. I mean"—she hesitated—"well, why shouldn't I come and live with you?"

Brusquely he announced: "We've been into all that so often."

"Well, why shouldn't we go into it again? . . . Oh, I know how you despise me. You think that I'm pampered and useless, and that I couldn't live your sort of life. You haven't given me a chance. I like money and the things money buys—yes, I admit it. But money's not essential to my life, of course it's not essential. You—you are essential. Oh, my dear, if you only understood how I——"

"If you're ready, let's go."

"Oh, you're so cold, and unsympathetic, and—and inhuman! 'Let's go'——" she made an attempt to imitate him, and then gave a melancholy laugh. "One day I think I shall kill myself because of you."

"What on earth are you doing now?"

"Pinning on that brooch."

"What brooch?"

Again she gave the same unnatural laugh as she answered: "That brooch he gave to her. Look!"

"But why on earth——?"

"Oh, I think it goes so well with your idea of what a woman should be—a household drudge to be made whenever the male animal feels like it. I'm sure you'd have loved her."

"I love you," he said softly.

When they had gone, Colin wrenched at the door, and finding it locked, ran out into the corridor and entered that way. He felt he must do something, but he did not know what. There was the jewel-case, carelessly left open, and there was the small cardboard box, with the name of the New York jeweller, in which his mother's brooch had always been kept. Now it lay empty. So she had, after all, gone out wearing it on her dress! In his rage he slapped the rumpled damask bedspread. They had kissed there. Who knew what disgusting, depraved things they had done there together? And, suffocating him, there was always the reek of her perfumes. Harlot, harlot, harlot! He strode over to the french windows, flung back the curtains, and pushed one half open. The night was vast beyond the floating terrace, and as he looked out on it, it brought a certain peace to his throbbing temples, heart and spirit. Tears came then and he did not attempt to check them. He wept for Max and his own behaviour that afternoon; he wept from an aching, outraged sense of decency; but above all he wept for his dead mother whom he had never known. She had died when he had been born, and he had always felt that it was he who had killed her.

Chapter Twenty-nine

THE following day Maisie took Colin and Pamela to a fair at Settignano.

The night before she had been out dancing with a colonel from the Air Training College, a corpulent little man with a tooth-brush moustache above excessively white teeth, a brown, wizened skin, and some thinning hair which he brushed over the top of his head to conceal a bald patch. "My dear, it was a priceless evening," she told Karen at breakfast. "All those elaborate compliments. He looked into my eyes and asked me whether they were brown or hazel, and then he looked at my hair and asked whether it was chestnut or brown. So I said plain mouse. And then there were a number of references to my age, which sounded less complimentary than he obviously intended. I mean, no woman likes being complimented on *looking* so young—on *being* so young, yes, but he didn't say that. And then he waited for me to say something in return about him, and I couldn't, so at last he said: 'Now what do you think about me?' And there he was sitting opposite me, so fat and greasy, with the sweat on his forehead and a lock of hair slipping from its place, and all I could say was: 'You have a nice smile.' But, my dear"—she leant forward to put one of her emaciated hands on Karen's wrist, as she whispered—"he was a superb lover."

"Oh, Maisie, you didn't!" But Karen said the words, only because she knew that they were what Maisie expected; her mind was busy with a wholly different problem. That morning she was going to tell Max that she wanted to join Ross out at his *villino*, and though this was what she had planned to do for many days past, her distaste for all scenes had already spoiled her breakfast.

When Maisie and the children had left, Karen went out for a long walk beside the Arno, and then, summoning her courage, hurried to Max's room. But Lena was with him.

"Oh, Lena," Karen said in a voice which fright made cold and spiky. "I have some things which I must discuss with my husband. Do you think you could leave us?"

Lena's face darkened as she picked up some papers. "Will you be long?" she asked, her breathing like a ground-swell under the mumbled words.

"I really don't know. I'll call you when I'm finished. Perhaps you'd wait in the upstairs lounge?"

"Is that all right, Mr. Westfield?"

Max's attention seemed to return from some far distance as he said: "Yes, yes—oh, yes."

"Then I'll leave you both," Lena said, going out and shutting the door quietly behind her.

"You know what I want to say?"

Max's face, now that the colour had all left it, glistened in a vaguely metallic way; and his small, green eyes were expressive of nothing but abject terror. Looking down at him and noticing how his hands trembled as he clutched them together, Karen felt all her previous nervousness evaporate and she continued decisively:

"It won't be a surprise to you. You must have known it was coming." She balanced herself on the end of the bed, and swung her legs back and forth; in comparison with his strained, urgent body, hers was beautiful in its ease, grace and litheness. "I want to go," she said.

"Leave Florence?" he said, momentarily enraging her with this deliberate refusal to face what she had to say.

"Don't be silly," she retorted drily. She undid the clasp of her elaborate gold bracelet, a present from him, and then clicked it shut as she said, "I'm going to live with Frank—Frank Ross."

"I see."

There was a silence until she said: "That's all. I'm going to go to-day."

Then he gathered himself to retaliate: "And I suppose he really wants you?"

She coloured as she retorted: "Well, of course he does."

"That's fine. That's really fine." The irony was pathetic in its feebleness and she despised him for responding with it, instead of with the rage which, unconsciously, her whole being would have welcomed. "And what do I do now?"

"That's up to you. If you want a divorce——" the bracelet again clicked shut.

"I must think," he said. "It's all so sudden."

"Of course it's not sudden! Good God, you've known for days now, haven't you?"

"Oh, I suppose so."

She longed to goad him out of this mood of defeat and weariness; she wanted him to fight her and to fight for her. "We made it obvious enough," she said. "You almost came in on us that day. Don't you remember?" He did not answer and she repeated: "Don't you remember?"

"What about money?"

"I don't want any." It was only two days since her allowance had been paid. "I have some pride, you know. And so has Frank."

"But he'll never be able to support you."

"How do you know? . . . Anyway, that's our affair."

"And the divorce? Do you want it? I mean, is he going——?"

Again she coloured as she gathered her strength to say: "He doesn't want to marry me. Or anyone, ever." She seemed to be defying him as she stared at him, while he in turn stared hopelessly at his locked and trembling fingers.

"Nicko will feel this," he said.

"Oh, please don't try the sentimental approach!" she at once exclaimed, and he knew that he had touched her. "I don't honestly believe that at that age children feel much. Besides I shall go on seeing him—if you will let me."

"Perhaps you had better take him."

"I can't decide everything at once—please, please!" All at once she seemed to lose control; but she regained it as she said: "Of course if you don't want him. . . . But Mother will always look after him, I know. She looks on him as her own. He's far happier with her than he ever is with me." Momentarily she thought back to the evening when she had found him crying and sleepless in bed, but she banished the memory. "But, of course, he's my responsibility and I acknowledge that, so if you'd prefer——"

"No, let him be."

"The other two won't care two pins whether I'm here or not."

Max did not contradict her.

"I hope you'll be happy," he said.

"Oh, what a conventional thing to wish the wife who's leaving!"

"I mean it."

When Karen had gone through the communicating door into her own room, she rang for Lena to be sent up to Max and then began to sort and pack her clothes.

"That'll do for to-day," Max said to his secretary. "I have to go out."

Lena looked at his slumped figure as he sat with his back to her,

one hand over his eyes, and all at once a wild, extravagant pleasure
tore through her whole being. "I'll take these home," she said and,
her large, competent hands all at once strangely incompetent, she
began to dither among the neat stacks of letters. "Shall I return
this evening?" she asked. "Mr. Westfield," she said gently, when no
answer came, "do you want me this evening?"

"Oh, Lena!" Suddenly he flung round in the chair and an arm
shot out. He looked up at her in misery, and then, his whole body
writhing, put his head on the table. She was at once terrified and
delighted when she heard his loud, gulping sobs.

"Karen," Mrs. Bennett said, entering her daughter's room more
than an hour later, "aren't you coming to lunch? I can't wait any
longer. Max has gone out, God knows where, and Maisie and the
children won't be home anyway. You know I hate eating alone!"
She was limping on a stick with a rubber ferrule, and her whole
body, normally so erect, was bent almost double.

"Aren't you well?" Karen asked. It was the first time she had
noticed her mother for many days, and the change had now
shocked her. "What's the matter?"

"Still this rheumatism. I don't think the damp from the river
suits me. Perhaps we shall leave soon," the old woman added.

From all this, Karen supposed that Mrs. Bennett had still to be
told the news, and she said: "Mother, I've something to tell you."
She hesitated, all at once filled with terror. "I've—I'm——" She
clumsily attempted to roll up some silk stockings. "I've decided to
leave Max," she said at last.

"Yes, he told me," Mrs. Bennett replied calmly. "Poor Max! He's
feeling it so. Don't you think it's terrible to have someone's life so
much in your power? That's always frightened me, you know—
the way that love gives us powers of life and death over others."
She seemed to be rambling, the words coming irregular and slow,
while her gaze moved round the room and she made vague, waver-
ing gestures with the stick. Karen said:

"I suppose you disapprove."

The stick made another small flutter.

"Well, do you?"

"Oh, my dear," Mrs. Bennett mumbled, "duty and love are both such awful things. Such crimes are committed in the names of both of them. And when one has to choose between them . . ." She shrugged one shoulder, almost as if it were a nervous twitch. "When I think of the years I wasted . . ." Once again her voice trailed into nothingness.

"You will look after Nicko for me, won't you?"

"After whom?" Mrs. Bennett raised her head which had previously seemed to weigh downwards like a too heavy flower.

"After Nicko," Karen repeated.

"Of course, my dear, of course."

Suddenly, and apparently without reason, Karen burst into tears. She threw herself on the bed, regardless of the clothes she had laid out, and sobbed: "I know you think I'm wicked and hateful. I know you think I oughtn't to go. Well, why don't you say so? Say so, that's all. It's so hypocritical to pretend to be—to be so impartial, when all the time I know you think me an absolute bitch for leaving the children like this. But I've got a right to my own happiness, haven't I? Haven't I?"

"Of course you have," Mrs. Bennett said, sitting beside her and putting a hand on her shoulder. Suddenly she laughed: "You sound just like Chris."

Karen sat up on the bed, in a frenzy, and shouted: "Leave me, leave me, leave me!"

Strangely, as soon as her mother had gone, she again felt wholly calm. She washed, made up her face and went downstairs to eat a large meal.

After lunch, she returned to finish her packing, and discovered a strange thing. The cardboard box, with the name of the New York jeweller, to which she had returned the brooch she had worn the previous evening, now lay empty. She was sure she had put the brooch back; and at this moment, as she looked down at the bed of cotton-wool, she remembered how, as she had taken it off, she had thought, "I'll leave it for Pamela. I'd better leave all *her* jewellery for the child, that's only fair." She had been happy and full of generosity towards all the world. "But how ugly it is," she had thought. "Why on earth did I wear it? It wasn't even a particularly effective gesture. . . . And yet it brought me luck. It certainly brought me luck. . . ."

Karen went to the bell and rang for the maid.

The girl, obviously frightened, at first could do little but repeat over and over again, in a voice of increasing shrillness, that she had taken nothing. Becoming more coherent, she pointed out that for weeks past she had looked after Karen and though jewellery was habitually left lying about on the table, not even a pin had been touched. She flung her arms about and her peasant face became more and more red in its bell of jet hair.

The old man who cleaned the floors and who had watched Colin at work on his jig-saw puzzle was next called in. In contrast to the girl, he was wholly unperturbed. He shook his whiskery, fox-like head, as he clanked down his bucket and rested his broom in the corner, and then stood, with a vague smile deepening the dirt-engrained furrows of his face, while he waited for Karen to say something further.

"You know nothing about it?" she pursued in her halting Italian.

The old man went through the gestures of wiping his twig-like hands on his green-baize apron though, in fact, they were dry, and then cocked his head so far to one side that his ear almost touched his shoulder. "Well, I wouldn't say that," he mumbled at last.

"What do you mean?"

He was reluctant to say what he meant, and coughed and pulled at his nose instead of giving an answer.

"Well? Please tell me."

"I can't say I didn't notice something," he brought out at last. "Mind, I'm not saying more. But I noticed something, that I did."

"Noticed what?"

"Well . . ." He swung his head from side to side, while his tongue licked at his dry lips. "It was those lads," he said at last.

"*Ecco!*" said the servant-girl as if the brooch had already been found.

"Which lads do you mean?"

"The Italians, the ones that play with the Signorino. They were here this morning," he said.

"Were they?" Karen had not seen them.

"Always here," he said. "Almost every morning. They go in and out of the hotel, free and easy as they please. Well, the Signorino was out this morning, wasn't he?"

"Yes."

"Well, they didn't know that, see." His voice all at once became confidential in its whisper, and his eyes glinted out of the recesses of his brown, wrinkled face. He had liked Colin; and had always resented the boys and the gifts Colin had lavished on them. "Mind, I'm making no accusation," he said, raising one hand, with its thumb that grew horizontally into the palm. "I'm just saying what I saw, no more, no less. They were waiting, see, out there on the terrace, because they didn't know when the Signorino would come back. And they began playing ball together—one of them little balls, ping-pong balls. And there was I, doing the Signorino's room, so I could see them, out of the corner of one eye, I could. Well—now mind. I'm making no accusation—but that ball bounced in here, and the big chap, the big one"—he raised one trembling hand to indicate Enzo's height—"he came in here, into this very room, and he didn't come out *for more than a minute*." He coughed with satisfaction as soon as he had finished his tale.

"You saw him come in here?" Karen pursued.

"With me own eyes. I could swear to that—on the Bible, if need be. There he was, and he came in here, and when he came out the other said: 'Got it?' and he said 'Yes'. At once they upped and hopped it."

Karen's face all at once became dangerously hard. "We've had trouble from them before," she said. "It was a pen last time. We were fools to trust them. . . . But you can swear all this happened?"

"I can swear, Signora." He crossed himself piously and then said: "It wasn't for me to say it, but I thought all along, I said to meself, well, I said, there's going to be a packet of trouble there, likes as not, having them boys off the streets to play in the rooms of decent folk. It don't work, never does, to make a——"

Karen cut him short.

Hurriedly scribbling a note to Max, she decided that she had already wasted enough time on a matter that was really of no importance.

Chapter Thirty

So, for the second time that week, the Rocchigianis were visited by the police.

Ever since Bella's death, Giorgio had been in bed with a slight, but perpetual temperature which rose in the evenings and prolonged attacks of coughing after which he would lie back exhausted, the tears streaming down his cheeks. At a first glance he did not look ill. His colour was good and when, in the heat of the day, he flung aside his bedclothes, the body thus revealed seemed healthy and sturdy. Yet his fever persisted and he seemed to have lost all will to conquer, or even to resist it. Sometimes he would play his mandoline but after a few minutes of strumming he would put it aside and once again stare at the cracked, blotched ceiling or out of the open window.

His mother would come in and put a hand on his forehead, sighing as she did so. "You've eaten nothing."

"I don't feel hungry."

"But just a little of that broth."

"I don't feel hungry. Please, Mother."

"Well"—again she sighed—"I must get to work."

On the day the brooch was stolen, Enzo was seated on his brother's bed, though many minutes had passed since either of them had spoken. They had never discussed Bella, but her presence seemed always to stand between them, making communication more and more difficult. Enzo had come to hate his brother, and Giorgio felt what was almost a hate for Enzo, as we always tend to hate those who have witnessed our shame. Yet neither of the boys admitted to himself that this hate existed.

"Why don't you drink the soup?" Giorgio suggested. "It'll get cold."

"You must drink it."

"I couldn't. Go on—go ahead."

"But you must eat something."

Giorgio's weak face became suddenly obstinate. "I tell you, I

225

don't want to eat anything," he said petulantly. He raised a hand
and slapped it against the wall, and then brushed off the tangle
of wings and blood that had once been a mosquito. "Brute!" he
said.

Enzo, who had not eaten all that day, took up the bowl. "You're
sure?"

"For the hundredth time, I don't want it. I don't want it!"

"It's good." Enzo began to drink, raising the bowl with both
hands and tilting it at his lips. The lukewarm soup made him feel
instantaneously stronger and more amiable. "You've missed something," he said.

"Well, good God!" Signor Rocchigiani had opened the door and
stood looking in, his grease-stained, blue-and-white trousers hanging low on his hips and his open shirt revealing a singlet grey with
dirt. He shambled forward, scowling from under the grey tufts
of his eyebrows and breathing so heavily, after his climb upstairs,
that the whiskers which grew from his nostrils vibrated and a kind
of grunt sounded from the recesses of his throat. "So that's why
Giorgio eats nothing. You come up and wolf it all."

"I didn't want it, Father."

"That's not the point. You ought to be drinking it." With one
hand he tousled Giorgio's hair, an action which his son particularly disliked. "How are you going to get well if you won't eat?" he
asked. To his elder boy he was always benevolent; secretly he was
a little afraid of him. "Eh?" he said. "Eh?"

"I shall get well," Giorgio said wearily.

Signor Rocchigiani began to tug something from his trouser-
pocket and at last produced a banana. "*Ecco!*" he said. "I bought it
as a present for you. Not for *you*, young rascal," he said, still maintaining this new mood of benevolence as he pointed the banana,
like a pistol, at Enzo. "And I bought you this, too." Once again he
grubbed in the trouser-pocket and produced a silver identity disc,
inscribed with Giorgio's name and the address in the Borgo, and
a silver bracelet on which he began to string it. It was a present
which, whether from accident or design, was exactly suited to the
tastes of the boy, and Giorgio was delighted. "Give it to me," he
said, and having fastened it round his wrist, he turned it this way
and that, cocking his head at the same time, like a woman examin-

ing a ring. For the first time for many days he smiled without an intense, suffering languor.

"Pleased?"

"Very much."

"And look—I bought myself this." Signor Rocchigiani displayed his own hairy wrist on which was fastened a watch. "Like it?" he asked.

"But good God, Father, where did you get the money?"

"That's my secret."

"I hope this doesn't mean that you've——"

"Now look, my boy, have you ever known me do a dishonest thing? Now, have you? I ask you, have you?" When Giorgio and Enzo could not restrain their smiles, he exploded: "What are you both sniggering at? What's the joke?"

"Nothing, Father," Giorgio said, beginning to cough and continuing to do so for so long that it was like a machine gone out of control. "Nothing at all." Between gasps, he said: "But tell us— where did you get the money?"

"Mind your own business," Signor Rocchigiani answered with an intense self-satisfaction. "Curiosity killed the cat," he added, in his childish addiction to proverbs.

Ten minutes later the police had arrived.

There was a wisp of a middle-aged man, who had the perpetually suffering expression of a martyr to dyspepsia, and with him a youth whose over-large hands and feet, sullen peasant's face, and a habit of walking with his head thrust forward, as if in aggression, lent him a kind of brutal charm. Both were in plain clothes, the senior man in a shiny blue suit and black shoes, now grey from having remained so long unpolished; the junior in a cheap grey-and-white striped cotton, a peculiarly bright tie of contrasting lines of green and purple, an artificial silk shirt and slipper-shoes of the grey, punctured suède then most in fashion among the men of his class. It was these men who had also come to the house after Bella's death.

The older man spoke, while the youth prowled about the living-room, lethargically opening drawers and boxes and even raising the lid of the teapot. They had both been suspicious of Enzo when

called to the dead woman, and though the verdict at the coroner's
court had been death by misadventure, they still persisted in con-
necting the operation the girl had attempted to perform on herself
with the young boy. They now not unnaturally felt that their suspi-
cions had been justified.

"You remember us?" the sergeant said; and each word seemed
to be impregnated with sourness, as if it were something brought
up from his stomach.

"Yes, I remember you."

"You had an easy time, last week," the youth drawled, turning a cup over in his hands which were remarkable for the length
to which he had grown the nails of the little fingers. "You were
lucky," he said.

"The court never——"

"We've come about the brooch," the older man said.

"What brooch?"

"The Englishwoman's brooch." The sour vomit again bubbled
effortlessly upwards and emerged from between his lips. "Where's
your pal?"

"What pal?"

"Come off it. Rodolfo Benelli. You know who we mean. He's
not at his home."

"How should I know where he is?"

Outside the door five of the inhabitants were already listening,
among them Signor Rocchigiani, who, when he heard this defiant
question, exclaimed with disgust. That wasn't the way to speak to
a policeman, he knew from experience.

"We must search you," the little man said. He beckoned the
other forward.

"I've stolen nothing."

"All right. We must search you."

"But why the hell——?"

"We must search you." He perched on a corner of the table and
began to fan himself with a paper he had drawn from a pocket.

The young man began to run his clumsy hands over Enzo's
body, standing close to him and looking into his eyes with his own
lazy, mocking ones. He had not shaved that day and there were
heavy shadows under both jowls. At one point in his examination

he touched and then made an obscene reference to a part of the boy's body, and Enzo suddenly leapt away from him.

"Come here," the policeman said quietly, in his soft, indolent voice, and he raised one hand and pointed to a spot between his feet.

"Not on your life."

"Come here!"

"Not if you give me that sort of stuff."

The policeman sprang at the boy and the two scuffled together, blundering round the room until they knocked over a table on which stood a bowl of gold-fish. The sight of the fish, gaping and thrashing their tails on the stone floor, at once quietened Enzo. He stood staring at them, and appeared hardly to notice when the panting detective slipped some handcuffs on his wrists.

"May I put them back?" he said.

"No, leave them."

"But they'll die."

"Let him do it," the sergeant said from the table.

Clumsily, because of the handcuffs, Enzo picked up one after another of the slithering fish and put them back in the bowl; then he carried it over to the tap and filled it with water. "Lucky it didn't break," he said. "That mat must have saved it." He was quite calm now, and spoke in an ordinary, conversational voice. "Well, what do you want me to do?" he asked.

"You're coming to the station."

"Do I—do I have to walk through the streets with—with"—he extended his hands—"with these?"

The sergeant lowered himself from the table as carefully as if he had a time-bomb inside him.

"Now don't be silly," he said. "We look after you well. We've brought a car for you—just think of that. A car for you, for you alone."

"What about searching the house?" his junior demanded.

"The other two can do it."

"Those two bastards? They wouldn't notice a thing."

"The other two can do it," the sergeant snapped decisively, irritated, as always, by his assistant's vigour and health.

When they went out, the junior wrenched so violently at his

own end of the handcuffs to get Enzo to hurry that the boy slipped
and fell on to his knees, bruising them on the stone. As the boy
raised himself, he noticed, lodged along the wall, a few scattered
pieces of brightly coloured confetti among the grey dust. "There
was a wedding here," he told his two companions; and then he
wondered what interest such information could possibly have for
them. They went down between the small, silent crowd who now
lined the stairs, and out into a glare which made all three of them
pause and blink their eyes. Enzo tried to raise a hand, but of course
could not do so. He could feel a trickling sensation on the knee,
and wondered if it were a fly or blood from his fall.

At the station he was again questioned, by the same sergeant
and later by a white-haired man of an extreme, if exhausted, cour-
tesy who, as he spoke, dug holes in his blotter with a tooth-pick.
They asked him what had become of Rodolfo, putting the same
question over and over again to him in different forms, and each
time he answered that he did not know. "But surely," the white-
haired man urged in his smooth, tired voice, "you must know what
has become of your accomplice."

"He is not my accomplice. I have no accomplice."

The white-haired man shrugged his shoulders and dug the tooth-
pick deep into the blotter. "That remains for us to see," he said.

"I know nothing about it."

"That, too, remains for us to see."

At the door one policeman was glancing vacantly at the ceiling
while another rubbed an eye on whose lid was an incipient inflammation; then they both yawned simultaneously and smiled as they
looked at each other, their hands over their mouths. The room was
suffocatingly hot, and its worn leather chairs smelled as if they had
just come from a tannery. There was a large red stain, like a pool
of blood, where some ink had been spilled on the beige carpet.
Two flypapers dangled above the desk, thickly encrusted, but the
air remained loud with an incessant buzzing.

"You spoke to the English family about going to Tunis with
your friend, didn't you? . . . Well, didn't you?"

"Yes." Enzo, who had no handkerchief, wiped the sweat off his
forehead on the back of his hand and then wiped the hand on the
side of his trousers.

"And you once stole a fountain pen?"

"No . . . it was . . ." He hesitated from a desire not to betray Rodolfo, and at last mumbled: "Anyway we took it back."

The tooth-pick again dug deep into the stained blotting-paper and the white-haired man again gave his exhausted, courteous smile as he looked up. "That'll do for now," he said, like a dentist to his patient. "Since you won't help me more. But I wish you would be reasonable. . . . All right." The two policeman stiffened from their slouched positions, and marched briskly forward.

Enzo sat on the uncovered wooden slats of the bed in his cell and, hands clasped between his bruised knees, let his feelings of despair and indignation rise over him like a suffocating cloud. In his mind there had been established a connection between the loss of the brooch and his father's sudden wealth, though there was a mystery here which he could not yet fathom, search it how he would. His father had never met the American family and, as far as Enzo knew, he had never even entered the Palazzo d'Oro. Yet he had stolen the brooch; of that the boy was certain. But how, how? And then through the thick cloud of his present mood an awful suspicion crept. His father had somehow forced his mother to steal it. True, she did not usually take the laundry upstairs to the guests' rooms—that was done by the chamber-maids and valets. But he now remembered that she had once told him of how, when a woman had been in a hurry for an evening-dress, she had herself carried it up. Would his mother ever do such a thing? It was incredible. No, no, there must be some other explanation; perhaps, after all, his father had had nothing to do with the theft. And yet—she was so weak; she would do everything her husband told her; it had been like that ever since he could remember. . . .

"Cheer up, son."

The *carabiniere* on duty had looked up from his English Grammar, and was smiling at Enzo. He sat, neat and small and handsome, on a rusty iron folding-stool, with his legs crossed before him and his cap on a peg behind. He was a young man, and he had about him an air of scrupulous cleanness. His ears were delicate and pointed; his hair, smooth at the sides where he brushed it in two glossy wings, frothed into curls at the top, in the manner of an Edwardian beauty. His hands, too, were delicate and beautifully kept.

Enzo smiled back gloomily.

The *carabiniere* folded his newspaper and put it into the breast-pocket of the tunic which hung behind him as he asked: "What's the matter? What did they get you for?" His voice was soft and low, and his beautiful dark eyes, under the arched brows, seemed full of friendliness and sympathy.

"I didn't do it."

He laughed. "Well, of course you didn't. They all say that."

"I didn't."

"You're the one who was supposed to have taken the brooch?" he said with sudden recognition. "They were talking about the American woman—seems she's quite a beauty." He leant forward, and asked in his soft, pillowy voice: "How did you come to meet her?"

"Rodolfo—my friend—met her husband first. They asked us back. We met the kids. They were decent to us—until this."

"Oh, you met the husband first." The *carabiniere* showed his small white teeth as he smiled, and then put his tongue roguishly between them. "It was like that, was it?"

"It wasn't like that at all," Enzo said with sudden anger.

"All right, all right," the *carabiniere* conceded, laughing. He looked up and down the hunched, despairing figure of the boy, and then exclaimed: "Your knees! What have you done to them?"

"It's nothing."

"You'd better wash them."

"It's only a graze."

"Wait a moment." He got up from the stool and, having taken a tin mug, filled it at the sink which stood at the far end of the corridor. "Have you a handkerchief?"

"No."

"This one's quite clean." He pulled a handkerchief from his trouser-pocket and unlocking the iron grille which served as a door, went in to the boy. Enzo made as if to take the water, but the *carabiniere* said: "No, no, I'll do it. You remain where you are." He rolled back his sleeves, knelt on the floor and dipped the clean handkerchief in the water. When he stooped over, Enzo noticed how clean the back of his neck had been shaved, as if he had just been to the barber. The *carabiniere* began to wash the grazes, saying in a voice as soft as the movement of his hands: "Tell me if I hurt you. It must be done, mustn't it? You've taken off the skin."

"You are kind," Enzo murmured.

"We are not all brutes here," the *carabiniere* said, looking up and laughing in his eagerly youthful way. He began to dry the grazes on another part of the handkerchief and asked: "Do you know who pinned this on to you?"

"Who——?"

"Who took the brooch?"

Enzo replied abruptly: "I think so." His face slowly darkened.

"You know where it is, you mean?"

"Yes."

"Where?"

Enzo shrugged his shoulders; and the *carabiniere*, glancing for a moment, with a peculiar intentness, at the boy's averted face, said lightly: "There! That looks better."

"Thank you."

"You're welcome." He gathered up the tin and the handkerchief, and went out, leaving the cell door open behind him. "Well, I suppose I'd better lock you into your cage again. That's orders."

"When will they let me out?"

"Who knows?" The *carabiniere* extracted a cigarette from a packet which lay on the table, lit it, and having puffed two or three times asked: "Care for a smoke?"

"I could do with one."

The *carabiniere* took the cigarette out of his mouth and put it through the bars, and thus they continued to smoke it, turn by turn, until it was finished. "Care to see the paper?"

"Thanks."

"Montevardia lost—two goals to nil. Does football interest you?"

"I play myself—for Castellocino."

"You do? I thought you looked like an athlete when I first set eyes on you. Those muscles in your legs. . . ." He glanced down. "I bet you're strong."

Enzo blushed slowly, without contradicting him.

A few minutes later the *carabiniere* was relieved by a middle-aged man who grumbled, for some time, in a bass voice, about the meal he had just eaten, and then took off his tunic and cap, revealing a shirt sticky with perspiration, lowered himself on to the stool, and having rested his head against the white-washed wall and stuck out his legs, at once began to snore. Enzo stretched out on the wooden slats but they pressed too uncomfortably into his back and his thoughts were too troubled for him to fall asleep.

More than an hour later, a *carabiniere* clattered down the stairs and unlocked his cage. "You're wanted," he said, still chewing on the remains of something he had apparently just eaten.

"What for?"

"How should I know?"

"When are they going to give me some food?" His belly had begun to rumble and ache with hunger.

"I don't know, brother. You'd better ask when you see the sergeant."

It was the same room in which he had been interviewed by the white-haired man, and the same two sentries still slouched on either side of the door; but it was the sour, dyspeptic little sergeant and the peasant detective who were now waiting for him. The peasant was swinging a key-ring round and round on its chain, as he looked Enzo up and down with his small, lazily malicious eyes.

The sergeant said: "Well, what have you got to tell us?"

"I?" Enzo pointed at himself in astonishment.

"Yes, you."

"Nothing."

"Look, Rocchigiani, you're being a bloody fool. You're wasting our time. You know where that brooch is?" The last sentence was a statement, rather than a question; but at the end of it the sergeant cocked one of his thin eyebrows in interrogation and added: "Well?"

"No."

"Now look here, Rocchigiani, you know where the brooch is. Tell us."

"I don't know."

"You're wasting our time—and of course your own. I have a note here"—he glanced down at a pink slip of paper, the size of a visiting-card, which lay on the desk, and held it to the light from the window, as he read out—"from Police Constable Gardini. He says that you told him at thirteen-forty hours that you had certain knowledge of the whereabouts of the brooch." The boy had gone white and one nervous tremor after another was making his right knee, recently so carefully washed and tended, flutter against his left. "Did you or did you not say that?"

In a voice attenuated by despair Enzo answered: "Yes."

"You know the whereabouts of the brooch."

"I said I thought I knew. I meant that I could guess."

"Well, where is it?" The right knee continued to tremble as the boy rubbed the palm of his right hand down the seam of his shorts; but no answer came. "Well?" the peasant put in, the twirling bunch of keys making a rotating shadow on the white-washed wall behind him. "Are you dumb?" At some slight indication from the sergeant, he eased one buttock and then the other off the table and, still twisting the keys, slouched over to Enzo. "Tell us," he said; and then, suddenly raising a hand, he slapped the boy five or six times back and forth across the face. Tears came into Enzo's eyes, not from pain but as a reaction to the swift, stinging blows, but he made no effort to move away or to resist the detective; he was filled with a profound, lonely despair which made even this humiliation seem unimportant.

But he still had obstinacy and the honour which forbade him to mention his father's name, even though that illogical connection between Signor Rocchigiani's extravagance and the theft persisted, as strong as ever, in the boy's mind. They did much else, in a mild, half-hearted way to force him to speak, and he endured it in silence. Fortunately it was too hot, and his persecutors were too lazy, for any systematic brutality to be practised against him. In the end, his nose having been made to bleed, the peasant administered a brisk, parting kick and the boy was led back to his cell.

He huddled his bruised and aching body on the hard wooden slats and covered his blotched face with his hands, as nervous tremor after nervous tremor made his whole body shudder. As he lay there, he looked like someone who is crying, but his was a dry, tearless grief. Uninterested, the *carabiniere* continued to snore, his head tilted against the wall and his vast thighs stuck out.

Later, this *carabiniere* was relieved by the smooth, clean young man, Gardini.

Gardini strolled over to the iron grille and rattled a foot along:
"Hey, there," he said pleasantly.

Enzo remained huddled on the bed, his face to the wall.

"Hey, there! Rocchigiani!"

When there was still no answer, the young man fetched the key
of the cell, opened it and went in. He put a hand on the boy's
shoulder and said: "What's the matter? Did they give you a tough
time? I've brought you something to eat. Otherwise they don't
feed you till six. Look"—he pulled a package from his tunic—"it's
bread and *mortadella*. Come on," he coaxed. "Eat it. It'll do you
good, Rocchigiani!"

"Go away," the boy's voice came sullenly. He still remained like
a sick animal, crouching, with his knees drawn up and his face
under his arms.

"But—look, son—you must eat——"

Suddenly Enzo's whole body opened like a spring, and he leapt
to his feet. The *carabiniere* drew away, made a sudden dash for the
iron grille and slammed it behind him. There was a rattle, as with
agitated fingers he turned the key in the lock. "What's the matter?"
he asked, his face yellow under the glossy black wings of his hair.
"What's up?"

"You know perfectly well."

"I know?"

"You told them—what—what I'd told you," Enzo said bitterly, holding his blotched, swollen face close to the bars while he
gripped them with both fists.

"But look, I never——"

"They told me you had."

"I have to do my duty," the young man replied and as he spoke
his face turned rapidly from yellow to crimson.

"Oh, I see that!"

"They asked me if you'd said anything, and what could I do? It
wasn't that I wanted——"

"Shut up!" Enzo turned his back on him and returned to the
wooden bed. He heard the *carabiniere* say in a frightened, plead-
ing voice: "Anyway, eat what I've brought you," but though he
felt agonizingly hungry, he made no move to take what was being
proffered through the bars.

"I'm sorry," the *carabiniere* said. "I suppose it was a shit's thing to do."

Again there was no answer; and having taken off his tunic and hung it on a peg behind him, the *carabiniere* continued learning English from his grammar in apparent composure.

At half-past five the peasant detective clattered down the stairs with an uncharacteristic nimbleness and announced to Enzo, as if he were an old friend: "Good news, Rocchigiani! You can go home." The grille having been opened, he grabbed Enzo by the hand and shook it, saying: "No hard feelings. We have to do our duty."

Enzo looked at him in complete bewilderment.

"But come and eat first."

Colin had returned home.

Late that evening, Giorgio said to Enzo: "You'll never believe how Father got that money. I managed to drag the story out of him. You know, he does some pretty shabby things." He cleared his throat and spat into a small enamel bowl in which frothed a mixture of disinfectant, phlegm and streaks of blood. "The day after—after Bella's death, I remember hearing him and Ma Kohler argue, and I wondered what it was all about. Well, he was asking her for compensation. Can you beat it?"

"Compensation?"

Giorgio nodded his head as he again began coughing. "Yes, compensation," he said breathlessly. "The chair to be re-covered, the carpet to be cleaned. God knows where she found the money, but to-day she gave it to him. And of course the chair and the carpet will remain exactly as they are." Suddenly, in soft, plaintive reiteration, like a man in a delirium, he said: "Oh, Bella, poor Bella . . . poor Bella . . . poor Bella. . . ." He had closed his eyes and the long, fair lashes made deep fringes of shadow on his smooth cheeks. He put out a hand and suddenly gripped his brother's.

Chapter Thirty-one

THERE was a small, white-washed room at the end of the *villino* in which stood a plain deal table, a rush-bottomed chair and along the wall a number of dusty packing-cases which gaped splintered wood and rusty nails. There was a lamp on the table and Frank Ross was working there. He wrote slowly, and with few corrections, in a small, rounded handwriting, using Greek *e*'s and showing a complete disregard for the lines of the foolscap paper on which he was working.

Karen knocked at the door and, before he answered, came in, wearing slippers and a silk kimono over which she had tied an apron of coarse brown cotton, one of her acquisitions in the market. "It'll be ready in five minutes," she said.

"Oh, I can't come now," he replied without looking up.

"But you must. It'll spoil."

"Of course it won't spoil," he said, gazing fixedly at the blurred cone of the lamp.

"But you know, darling . . ." She came across to him, put a cheek against his and an arm round his shoulders, and then, kissing his ear, said: "You're such a cross-patch if the dinner isn't nice."

"Look . . ." He extricated himself from her and dipped his pen in the ink-well, preparatory to writing. "You run along and call me in half an hour. All right?"

"Well, don't blame me if the meal tastes awful."

He did not answer; and soon, to her irritation, she could hear his pen scratching on the paper as he continued with his work. She sighed and went out.

When she had served him, in the kitchen, with one of the slices of beef-steak she had fried over the charcoal burner, she stood and watched as he plunged in his fork and began to cut a section. "Well?" she said.

He masticated, the light from the lamp gleaming on his ceaselessly working jaws; then he swallowed, and gulped at some wine.

Wiping his mouth on his napkin, he said: "It's not the waiting that spoiled it."

"What do you mean?"

"There was nothing to spoil." He looked up at her and smiled; but his eyes were strangely cold, even hostile as he asked: "Where on earth did you buy such a hunk of meat?"

"At the butcher where I always go."

"And you paid——?"

"Four hundred lire. For the two pieces."

"Four hundred——! But, my dear Karen!" She had already discovered that meanness was one of the essentials of his character, and since she herself was naturally extravagant, she was often to be irritated by remarks of this kind. She knew, of course, that between them they had little money and must therefore economize; he was always telling her so. But for her to economize was to eat an expensive tea at Doney's and then, in a rush of conscience, to leave ten lire instead of fifty as a tip. Unfortunately Frank's economies were of a more logical nature.

"I can see that I'll have to do the household shopping," he said, chewing heavily. He put his hand to his mouth and drew out a long piece of sinew. "I bet this is horse . . . Well, aren't you going to eat yourself?" he asked. Karen had remained standing before him, the frying-pan in her hand, while on her face was the expression of love mingled with exasperation with which she now usually confronted his moods. "Come along, sit down!"

"Do you really think it's horse?" she asked, turning the pan from side to side and peering at the chunk of coarse-grained flesh. "Because if it is . . ." She shuddered slightly. "I just couldn't."

"Now don't be silly. Come and eat."

"But I couldn't."

"Very well, it's not horse."

"If you say it like that . . ." She flung the pan down on the kitchen-range.

"Now don't be silly," he repeated in a quietly ominous voice, laying his knife and fork down. "You can't waste it, and you must eat something. Bring it here and eat it. Bring it here."

She hesitated as if about to challenge his authority and then brought the pan over and speared the meat with her fork. They both ate in silence, she forcing herself to swallow lump after lump of the resilient, crimson flesh, though at each mouthful she felt she must retch. When she had consumed half the steak in this manner, he said softly: "Good girl. You can leave the rest if you like."

She wanted to reply "Thank you" with all the irony she could. But the words when they came out sounded ineptly docile. She even found herself closing her hand on his, as:

"How's the throat?" she asked.

"The——?"

"The throat. This morning you said your throat was sore. Remember?"

"Oh, I'd forgotten about it," he replied with the staccato abruptness he used when he did not wish to discuss anything. But she knew that he lied. She had watched him gulp his wine, and by now the way in which he did so had become so familiar to her that she could notice the smallest difference.

"That's good," she said. "I bought some gargle at the English chemist's, just in case. But you won't need it now."

"That was one way to waste more money," he retorted; and again her face assumed that expression of irritation which dare not express itself because of the restraints of love. "There's only one good gargle—salt and water. Salt's good for most things; we found that in the jungle." She had heard this eulogy of the medicinal value of salt many times before. "There's no point in buying expensive gargles when you can do the same job with a teaspoonful of salt in water. And why go to the English chemist?"

"You know my Italian——"

"But heavens above, you can speak the language—after a fashion."

"Yes, but they're always so helpful there—they're like old friends."

He smiled sardonically and shrugged his shoulders as if this last remark were too fatuous even to be worth an answer.

Then, as so often, he all at once changed. He checked her, as she rose to fetch the fruit, and carried it himself from the sideboard. "Peach?" he asked. "Or banana?"

"Peach."

"Shall I peel it for you?"

"Please."

She watched him as he took a small silver penknife which hung from his belt, opened it and began deftly to remove the skin between his brown fingers. The juice trickled down one arm and cascaded in a number of opaque pearls on to the marble-topped table. He cut the peach into slices and fed them to her one by one. Suddenly he seemed to be overflowing with tenderness and consideration, and when the peach was finished, she rose and sat in his lap, her head on his shoulder. "You find me a terrible slut," she said.

"Yes." But the words lacked any sting. He kissed the back of her neck, and said: "I don't suppose that you'll ever learn. And I don't really care. I like you as you are; with the kitchen dirty, and a hole in your stocking, and this awful dressing-gown thing which you will always wear." He pulled the kimono open. "I don't care," he repeated, as he slipped it from her shoulders. She sat staring at the lamp, impassive as a doll; but her whole being was waiting for him and she gave a small cry when at last his touch came.

Afterwards he told her that he was going to scrub and tidy the kitchen. "But I only did it two days ago," she protested.

He laughed. "Now you run along; and come back in an hour and you'll see how a kitchen should really look. All right?"

She pouted as she replied, "You make me feel so useless."

"Absolutely useless!"

"Let me help," she urged.

"God forbid! Have you forgotten when you helped to paper the room? No, you go and see to those letters you always complain you haven't the time to write. And try not to get ink on your fingers," he added, in the same jocular mood which nevertheless filled her with a vague resentment.

She did not write the letters; she wandered out into the overgrown garden, one corner of which Frank had already begun to tame, and made her way along a path flanked with straggling box hedges, to the wall above the river. It was a night without a moon, but the whole garden and the sky round it gave off a subtle radiance. The box hedge scratched at her kimono and her slippers, flapping at the heels, seemed to make an unnaturally loud clatter in all that silence. She stared down for a moment at the sunken rectangle of stones, like the foundations of some miniature house, which had caused her and Frank so often to wonder; he said that there had once been a greenhouse there and she, more imaginatively, a tomb. None of the villagers appeared to know anything about it.

After the heat of the day the stone balustrade over the river still felt warm. She perched on it, leaning forward as if she expected to have to jump off at a moment's notice, and looked back at the *villino* where she could see the lamp still burning on the kitchen dresser and Frank moving briskly about his tasks. She took a childish pleasure in seeing him thus when he could not see her. He had taken off his coat and rolled up his sleeves, and a lock of grey hair had fallen across his forehead. Suddenly she felt the impulse to go to him again and put her arms round him, but she knew he would be angry.

Beside the *villino* was the tall shell of what had once been the big house, destroyed in a bombardment. There were two walls, stretching as high as the highest trees, and a few heaps of rubble, buried in dock, nettles and bindweed; and sometimes, in the stillness of such nights, if one listened, one could hear a sudden plop and rustle as yet another fragment of stucco crumbled away. The peasants said the old house was haunted, because in the bombardment some Germans had been killed, and certainly now it was eerie, rising up like a blank wall notched with narrow spaces of black where the windows once had been, and housing stray cats, birds and some strange yellow-winged insects which had flown up into Karen's face, buzzing loudly, on the only occasion when she had dared to penetrate within. No, it frightened her; and she gave a little shudder as she twisted round from it to gaze at the river.

The Arno here curved wide and shallow, and in its crook were the marshes from which, throughout the day, there would ring the shots of those who came out from Florence on their bicycles and *vespa*'s with guns strapped on their backs. A bright yellow under the sun, the water now spread grey, with a few wisps of mist clinging to it and meeting the vertical black of the trees which fringed its distant edges. Some kind of river-fowl was calling through the greyness with an insistent, plangent note, and then over her head Karen heard a sudden flurry and creak of wings.

She looked back at the old house, with its blank, imperious façade, and all at once her mind returned to the Palazzo d'Oro. She had left without saying good-bye to any of the children, because she had feared the "scenes" which, all her life long, she had done everything to avoid. "Say good-bye to them for me," she told Mrs. Bennett and her mother had answered with the indifference which now seemed to govern all her actions: "As you wish." . . . Staring at the white ruin for which Frank was always elaborating plans—he would pull it down and use the bricks to build another *villino*, or he would train vines or some other creeper to cover it picturesquely—Karen felt a desolation strike at her heart. When she walked out of the hotel, she had so gladly divested herself of all that had belonged to that former life; but, from time to time at moments such as these, she would be visited by an intense, parched regret. It was of Mrs. Bennett and Nicko that she chiefly thought. There was nothing to prevent her seeing either of them whenever she wished it, but she had discovered that Frank nursed a secret jealousy of whatever belonged to her and could not belong to him, and he discouraged her, more by an attitude than any actual words, from too often going into Florence to see her son or her mother. Besides, after such visits she returned to the *villino* full of a vague, nagging restlessness and it would take many hours before she was once again lulled back into her former well-being.

"Did Nicko cry when you told him I'd gone away?" she had asked Mrs. Bennett at their first meeting.

"Well, what do you think?"

There was a silence, and then Karen asked: "And Max—how did he take it?"

"How angry you'd be if I told you he hadn't cared!"

"Oh, you're so unsympathetic, Mother. You usen't to be like this."

Mrs. Bennett had shrugged her shoulders, and then stooped over the cup of chocolate the waiter had brought her.

. . . Now, as once again there was that wild, plangent note of the bird calling out from the marshes held in the dark elbow of the river, Karen felt her eyes fill with tears. She was even thinking with tenderness of Max: of the small, daily decencies of their life together, of his consideration and his tolerance for all she did. It was absurd never to be satisfied. But I am satisfied, I am satisfied, she said over to herself in a passionate agony of spirit. I love Frank. I am happy with him. I want nothing more. And as if to reassure herself of these facts, she sought reassurance in the way she always sought it from him; from his mere physical presence. He was still there, moving back and forth across the small, square window, and his shadow moved behind him on the white-washed wall. She plunged down into abysses of fierce, aching longing. But she must wait; he would finish his job, and then, the kitchen scrubbed and tidy, he would come out to her or call to her to go in to him. She must wait.

Suddenly she turned in horror. Without a sound the whole high, blank face of the old, bomb-dilapidated shell of a house was slowly curling forward. It seemed to stretch itself, like a vast piece of rubber, and then, with a noise like the explosion of a high sea on shingle, it plunged downwards, as Karen covered her head with her arms. Stones scattered around and she could even feel them stinging her own body. Trees cracked and split and were wrenched from their bases; the old wall parted like a wooden fence, buckling inwards to let a cascade of masonry slither with a crashing recoil of water into the river. A cat, pinioned somewhere in the darkness, screeched like a child in pain, through the strange crescendo of noise made by birds racing across the river into the safety of the marshes. Then, when Karen looked again it was as if a ghost of the old house were slowly rising up to take its place. A wall of glimmering white dust slowly unrolled upwards from the ruin, until bursting through it, she saw Frank racing towards her. "Karen!" he was calling. "Karen, where are you? Are you all right? Where are you? Karen?"

She could say nothing; could not even move. When he found her and gripped her convulsively to him, pressing his lips on her face and saying over and over again, "Thank God . . . thank God . . ." she remained stiff and silent. "Oh, I was so afraid, so terribly afraid. It was hearing that cat—it sounded almost human."

Still she did not answer; and looking down at her rigid, strained body he said with a tenderness she had never before known: "My poor darling. I'm afraid it's been a terrible shock for you."

Suddenly she burst into a hysterical weeping. "That cat . . . find that cat!"

Chapter Thirty-two

PAMELA was stitching the nightdress she had long ago cut out, with Lena's assistance, for the music-mistress, Miss Preston. She sewed clumsily and the seam of white chiffon was grey where her hot hands had clutched it. Her hair kept falling across her face, making her brush it away at intervals with a gesture of impatience. "Oh, don't be so restless," she suddenly exclaimed to Colin, who was wandering about the lounge. "What's the matter with you?"

He had raised the lid of the piano which stood, untuned, in the corner of the room and was picking out "Auld Lang Syne", the tune which Enzo and Rodolfo had always been singing, with the fingers of one hand. "It's so lonely," he sighed. "There's nothing left to do."

"You miss them, don't you?" she said. He did not answer, and after a moment she looked up again from her work: "Colin?"

"I wish we could leave here," he burst out, slamming the lid of the piano.

"So do I."

"Everything seems to have gone wrong, and I'm mostly to blame. *She's* left, and Granny's unwell, and Daddy is miserable."

"Why did you do it, Colin?" his sister asked softly. It was the first time she had ever mentioned the theft of the brooch, and she was not surprised when he turned on her:

"Oh, mind your own business!"

"I remember when Rodolfo took Granny's pen and you said——"

"Shut up, shut up!"

"All right. Keep your hair on." She half-smiled to herself in satisfaction at not having lost her own temper. "You do get easily upset these days. . . . If you're so bored, why didn't you go with Maisie to Rome when she offered to take you?"

"Because she's a fool. And I can't stand her voice. And anyway, she didn't really want me. She offers these things and then she regrets them—and then she takes it out of one."

"I thought you liked her."

"Well, I don't!"

"Dear, dear," Pamela said in a maddeningly restrained voice, as she reached for some pins.

The children did not again talk until Signor Commino arrived, his portfolio in one hand and a pile of books, tied with string, dangling from the other. His collar was yellow, rumpled and soggy round his neck and there were beads of perspiration along each of his shaggy eyebrows. "Lena?" he asked, sinking into a chair and drawing out a handkerchief with which he proceeded to mop his face.

"I think she's still with Daddy," Pamela said, and added when Signor Commino pulled his watch from his pocket: "I know she's meant to finish at half-past but it's always nearer six. . . . Where are you taking all those books?"

"To a bookseller."

"Oh, are you going to sell them?"

"Yes," he said simply. "I am short of money—again." He slowly brought his two podgy hands together, as if he were playing a concertina, and emitted a long sigh as he added: "Money, money, always money."

"How are you going to marry Lena, if you haven't any money?" Pamela pursued ruthlessly.

"How indeed!" Then, all at once he looked cross: "You are extremely impolite. I suppose it is the American way of bearing. You must not ask such questions."

Pamela laughed; she could not help herself: "Why ever not? It's true, isn't it? You want to marry Lena."

With an exclamation of disgust Signor Commino gathered himself and went to the open window. Once there, he stood for many seconds, tapping his foot on the wainscot and clicking his fingers. Surprisingly, when he turned, his resentment had gone. "I have an invitation for you," he said. "For all of you. Saturday is for me an especial day, a day of much importance."

"Why?" Colin asked.

"Because on that day, forty-one years ago, Mino Ignatius Loyola Commino was given to the world! And next Saturday, in the Cloister of the Oriouli, they sing *Tosca*—you know *Tosca*?" He began to sing the famous love-duet from the first act in a thin falsetto, swinging from side to side, his hands clasped, until the children both had to burst into laughter and he joined in. *"Dunque*—we shall be a party—your daddy, your grandmother, Lena and you— and me! Is that good?"

"Colin is mad about opera," Pamela said, who hated it.

"Is ——?" Signor Commino did not know the expression.

"He loves it. Don't you, Colin?" Colin nodded.

"Ah, Lena!" Signor Commino greeted her, as she at that moment entered. "I have spoken to them about the opera, and they will come. Good afternoon, Mr. Westfield," he added, swinging round with both heels together, to greet Max, and then bowing and making small flustered movements with his hands. He repeated the invitation.

Max accepted; and at once Signor Commino again began to bow, murmuring over and over again, "Delighted . . . most honoured", until Max cut him short by exclaiming: "Oh, I feel done in!" He yawned, stretched and then slumped into a chair, covering his face with his hands.

Lena looked at him for a moment, her beautiful dark eyes expressing a mixture of sympathy and exasperation, before she said: "Pamela, you must make your father work less. It is not good for him."

"It's nothing to do with me." Pamela was secretly jealous of the devotion she guessed that Lena felt for Max. "Why don't you try to persuade him?"

Lena coloured as she said: "Because that is not within my province."

"You buy his socks," Pamela said, half as a joke and half in resentment.

"Because her taste is excellent," Max said. "I have yet to meet a woman who can buy socks as Lena can."

"Oh, nonsense, Mr. Westfield!" Lena's eyes darted in embarrassment about the room, as she fingered the belt of her dress. "I am always willing to help," she added. "But seriously, Mr. Westfield— you must not drive yourself so hard. It is not good for you. No, seriously."

Max laughed; and Signor Commino glanced at his watch and

then put in, as if expecting a rebuff: "Lena, if we are to be at the station in time we must go now."

"Oh, I don't know that I want to go to the station," Lena said, who only knew that she wanted to stay with Max.

"Are you going away for the week-end?" Colin asked.

"Good heavens, no. Your father wants me to-morrow morning. We still have a lot to do, haven't we, Mr. Westfield? No peace for the wicked. . . ." She brought out this last phrase a little dubiously; she had only just learned it. She went on: "No, it is those two Americans and the English lad. They are leaving and Mino said that we would go and see them off." She smiled as she added, in a manner which she knew would wound Mino: "He said it, without even asking me. And now I suppose I shall have to go. . . . Oh, I can't!" She flopped into the chair beside Max's and, all unconsciously, imitated his exact gesture as she put her hands over her face, in a pretence of being tired: "You must go without me, Mino."

"But, Lena——"

"No, I can't, I can't. They bore me so. And I do not even like them."

"Where are they going?" Colin asked.

"They say they are going to Paris. They think they will like Paris better than Florence. But they won't. They will go to America. . . . Quick, Mino, or you will miss them." She laughed: "And give them my love, and my apologies, and *buon viaggio.*"

"If you do not go, then I do not——" Mino began.

But: "Yes, yes," she urged him. "They are your friends. You must go. Of course you must go."

"When shall I see you? Shall I come back here?"

"Oh, I expect I shall be gone by then."

"Then to the house?"

"Yes—no. I don't know where I shall be. I may be there. I don't know. I feel too tired at present to make up my mind."

Mino shrugged his shoulders hopelessly, and picking up the books in one hand and the portfolio in the other, lumbered towards the door. Suddenly he dropped the books, and slapped his forehead with his hand: "I have forgotten, I have forgotten! My mother keeps remembering me. Children, have you still the music-box?"

Colin and Pamela exchanged glances, and Pamela at last said: "Oh, Signor Commino, we've been meaning to tell you. The spring went and broke. It wasn't our fault, it wasn't anyone's fault." She hurried on, the colour deepening in her cheeks. "One of the boys—the Italian boys—was winding it up and it just made a funny click, and that was that."

"But we're going to have it mended," Colin put in, stricken by the look of dismay on Signor Commino's face. "We took it to all sort of shops in Florence, but none of them could do it. So now Maisie says she'll take it with her to Switzerland when she goes next week. It was made there, and she's certain they can mend it."

"It belongs to my mother," the Italian said pitifully.

"Yes, we're awfully sorry."

"Of course it was very old. But it worked for so many years."

"It wasn't the children's fault," Lena said sharply. "They're doing all they can."

"Yes, I know, I know. But I cannot help feeling sad."

"These things happen," Lena said.

"Yes, that is true. These things happen. They are always happening."

It was absurd, the children thought; as he hurried from the room, his eyes were full of tears.

"He *is* odd," Pamela said. "So sentimental."

"But I like him," Colin put in. "Before I thought him awful. Now—I don't know——"

"Oh, don't let's talk about him!" Lena exclaimed. "He gets so on my nerves. And he should be ashamed to go about like that—like a scarecrow. And that terrible portfolio—and all that scurf on his coat——!"

Both children were shocked by this outburst, and Pamela said: "Don't you feel in the least bit sorry for him?"

"No!" Lena was emphatic. "Why on earth should I?"

"Because—oh, it doesn't matter. You'll only say I'm being impertinent."

Lena hardly heard this last remark, she was so intent on watching Max, as he lay, eyes closed and hands over his stomach, in the arm-chair into which he had at first slumped. He had told her that he was not sleeping well, and she noticed, with a deep, thrilling pang of sympathy, how now that he was relaxed, all the lines of his face sagged downwards. Perhaps it was only the way in which he was hunched, but his clothes seemed far too loose for him and there were bruise-like patches under each of his eyes. Poor Max! She watched him as a mother watches a sick child; and yet she was, unconsciously, a little glad of that sickness because it made the child depend on her.

Suddenly Max opened his eyes and said: "Oh, I must have some fresh air. It's days since I took any exercise."

Lena waited; she almost said, "Let's go for a walk," but she left it too late. Max was looking at Colin: "How about a walk, Colin?"

"Yes—if you like."

Max, in the abnormal sensitivity from which he always suffered in his relationship with his son, said: "Oh, not if you don't really want a walk."

"Yes, I should like a walk."

"Good."

"And Lena can help me with this hem-stitching," Pamela said, not without a certain artful malice. "Would you, Lena?"

"Well, of course, dear." Lena smiled at Pamela and she smiled at Max, and then she smiled at Colin; but there was an intense exasperation on her face when she picked up the work.

Colin and Max said little to each other in the tram which they took to Settignano; from there they were going to walk by the hill road to Fiesole. "You buy the tickets," Max said. "Your Italian is already much better than mine." He added with mock ruefulness: "You see, you're already far too clever for me."

Colin remembered the remark; he felt it was almost a reproach, though his father had said it in joke, and when having descended from the tram, they began to trudge, in silence, up the dusty road, the boy suddenly said: "Do you think I'm conceited?"

Max laughed: "No, of course not. And even if you were, you'd have good reason to be."

"I feel—oh, I can't say it!"

Max's whole being shrivelled, but he forced himself to pursue: "No, please say it." Since he was sure his son was going to attack him, it was with a pleasurable relief that he at last heard:

"Oh, it's just—sometimes I think that you think that I—I despise you. And I don't! It just isn't true. I—I only despise myself." Max did not answer and they continued to trudge upward, passing cars choking them with a dust that had a vague taste of sulphur, until Colin gathered himself and said: "You do think that, don't you?"

"No, of course not." And then feeling that his son's courage had earned a like courage from himself, Max said: "But sometimes I feel sad that we care about such very different things. I know that it can't be helped. Music and books and pictures—I know that to you those things already matter much more than they have ever done to me. And so perhaps"—again there was that taste of sulphurous dryness in the mouth as another car passed—"perhaps, in a sense, you have outgrown anything I can do for you."

"But it's not true—it just isn't true!" Colin halted, and turning to his father a face blotched with perspiration and dust, protested: "I've never felt like that." Then he looked away at the falling land-scape, shimmering in the heat-haze of the late afternoon; to gaze for long at it made the nerves of the eyes ache: "There are so many things at which I am useless—which even Pamela can do better than I can do." He smiled: "Mending fuses, and throwing cricket-balls, and riding bicycles—oh, hundreds and hundreds of things. I'm such an awful coward," he added in a low voice. "You know that, don't you? And I've thought that perhaps you must hate me for it."

"Of course you're not a coward—and of course I don't hate you!" What had before seemed difficult now seemed easy, and Max slipped an arm through his son's arm, as he laughed:

"Imagine Lena recommending this walk! She must have been crazy. All this traffic, and the sun beating down on our heads. . . . Perhaps it's different in the spring and autumn. . . . Let's find some-where cool."

They turned off the road and having followed a path up a hill-side until their shoes became white with dust, they at last threw themselves down in the shade, and stretched to full length. Their heads throbbed, and they felt their hearts beating with an unnatu-ral loudness against the baked soil. The air was loud with cicadas.

Colin covered his face with his arm, because a spear of sunlight had pierced the overhanging leaves, and asked: "When do we leave Florence?"

"I don't know." Max sat up and twisted a dead branch, with a single shrivelled leaf clinging to it, between two fingers. "Do you want to leave?"

"Yes, I think so."

"I thought you and Pamela were both so anxious to stay."

"We were—before. Not now."

There was a pause, and then, the dead branch still twisting in and out of the sunlight: "I'm sorry about that business with the Italian boys."

"It was all my fault. I don't blame Enzo for feeling he never wants to see us again."

"I wrote to him," Max said quietly.

"You wrote to him?" Colin was astonished; he at once sat up.

"Yes. I don't know if I did right. But when you wrote twice and he still didn't come—and I knew you wanted to see him . . . I thought it might help if a letter of apology came from me. But"—Max suddenly snapped the twig between his fingers—"I'm afraid it didn't work. . . . You don't mind my having written, do you?"

"Well, of course not. It was jolly decent of you."

"Because I guessed that you were unhappy about it. . . . Tell me, Colin"—Max screwed up his eyes as he gazed down at the shimmering white of the road—"why did you take the brooch?"

"You've never asked me that before," Colin said with a sudden tightening of his whole body. He rolled over on his stomach.

"No. Mummy said you wouldn't tell her and so I thought there was no point in my asking."

"Then why—now——?" Colin queried; and then added with a laugh, in case Max should think this was a snub: "I don't mind trying to explain, only I don't know that I can. I don't know that I understand it myself." Briefly, and with difficulty, he told the story of how he had overheard Karen and Frank through the communicating door, and as he did so his face unconsciously assumed an expression of disgust and hatred. "I couldn't bear to hear her speak like that about—about *her* brooch. Well, after all, it was she who stole it in the first place; it was always meant for Pamela—wasn't it?" Max had given the brooch to Karen but he now made no attempt to refute the injustice of his son's accusation. He merely nodded his head as Colin continued: "I didn't decide to steal it, it was just an impulse, it just happened. I saw her door open and there it was, and I went in and put it in my pocket. I don't know what I meant to do with it at that time. . . . But then, driving in the car with Maisie, I suddenly thought of how Enzo and Rodolfo had said that if only they had fifty pounds or so, they would be able to go to Tunis, and I—I decided to sell it. And so at Prato I went to that little shop, and as you know, he would only give me that fifteen thousand lire. He said it wasn't worth more, and he wanted to know where I'd got it; so I had to make up some story about selling it for my mother, which I knew he didn't believe." Colin sucked a blade of grass, his face curiously still after this confession, and then went on: "Driving home I wasn't at all frightened or ashamed. Oh, but I was mad to think she wouldn't notice. By then, you see, I'd persuaded myself that I'd originally stolen the brooch in order to help Enzo—and Rodolfo," he added as an afterthought. "I liked to think that; it seemed somehow brave and noble to have committed something wrong because one wanted to help someone whom one—loved." He pondered, his brows drawn together: "Perhaps, really, that is why I stole the brooch, and then perhaps—oh, I don't know!"

"Thank you for telling me," Max said quietly. "Of course, at the time, I couldn't have cared less," he went on, once again screwing up his small green eyes under their red-tufted eyebrows as he focused them on the road. "It seemed terribly unimportant that you should have—have done something like that, when—when so much else was happening. But of course it was just as important, in its own way."

Colin braced himself: "Are—are we staying on in Florence, because you hope—that perhaps——?"

"Yes."

"That's what Pamela and I both thought." Again he braced himself: "You want her back very much, don't you?"

"Yes."

"Do you think there's any—any chance?"

Suddenly Max turned over on his stomach and put his head in his arms; he lay very still.

He was thinking of a visit he and Karen had paid to Blenheim four days after Karen had heard the news of her lover's death. They had driven in silence, out from Oxford through the close, winter lanes, and when they had arrived it was to find the sun already sinking. Momentarily the palace caught its rays and brimmed with fire, so that it seemed as if, even while they watched, the flames would burst through, the roof would collapse, and the whole vast edifice would disrupt, tumble, subside in a million particles of light. But in a few seconds all was over. The sun descended into mist; the fire ebbed; everything became bare, moist and cold.

All that day it had been thawing and now, as they began to tramp through the solitary park, the slush wet their feet and the trees wet their clothes. Noises of invisible dripping were all round them. Far off, they could hear a roar of water descending into "Capability" Brown's artificial lake. Yet, for all the melancholy and dampness, the place had its beauty; the lake, stretching on into the mist, the faint, barely perceptible outlines of the trees and, beyond, the fantastically uncertain silhouette of the Palace—all these things by their fugitive and unemphatic presence combined to make a profound impression on his mind. Now his grief and resentment over Karen seemed to have taken on an external form, and viewing it thus, he felt somehow comforted and assuaged.

All at once Karen's foot touched ice; she slipped, lost her balance, and was only saved by the hand he put out to help her. How it happened then he did not know. "Take care!" he cried out; and a moment later they stood clutching each other through long, aching seconds, tensed, waiting, as if a bomb were about to explode; terror, not joy, seemed to hold them there. Karen's face was pressed against his coat; ceaselessly the trees dripped water down on to their rigid bodies.

Then as it were nerve by nerve that wild, unreasoning panic left them. She was pushing him away from her: "No, no! I can't! I can't!" She was sobbing and a wet strand of hair clung to her cheek. Through the years of separation he had waited for this embrace, and its difference from what he had imagined left him stunned and appalled.

They walked on; and as they walked, he seemed to descend, step by step, into a profound darkness beyond all hope of escape or rescue. This was the woman, he knew now, for whom he would sacrifice himself, not once, but a thousand times over; and the bitterest irony was that that sacrifice would never have the smallest value in her eyes. And yet—desperately he sought for some light through the black gloom in which he found himself—was not love like charity, supreme when it was expended without either possibility or expectation of return? Was not that the largest triumph? And under the dripping trees he again and again pressed that icy comfort to him.

As now, once more, with the cicadas loud in his ears, his being reached to enfold it. In the long, unsleeping anguish of nights without Karen; in the persistent desolation of days spent in attempting to concentrate on things which seemed all at once to have lost meaning; in those sudden, yet more terrible, moments of night or day when he seemed to topple, to fall, as from some abruptly subsiding cliff, down and down through limitless gulfs of pain and humiliation: always he sought that same illusory refuge.

As now he did. But no, no, no. He flung round on his back, an arm over his eyes, and put the comfort from him.

He heard his son's voice say "Daddy?"

There was no answer; and after having extended a hand which he at once withdrew, Colin sat and waited in silence for the end of this grief.

Chapter Thirty-three

"It's not very good," Frank Ross said. Seated in nothing but a pair of shorts, he was painting the river.

The flesh of Karen's bare arms and legs seemed strangely white against his brown as she leant over his shoulder and said:

"I like it."

He had never had any use for the admiration of those he had enslaved and he now said: "Yes, but it's not very good."

"Meaning that I know nothing about painting?"

"Meaning precisely that."

She laughed, but once again he had wounded her. "You are funny with your crazes," she said.

"My crazes?" he asked coldly.

"The way you take up things for a few months and drop them.

Or even for a few days, or a few hours. When we first came here, you would do nothing but potter about the garden. And now all the weeds are up again."

"You know I haven't been feeling any too well these last days."

"Yes, I know, darling," she conciliated. But she could not resist once again playing on this sensitive place she had discovered for herself. "You said it was the same with the piano—do you remember?"

He thought for a moment, turning the canvas this way and that in his strong, competent hands and then said: "Yes, I suppose it is true. I'm only interested in mastering things—and once I have the mastery, I don't want to use it any longer. It cloys the palate." He looked at her so closely with his sharp, glinting eyes in his burned-up face, that she felt herself redden, she could not have said why. "It took me six months to be able to play averagely difficult music at sight. That was enough."

"And when you can paint averagely competent pictures, that will be enough too."

"Perhaps." He yawned and stretched, wriggling his bare toes, and again concentrated on the picture. After a while he said: "It was your mother who gave me the idea. Do you remember—that wonderful sketch of the two sleeping boys? If I could do something like that, I'd never want to draw or paint again."

"Why wouldn't you accept it, when she said you could have it?"

He shrugged his bare shoulders. "Oh, one has one's pride," he said. "Did she mind my not taking it?" he continued.

"No. She has no pride."

He was tenderly pressing the finger-tips of one hand against the sides of his throat, and she said: "It's hurting you."

"No."

"I know it is. What's the use of pretending? Let me paint it for you again."

"Oh, don't fuss so!" he exclaimed irritably.

"But I'm worried. Why won't you see the doctor? It's not fair to me. I know that you're ill."

"I've been iller than this. In the jungle. Where there aren't any doctors even if you're willing to see them. I shan't die."

"I wish you wouldn't talk like that. If only there was something I could do for you."

His teeth glittered in his burned-out face as he smiled and said: "There is something. Cook me something which I can swallow with ease this evening." He was referring to a disastrous soup of the night before in which most of the diced vegetables had proved to be as hard as pebbles. "Will you do that?"

"I think it's beastly of you to go on about the soup."

"I never mentioned the soup," he said with feigned surprise.

"But that's what you meant."

She went angrily into the house and threw herself on to the bed with a book he had lent her: Doughty's *Arabia Deserta*. She could not read it, and after a few minutes she went to the window where she leaned on the sill and watched him at his work. The heat was intense, and her whole being seemed about to faint from the mingled remembrance and expectation of his body.

That night she again applied the Mandl's paint she had bought at the English chemist's. She was nervous as she did so, and she did not wish to look closely at the slough, like yellow cotton-wool, on either side of his swollen throat. A number of small ulcers had begun to make his mouth painful. Her hand shook and he exclaimed: "You'll make it so much sorer if you're not careful. Besides making me retch. It really can't be all that difficult to get the brush in the right place."

"I'm sorry," she said in exasperation.

"And then you at once fly off the handle."

"I'm sorry, I can't help it. I'm so worried about you."

"Oh, for heaven's sake——!"

"I'm sure you have a temperature." She put a hand on his forehead: "Yes, I know you have."

"Well, you're not going to take it. That's one thing I won't allow. I don't believe in it, never have." His cheeks were flushed, his eyes glittered with obvious fever. "It's probably my old malaria. I can never quite shake it off. Perhaps I'd better stay in bed to-morrow. I think I'll go on a fruit diet, that always works. Yes, that's a good idea. Just fruit, fruit-juice, nothing else."

"Can't I get the doctor?" Karen again pleaded.

"No! I will not see a doctor."

"If it's the money——"

"The money!"

She said no more.

Waking in the middle of the night, she found that in spite of the August heat which was making her sweat, his body was being shaken by convulsive tremor after tremor. She put out an arm and attempted to draw him towards her, as if contact with her own health could somehow destroy his illness. But, whether in sleep or not, he at once pulled away. Soon she could hear his teeth grinding together. It was a sound which filled her with an inexplicable terror and yet she dared not wake him. She sat up on her elbow and peered at his face, working so noisily in the summer moonlight, and then she attempted to go to sleep and pay no attention. But she could not do so. At the last she had to get up and go and sleep on the sofa in the drawing-room. She crept back into the bed in the early morning so that he should not notice.

There was no doubt, when he woke, that he was really ill. He could only swallow with difficulty and rather than force his saliva, with agonizing effort, back down his throat he preferred to spit into the basin which she had given him. She felt physically nauseated when, as she ate her own breakfast in the kitchen, she could hear his repeated attempts to clear his throat, followed by the sounds of expectoration. Again she pleaded that she must get a doctor, and again, this time with a kind of weary but terrible anger, he told her to mind her own business. She painted his throat and saw that it was almost closed. She was tearful with frustrated anxiety and kept repeating, though she knew it annoyed him: "You poor darling . . . you poor thing . . ."

"Oh, shut up!" he shouted at her in the end. "Who's ill? You or I? . . . Fetch me my sketching-block."

"Do you think you really ought——?"

"Oh, very well." He swung his legs out of the bed and she at once went and fetched it.

She had arranged to meet Mrs. Bennett in Florence that day, but she told Frank that she could, of course, put her off. But she had looked forward to the encounter, as she had never done previously, feeling for the first time in her life the need to confide in, and lean on, her mother.

"You must go," Frank said, when she told him that she was going to telephone to the hotel.

"But how can I? I can't possibly leave you——"

"Don't be silly," he croaked. His voice had almost gone. "The woman comes to clean to-day, doesn't she?" Exasperated by Karen's failure to keep the house tidy, he had recently engaged a peasant woman to come in twice a week. "She can fetch me anything I need."

"But she's dirty! And she never hears what one says. You can call and call and she won't come to you. No, really, Frank——"

"You're going into Florence," he said. "Now please don't argue. My throat is too sore. . . . Perhaps you'd just tidy the bed first, though?" Once again her nervousness made her clumsy, and as she pulled one of the pillows from under him she accidentally pulled the other too, thus making his head jolt downwards. He said nothing, but she saw his face tighten with pain and displeasure.

Florence was suffocating, and she dragged listlessly from shop to shop paying more for things than she knew Frank would allow. When at last she met Mrs. Bennett at Doney's, she had made a number of useless purchases and had at the same time failed to buy at least a quarter of the items on her list. She had feared that her mother, in the strange mood of fatalistic indifference in which she now seemed to exist, would show little sympathy; but in that she had been wrong. True, Mrs. Bennett had no practical suggestions, beyond gargling with peroxide, and she did little more than listen as Karen unburdened herself of her misery. But her ancient eyes seemed to express an immeasurable pity and even love for the daughter whom, she had so often confessed in the past, she had never understood. She held the girl's hand in her own and said: "Poor Karen, my poor Karen . . ."; and the words themselves, spoken in a husky voice which seemed only a shadow of the decisive voice of the past, somehow had the power to heal and to allay fear.

"It's been so wonderful, seeing you, Mother," Karen said. "I feel so much better."

In the rush of her anxiety and grief she had failed to notice that Mrs. Bennett was herself looking extremely ill.

"Well, how's the patient?" Karen asked on her return. She

put a hand on his forehead, to which a few strands of hair had stuck, and then said: "You're wringing wet. You'd better change those pyjamas." Then, as she stooped above him she could hear a strange, guttural rattle in his throat. "Do you feel bad?" she asked.

"Oh, don't go on asking such silly questions! Fetch the pyjamas."

When she returned, she noticed that an earthenware bowl was standing on the bedside table, with a black sediment at its bottom; she tilted it to the light as he explained: "It was some concoction of Anna's—herbs and mulled wine."

"Wine—with a temperature!"

"It made me feel much better. Why not? These peasant women know far more about nursing than we do."

"Nonsense! You'll have her bringing in a witch next."

He smiled weakly. "She made me wear this." And as Karen helped him off with his pyjama jacket she saw that he was wearing an amulet round his neck: what looked like a worn penny, with a lamb on one side and a hand raised in a blessing on the other.

"It's absurd!" she exclaimed. She dried his body with a towel, reiterating, "It's absurd . . . such superstition . . ." and then clumsily pulled the pyjama-trousers over his loins. "You'd better gargle now and then I'll paint your throat."

"Oh, she can do that," he said, sinking back on to the pillow, his hands crossed over his stomach.

"Who can?" Karen asked sharply.

"Anna."

"Anna!"

"She did it when you were out."

"But the woman's filthy. And she can never have painted a throat in her life."

"Well, she did it as if it were the commonest thing in the world." He closed his eyes, and gathering all the husky remnants of his voice, commanded: "Please send her."

"But an ignorant woman like that——! You must be crazy. No, really, darling, why can't I do it?"

Without opening his eyes again he said: "Because you don't do it nearly so well. And because you know you hate doing it. You do, don't you?"

"Well, there's gratitude for you!" She went out, slamming the door, and then crossed the narrow, white-washed passage to the kitchen: "Oh, Anna," she said. "The Signore wants you."

The peasant woman was about thirty, the unmarried mother of two children, one of whom had had a German father and the other an English: she looked much older and there were already streaks of grey in the black, greasily dull hair which straggled to a bun at the nape of the neck. In the house she worked barefoot, with a rag tied over her ears. When she talked it was her habit to run the palms of her hands over her massive breasts and down her thighs, as if she were attempting to mould her far from shapely figure. Karen instinctively distrusted her; and now, absurdly, she had begun to feel jealous. "What was that drink you gave him?" she asked. She had heard that in country districts the peasant women were always administering love-potions of catamenal blood, and she suspected that, like most women, Anna found her exuberant temperament responding to Frank.

"For fever," the woman said simply. "It cured my youngest *bambino* when he had the same kind of malady."

"Have you scrubbed the bath as I told you?"

"Not yet."

"Not yet! But it's past seven o'clock."

"I can stay later," the woman said calmly. "I was busy with the Signore."

"Well, go to him now, please. He wants you to paint his throat."

After Anna had been away for over five minutes, Karen was about to go after her when the peasant woman returned, carrying some cotton-wool, which Karen knew she had taken from her own table, a handkerchief torn into strips, and a silk scarf of Frank's. "What are you doing with those?" Karen demanded.

The woman began to fill a kettle as she said: "I thought I'd give him a fomentation—get some of that muck away. No wonder the poor thing can hardly breathe." She turned her back on Karen and began to rake the charcoal burner.

"Did he say he wanted a fomentation?"

"Yes," the woman replied, continuing with her job.

"Now what are you doing?" Karen asked, as a few minutes later the woman unwrapped some newspaper and began to pick at the green leaves thus revealed. "What are those?"

The woman mentioned the names of some herbs of which
Karen had never heard and then went to the cupboard and took
down a bottle of vinegar with which she proceeded to scatter the
leaves after she had put them in a saucepan.

"Does he know about all this?" Karen stood with her hands
deep in the pockets of her suit. She felt an intense, helpless frustration; she hated the woman—her calmness and competence and
the dirty, vivid charm of the body which seemed about to burst
through the rags in which it had been clothed. The woman was
exploring one ear with her forefinger while she waited for the
kettle to boil, and she now said:

"Don't take on so, ducky. It's the best thing. He'll be as right as
rain to-morrow."

"Please don't call me 'ducky'."

The woman shrugged her shoulders, and smiled as she peered
down at the forefinger she had now removed from her ear.

"You're extremely insolent," Karen said.

The woman said nothing; and in the end the English girl went
out on to the terrace where she sat slumped in a deckchair, glaring
angrily at the river.

The next afternoon Frank, who was no better in spite of Anna's
ministrations, banged on the wall between his room and the kitchen
as a signal that he wished to speak to Karen. His voice was almost
inaudible, and the rattle of mucus in his throat oppressed her as if it
were in her own. "Look," he whispered. "I've been thinking. You'd
better sleep in the room upstairs to-night. Have Anna make up the
bed."

"Upstairs!"

"Now don't argue. Please. I know you hardly slept at all last
night—I'm so restless when I'm like this. And besides I like having
the bed to myself when I'm ill. That's not unreasonable."

"Well, let me sleep in here on two chairs."

"No."

"But why on earth not? Suppose you want something during
the night? I might never hear from up there. While if I sleep in a
chair——"

"That's all right. I've seen about that."

"Seen about——?"

"I've asked Anna to stay the night. She says she'll sleep in the kitchen, and I can bang if I want anything."

"But there's no need," Karen burst out; and then in a quieter voice she asked: "Can't I sleep in the kitchen?"

"No, you're tired out."

"But don't you see that I might want to—that"—her voice broke—"that I should regard it as my right to nurse you myself. I want to nurse you!"

"That's very sweet of you." But he destroyed the appeasing words by suddenly twitching his mouth. "I'm touched," he said.

"Oh, no, you're not! Because you're hard—you're utterly hard—and ruthless—and selfish! It matters not a damn to you that I—I—— Oh, what's the bloody use?"

Again his mouth twitched, the strange vertical lines on either side of it deepening in the haggard face. "Nursing is a matter of skill, not of sentiment," he whispered.

"Skill—sentiment! You mean that Anna has the skill, while I have nothing but——"

He raised a hand to quieten her. "It's better to be nursed by someone impersonal. You're all strung up—look at you now." He indicated her trembling figure and pinched, white face. "Besides, she's had so much practice. She's nursed her children and her father, and after the Armistice she nursed the wounded German who was hiding with her. She was telling me about that. You must get her to tell you the story, too—I think it might amuse you."

"Impersonal," Karen said bitterly, sinking down on a chair and drawing her hands down her dress. "So Anna is impersonal—that sly, lousy trollop."

"My dear Karen!" he laughed.

"She's in love with you."

"Oh, don't be so silly."

"Well, of course she is. Anyone can see that. Why else should she offer to sleep in the kitchen? Just to keep an eye on you? She has her own family, hasn't she? Her two little bastards who presumably need her care? Oh, I've watched her looking at you when she didn't know I was watching. There's only one thing in life that interests her, that's quite obvious. And how you love it—to be worshipped and flattered and have her cringe before you! Of course, you love it!"

He had shut his eyes at the beginning of this speech and he kept them shut until she had finished. Then he said quietly: "Tell her about the bed, will you? Don't forget." He again closed his eyes.

Karen stared at him for many seconds, biting her lower lip in rage and picking with a forefinger at the skin around her thumb until it began to bleed; then she got up and dragged out to the kitchen.

"You're to sleep in here to-night, the Signore tells me."

The woman had the damper of the fire open, and her face and the arm with which she was putting in the charcoal were both ruddy in its light; triangular shadows flickered upwards from the eyes she turned on Karen. "Yes, my sister-in-law will take the *bambini*." She looked even more closely at Karen and said: "The Signora is tired."

"I'm not in the least tired!"

Late that evening, on the pretext of fetching herself a drink of iced water, Karen came down to the kitchen and found Anna asleep in one corner, like an animal, her knees drawn up to her breast so that both the blackened soles of her bare feet were visible. She was curled on the threadbare mat which usually lay before the doorstep of Frank's room and she had rolled up another mat and put it under her head. The room was full of the smell, in no way unpleasant, of stables and kennels, for even on this hot August night she had closed every window before retiring.

As Karen turned the tap and the water, lethargic after a long drought, began to trickle into the tumbler she had fetched herself, the peasant woman gave a snort and a shudder, and at once was awake.

"I came for an iced drink."

"Let me, Signora."

The woman at once took the glass from Karen's reluctant hand and, going over to the ice-box, picked out some chips of ice, not with the tongs, but with her own bare fingers. Karen did not protest; but when she reached her own room again, she could not drink the water. She put the tumbler on the window-sill and then drew up a chair and sat there, watching the glimmering sheet of the river under the moon. Soon she began to feel a little light-headed, as if from an excess of air or of moonlight, and her resentment against Anna and Frank began to seep away. She seldom thought of others, even those to whom she was attached, when they were absent, but now, curiously, her mother came to her mind and she wondered, drowsily, whether she, too, were asleep or whether, as so often, she lay awake in spite of the luminal or barbitone the doctor had ordered. And then Karen remembered another night such as this, spent sitting at an open window. It was after she had first met Max, and full of a vague, romantic ardour she had felt she could not sleep while the memory of him so oppressed her. She had drawn a chair up to the window just as she had done now, and had looked out on to the school garden, vast and secret in the autumn moonlight, and then along the windows of the main wing, each glimmering like ice, until, suddenly, she had caught her breath. Someone else was seated at one of the windows and was gazing into the moonlight, and she guessed that it was her mother. It was strange, the other woman's face, like the reflection in a dim mirror, and all about the silence and loneliness of night in the empty school; but Karen had never spoken to her mother about it, had never asked her what had kept her up or whether she had noticed her fellow watcher.

She could hear Anna move about below and she supposed that Frank wanted something. Perhaps this was the crisis of his illness; perhaps he was really ill. But she stayed where she was, her arms along the window-sill and her head on her arms. She was empty of all desire to go to him and if someone had then said to her, "Is he to live—or die?" she would probably have shrugged her shoulders.

When she came downstairs early the next morning, she met Anna in the hall. "Well, how is he?" she asked.

The peasant woman shook her head. "It was a bad night. Didn't you hear?" she added.

"I heard nothing. You should have called me."

"What would have been the use? It was better for you to sleep."

"Did you sleep?"

Anna laughed; and Karen was conscious that while she herself, in her silk dressing-gown and slippers, must still look haggard and limp from her vigil at the window, the peasant woman, on the contrary, seemed to have opened to the morning light, like some rich flower, in the full ardour and vitality of her nature.

"Shall I go into him?" Karen said, feeling the ignominy of having to ask such a question.

"Better later. He's at last got to sleep. He was fighting for breath all night, poor soul." Anna had gone into the kitchen, where she began to rake the ashes from the fire, and Karen now followed her. "The things they think of, when they're like that! It was ants with him—ants the whole night. He kept telling me they were crawling all over him. It was all I could do to keep him in bed. And then there was a lot of gibberish, English maybe, and then those blessed ants again. There was no end to it. Now with my boy"—she always spoke of her German as *il mio ragazzo*—"when he was taken bad—his wound green and purple it was—bless me if it weren't rats. They were gnawing him, see, all the live-long night. . . ." She went on talking in her guttural peasant voice, Karen understanding only a word here and there, while she energetically raked out the ashes and began to crack some sticks between her strong brown fingers to lay the new fire. Karen noticed that where the seam of her blouse had split a substantial part of her breast was visible to the eye. "Oh, he has it real bad," Anna ended up. "The poor pet!"

Frank continued to "have it real bad" for the whole of that day, lying on his back with his eyes closed and that perpetual bubbling, snorting noise in his throat, except on those occasions when his fight for breath made him suddenly raise himself on one elbow and hawk violently until he had spat mucus into the enamel bowl on the bedside table. Every hour Anna would go into him to renew the fomentations, carry him some drink which would with difficulty penetrate down his throat, or pull straight the moist sheets, now tangled about his body. He would look at the peasant woman with tired, suffering eyes in which Karen, in her jealousy, always detected some gleam of interest or even admiration. At Karen herself he never looked, keeping his eyes closed or staring fixedly at the ceiling whenever he spoke to her.

She had decided that if he did not improve by the evening she was going down to the village store, without telling him, to telephone for a doctor. But as she changed from the slippers which she had worn all day into a pair of sandals, Anna appeared in the doorway, the enamel bowl in one hand, to say: "He says he's feeling better. Look what he brought up." She tilted the bowl towards Karen who had no desire to look.

Karen went down, and Frank said weakly when he saw her: "I think I'm better. I feel much better. The temperature seems to have gone."

"Then you do admit you had a temperature? In that case, why wouldn't you let me take it? . . . May I take it now?"

"Oh, if you wish," he said between teeth which had suddenly started chattering.

"It's sub-normal," she said, when she had gone to the window with the thermometer and held it to the light. "Let me see the throat."

"You don't want to look at it. It's not a very pretty sight. Anna says a lot of the mucus has cleared."

But for this mention of Anna she would not have persisted as she did now: "Let me see," she said. "I'd like to see." She looked, using a spoon as a spatula, and then gave an involuntary shudder. The whole mouth was ulcerated, the throat thick with mucus. "It looks much the same to me."

"No, it's easier," he said. "It's easier to breathe."

From then on he improved slowly, though for the next two nights, in spite of Karen's protests that she could look after him, Anna continued to sleep on the mat in the kitchen while she herself slept upstairs. On the third day he went out on to the terrace for a short time, but he was so weak that he had to be supported between the two women. When they had placed him in a wicker-chair he looked from one to the other and then, with what appeared to be a deliberate cruelty, said: "Poor Karen! I'm afraid I've fagged you dreadfully. You're almost done in." This concern for her breathlessness over such a trivial physical feat inevitably implied a comparison with Anna who had carried Frank as easily as if he were one of her children.

After the peasant woman had gone, Karen sat on the arm of his chair and said: "Glad to be up?"

"I feel terribly weak."

"Well, of course you do, you poor darling." She attempted to put an arm round him and kiss him but he said fretfully:

"Don't suffocate me—please." He added: "I think I'd like my sketch-book."

"You are a funny old thing."

The following day she said: "I'm telling Anna to make up my bed with you again. Is that all right?" She had missed not sleeping with him and her whole being now craved for a renewal of their intercourse.

"If you don't mind I think I'd rather be alone just at present," he said, without looking up from his sketching.

"Oh." She placed herself on the ledge of the terrace, her back to the view, and then said: "Why?" as calmly as she could manage.

"Why?" he repeated. "Oh, because I do—that's all."

She did not realize that he had always been unconsciously disgusted by the sexual act, and that he regarded it as an evil necessity rather than as a source of light and joy. Now, illogically, in the secret recesses of his personality, there had been established some connection between his illness and the hours of intense, unthinking pleasure he had snatched with Karen. The illness had been a retribution; he did not say that to himself and consciously he did not even think it. But he felt it in his whole immature, twisted being; and perhaps he was right. The subterranean guilt may have at last chosen to erupt in this manner.

"All right," she said listlessly. "I'll stay upstairs. For how long?"

"Oh, I really don't know. Do you mind?"

"Well, of course I mind!"

"It matters so much to you?" he said with a mixture of astonishment and repugnancy.

"Yes. . . . You seem to think that I should be ashamed. You know it's a Victorian notion that women endure that sort of thing but don't really enjoy it." But for "that sort of thing" she used a far cruder word.

He looked up at her now for the first time and stared at her. Then he suddenly burst into laughter; and that was his only comment.

For the next few days they ate together and sat together, as they had done in the past, and Anna ceased to spend her nights at the *villino*; but Karen felt that he now only tolerated her presence whereas before he had taken pleasure in it. He would go about his occupations of painting, reading and writing, and she herself would attempt to concentrate on some task which kept her beside him. But sooner or later, while she was darning socks, or shelling peas, or writing one of her short, illiterate letters, she would find herself watching his absorbed face with a bitter mingling of impatience and regret and a longing to be possessed by him. She would say something, and he would answer, briefly, in his staccato voice, and then he would return to what he was doing as if a door had been quietly locked in her face. One morning, as she finished a late breakfast, she heard him laughing with Anna on the terrace as she beat one of the mats, and then their voices, speaking Italian, began to weave an invisible net of sound in which she felt that her whole being was struggling for life and freedom. She held her coffee-cup in trembling hands and stared into its depths; until she noticed, with revulsion, that a black hair, obviously Anna's, was clinging to one side. She thought, I knew the woman was dirty; and it was as if she had succeeded in scoring some immense, if subtle, triumph.

One day Frank decided to go out shooting, and slinging a rifle he had borrowed across his shoulders, he set off towards the ferry which would take him from their side of the river to the marshes on the other side. He wore khaki shorts and a khaki tunic whose breast-pockets were swollen with the cartridges he had put there; his brown, sinewy legs were bare except for some army boots and the short, thick army socks he had folded over them. He wore a straw sun-hat on his head.

When he had gone, Karen wandered out into the garden for the first time since the old house had fallen, and she was at once sickened by the sweet, pervading smell of corruption which hung on the air. It came from one particular spot under the rubble, and she guessed that there the carcase of the cat was dissolving in the summer heat. But she stayed out on the parapet, in spite of her nausea, because she wanted to see Frank. Far away the ferry began to move, with short jerks, across the shrunken waters; and he— how typical!—was helping the old man to tug at the cable, their two bodies straining side by side. He was always achieving this kind of simple comradeship with others, she thought; with men particularly and with those who were his inferiors. But with her it had seldom existed. And then, all at once, she remembered what he had said about the tedium he found in doing a thing once he had mastered it; and she supposed that she, too, was being relegated to the limbo which had swallowed up music, chess and flying. It was with a savage kind of relief that she at last faced this conclusion.

She heard two shots from the marshes and the whole sickly air seemed to jitter and sway. A covey of birds were blown upwards, as if by the force of the explosion, and then drifted across the river, while the ring of the shots still persisted in her head. Again the air swung hither and thither; it made her feel vaguely giddy, like a stunning blow. He was a good shot, and seldom failed to bring down a bird. Out of the bamboos and dwarf shrubs a number of small whiffs of smoke were wriggling, like grey worms, up the intensely blue sky behind. The reverberation was now almost ceaseless.

She turned to go in and then stopped appalled. Something large and almost the same colour as the rubble was picking its way slowly over a fallen column; and then, almost as if it knew she was watching it, it whisked away. After several seconds another grey form—or perhaps it was the same—appeared on another heap of stones. Its tail, like a length of wet string, seemed to be plastered to the masonry. Then it too disappeared. Somewhere in the depths and silence of the ruin the putrefying carcase was being devoured.

"Anna!" Karen screamed. "Anna, Anna, Anna!" But the peasant woman had long since gone home. Once again the air swayed from side to side like a suffocating curtain in a wind.

When Frank returned that evening she noticed, with joy, that he was changed. "A wonderful day," he said, flinging down on the terrace the birds he had shot in a bedraggled jumble of feathers, beaks stuck together with blood, and rigidly grasping claws. He put out his arms and she went to him, with the mingled fear and fascination of an animal lured into a snare. "Oh, Frank!" she whispered; and then mutely she welcomed the destructive rage of his passion as she welcomed the sweat of his body and the grime of his face and the blood of his hands. She felt she had never been possessed so utterly; so utterly annihilated by another human being. Until, all at once, she was alone on the wicker couch on the verandah, with her torn and aching body, and he had gone. She got up to find him again, but when she tried the door which led to his room, she could not get it open. She banged on it and called his name, and then walked round to the other door. Both doors were locked.

"Frank!" she called. "Frank! What's the matter? Let me in!" And then in desperation, on a single repeated note: "Frank, Frank, Frank."

She heard him move about and at last he came to one of the closed doors and said through it, in a level, authoritative voice: "Please don't interrupt me. I'm trying to do some work. I want to be left to myself."

Chapter Thirty-four

"WHY won't you come to the opera, Granny?" Pamela asked. Mrs. Bennett was sitting in dressing-gown and slippers, *Emma* face downwards in her lap. Her grey hair, brushed loose about her shoulders instead of being screwed into a bun, made it seem as if she were failing in a grotesque attempt to recapture a lost youthfulness. But the truth was that she had undone the hair and had then felt too tired to do it up again.

In answer to her grand-daughter's question, she said: "Oh, for lots of reasons."

"Such as?"

"I feel weary, and I don't like music, and I don't like crowds. And I want to be alone and read my book. And besides there is Nicko."

"Nicko! That's all you ever think about."

"Someone must think about him, dear."

"Yes, I suppose so. . . . Somehow I don't think it'll be much fun."

"I don't see why not." The old woman gave a small, twitching smile as she added: "You don't miss me all that much, do you?"

"What a thing to say!" Pamela exclaimed, putting her arms about Mrs. Bennett's shoulders and kissing her on one cheek. "You do say such odd things." She turned her head sideways to read the tide of the book and then said: "You're breaking your resolution."

"My resolution?"

"Last year you said you were never going to read another Jane Austen book until you were on your death-bed. You said you wanted to save her—remember?"

"Oh, I think that was rather an affected thing to say," the old woman replied with what was almost crossness. She gave a jerk of her bony shoulders as if to push her grand-daughter away from her, and then looked up to Colin who had just come in: "You do look the little man-about-town," she said, maintaining the same sharpness.

"Do I?" Colin did not know whether to be flattered or riled at this comment on the suit which his father had recently had made for him by Rossi. "It fits well, doesn't it?"

"Far too well for a boy of your age."

But Colin was too busy peering at himself in the mirror which hung in one corner of the room to hear this last comment. It was a long, rectangular mirror, in a dark brown wood frame; and after the manner of many old Italian mirrors, particularly in the country, it was divided down the centre by a crucifix, carved from the same almost black wood. Colin looked from the expert cut of the shoulders of his suit to the grotesquely sagging shoulders of the writhing Christ, and said: "What an odd mirror—I've never noticed it before." There, in the left panel, was himself with his small, compact body and enormous eyes; and there, in the right panel, was his grandmother, her white hair straggling about her face, and Pamela still behind her; and there, in the centre, the crude Christ twisted in agony, black on his black cross. It was as if they had been snatched up into a timeless state, he and the two women frozen on either side of the frozen agony of the Christ, as in a nightmare where, try as one may, one cannot move an inch. He wanted to move but he could not do so; he could not even raise a hand or nod his head.

Suddenly the whole of Mrs. Bennett's body jerked as if she had been pricked by some invisible instrument; her book tumbled noisily to the floor as, "Oh," she said. "Oh. . . ." She was still staring ahead of her.

"What is it?" Pamela asked.

"I don't know. . . . The back of my head. . . . I had such a strange feeling. And I was looking in the mirror, and it seemed . . ." She began to cry, wrinkling up her face so that she looked like an aged monkey and making no attempt at concealment. "It's horrible," she said; but they did not know whether she was referring to the mirror or to an experience which she appeared to be incapable of describing in spite of their repeated questions.

"I've never felt less like the opera," Pamela whispered to Colin as they waited for Max to bring the car to the door of the hotel.

"Why on earth?"

"Oh, I don't know—Granny being so odd, and . . ." Her voice trailed off, because she could never express any but the simplest of her emotions. The truth was that she was feeling a mysterious kind of dread, not unlike what she had experienced before going to school for the first time; but this was worse, because she could not guess its cause. "Anyway, you don't like opera yourself, do you?"

"Who said?"

"You came back jolly quick from that performance of *Madame Butterfly*."

"That was because the singing was so bad."

"You mean you were bored."

Colin did not bother to contradict her because the true explanation seemed even more discreditable to him. He had gone alone to the opera and, arriving early, had found himself sitting next to a young couple who, he decided, must have only recently got married. They scrutinized him, not surreptitiously as two such people would have done in England, but with so bold and frank a curiosity that they at once made him blush. Then they began to talk about him. They spoke fast and he could not understand all that they said; and though, in fact, they were commenting admiringly on his English clothes, he assumed that they were jeering at him. He attempted to outstare them but after a few seconds his eyes fluttered downward; he attempted not to listen; he looked at his watch and looked at the proscenium and looked at the other people filing in. At last, in a panic of self-consciousness, he rushed from the theatre.

It was not an incident of which he now felt proud.

Signor Commino, in a dinner-jacket green with age and a shirt whose soft collar had obviously been worn before, was rubbing his hands together and swaying back and forth, on his toes, like a balloon in a high wind. "You look wonderful, Lena," he said. He scratched the top of his head with his forefinger as he repeated: "Wonderful." Lena took no notice.

When Max drove up, Mino continued: "You should always wear beige." With her sallow complexion, this was one colour which Lena should obviously never wear. "There is something very chic about you in beige—something almost Parisian. And those furs of your mother's add just the right touch of sophistication. Yes, they are a great success, a great success."

"Oh, shut up!" Lena said, as she climbed into the car. It was not so much the absurd compliments that angered her as his thus gratuitously informing Max and the children that the furs had been borrowed.

Mino, not at all defeated by her last remark, climbed into the car between the two children, and wriggling his body as if he were itching all over, chuckled: "How do you say in English? A rose between two—two spines."

"Thorns," said Colin.

"Ah, thorns, thorns, thorns."

"Take care, take care!" Lena exclaimed to Max, and she gripped his arm, as he swerved to avoid a lorry.

"Sorry, I'm driving abominably," he said gloomily. "I wasn't thinking. I was thinking of something else."

She looked for a moment at his face in profile. Her hands, the square nails of which she had painted especially for this evening, were holding her furs together in a gesture which, though she imagined it to be seductive, in fact only served to emphasize the raw-boned ugliness of her shoulders. Her lips were apart, their outsides crimson and their insides pale pink. There was lipstick on her teeth. "I hope you will enjoy this evening," she said; and the strange thing was that in spite of all the grotesque details of her appearance, her love for Max lent her at that moment what was almost a grave beauty. Her dark eyes had never seemed more tender, or the irregularities of her face more attractive.

He suddenly said: "You have helped me so much, Lena," taking advantage of Mino's uproarious laughter with the children in the back of the car.

"I?"

"Yes, you." He was naturally sentimental and he added: "I look upon you as another daughter, you know—a grown-up daughter."

Anyone who was not in love with him might here have flinched; but Lena only said: "I'm glad, Max." He had asked her to call him Max the day before.

The performance was to be held out of doors, and they had to make their way to their seats down a narrow lane of canvas sagging inwards on rickety bamboo poles. Mino who, for some inexplicable reason, had brought a large umbrella with him on this hot night of August, began to run it along the canvas as he walked so that it made a loud, rasping noise. "What are you doing?" Lena said crossly; but he was in such high spirits that he only guffawed like a naughty child and continued the action. "Why bring an umbrella, anyway?" she demanded: and when he did not answer at once, she snapped: "Mino! Listen to me!"

"Because it matches my evening-dress," he explained gaily.

"No, it doesn't. The umbrella is black and your evening-dress is green," she retorted rudely.

Suddenly his laughter died and the umbrella fell limply from the canvas. But that evening he was irrepressible and no sooner had they seated themselves than he began to ask the children Italian riddles which he invariably had to explain to them, at great length and to their obvious boredom. At last, more to escape from him than from any real inclination, they announced that they must be excused before the performance began and chased each other, giggling wildly, along the canvas lane which led to the cloak-rooms. Lena was looking over Max's shoulder at the programme, and Mino was now meditatively rubbing the handle of his umbrella, stained black with sweat, as he gazed in turn at the curtain and at the two others. It was a strange handle which just failed to make a proper curve owing to some fault of seasoning.

Mino suddenly said: "Look at my umbrella." He held it high; and Lena at once knew, from a familiar glint in his eyes and an expression of suppressed mirth, that he was going to make a witticism. When the witticism came, it was even more appalling than she had imagined possible: "My umbrella has no self-control." He indicated the outward thrust of the handle. "No self-control," he repeated; and Lena and Max both stared at him with expressionless faces while he chuckled, checked himself, and then slowly began to go crimson with embarrassment. From time to time it was his habit to come out with some ribaldry of this kind.

Colin and Mino evidently enjoyed the opera, though it made Max and Lena yawn, and Pamela giggle. The stage was so narrow that the singers kept colliding with each other, the back-cloth suggested the tour of a musical comedy in the Far East, and the tenor, who was some five feet high, was wearing high heels. But Mino hummed the music to himself, falsetto, with his hands clasped between his knees, and Colin nudged Pamela indignantly when she lost all control of herself. Lena gazed occasionally at the stage, but more often at the sky above her, at the audience before her, or at the face at her side. Max shifted uneasily because the wooden slats of his seat were pressing into him.

After the first act, Mino bought them glasses of a sticky orange-ade which Max and Lena placed surreptitiously under their seats after they had drunk no more than a quarter; fortunately Mino was too busy making gurgling noises in his own glass with a straw to notice this abstinence. He had also bought some equally sticky nut-brittle, which he twisted this way and that in his perspiring paws in an effort to break it into pieces. He laughed and gesticulated and continued to make outrageous jokes, but some part of his gaiety seemed to be incessantly trickling away, as if through an invisible puncture. One end of his black tie was beginning to work loose.

At the conclusion of the second act, Lena whispered to Max: "Let's go out. I shall need something more intoxicating than that filthy *aranciata* if I'm to survive. . . . No, don't ask him too," she at once checked Max. "Let's go alone. He can keep an eye on the children. We're just slipping out a second," she announced to the others. "Good-bye." She waved a hand, and as soon as she and Max were out of the row, exclaimed: "Saved! I was sure he would follow us."

"Where shall we go?" Max had not failed to notice how Mino, having gathered himself to follow, had then sunk back into his chair on realizing they did not want him. A rush of guilt made him answer sharply: "There's such a crowd! We'd have done better to stay where we were."

"Now don't be so grumpy. We can slip out through here"—
Lena pulled apart two of the flapping canvas sheets—"and there's
a little bar just across the road. I know it well." She laughed: "It will
be good for you to see how we of the other half live. Come!" With
a certain self-consciousness she linked her arm in his and drew him
through the crowds.

"What will you have?" she asked when they were standing
before the veined marble counter.

"Damn!" He had placed his elbow in a smear of coffee and
began to mop at himself with a handkerchief. "Let me do this," he
said.

"No, no, of course not. I asked you."

"Well, what do you suggest? I'll have what you have."

"*Due Americani*," Lena said to the man behind the bar. They carried their glasses, misty with ice, over to a small wicker table and
sat down, Lena slipping off her furs to reveal shoulders in which
she obviously took an unaccountable pride. She was aware that the
crowd round the bar and the four men playing cards at the next
table were all watching her, and she experienced a fierce joy. She
sipped at the bitter drink and said: "This is fun. Isn't it?"

"Yes," Max said. "Yes, it's gay here—gay and"—he sought for an
adjective—"and kind of colourful. It's the real Italy, I guess. One so
seldom sees it."

"I am always seeing it," she said. "To-night it seems gay, but it
does not always seem so. I think I prefer the Palazzo d'Oro. But
of course for you Americans it must be fun to go slumming every
now and then." Suddenly there was bitterness in her voice, as if
she were attempting to provoke him to some emotion, no matter
what. "I used to work in an office next to this bar and sometimes I
came here for coffee. It was warm in winter, that was why I came."

"Tell me about your life," Max said. "You know, I know absolutely nothing about you."

She sighed and shrugged her shoulders: "Oh, there's nothing to
tell. My father was an army officer and he died in Somalia when I
was six. Once we had money, then we had less, now we have almost
none. I work for you and I keep my mother who is always ill—and
Signor Commino wishes to marry me," she added with a sudden,
artificial laugh. She stared down at the glass and he thought she

was going to burst into tears; but instead a blush, agonizing in its intensity, swept up from her bare shoulders. "I shall not marry him," she said.

"And what work will you do, when I go?"

"I don't know."

"I must do what I can to find you something else." He looked at her and added: "Unless you would like to come to England to work for me there."

"I? To England?" She was incredulous. "But how can I possibly——?"

"Why not?"

"But my mother——" she began. "Oh, there is nothing I should like more, nothing, nothing! But it is all so difficult. You do not understand how difficult it is."

"Well, think about it."

"Of course I shall think about it." She gulped what was left in the glass and said: "You are so kind to me. And I have always wanted to visit England. But——" she stared down at the sawdust on the floor and then twitched at her furs—"it is my mother," she said. "No, it is impossible. Impossible," she repeated on a strange, dying note.

"You are the best secretary I have ever had."

"Oh, nonsense!"

"I mean it, Lena."

She looked at her watch, her face still expressing pleasure at the compliment, and then said: "I suppose we must go back."

"Oh, must we? It really is torture. . . . Listen!" He cocked an ear and said: "It's already begun. Can't we stroll until the others come out?"

"Why not?"

Suddenly a scruple overcame him: "But Mino——?" he said. "Won't he be hurt?"

"Oh, let him!"

They walked arm-in-arm up and down the street, and then round the Duomo, gazing from time to time at a sky that was brilliant with stars. Because they were in evening-dress they were stared at, but neither of them cared. Lena was telling him about her father and how the few of his relics that had been sent back from Somalia had been stolen in passage, and then she described her life with her ailing mother and her one brief love-affair with an English clerk who had been stationed in Florence and had later turned out already to have a wife. "Poor Lena!" Max exclaimed. "What a life you've had."

Meanwhile Mino fidgeted in his seat, incessantly turning round to see if they were coming in; he had bought them an ice each, but the two packets were already limp and soggy. At last he got up and went to the back of the ramp on which the seats had been placed, and stalked up and down, peering in all directions. He explored each of the canvas lanes. No, they had gone, they had left him, they had been bored. Someone in the audience hissed at the sound of his ceaselessly plodding feet, and he stopped, ineffectually pushing the end of his black tie under his collar and staring at the monstrous shadow which his body cast on the canvas screen beside him. From the stage poured light and noise and movement; in himself there were darkness, silence and death.

After the performance he did not show his disappointment and even if he had, Lena was too happy to have noticed it. As she said good night to Max she whispered: "I shall think of that idea. I shall try to make it possible."

"Yes, try," he said. He walked up the steps of her house with her, and kissed her, briefly, behind the door, where the others could not see them.

When he reached the hotel there was a letter for him, with a Swiss stamp:

DEAR MAX,

You see that I am here in Zurich, where I came to find Maisie. But she left unexpectedly for Salzburg yesterday and I haven't a bean. You said if I ever needed money you would let me have it and that is why I am writing. You were right about Frank. He tired of me, and though he never told me to go, I knew that was what he wanted.

I didn't intend to ask for money but there's nothing else for it. Is there?

KAREN.

PS. How's Nicko?

Chapter Thirty-five

"ANOTHER, another!"

"But, my dear, I have no more paper."

"You have *that*," Nicko said, pointing at the sketch-book which lay among the other odds and ends in Mrs. Bennett's string-bag.

The old woman hesitated, and then pulled off the elastic band which clasped the book together and ripped out a sheet. "What is it? What is it?" the child demanded. "Let me see!"

"Rodolfo and Enzo." She stared down at it for a moment, bunching her lips so that the deep furrows around her mouth all at once deepened; then, swiftly, she began to fold another boat.

"Don't you want it, Granny?" Nicko asked; he had not imagined that she would take the suggestion seriously.

"No, I don't want it."

"It was a beautiful drawing."

"No, it wasn't," she said gruffly. "There! Take it. But don't fall into the water."

She watched the child as he scrambled down an incline strewn with fragments from the destroyed bridges, and called: "Be careful, Nicko! Be careful!" He was going to the place where an endless gush of water foamed and roared out of a tunnel to join the sluggish river; he had discovered it for himself, and now always insisted that she should take him there when they went on their walks. She made him paper-boats and he would launch them in the rushing waters; and then he would stand, one hand shielding his eyes, as he watched them sweep into the river, bobbing up and down, whirling round, and in the end either sinking or travelling so far that they were lost to his gaze. He did not know, as she did, that the water, glittering so beautifully in the sun as it poured from the hillside, in fact came from a sewer.

After he had launched the boat, he still watched the water, rapt away by its speed and noise and power; and she still watched him. Though it was now late afternoon, the sun made her head ache and gave her a tight pain between her eyes, as if from too much scowling. But from here, among the scattered chunks of masonry, the sewer looked pure as it flashed into the sunlight from the dark of the tunnel. It looked beautiful, as the child looked beautiful, with one brown arm raised to his face, his legs sturdily apart, and his fair hair gleaming. Beyond him the semi-naked children of the city splashed and shouted in the brown scum of the river; and beyond them was the outline of the city, dissolving in a heat-haze, the blue mountains and an intense blue sky.

. . . The water was clear and cool, she thought, it was aerated, coming like that from the hillside, and ice-cold; it would sting the tongue and make the teeth ache, and afterwards it would leave a delicious feeling of satisfaction. So many years ago they had drunk at the stream at Fiesole, he cupping his hands over the thin spirt of water and then raising them to her mouth. The carriage had been left where a cart-track led off the high-road and the three of them, her friend, the man who was to become her husband, and herself had trudged up through the dust and heat and incessant shrilling of cicadas to find the "view" which had at first sent them on the errand. He and she had never found it; they had found the stream instead.

Afterwards they had sat on a rock, and suddenly out of the burnt clusters of broom two figures had emerged, their arms intertwined. They were girls, in the blue frocks and black stockings of an institution, and they had hideous, simian faces in which there were no eyes. They chattered to each other, led unerringly by the low murmur and lisp of the spring, until they had reached it. Then, as if they were re-enacting the scene which had already passed, one girl lowered her coarse hands and cupped them for the other. The two unseeing faces were close, while the lips gulped greedily, like an animal lapping from a bowl. Now they changed their rôles, and the girl who had lapped in turn cupped her hands to the flashing water.

At first it had been a scene of an ugly, and even grotesque, pathos. But there was something monumental in the pose of the two figures, in their blue uniforms; something so little human that the young girl who watched them had the feeling of watching while two wild beasts quenched their thirst in what they imagined to be an unbroken solitude. Five minutes previously, his hands with

the small, beautifully manicured fingers and the narrow wrists had
been raised to her mouth; and when she had performed the same
service for him, he had suddenly caught the tender flesh of her
palm between his white teeth. . . . One of the blind girls put her
face to the spring and the other gave her a push. They laughed, and
then, their arms once again intertwined, they disappeared down
into the silence and heat below.

"Come, Nicko, come!" she called; and it cost her an immense
physical effort to shout even that distance.

"In a minute."

"No. Come now!"

But she knew he would come only when he wanted to come,
and she felt too tired and ill to shout any more. She perched on
one of the jagged lumps of masonry and looked about her, twisting her bowed head as if it were a too heavy flower withering in
the sun. In its noisy confusion the water seemed to be pouring
through her body; but it was not cool, as she had imagined, but
hot, hot, hot. She swept her bloodshot eyes from side to side and
suddenly let her string-bag slip to the ground as she gazed at one
spot. Someone was asleep, where the last row of a plantation of
Indian corn cast a brief shade. She thought it was an old man, and
she guessed which old man it would be. He lay, arms outstretched,
on his back, like a wax effigy slowly dissolving in the heat. There
was no bridge to his nose and his red-rimmed eyes stared, sight-
lessly open, at the blue of the sky above him. The long, curving
nails of one hand glittered like claws in the sunset. She stared, fascinated, while the water seemed to pour faster and faster through
her. Then she looked wildly about her, half-rising as if to summon
assistance, and saw—Enzo. . . .

"Oh . . . Oh . . ." she said. She put out both hands, seemingly
in entreaty, to the Florentine whose half-naked body glistened
with water. "Oh . . . save me . . ." she said in English. She pointed:
"There! Look! The man . . ."

"Sì, sì," the Florentine said, nodding his head energetically. He
had not understood. "My clothes," he explained in Italian. He
pointed to the spot and smiled, and then brushed back a lock of
wet hair which had fallen across his forehead. He had vowed to
himself that he would never again speak to any member of the

family; yet now he welcomed this encounter with joyful exhilaration. Once again he smiled.

Mrs. Bennett stared at him and then at the spot where the man had been sprawled; and as she did so, Enzo sprinted off to fetch his towel with a murmur of excuse. There could be no doubt; she had been mistaken. And yet . . . She felt almost tearful with mingled exasperation and relief.

Enzo sauntered back, drying himself as he did so; and, seeing the Italian, Nicko at once let out a squeal and bounded up the incline. He flung himself into Enzo's arms and Enzo lifted him off his feet and swung him round and round in a circle, both of them laughing. "Take care, take care!" Mrs. Bennett warned. Nicko's shirt was now covered in patches of moisture from the other's wet body.

The Italian and the English child played together for many minutes and Mrs. Bennett lost all interest in them. She remained perched on the slab of masonry, her legs, with their grape-like veins, crossed one over the other, and her eyes staring vacantly at the brown water or at the outline of the houses on the other bank. There was the *pensione* at which they had stayed; and there was the balcony . . . "Are you happy?" he had asked, and she had seemed to be suffocating in the cool night air as his body had shuddered against hers. "I don't know." And she had never known. When he was dying, they had seemed to act the same scene all over again, with her arms once more about him and his body straining against hers, as her whole life seemed to issue out of him in spasm after spasm. She was suffocating in the odours of illness, and he had gasped: "Have you been happy? Have you been at all happy?" And there was no reply she could make but the old "I don't know. I just don't know." . . . For the things most important to her in life were physical health and physical beauty; it was immoral but there, it had always been so and she could not help it. . . . Health and beauty: her whole being embraced in a dying tenderness the fair-haired child and the dark-haired boy moving in the unconscious perfection of their youth as if to enact some last ritual before her. Enzo held Nicko in his arms and was swinging him from side to side, the muscles in his legs and belly straining. And now she felt for this ill-educated, uncouth stranger what in her whole life she had never once felt for her husband; she knew that she loved him.

"*Basta, basta!*" Enzo laughed to Nicko. He came over to Mrs. Bennett and stooped down to speak to her, his hands on his knees: "I am going to sleep," he said in his guttural Italian; and because she looked at him with so vacant a gaze, he repeated: "I am going to sleep, sleep."

She put out a hand and ran it slowly down his face, neck and glistening shoulders in the gesture with which she had first acknowledged his beauty when Max had brought him to the hotel, and she had tried to draw him. Her mouth twitched, as if she were either about to laugh or burst into tears, and suddenly, in her appalling Italian, she said: "My grandson—Colin—he's very sad. He so much wants to see you again—so much, so much. Please—please—go and see him. Forgive him. Forgive." Her nails dug into the flesh of his shoulder as she said the last three words with immense emphasis. For the first time in her life, whether by accident or intention, she had used the *tu* form in Italian.

"*Sì, sì.* I'll go. I'll go this evening."

She closed her eyes, rocking from side to side on the piece of masonry as she said: "*Va bene, va molto bene.*"

Enzo strolled away and pillowing his head on his heap of clothes, soon fell asleep. Nicko came to Mrs. Bennett and said plaintively, "I'm tired." She put out her arms and he clambered into them, curling up like an animal, his cheek against hers. "Sleep," he said.

"Yes, sleep, sleep."

The sun shifted and after many minutes the old woman and the sleeping child were in its full glare. But Mrs. Bennett did not move, though her whole body seemed to be shrivelling in the heat. Now the only coolness was where the child's breath issued gently against her throat; everywhere else was fire. And from that one spot the child seemed to be drawing out her whole life with each gasp of air. She looked for the balcony but it was now no more than a glittering bar of light. She looked for the *pensione* and all at once it seemed to burst into flames. She looked for Enzo, and under the shadow of the Indian corn saw the effigy-like figure, now purple and swollen to an enormous size, as she had once seen a corpse when nursing in the Great War. . . . She looked down at

Nicko; and he at least was safe. His breath came easily and one of his hands was opening and shutting rhythmically over her withered breast. There was moisture on his lips, as if he had just licked them, and innumerable small beads of sweat at his temples and each of his eyebrows. Once again she felt her whole being envelop him in a last embrace.

When Enzo woke, he dressed himself, combed his hair and then slouched over to say good-bye to the old woman and Nicko. They now sat in shadow, and Mrs. Bennett's head had lolled forward so that it almost entirely covered the sleeping child. No, he would not disturb them; they both were asleep. . . . A smile, full of the tenderness which lurked, so often hidden, in the Italian boy, now transfigured his dark, sunburned face. Until he stooped. A trickle of dry blood gleamed black on Nicko's cheek and throat.

It took Enzo a long time to separate the old woman's locked fingers and remove the by now screaming child.

Chapter Thirty-six

It was the loneliest hour of night.

Since Karen's train from Switzerland was due to arrive at half-past three, Max had decided that it would not be worth his while to go to bed before he had met it. He wandered from street to street, oppressed by the sense that the whole city was dying all about him; lights went out, shutters were drawn down over bars and even the beggars, usually so importunate, curled up on benches and in corners and dropped into sleep. He could not stop thinking about the dead woman, but all the wildness of grief had spent itself and as he listened to the echo of his own feet in the silence and solitude, there was nothing now but a vague and tender sadness. He had not imagined that he would care so much and only now realized how, in these last days without Karen, his spirit had been bound to Mrs. Bennett's no less securely than to those of the children.

It was not cold, but as he thought of her, it was as if the circulation of the blood in his veins were slowing as it slowed in the empty streets. Everything seemed to be coming to a standstill, and his pace slackened too until, almost unconsciously, he was leaning above the river. Down below, in the brown undergrowth, two shapes were huddled together, but even they were motionless. A solitary figure crossed the Grazie bridge as if in a dream, and a long tapering shadow swung from side to side with each step it took. They would bury the old woman in the English cemetery and the archdeacon's tenor, richly valedictory, would say the service for her. They would throw earth on her, and then . . . no, no, he could not think about it.

In the vast, glittering hall of the station two soldiers slouched in one corner on their kit-bags; dark, pigmy figures with blank faces and eyelids drooping with sleep. In another corner, a woman leant against the closed shutters of the tobacconist's kiosk with a suit-case beside her and a cigarette hanging from her mouth. She was waiting for someone, in silent patience, and all the time that Max watched her she never once moved. From time to time a voice came over the station microphones, sounding as if a piece of celluloid were being crackled in imitation of human speech, and one or other of the isolated travellers would stir from his stupor.

There was only one other person on the platform to which Max went, and he was a little, old man, beautifully manicured and dressed, with a white, clipped moustache, white hair and a rosy complexion. He sat on a bench, and he all at once unlaced one of his black patent-leather shoes, pulled it off and began to stare into it, turning it this way and that to catch the light better. He was completely absorbed, though it would be impossible to say for what he was searching. Some porters, clustered round a trolley, were smoking in silence and their cigarettes, glowing in the shadows of an unlit corner, seemed even brighter than the stars which stretched, in parallel sheets, between the roofs of the station.

Karen was almost the last to descend from the train, and she looked white and ill. Without returning his greeting, she said: "I've lost everything."

"What do you mean?"

"All my suit-cases—they've been stolen." She spoke with a quiet, hopeless melancholy, her voice almost inaudible and her face without expression.

"Stolen!"

"I changed carriages before Verona, because there was a man

I didn't like—he gave me the creeps. I didn't bother to move the cases, I thought they'd be safe. They must have been taken at Verona."

"Oh, my God! . . . Have you told the guard?"

"Yes, I've told all sorts of people. Now I've got to see the station police. It's lucky I left all that stuff at the Palazzo d'Oro. But my most precious things . . ." She stopped, because she was going to burst into tears.

Max attempted to take her arm as they walked away up the platform but she drew away from him, with no more than a light sigh. They continued to walk in silence, until she said: "I came as soon as I got the wire. I'm glad it was like that, sudden and without fuss. She hated illness, and she'd had twenty years of Father." She asked questions in the same soft, tranquil voice until they reached the office where they had to report the theft. Then sinking into a chair and leaning forward, her hands clasped together, she allowed Max to talk for her; nor did she again look up until some question was asked to which she alone knew the answer.

"Well, that's that," Max said as they left the office. "We must hope for the best."

"Where are you taking me?"

"To the Palazzo d'Oro, of course."

"There was no need to book me a room there. You could have sent me to somewhere cheaper."

"It's the old room."

"Oh, no—Max, no." She stopped. "I must be by myself—alone. I don't mind where I am, but I must be alone. I—I haven't come back, you see. Not like that."

"That's all right," he said softly. "I've asked for a room for myself on another floor."

"Thank you," she muttered, again almost inaudibly. Many seconds later she said: "We have so much we must discuss—so many decisions. About Nicko, above all. Poor Nicko! What a terrible shock it must have been for him." Suddenly she began to bite savagely at the nail of one thumb: "I can't think at the moment. I can't decide anything. All through the journey, I was only thinking. . . ." Her voice died and her expression seemed to die with it, leaving her face still.

"We have plenty of time," he said.

In the car he noticed how she kept touching her throat with one hand as if it were tender, and he asked: "What's the matter? Have you a sore throat?"

"A slight one. It's the dust from the journey."

She had a headache too, though she did not tell him so; but the next morning she could not go to the funeral. The doctor took a swab and announced that she had diphtheria.

She had evidently caught it from Frank.

Chapter Thirty-seven

MAX was preoccupied. Having dictated two letters, he said to Lena: "You can deal with the rest yourself, can't you?" He strode over to the french windows and gazed out, his hands in his pockets and his shoulders slouched.

"Please do not worry," she said. "Of course I can do them."

"Probably better than if I dictate." He swung round: "Did you remember to order the flowers?"

"Of course."

"And you rang up Seeber about the two books?"

"I fetched them myself on my way over here."

"But there was no need," he began; and then he added awkwardly: "You've been wonderful to us all through this."

"Don't use the plural," she said quietly; and all at once, a blush sweeping over her, she began to fiddle with the typewriter roll, as if in an attempt to distract his attention from this last remark.

"The—plural?" he asked, in slow bewilderment. "What do you mean?"

"Nothing." Her hands were so clumsy that one of the sheets of paper with which she had been fiddling slipped to the floor. Her face became even redder as she stooped to pick it up.

Max appeared to be about to say something, as he stood looking at her, his hands still deep in his pockets and his sandy eyebrows drawn together in a scowl above his small green eyes. But instead he turned away and went back to the window. Mournfully he whistled a few bars from the first act of *La Traviata*, swinging the sash of the blind in one hand as he did so; then he said: "Can you be responsible for Nicko until we get back?"

"Of course."

Bitterly she thought that the only use he would ever find for her would be this of substitute. While Karen was away, she was the substitute wife who encouraged him and told him he looked tired and ought to rest, and went out to buy him a new pair of socks. Now, with Karen ill and Mrs. Bennett dead, she was no longer the substitute wife but the substitute mother. It was she who woke Nicko at ten o'clock and put him on the pot, who took him to sail his boats by the river, and who checked Colin's and Pamela's clothes when they returned from the laundry. Lena knew now that she would never achieve anything more than this kind of usefulness; and the despicable thing, which filled her with fury against herself, was that she accepted the rôle and would not rebel against it, just as, during the occupation, she had accepted the humiliating discovery that the man who had professed to wish to marry her was, in fact, already both husband and father. Yes, she already knew, as she looked at Max's slouched figure, that, to the end of her days, she would always rather beg for a few crumbs from his table than eat a banquet at Mino's. . . .

"I've been thinking," she said. She clicked a few letters of the typewriter and then looked up. "I've been thinking," she repeated.

"Oh, yes—yes?" he murmured absently. He turned, but instead of looking at her, gazed fixedly at one point on the corner of the desk. "Yes?" he said.

"Perhaps, if you really wanted me to go to England, I could manage it. I do not know. First I must speak to my aunt and see if my mother can go and stay with her. Then I must——"

"Oh, fine, fine," he cut short this laborious explanation. "That's fine. Yes, do that, do that." But of course he was thinking of Karen.

Then Lena did an extraordinary thing. She rose to her feet, and supporting herself with the desk, the fingers of one hand white as she clutched it, she said in an even, but curiously intense voice: "You do not really care. And you have not understood. And you never will understand. 'Yes, do that, do that.'" She mimicked his intonation with surprising skill. "And so I leave my mother, and my home, and my—my chance of happiness"—she flung out the hand that had been gripping the table—"and all—all for what? For what?" No less suddenly she crumpled up before his astonished gaze, and collapsed back into the chair from which she had risen. She placed her elbows on either side of the typewriter and rested her head in her hands, so that her hair fell over her burning cheeks. She gazed down at the letter she had begun: "Dear Sir, Mr. Westfield asks me to thank you . . ." She waited and at last she felt Max's hand on her shoulder.

"I don't understand," he said. "Lena—I——"

"There's no need to understand," she said in a faint whisper. "I'm sorry. . . . No, please do not say any more," she checked him. "Please!"

"But look, Lena——" Of course he had long since known she had loved him. But he was not very imaginative, and it was the first time that he had fully realized the depth of her devotion; the discovery at once touched and appalled him. "Lena——".

"Please!" she exclaimed again.

He put his hand on her shoulder, and then with hesitant footsteps he made for the door. Lena rose and said calmly: "I'll give you the books. And I have a little present here for Mrs. Westfield from myself. Perhaps you would be very kind and take it for me." Nothing betrayed her previous emotion except the shiny flush of her cheeks and the way in which she spoke, through barely parted lips. "My best wishes to Mrs. Westfield," she said.

"Can we see Mummy?" Pamela asked when she, Colin and Enzo had piled into the car.

"What?" Max was still preoccupied—with Lena now, not with Karen. "No—no, I'm afraid not. The doctor says not. She's still infectious."

"I'm not afraid of infection," Pamela said. "If I'm going to become a doctor I shall have to get used to it."

"Plenty of time for that."

The nursing-home was out on Bellosguardo and Max left the three children in a garden which fell, in a number of terraces, down a steep hillside. They sat round a gold-fish pond into which Enzo began to spit, making the gold-fish huddle together with darting tails and gaping mouths as they fought to devour each blob of saliva. The English children laughed uproariously and then they too began to spit, until the game tired them. Pamela said: "Do you suppose Mummy has been in great pain?"

"They say diphtheria is painful."

"You know, in a way, I rather hope she has been in pain."

"Pamela!"

"I do. It's a punishment for her. It's a kind of visitation from God. He did it to her to send her back to Daddy. And I'm glad she suffered, because she made Daddy suffer." Her eyes glinted and her cheeks were suffused as she tugged at the clumps of grass which straggled round the pool. "Oh, don't look so shocked!" she burst out at Colin.

"Well, it does shock me when you say things like that."

Meanwhile, upstairs Max had been greeted by the doctor who had set Colin's leg. The Italian was justifiably pleased with the rapidity with which Karen had made her recovery, and being young and intensely interested in his work, he proceeded to describe in detail the whole of her treatment. His smile was brilliant and his manner almost hysterically gay, as he sat on an edge of his desk, in a white coat with a stethoscope dangling round his neck, and kicked his legs back and forth as if in time to some invisible music. The contrast between his exhilaration and the sluggish melancholy of the American was extreme.

At last he led Max to Karen's room and after a few encouraging words, most of them delivered while he took deep gulps of air at the open window, he left them alone together. Without saying anything, Max put down the parcels he had brought and began to fill a vase with water to hold the flowers. Karen watched each of his movements, as if she were puzzled by them. Her blonde hair looked white on the pillow, and her face seemed to have taken the impression of a number of minute furrows, as if old age had come on her suddenly, like a fall of snow in spring.

"Well?" he said, when he had finished arranging the flowers. He came and stood beside her, and looked down at her small, triangular face, as he asked: "Better?"

"Oh, I think so."

"Antonini was saying that you'd made a wonderfully quick recovery."

She gave a sudden, small smile: "I don't feel as if I'd recovered."

"You're weak, I expect."

"Sit down," she said. "Sit here, beside me. . . . No, perhaps you'd better go and sit by the window."

"Oh, that's all right," he said. "I had diphtheria when I was a kid."

"I never knew that. I've never bothered to know much about you." When he had placed himself on the bed beside her, she said: "Max, what are we going to do?"

"Do? . . . Oh, let's discuss all that later."

"No, now. I can't stop thinking about it, and I must get it all straight." She spoke in a tranquil, slightly husky voice, her small, urchin's hands resting outside the sheet.

"Well, what do you want?" he said.

"What do *you* want?"

"Is—is it all over with Ross?"

Momentarily she pulled in her lower lip: "Yes, all over." And then she added in the same quiet tone: "It was ghastly, leaving him, but there was nothing else for it. You can't imagine the loneliness when I reached Zurich, and found no Maisie there."

"Yes, I can imagine," he said; but the irony was lost on her, for she would never learn to identify herself with others, least of all with him.

"The hell of caring, caring, caring, when you know it's all for nothing. When you're despised and, in the end, even hated for asking for what you know you'll never get. Oh, I want to forget all that!" She brushed her hair away from her forehead: "And then Mother . . ."

He wanted to take her hand in his, but did not dare to do so; he tried to speak, but no words came to him, until at last he said: "I know you've had the hell of a time." And then he realized the inadequacy of that comment.

"Will you have me back?" she suddenly asked, "Max?"

"Of course," he said, simply and without hesitation.

"I don't know if it's fair to ask that, because I don't know if it'll really be awfully different. But I'll try, I promise I'll try. And there's Nicko—we must think of him. I thought I liked being alone, but that week in Zurich made me want never to be alone again. And

Frank has done one thing for me—I don't think I shall mind your making love so much now. I don't *think* I shall. But you do see that I can't promise ever to love you? In fact, I know I shan't—ever, ever. I can't say why, but it's as if I could love only those who don't love me—those who make life hell, as Frank did, and who end up by hating me." With a clairvoyance rare in her nature, she said: "Like you with me. Because you go on loving me, and all the dreadful things I do to you only make you love me more. Frank, for instance. I believe you love me more now than before I went away with him. You do, don't you?"

It was the cruellest of questions, but he answered truthfully: "Yes."

"And now you'll take me back, and you'll be glad to take me back. I can't understand it! Why do we cling so to people who make our lives miseries? Cling so to our crosses instead of climbing off them?"

"I'm happier with you than I've ever been without you."

She smiled, as if at something peculiarly ingenuous, and then said: "Very well. Next week we'll go back to England—shall we? The children are already terribly late for school. And we'll try again. *I'll* try again." She sighed: "But don't expect too much, will you? Deaths and illnesses and things like that bring people together— but seldom for long, so I don't expect it'll really be much different. I expect it'll always be much the same, right to the end—to the bitter end."

"I'm prepared for that." He clasped both her hands in his, but he lacked the confidence to take her in his arms, and after a few seconds of silence, he got up and went to the open window and looked out. "The children are in the garden," he said, "with Enzo. They patched it up with him. I'm glad, because Colin was kind of upset about all that. But I guess he'll miss Enzo."

Only the two boys now sat beside the gold-fish pool, for Pamela had wandered off on her own. They were talking to each other and they looked happy there, with the sun glinting on their hair and their bare knees and the water between them.

More Award-Winning Fiction from Valancourt Books

DAVID STOREY

Saville

WINNER OF THE BOOKER PRIZE

"The leading novelist of his generation." *Daily Telegraph*

BARRY ENGLAND

Figures in a Landscape

SHORTLISTED FOR THE BOOKER PRIZE

"Achieves a tension that is almost unbearable." *Daily Mail*

JENNIFER DAWSON

The Ha-Ha

WINNER OF THE JAMES TAIT BLACK MEMORIAL PRIZE

"A novel about madness which succeeds completely." *Daily Telegraph*

PIERS PAUL READ

Monk Dawson

WINNER OF THE SOMERSET MAUGHAM AWARD AND HAWTHORNDEN PRIZE

"A remarkable novel. . . . [P]rofoundly moving." *Graham Greene*

PETER PRINCE

Play Things

WINNER OF THE SOMERSET MAUGHAM AWARD

"[E]xciting, relevant, a wholesale gift for the top-notch department."
Books and Bookmen

STEPHEN GREGORY

The Cormorant

WINNER OF THE SOMERSET MAUGHAM AWARD

"An extraordinary novel—original, compelling, brilliant." *Library Journal*